FORGOTTEN SISTER

The FORGOTTEN SISTER

MARY BENNET'S
PRIDE AND PREJUDICE

Jennifer Paynter

LAKE UNION
PUBLISHING

First Published by Penguin Group (Australia), 2012
Published by Lake Union, 2014
www.apub.com

ISBN-13: 9781477848883
ISBN-10: 1477848886

Library of Congress Control Number: 2013910957

For Caro

Part One

1.

For the best part of nine years—from the age of four until just before I turned thirteen—I prayed for a brother every night. My two elder sisters also prayed. They felt the want of a brother equally keenly, for our father's estate was entailed upon a male heir and (as our mother never ceased to remind us) without a brother to provide for us or a rich husband to rescue us, we would all be destitute.

But if my Aunt Philips is to be believed, our parents in the early years of their marriage scarcely gave the entail a thought. When my eldest sister was born my father was philosophical. As Aunt Philips tells it, Jane was the most beautiful baby with an angelic disposition and Papa was prodigiously proud of her.

He was disappointed when my second sister was born, however. But then according to our neighbor Lady Lucas (or Mrs. Lucas as she then was), Elizabeth was such a charming child that Papa was very soon reconciled to her existence—more than reconciled, he rapidly came to dote on her. Her favorite trick was to creep into his library with her linen blanket and make a nest for herself beneath his kneehole desk. Whilst ever he was reading she would be quiet as a mouse but as soon as he closed his book she would call to him in shrill imitation of our mother. Apparently this so amused my father he began to close his book more often. He would go down upon his hands and knees to play with her and the two of them would then romp for half the morning.

Later, he taught her to read, and so delighted was he at her progress that if there was company present he would call on her to display her precocious talent. Mama's old friend Mrs. Long remembers Elizabeth chalking words on a slate and lisping "Sally in Our Alley" when she was but two years old. She also recalls the infant prodigy performing a sailor's hornpipe while my father beat time on the arm of his chair and cheered her on. (I believe at one stage he even considered teaching Elizabeth Latin but nothing ever came of it.)

My mother not unreasonably took exception to all this. "You will turn the child's head, Mr. Bennet. She will be so puffed up that soon there'll be no teaching her anything." My father would laugh and return to his book. In those days he did not expose his wife to ridicule. That came a little later, after I was born.

Mama's joy at the prospect of a third child was known to most of the good people of Meryton, and so certain was she this time that the Bennets were to be blessed with a son that she arranged for his initials to be embroidered on a fresh supply of baby linen and for rosettes of satin ribbons to be affixed to the left-hand side of all his caps. Papa too looked forward to the birth, anticipating the cutting off of the entail and the disappointment of his cousins, the Collinses.

"And how will you like having a little brother, Lizzy?" he would say, whereupon Elizabeth would clap her hands. "But it may be you'll have to make do with another sister." At which Elizabeth would frown and shake her head. I am told this caused my father much amusement.

He was not amused, however, to hear of my own arrival— telling my aunt when she tried to sympathize: "Mrs. Bennet will bear me a son eventually, depend upon it. And if she does not I can always divorce her, like King Henry the Eighth."

I am told Papa made these sorts of remarks more often after I was born. He had always enjoyed teasing Mama but hitherto his jokes had been good-humored. Mama of course was incapable of laughing at herself even at the best of times—a failing my father believes I have inherited—and soon tears and hysterics became the rule at Longbourn, my father spent more time than ever in his library, and the Bennets could no longer pass for a happy couple.

When I was about a month old my father's old friends, Mama's nerves, took a hand in my fate. Out of consideration for them, I was farmed out to a wet-nurse, one Mrs. Bushell, whose husband was gamekeeper at the Great House of Stoke. After I was weaned I still remained with Mrs. Bushell, and when at last I returned home to live, Mama was once more in an interesting condition.

I have no memory of Kitty's birth but Lady Lucas recalls both Mama and Papa greeting the arrival of a fourth daughter with amazing fortitude. In the months before the birth Papa forbad any embroidering of new baby linen but at the same time he was more patient with Mama, taking care not to provoke her. He even made her the present of a brooch of two gold doves set in a circlet of seed-pearls.

Kitty was a sickly, fretful baby, however, and soon Mama's nerves were being chafed by her constant crying. Once again Mrs. Bushell's services were called on, only this time Mama decided that her infant daughter should not be living quite apart from the rest of the family. Arrangements were made for Mrs. Bushell and her two children to be installed in Collins Cottage, a little house on the Longbourn estate that had once been the home of Papa's poor relations.

And now I come to something I remember clearly though I was not three years old. I remember accompanying Kitty to

Collins Cottage with the nurserymaid, and young Peter Bushell opening the door to us without any shoes on. I remember Mrs. Bushell's husband shouting at us to shut the door—he was cutting up wadding for his gun—and I remember at sight of him finding it impossible to draw breath.

Afterwards, the nurserymaid told me that I had held my breath till I was blue in the face and that God would surely punish me if I ever did it again.

Eventually of course it all came out—how Mrs. Bushell's husband had been dismissed from the employ of Sir John Stoke and was now living permanently at Collins Cottage, doing nothing all day but drink and (as I would later discover) turning his hand to poaching by night. Mrs. Bushell was no longer able to check her husband's drunken outbreaks—on one occasion when Kitty would not stop crying he had actually picked her up and shaken her, and it had been six-year-old Peter who had persuaded him to stop. Shortly afterwards, Mrs. Bushell had confessed the whole to my father, and what he felt and how he acted may well be imagined. Certainly, I saw no more of the Bushell family, although Mrs. Bushell's husband visited me frequently in dreams.

Everyone then had been amazingly kind to me, especially Papa. He would take down a picture book and sit me on his knee and I would perch there, stiff and shy, until the ordeal was over. He saw that I was afraid of him, I suppose, but then at that time I was afraid of all men.

I was also frightened of raised voices and sudden movements, and it was now that my eldest sister Jane (dear Jane!) saw that music calmed me. She herself was only eight years old but already acutely aware of the feelings of others. She would have me sit on a little stool beside the pianoforte while she practiced, and wonderfully soothing I found it to watch her sweet face frowning over the keys and to listen to music, however imperfectly executed. (Elizabeth would also let me sit by her, but would hush me if I hummed a bar in accompaniment.)

It was at this time too that I learned to read, although here my progress was disappointingly slow because of my poor eyesight. Mama spoke the literal truth when she said of me that I always had my nose in a book. (I did not begin wearing spectacles until I was eight.)

But I have not yet mentioned Lydia. She was born just two years after Kitty on the first day of June—the fourth anniversary of the Glorious First of June, the day of Admiral Lord Howe's victory over the French, as my father jokingly reminded the London accoucheur in the hours before her birth. (This time, for a wonder, it was Papa who was confident of having a son.) It was my Uncle Philips who announced her safe arrival. Jane, Elizabeth, and I were summoned to the dining room, where he was finishing his dinner, and I remember him luridly lit by the setting sun (the windows of the Longbourn dining room face full west), pulling sugarplums from his pockets and pretending to be cheerful.

None of us were taken in, and my uncle did not try to maintain the charade. He left, muttering something about having to wet the baby's head, and shortly afterwards I descried Papa through the window walking across the lawn towards the little wilderness.

As he passed, I had a clear view of his face—lines running deeply from nose to mouth, set and despondent. The shock of seeing him made me cry out and Elizabeth ran to the window saying: "Oh! I must go to him." And although Jane tried to prevent her, she unfastened the window and sped out onto the terrace.

I saw her chase after him and catch at his coat. I saw him turn his head and for a moment I was terrified—I thought that he might strike her—but then his face softened and I saw him take her hand.

2.

About a week after Lydia's birth, my Uncle Gardiner visited Longbourn. If he had expected to find his sister weeping and hysterical as had been the case after my own birth, he must have been pleasantly surprised. Although Mama spoke of disappointment, her face whilst nursing Lydia belied her words. She was very angry with my father, however. "I vow I have no patience with Mr. Bennet, Brother. Does he imagine he is alone in his disappointment?"

My uncle then endeavored, not for the first time, to explain to her the nature of the entail.

"He has not been near this child in two days. Is *she* to be held responsible for the entail, pray? Why does he not *do something* about the entail?"

Again my uncle attempted to explain but Mama cut him short: "And in the meantime this innocent child is blamed. Only look at her. Is she not the most beautiful child you ever beheld? Mrs. Long says she has never seen such a beautiful child, not even excepting Jane. But Mr. Bennet will have it that she is nothing very extraordinary."

I confess I resented Lydia from the first. Mama made such a ridiculous fuss of her, and the new nurserymaid, a Kentish girl, Nan Pender, also favored her, and altogether she grew to be such an obstreperous child that I soon wished to have as little to do with her as possible.

Shortly after my sixth birthday, that wish was granted. I contracted measles and was removed from the nursery I shared with Kitty and Lydia to an attic room that, as soon as I was recovered enough to take cognizance of my surroundings, suited me very well. It was a long, south-facing room with a sloping ceiling and dear little diamond-paned windows, and during a protracted convalescence all my books and belongings were brought up and arranged to my great satisfaction.

And one memorable day Mama said I might have the room for my very own: "To my way of thinking it will be pleasanter for you to remain up here, Mary. No little people running about disturbing your studies and breaking your precious things. And Lydia and Kitty have quite grown used to having the nursery to themselves now." Mama also promised that a pianoforte would be placed in my new room: "Only you must not always be playing your scales up and down."

Jane was the only one to question the arrangement. "But will you not be lonely up here, Mary, all by yourself?"

I told her I preferred being alone so that I could read and work in peace. "And besides, Mama has promised me a pianoforte to have for my very own. And nobody will be allowed to touch it unless I say they may. Lydia will *certainly* not be allowed to touch it."

"But when you have put away your books, you must come and play with Lizzy and me. You must not shut yourself away from us, Mary dear."

Elizabeth walked in on us then—she could never bear to let Jane out of her sight for long—but when I told her of the pianoforte she merely raised her dark little eyebrows in the superior way I so disliked and reminded Jane that they had yet to write to Uncle Gardiner.

Jane patted my hand. "You are old enough to keep a secret, Mary, are you not?"

I saw Elizabeth looking doubtful and I said (very indignantly) that indeed I was.

"Uncle is to announce his engagement, dear. He is to marry a Miss Bellamy who comes from a very respectable family in the north of England."

"Miss Bellamy used to live in the village of Lambton," said Elizabeth with insufferable self-importance. "In Derbyshire."

"It is to be a London wedding, however, and I expect we will all be invited."

But we were not all invited. Kitty, Lydia, and I were not invited. And in the months before the marriage little else was talked of at Longbourn other than Miss Bellamy's wedding clothes and whether she would choose to live in Uncle Gardiner's house in Cheapside or in a more fashionable part of London, as she was so very fashionable herself—but at the same time immensely clever and charming—and how she had made Uncle Gardiner the happiest of men.

My first feelings of envy and disappointment were acute but I comforted myself by committing to memory Alexander Pope's "The Quiet Life." Unhappily, Lydia had no such resources, and on learning that the wedding was to take place on the Glorious First of June, the date of her fourth birthday, she had been inconsolable. She waited, however, until the afternoon they were all set to return from London before avenging herself—going first to Mama's dressing room and taking down Grandmother Gardiner's box of pomatum and hair-powder. After plastering the looking-glass with pomatum and scattering powder everywhere, she locked herself away in Papa's library to wreak further havoc—something, alas, we did not discover until too late.

I shall not easily forget my father's face as he stood amidst the ruins of his sanctum sanctorum—still wearing his caped traveling coat and holding a branch of lighted candles. The room looked as if a storm had blown through it—books strewn about with the pages torn out, the ink from the standish on his desk splattered on his favorite wing chair, and over everything a coating of powder. In the middle of it all lay Lydia, curled up in Elizabeth's old nesting place under his desk, fast asleep.

3.

This childish escapade of Lydia's was to have most serious consequences. My parents in their response to it were no longer able
to maintain even a semblance of conjugal unity. There was a very
public disagreement after Papa ordered Nan Pender to take
Lydia upstairs and put her to bed without supper. Mama had
become hysterical, attempting to snatch the still sleeping Lydia
from Nan's arms: "I am not about to let my child starve, sir!
Whatever you may have to say about it."

Papa was gathering up the torn pages of his books—his
favorite novel *The Life and Opinions of Tristram Shandy, Gentleman* was amongst the fallen—but now he turned to her with a
dreadful, fierce coldness: "Madam, I would speak with you in
private."

He then ordered the rest of us out of the room and shut the
door. Neither of them joined us afterwards for supper, and later
when Mama was up in her dressing room I saw that she had
been crying.

Once the hollowness of their marriage was exposed, perhaps my father felt compelled to act accordingly. I was too young
to understand the significance of his removing to a smaller bedchamber quite separate from Mama's apartment, but I saw—we
all saw—his attitude towards her becoming increasingly disre-
spectful. (Of course we could not know then that there would
be no more children, no son to join in cutting off the entail and

ensuring Longbourn would not fall into the grasping hands of the Collinses.)

A further consequence, though not an unpleasant one, was that we saw a great deal of the Gardiners. Mama may have hoped that their presence would deter Papa from making sarcastic remarks: He was always more agreeable when the Gardiners were at Longbourn. We all were.

Elizabeth was particularly taken with Mrs. Gardiner, or *Aunt* Gardiner as we now called her. And when it became known that Aunt was with child, she became an even greater object of interest, and not merely to Elizabeth.

The fact that Aunt was breeding was supposed to be a great secret, but I overheard her talking about it with Jane and Elizabeth one evening when the three of them were in the breakfast room making clothes for the poor. For the first time I had been allowed to help: Aunt had set me to cutting lengths of ribbon. But after a while I became sleepy—I was not yet nine years old and it was well past my bedtime—and the warm and tranquil room, the murmur of female voices, had lulled me into a sort of trance.

And in this trance or waking dream of mine the following exchange occurred, or something very like it:

"Dear Aunt, only look! Mary has cut this ribbon into such short lengths that it is now quite good for nothing."

"Oh, I'm sure we shall find a use for it, Lizzy. Perhaps I shall use it to trim Baby's caps."

"I know Mama means to make you a present of a christening cap and robe, dear Aunt." (This from Jane.)

"Do you wish for a boy or a girl, Aunt?"

"A healthy child is all I would wish for, Eliza."

"Ah, but supposing Uncle's property was entailed away from the female line, what then?"

There was a pause and then my aunt spoke very quick. She thought that there had been quite enough said on that subject already. And then: "Poor Mary. She will have to be carried upstairs to bed. Do you ring the bell for Nan, Lizzy."

This conversation gave me much food for thought, and I confess to my shame it also gave me a taste for eavesdropping, for a few days later I deliberately listened to another conversation between the three of them.

I had not *intended* to eavesdrop precisely—I had gone downstairs in search of Lydia's new kitten—but in passing the breakfast room I noticed that the door was ajar and a sudden burst of laughter roused my curiosity. What on earth did they all find so amusing? Even Jane was laughing loudly. And it occurred to me (as I crept ever closer to the door) that the lost kitten would serve as an excellent pretext if anyone were to ask what I was about. It was soon clear that they were talking—and laughing—about Mr. Benjamin Knowles—the young curate Mama had recently engaged to help me with my studies.

"He claims to have had *visions*, Aunt! He once told Jane he had conversed with an angel!"

(More laughter.)

"He is undoubtedly a pious young man, Aunt, but I fear he is misguided."

"Papa thinks him the stupidest young man he has ever met."

"We are a little concerned that Mary's education will suffer. It seems to consist entirely of religious instruction."

"He has her reading the Bible morning, noon, and night—the Bible and *Fordyce's Sermons*. As for geography, it is all the Holy Land. They are forever poring over maps of the Holy Land."

"But my dears—" Aunt had been laughing but now she sounded serious. "It is your parents to whom you should be addressing these concerns, not me."

"No, it is of no use. It is the one thing they agree upon: that Mr. Knowles must stay."

"Mary is so attached to him, you see."

"I daresay you have heard of the Bushells, Aunt? Of Mary's experience in that family?"

Aunt said that yes, she had heard about Bushell's mistreatment of myself and Kitty: "A shocking thing to have happened."

There was a pause during which I felt my heart beat fast. The name Bushell invariably had that effect on me. But I also hated to hear poor Mr. Knowles traduced, for to me he had been unfailingly kind and gentle. And I was especially grateful to him for perceiving that I needed spectacles. He himself needed always to wear spectacles.

"And Mary's progress in other subjects?" Aunt was again speaking. "Arithmetic, for instance?"

"She cannot cast up a single sum with accuracy. She is completely ignorant of the rudiments."

"I fear she has been hurried through the different rules."

Aunt spoke again. "Yet Mary is so very attached to him."

"And I believe he is sincerely attached to her," said Jane. "I know he considers her to be amazingly clever."

There was a moment's pause and then all three of them exploded into laughter.

4.

I could scarce believe my ears. And my father undoubtedly shared this view of my abilities! My first reactions were passionately contradictory. I would prove them wrong if it was the last thing I ever did, confound them all with a dazzling display of genius. In the next breath I resolved to be completely idle—leave off my studies, burn my books. Since I was so stupid, what did it matter?

But the last part of their conversation was every bit as hurtful as the first. Aunt had told Jane and Elizabeth she believed I was lonely, that I lived too much apart from my sisters: "It must be hard for Mary, situated as she is. You two are exceptionally close and Lydia and Kitty are inseparable, but she has nobody. It must be very hard."

Elizabeth then spoke in a tone uncharacteristically serious: "What you say is very true. I wonder it had not occurred to me before."

"But Aunt, whenever Lizzy and I ask Mary to come on walks with us or to join in games with the younger ones, she nearly always refuses."

"That is to say whenever *you* ask her," said Elizabeth. "The truth is I never do. I find Mary's company tedious."

"My dear Lizzy." Aunt's tone was both amused and disapproving. "If Mr. Knowles is as you describe and Mary is with him for the chief part of every day—"

"I know, I know, I see that now. I have not been kind to her. But I shall try to do better. I shall make amends."

And Elizabeth did try to make amends, unquestionably. She invited me to walk to the farm with her, to practice duets with her, and on several occasions—with real heroism—offered to accompany me when I sang. She also made me a present of an old and much loved doll I had coveted when I was seven but now no longer wanted.

But I could not allow myself the luxury of loving Elizabeth; I could not respond to friendly overtures now that I knew my company was so irksome to her. Also, it struck me that she was herself a little lonely at this time and less likely to be discriminating. Jane was beginning to put away childish things.

Like most such transitions, it was uneven. One day she would be playing at hopscotch with her skirts tucked up, the next would see her blushing and looking conscious when a clerk from Uncle Philips's office stared at her. Jane had always been a remarkably pretty girl with a great sweetness of expression but she was now becoming quite beautiful. When we walked into Meryton people would look at her so, it was embarrassing—and not men merely; she had the sort of face that also charmed women.

My mother of course took a vicarious delight in this admiration, prophesying to Lady Lucas that Jane would marry a duke someday: "There's no denying she has a higher claim than most by virtue of her sweet face, and I've not the least doubt she would make a charming duchess. And then, you know, she would be waited on by liveried footmen and I daresay dine off gold plate every day. Not that I would wish her to marry without affection of course."

Absurd as it might seem, I believe Elizabeth too saw Jane as somehow set apart from the generality of girls—if not destined to be a duchess then certainly deserving homage as a superior being. But for whatever reason—loneliness, ennui, disgust at Mama's vulgar aspirations for Jane—Elizabeth at this time began to read and study a great deal more; a master was engaged to teach her the Italian language, and she practiced her music assiduously. She also persevered with Aunt Gardiner's work for the poor families in the parish, as indeed did Jane.

Meanwhile, the Gardiner family continued to increase—there were now two little girls, Susan and Virginia—and perforce their visits to Longbourn became less frequent. But Jane and Elizabeth had both been to stay with the Gardiners in London, and more recently Jane had visited on her own.

It was on this last visit when Jane had just turned fifteen that she met a very eligible young man, who—if Mama is to be believed—fell in love with her. His name was Mr. Leigh Stanley and although he was not, alas, a duke, he was heir to a baronetcy and stood to inherit a sizeable estate in Gloucestershire.

I never heard the full story of Mr. Stanley. I knew that he had sent Jane some verses but Jane seemed her usual serene self when she returned home, and I remember thinking that she could not have been very much in love because she laughed when Elizabeth made fun of Mr. Stanley's poem.

The poem had half a dozen verses but I can recall only one:

I saw her first in Gracechurch Street
One hot bright August morn.
She wore a chipstraw bonnet
And kirtle of pink lawn.

I remember Elizabeth laughing as she read it out to me. She had come to the breakfast room where Mr. Knowles was giving me my scripture lesson—she had not yet given up trying to make amends.

"Dear Mary! Have you ever heard such *stuff*?"

"Now then, Miss Lizzy," said Mr. Knowles. "We must not be too ready to ridicule."

"What is a kirtle?" I wanted to know. (I did not think the poem at all bad.)

"Oh! 'tis an archaic word for a gown—and Jane does not even own a pink gown. It is the most absurd thing."

Mr. Knowles then said that his late father had once written a poem: "A lovely little acrostic upon my mother's Christian name it was—my dear mother's Christian name is Imogen—I wish I could remember it. He composed it when they were courting."

Mr. Knowles had taken off his spectacles, closing his eyes in an effort of recall and I saw that Elizabeth was having difficulty keeping her countenance. After a moment she turned to me: "Jane and I plan to walk to Clarke's Library. Do you care to come with us?"

I wanted very much to go but her attitude towards Mr. Knowles had unsettled me; it reminded me of her earlier scornful comments. And my loyalty to Mr. Knowles was now absolute. I said: "I am afraid I have a great deal of work I must attend to."

"Just as you choose."

It would be the last time for a long while that Elizabeth asked me to go anywhere or do anything with her, and I wish now that I had accepted. If the two of us had been better friends it might have made a difference later when Netherfield Park was let—not, I hasten to add, to Mr. Bingley; we have not yet come to Mr. Bingley—but to a very personable and clever man called Jasper Coates.

Elizabeth conceived a violent infatuation for Mr. Coates—she was fourteen at the time—and if she had been in my confidence, she might have been spared a deal of heartache, for I knew a thing or two about Mr. Coates that she did not. But the manner in which I came by this knowledge—and the threat it posed to my own peace of mind—will take a little time and paper to set down.

5.

Stories about Mr. Jasper Coates began to circulate long before he arrived at Netherfield. He was reported to be a single man of about eight and twenty, living in London, a writer of novels but with an independent fortune of some six thousand a year. His widowed sister and her two young sons were also to live at Netherfield, and this same sister was to keep house for him.

Sir William Lucas was the first to visit the newcomer; he called at Longbourn later to tell us what he had learned.

Yes, he assured Mama, Mr. Coates was a single man and a fine young man too, very handsome—if Sir William was any judge—with an affable, well-bred manner, although a little too informal in his dress (he had been in his shirtsleeves, supervising the unpacking of a crate of books when Sir William called).

However, when questioned further by Jane and Elizabeth as to what sort of man Mr. Coates *really* was—his interests and pursuits—Sir William could offer little: He guessed Mr. Coates's age to be thirty or thereabouts, and his weight to be about thirteen stone.

But then Sir William recalled that while the crate of books was being emptied, Mr. Coates had set aside several identical three-volume sets in red leather, all with gilded page fore-edges, and ordered that they be placed under lock and key.

"His own work!" exclaimed Elizabeth. "And what was the title, Sir William?"

Sir William could not recall the title except that it was encased in a scroll and the lettering was in gold.

"And what of this man's sister?" Mama wanted to know. "And her little boys?"

Here, Sir William was better informed. It was Mr. Coates's *step*sister, a Mrs. Rovere, who was the mother of the boys, and it was *her* mother who would be keeping house for them. As to the boys, Sir William had met them both; their names were George and Samuel—remarkably well-grown, rosy-faced fellows, and the older boy, George, a talented young musician. Their ages were twelve and eight.

"The exact same ages as Mary and Lydia! Well, and so what of the mother? Did you meet her?"

"No, I did not have that honor—although I saw a lady as I was leaving—a remarkably fine lady on the stairs as I came away, whom I assumed to be Mrs. Rovere—dark hair and eyes and a decided air of fashion."

"Well, Mr. Bennet is to call on Mr. Coates tomorrow—if he does not put it off again—and after Mr. Coates has returned the visit, I shall invite them all to dinner."

Mama was as good as her word, and one week later the Bennet family gathered in the Longbourn drawing room to await the arrival of the guests. It was but a small dinner party—only the Netherfield family and Sir William and Lady Lucas had been invited—but Mama had also asked the two Rovere boys, observing to my father that today's childhood playmates often became tomorrow's beaux.

We younger children would not be joining the rest of the company in the dining room of course—we would be eating quite apart in the breakfast room—but for the first time Elizabeth was to dine with the adults, and I saw that she was quite excited at the prospect. Her face, bent over her needle-work, had a heightened color and she was behaving in an unusually quiet and decorous fashion.

I also noticed that she was wearing a new gown—white with a sort of silvery trim—and as I watched her sewing, it seemed to me that she had become all at once maidenly and mysterious, that she had joined Jane in an esoteric world to which as yet I possessed no key.

Perhaps my father sensed something of this too, for he said suddenly: "That is a new gown, Lizzy, I think?"

"Yes, Papa. Do you approve?"

She was looking at him and smiling in her usual way, and he—possibly reassured—returned to his book.

My mother meanwhile was becoming restless. "The Lucases are late. And Sir William promised me they would come early."

And then when nobody spoke—Kitty and Lydia being engrossed in a game of spillikins in the corner—she again burst out: "I do so hate it when people do not keep their word. And nowadays that man thinks of nothing but his own importance. His head is full of the Court of St. James's—everything is the Court of St. James's—"

"Of whom are you speaking?" My father's tone was decidedly unfriendly.

Mama for once took the hint: "Nothing, nobody. 'Tis of no consequence."

But then her angry, restless glance fell on me. "For heaven's sake, Mary, that gown if I do not mistake is the one I told you to leave off wearing—it is by far too tight and now look, look!" (pulling at my sleeve) "Here is the seam split open entirely."

"Mama," said Jane. "I believe I can hear a carriage."

But Mama's attention was now fixed on my split seam: "I cannot pin it—there is not time enough to pin it—you will have to go and change. Go put on your blue checked muslin. Ask Nan to help you. Go *on*, girl! Hurry!"

6.

I did not hurry, I dawdled. And I did not ask Nan to help me change my gown. I was very angry with my mother. There had been something about her treatment of me, a contempt, which I very much resented and vowed I would make her sorry for.

I knew such a thought was sinful, that Mr. Knowles would be shocked, but the idea of making Mama sorry was too sweet to relinquish in a hurry, and while I removed my spectacles and polished them (slowly) and stared at my reflection in the glass, I meditated on how best I could punish her.

Meanwhile the guests had arrived—and by the time I fixed on a most exquisite punishment, they had all left the drawing room and gone in to dinner. The punishment was nothing more than that I had determined to return downstairs still wearing my torn gown—in fact I had made the split rather bigger.

Nan was serving soup to Lydia and Kitty and the two Rovere boys when I entered the breakfast room.

The younger boy said: "And who might you be, Miss?"

Lydia thought this so amusing she spluttered her soup: "That is my sister Mary, you rude boy."

The boy was cramming bread into his mouth and talking at the same time. "Why is she dressed in rags then, pray? I thought she was a maidservant."

More spluttering from Lydia, with Kitty copying her as usual, but now the other boy spoke up sharp: "Stow it, Sam!"

And then turning to me: "I am George Rovere and I apologize for my brother's manners."

He had a very pleasant, albeit foreign-looking face, red-cheeked and full-lipped and with beautiful dark eyes—so dark it was hard to tell where pupil and iris met. His manner too seemed slightly exotic; he inclined his head when he spoke and used formal phrases. But at the same time he was eager to talk and full of questions. And while Lydia and Sam and Kitty sniggered and spluttered and when Nan's back was turned rolled pills of bread and threw them at each other, George cross-examined me:

Did I enjoy living in the country? Did I have my own pony? Was I interested in music? Did I sing or play the pianoforte?

After I answered these questions and a dozen more besides— he was disappointed to learn that I did not own a pony and had never been taught to ride—I ventured to ask a question of my own: Had he and his brother always lived with their uncle Mr. Coates?

His reply surprised me. No, it was only in the last four years that he and Sam had lived in London with Mr. Coates—who by the bye was their step-uncle, not their real uncle. Before that, they had lived in Italy, in Florence.

"My grandmother is Italian," said George. "But her English is excellent, I promise you. Two of her husbands were English, you see."

"*Two* of her husbands!"

He nodded, smiling, but did not elaborate and soon after-wards the lady herself marched into the room, clapping her hands and calling: "Jasper! Christina! I have found them. Here is the room."

For a grandmother, Mrs. Falco was amazingly youthful look-ing. Her hair was silver but scissored into a fashionable feathery style and her figure was slender, her skin remarkably unlined, and she had the same black eyes and full red mouth as George.

"This is Miss *Mary* Bennet, I think it must be? No, do not stand up. I am Giulia Falco and the mother of these boys' mother, and now you must call me Nonna too."

She gave me a glorious white-toothed smile and then turned her charm on Nan Pender, asking whether she found the Bennet children extremely naughty ones. "Especially little Miss Lydia, the most naughty one of all."

Poor Nan of course could not deny this, whereupon Mrs. Falco laughed and ruffled Lydia's hair and again called: "Christina! Jasper! Where are you? I am in the room here!"

When at last Mrs. Rovere and Mr. Coates walked in I had the impression they had been quarrelling. Mrs. Rovere was saying something in a foreign language and then too suddenly she gave us all a public smile.

Until she smiled, I thought her the most beautiful woman I had ever seen. She was more voluptuous, more slow-moving, than Mrs. Falco, but there was a strong resemblance to her mother about the eyes and mouth. Her smile, however, in contrast to the gleaming energy of Mrs. Falco's, was disappointing: even-toothed but small, even a little sly.

Mr. Coates was beautiful too, in a manly sort of way. He stood silently observing us—as acute and unembarrassed an observer as Mr. Fitzwilliam Darcy would later prove to be. (He looked very much like Mr. Darcy too, his person being equally fine, tall, and well-made.)

"Here is a person you do not know, Christina." Mrs. Falco placed her hands on my shoulders. "This here is Mary Pender. And there is Nan Bennet."

I did not like to correct her for fear of being thought impertinent. Bennet and Pender are similar-sounding names and

Mrs. Falco spoke with a strong accent. But Mrs. Rovere was not paying attention anyway: She was talking to Mr. Coates.

He for his part continued to observe us—studying his fellow creatures as befits a writer of novels—when suddenly something made him laugh. It was an odd laugh—high and slightly cracked— an imperfection that made him more attractive (to me if not to Elizabeth). He laughed in response to something Lydia said. When Mrs. Falco had announced that George was to play Haydn in the drawing room, Lydia had understood her to mean the game of hide-and-seek: "In the drawing room! Mama will never give him leave." But on learning her mistake Lydia was not at all abashed, saying merely: "Oh! well then, Mary must play Haydn too. Mary is a capital player."

Altogether it was an evening for misunderstandings, for I later learned that Mrs. Rovere believed me to be Nan Pender's daughter. And although George would eventually set her right as to my parentage, I am convinced she persisted in seeing me as some sort of under-nurserymaid employed to help look after Kitty and Lydia. It is hard to completely disabuse people of faulty first impressions: Having consigned me and my torn dress to the servant class, Mrs. Rovere was content for us to remain there.

I do not think I would have learned the true state of affairs at Netherfield if Mrs. Rovere had not entertained this view of me—that somehow I did not count. I was soon to become a regular visitor to the house, and in the ordinary way of children I became privy to many family secrets. But their most closely guarded secret I should never have learned if Mrs. Rovere had not been quite unconcerned about what she said and did in my presence.

7.

Considering how little practiced I was in the art of making friends, my friendship with George Rovere bloomed amazingly quick. Within days of our meeting, we were practicing duets together and sharing the same music master. Mama was eager to promote the acquaintance, as was Mrs. Falco (or Nonna, as I came to call her), and soon it was Netherfield for me every morning, where the music master would give us our lesson before breakfast.

At first, Kitty and Lydia accompanied me, but this arrangement did not last. Lydia and Sam were too alike, both spoilt and self-willed, to endure each others' company for long; and after the sport of baiting and bullying poor Kitty lost its savor (and after Kitty refused point-blank to go to Netherfield) I always went alone.

During this time I hardly ever saw Mrs. Rovere. She rarely rose before noon and George always kept the doors to the music room closed so that she would not be disturbed. But one morning after I had been a regular visitor for several weeks, she stormed in when George and I were playing a duet in the absence of the music master.

We had our backs to the door, deaf to everything but our own noise, when she descended, knocking George off his stool and crashing the lid of the pianoforte down upon my hand.

The pain was terrible but I dared not cry out. She was standing over me like a mad person with her hair tangled up like serpents. George picked himself up and began brushing off the sleeve of his jacket while she stood there panting as if she had run a great race. After a minute she asked me if she had hurt my hand.

"It is of no consequence, ma'am." (If George could be calm in the face of her intemperate behavior, then surely so could I.)

Next thing, Mr. Coates came running in. He must have heard her screaming. "What is the matter? What is it, Christina?"

"Oh." (shaking back her hair and smiling) "Nothing, nothing. The music was so very loud." She reached for Mr. Coates's hand and then suddenly, convulsively, burst into tears.

"Hush now, Tina." He was holding her and patting her, his expression a curious blend of impatience and resignation. He then jerked his head at George in an unmistakable signal for us to leave.

I almost ran from the room but George took his time and when he reached the door I heard him mutter something in Italian. Whereupon Mr. Coates strode over and pulled him back and shut the door in my face—only to open it a moment later and say: "Run along to the library, Mary. You'll find Nonna there." And then, perhaps seeing I was close to tears: "George will join you later."

There was no sign of Nonna in the library, however, and George did not join me later. I must have sat there for the best part of an hour before one of the maids came to tell me that the carriage had been brought round.

Next morning George was not waiting for me in the music room as usual; he was in the breakfast parlor. But before we could talk, Mr. Coates walked in and made a great show of welcoming me. "I expect you're famished, are you, Mary? There's a very decent ham—shall I carve you a few slices?"

Normally I ate a hearty breakfast at Netherfield but this ostentatious hospitality quite took away my appetite. George sat in silence while Mr. Coates carved and set down my plate. "Now let's see how good a trencherwoman you are. *Buon appetito.*"

He then turned his attention to George. "You'll be pleased to hear that the new mare has arrived." (George had been promised the gift of a horse for his thirteenth birthday.) "Sam is down there with her now, getting acquainted."

George said quickly: "But you've not given him leave to ride her, have you, sir?"

"No, no." Coates laughed his odd cracked laugh. "She's your horse, never fear." He turned back to me. "Do you drink chocolate, Mary?"

I shook my head, feeling my face grow hot. I was sure now that he had sent Sam off to the stables so he could talk to me in private—to apologize for Mrs. Rovere's behavior—but in response to a question from George, he began talking about the new horse: "She's a lovely little creature—legs of iron and a wonderful bold eye."

During the ensuing horsey conversation I fancied Mr. Coates was glancing at me from time to time, and once when I dared look up he was certainly looking at me, although he immediately smiled and left off.

It struck me then that he was a perceptive man, and tactful withal—and it helped too that he had a charming, rueful-seeming smile.

The apology came when I least expected it. One moment he was refilling his coffee cup and telling George how to mix a linseed bran mash, the next he turned to me and spoke the words in an awkward little rush: "I am really very sorry about yesterday, Mary."

He stirred his coffee, his color somewhat heightened. "Well. Now that that fence has been cleared."

We all laughed but I saw George looked uncomfortable. Mr. Coates continued to stir his coffee. "I don't know how it is in your family, Mary, but in this household—I suppose you could say we are less 'English' in our ways, and when feelings run high, we are apt to—to *vent* those feelings, and afterwards we may regret—very much regret that we have hurt someone or made them unhappy."

I did not know what to say. I was not so much embarrassed as confused: He seemed to be taking responsibility for someone else's bad behavior. And while Mr. Knowles would have said that that was following the example of Jesus Christ, still I found it unsettling. It did not suit my child's sense of justice.

George must have felt as I did, for he said: "But it wasn't *you*, sir!"

Mr. Coates ignored this. "Let me see your hand, Mary. Does it still pain you?"

"Oh! it is much better this morning, sir, truly."

George muttered something in Italian that sounded like "*Ma va'.*"

"These sotto voce remarks, George—I thought I made it clear to you yesterday—if you have a grievance, for God's sake speak it directly."

"Very well then, sir. I think my mother should apologize to Mary."

"Well she won't, and there's an end to it!"

There was a pause, dreadful to my feelings, with Mr. Coates looking annoyed and George picking up his cup with a sulky sort of dignity.

I said: "Perhaps it would be better if I didn't come here any more. For my music lessons, I mean."

"But you like coming here, don't you?"

"Oh yes, sir, I like it more than anything."

"I'm glad to hear it." He was smiling now. "If Mary Bennet were to cease visiting Netherfield, I for one should be extremely sorry."

I felt myself blushing. "You're very kind."

"Nonsense. You're always welcome here, my dear. Never doubt that."

He then turned back to George as if their earlier argument had never happened: "Of what were we speaking? Linseed, yes, you need to boil the stuff for at least four hours before you mix it with the bran mash. 'Tis poisonous unless thoroughly boiled."

8.

Everyone at Netherfield now seemed anxious to reassure me that I was welcome—even Mrs. Rovere. Nonna immediately set about teaching me Italian, in which I made such rapid progress that my grasp of the language soon rivaled Elizabeth's. But when Mr. Coates tried to teach me how to ride, the outcome was less happy. I simply could not conquer my fear of horses, their snorting and eye-rolling and unpredictable tricks, although for George's sake I persevered for several weeks.

Fortunately, this did not affect our friendship. By now, George and I absolutely confided in each other. I could tell him about my sisters—how I felt excluded from Kitty and Lydia's juvenile pursuits and equally shut out from Jane and Elizabeth's new adult world, or worse, included as an act of charity. George for his part could talk to me of Sam's oafishness and childish clowning. There was also the comfort of complaining about our respective mothers, their partiality and caprice. And George even confided—swearing me to secrecy—that his mother was now a "proper" widow, his father having died six months ago in Florence. Before that, his mother had only pretended to be a widow when they had all come to live in London.

But over and above everything, George and I had our music—an *excess of it* so far as Mrs. Rovere was concerned— and it was now that we started to rehearse Mozart's *Sonata for Two Pianos in D Major*. Not long afterwards Mr. Coates decided that a musical evening must be held at Netherfield so that George and I could perform the sonata before an audience. A date was accordingly fixed and then came the business of deciding who was to be invited. It was during the course of these preparations that I witnessed a dreadful quarrel between Nonna, Mrs. Rovere, and Mr. Coates.

George, Sam, and I had been in the library transcribing under Nonna's supervision the names of guests on cards of invitation when Mr. Coates and Mrs. Rovere walked in. They had been out riding and looked hot and untidy and—in Mrs. Rovere's case—out of temper.

"Good God!" said she. "Have you not finished yet?"

Nonna was indignant. "We have *twenty-six* invitations to be writing, Christina."

Mr. Coates came to stand behind my chair. "Very elegant handwriting, Mary."

"What about *my* handwriting, Uncle?" Sam held up a barely legible specimen.

"Agh!" George scoffed. "Yours is good for nothing. You scribble so and make great blots."

"Well, well"—this from Mr. Coates—"I'm forever blotting my copybook too, Sam."

Mrs. Rovere had picked up the list of guests. "How is it that Mr. Frederick Purvis has not been invited?"

"The old fellow who dyes his hair?" Mr. Coates gave one of his cracked laughs. "Why the devil do you want to ask him?"

Mrs. Rovere answered him in Italian, perhaps forgetting I was now able to understand: "Because he has a lot of money."

She then spoke rapidly in Italian, only some of which I understood. It seemed that two distinct classes of guest were to be invited: The first lot were to come to dinner while the second, inferior group were to come in the evening merely to hear the music. Mrs. Rovere now wanted Mr. Purvis to be included in the first group.

"I notice," said she, now speaking in English, "that Jasper's beloved Bennets are asked to dine."

Mr. Coates looked annoyed but it was Nonna who exploded. "It is me who is asking the Bennets—not Jasper." (placing a hand on my shoulder) "The parents of this little person—of course I ask them. And I ask her two old sisters also."

"Well, Mama, provided Elizabeth Bennet sits next to Jasper and Mr. Purvis sits beside myself—"

"Tina. That's enough."

I had never heard Mr. Coates speak so sharp. He had taken Mrs. Rovere's arm, not ungently, but she at once accused him of "threatening" her. "Oh!" said she with a little laugh, a mere *ha* of furious breath. "I know you want to be rid of me. First my mother, then me." She struggled now to free herself. "*Unhand* me, Jasper!"

Mr. Coates immediately spoilt the effect by laughing— although he did not let her go. "Don't write any more invitations," said he to Nonna. "Tina and I will be happy to finish them, won't we, Tina?"

Mrs. Rovere's reply was in Italian but unfortunately I did not understand a word of it.

Afterwards, I wondered very much about this quarrel. It seemed preposterous that Mrs. Rovere should be jealous of Elizabeth—a fourteen-year-old girl with no particular claim to beauty and an inflated idea of her own intellect and powers of observation. But the more I thought about it, the more probable it seemed: Incidents that at the time had appeared trivial and unrelated now struck me as part of a pattern.

Mr. Coates often called at Longbourn to borrow books from my father, and I had observed how he enjoyed talking to Elizabeth, joking with her and teasing her. On a recent visit to Haye Park they had spent half the afternoon playing at battledore and shuttlecock together. And they frequently, inexplicably, laughed at the same things—things that to my mind were not in the least funny—such as when poor Mr. Knowles was scratched by Lydia's cat Beelzebub. (On being told that the sty on his eyelid might be cured by rubbing it back and forth with the tail of a black cat, Mr. Knowles had rather unwisely selected Beelzebub for the purpose.)

They were also very curious about each other, especially Elizabeth about Mr. Coates. She asked numerous seemingly casual questions of me. How did they all behave at Netherfield in private, and in particular how did Mr. Coates conduct himself? Was he good-tempered? Considerate towards the servants? Mr. Coates for his part often asked me whether *both* my elder sisters were to be present on such and such an occasion. And once when Nonna was praising Jane's beauty to the skies, he said (impatiently, speaking over the top of his newspaper) that yes, Jane Bennet was undoubtedly a very pretty girl but Elizabeth was infinitely more *taking*.

Reflecting on all this up in my little room, I was conscious of feeling out of all proportion vexed. I had come to regard Mr. Coates—indeed, everyone at Netherfield—as peculiarly my property. I was resigned to playing fifth fiddle to my sisters everywhere else, but at Netherfield it was *Mary* Bennet who was petted and preferred.

All my old jealousy of Elizabeth came rushing back. How did she contrive to so insinuate herself into people's hearts? Within our own family, she had all but annexed Jane and appropriated our father. And Aunt Gardiner too was fast becoming her exclusive property. Aunt was presently visiting Longbourn with her two little girls, and she and Elizabeth were forever walking together in the shrubbery, parasols held at the exact same angle and height. (Elizabeth had grown prodigiously in the past year.)

In an effort to check these envious thoughts, I opened my pianoforte. But even as I played the first bars of the Mozart sonata, my thoughts flew back to the morning's quarrel. Mrs. Rovere had accused Mr. Coates of wanting to be rid of her— "First my mother, then me." But Mr. Coates seemed sincerely attached to Nonna. And I had never heard him express dissatisfaction with the way she ran his household. On the contrary, he was always thanking her, grateful for the least little thing. Why should Mrs. Rovere make such an accusation?

I was no closer to solving this riddle by the time I went down to dinner. It was Aunt Gardiner who unwittingly provided me with a clue. Aunt had not yet met Mr. Coates—but she had read his very first novel.

"I may say I read it 'hot off the press.' A friend of Edward's has an interest in a publishing house and he gave us a copy. I enjoyed it immensely. All about a young man who falls in love with an Italian lady, a widow, many years older than himself. But the lady happens to be the widow of his own father—"

Papa said: "I take it this is Mr. Coates's version of Oedipus?"

Aunt laughed. "The lady was his *step*mother merely. But then a little later he falls in love with her daughter by a previous marriage." Aunt paused in her recital, perhaps belatedly conscious that the story was not suited to the dinner table, where there were children present.

Mama had no such reservations. "Go on, Sister. What then?"

"Oh! the usual vicissitudes. It's a great while since I read it."

Mama was peeling an apple for Lydia. "I daresay it was a bit warm, was it? Most of your novels are."

Aunt and Elizabeth exchanged smiles (they were constantly exchanging smiles) but Aunt said merely: "I daresay. But very convincing nonetheless."

My father was also smiling. "Founded upon his own experience perhaps."

Mama cried out: "My dear Mr. Bennet! You're not suggesting that Mrs. Falco—"

"What was the name of the book, Aunt?" Elizabeth was adept at heading Mama off whenever she sailed too close to the wind.

"It was called *Paola*. But you won't find it in the circulating library. The author had a change of heart shortly after the book was bound and tried to arrest publication. When that failed, he bought up every copy he could lay his hands on."

I sat very still, experiencing one of those moments when one recognizes a truth both logically and intuitively. Nonna's second name was Paola and Mr. Coates not infrequently called her by it. And innocent and ignorant as I was, I had long sensed that Mrs. Rovere's hostility towards Nonna was founded on jealousy.

9.

"What is it you are reading, Mary, pray?"

Mrs. Rovere, still wearing her dressing gown, had entered the Netherfield library just as I was turning the first page of *Paola*. Concealment was impossible: She had already plucked the book from my grasp. All I could do was wait, speechless and trembling, for her anger to break.

And I had been so certain I was safe! Mr. Coates had left for London, Nonna had gone into Meryton to shop, and George and Sam were out riding. I had watched both boys out of the house before going to the library and unlocking—with shaking hands and pounding heart—the big break-front bookcase where Mr. Coates kept copies of his own works. But now as I sat, head bowed, I heard only the rustle of swiftly turned pages and then—incredibly—a burst of laughter.

"Good God!" (seating herself beside me) "I had quite forgotten."

I glanced up at her. She was utterly engrossed, smiling as she read. Several minutes passed and I was beginning to breathe more easily when she said, without lifting her eyes from the page: "How came you by this? Did Jasper give it to you?"

"Oh no, ma'am!" I struggled to speak collectedly: "The key had been left in the bookcase and so I—I know I oughtn't to have opened it without Mr. Coates's leave but my aunt— yesterday my aunt spoke of the book so highly, that I ventured—"

"Your aunt? Your mother's sister? The one who lives in Meryton?"

"Oh no, that is my aunt Philips. No, I was speaking of Aunt Gardiner—she is a great reader, my aunt Gardiner—"

But her attention had returned to *Paola*. She must have read for five minutes—it seemed an eternity—and then she laughed an embarrassed, groaning sort of laugh such as a poor joke might elicit and looked at me.

Her look was not unfriendly. She was happy to have an audience—a sycophantic servant would have done as well as a docile child. She wanted to talk.

"Very few people have read this novel, you know, Mary."

"Indeed?" (I thought it best not to repeat what Aunt had said.)

"Jasper sent it to a publisher—*fare un esperimento*, you understand? He thought nobody would want it. And then they offered him a hundred guineas. That's a lot of money, wouldn't you agree, a hundred guineas? Very hard to say no to a hundred guineas."

She was now tracing the gold scroll about the title. "He should never have accepted of course. He should have known that people would recognize the characters, the circumstances—everything pointed to Mama and myself. But it was very much a young man's novel, very *confessionale*. He didn't consider our reputations. Of course Mama—being Mama—declared she didn't care."

She paused, frowning, and then went on in a very passable imitation of Nonna: "Reputation is no matter when a person is making *art*."

I laughed—I knew it was expected of me—and she continued: "Yes, well I happen to think it does matter. And Jasper eventually came round to my way of thinking—too late of course—he then had to spend a small fortune buying up the publisher's stock."

"Yes, my aunt did mention—"

But she was not listening, intent on justifying herself: "We all have to live in the world, Mary, and I had my boys to consider. And I have no assets—no capital—apart from my good name." (giving me one of her disappointing smiles) "And my good looks."

"Nature's coin," I murmured. I was then afraid she would think me impertinent. "Mr. Knowles had me learn many such aphorisms—on account of my plainness and my sisters' good looks."

"No, you'll never be a beauty, that's certain." She rose and walked to the bookcase and took down the second volume of *Paola*. "You must cultivate your talents, your music—you must study to become *interessante*." (leafing through the book as she spoke) "Perhaps you will write a novel yourself one day, who knows?"

"You're pleased to make fun of me, ma'am."

"Not at all." She laid aside the second volume and took down the third. "It's next to impossible for a woman to make her own way in the world, but if I had the least little talent I assure you I'd be laboring night and day to turn it to good account—to earn some money for myself. As it is, I'm reduced to muddling along with Jasper—who will never marry me now—or accepting an offer from Fred Purvis."

I was astounded. "But Mr. Purvis is so . . . so . . ."

She laughed. "So so *rich*, Mary! I have it on good authority he's worth twelve thousand a year."

"But ma'am." The image of Mr. Purvis—an elderly dandy with dyed caramel hair—was so strong I could not believe her to be serious. "You would have to *live* with him."

"Ah, but not for long. I have it all planned. I shall engage an Italian cook—and Purvis will then gorge himself. Oh! he will pop off within a year."

I could not laugh with her. That she should think of marrying Mr. Purvis solely for his money was bad enough, but to plan his death—to *joke* about it!

"What a solemn little creature you are." She was now holding all three volumes of *Paola*. "You peer at me through your spectacles so that I feel quite . . ." (shaking her head at me, and then when I failed to respond): "Such an unforgiving *basilisk* stare—you look just like your sister Elizabeth. But really, you must not judge me, you know. 'Judge not, that ye be not judged.' I feel sure your Mr. Knowles has impressed that upon you. Should you like to read this then?"

Incredibly, she was handing me the volumes. "I really don't think it will corrupt you—the whole thing is such ancient history now. It may even help you to understand us better. God knows we're all of us in need of understanding. Only you must not tell them at Longbourn that it has any *factual* basis."

"No indeed, ma'am. Thank you. I shall never let it out of my hands, I promise."

"Oh, I shouldn't object to your older sister's reading it. Elizabeth is a great reader, is she not? I would be interested to know what Elizabeth Bennet thinks of *Paola*."

10.

Strange to say, once *Paola* was in my possession I no longer felt eager to read it. I had begun the first chapter that same evening—a lengthy account of a rough channel crossing, it was all cresting swells and creaking masts, the stuff that boys delight in. Afterwards, having consigned the volumes to the depths of my bureau drawer, I was not impatient to take it out again. (At the same time, I was not about to let Elizabeth read it either.)

But in the days that followed, the secrecy of the whole business began to weigh on me. While I had grown used to concealing my thoughts from the members of my family, I was not comfortable hiding anything from Mr. Knowles—still less from George. But if I were to confide in Mr. Knowles, I was afraid I would never be permitted to go to Netherfield again. And I could not, in conscience, unburden myself to George. This then was the end of the perfect confidence that we had hitherto enjoyed. Now, when we were practicing together, I was in constant fear of Mrs. Rovere walking in. She would invariably ask: "Well Mary, and how are you progressing?" And such was my shame at having to prevaricate—knowing George believed her to be alluding to the Mozart sonata—I could not answer without blushing and stammering.

Images of the three red leather volumes in my bureau drawers (wrapped now in petticoats and covered with a cunning latticework of handkerchiefs) began to surface in my dreams. Indeed, I am convinced that the melancholia that was later to afflict me had its roots in this experience. But I am getting ahead of myself. For the most part I was cheerful enough. I constantly practiced the Mozart sonata, with and without George, and that helped to preserve my peace of mind.

My father meanwhile had forbidden all discussion about the musical evening (I suspect because it was of such concern to my mother), but on the morning of the great day just as we were sitting down to breakfast I saw Jane go up to him and whisper, and shortly afterwards he turned to me and said: "So, Mary. Your concert is tonight, I understand. And are you thoroughly prepared for your ordeal?"

"I hope so, sir." (I never knew how to respond when he quizzed me thus. Elizabeth was able to deflect his irony, challenge his assumptions—always with grace and good humor of course—and he permitted it because he loved her. The rest of us were not granted the liberty.) "We are to play Mozart's *Sonata for Two Pianos in D Major.*"

He nodded. "George is to play the other instrument, I take it?"

"Yes, sir."

As always when he gave me his attention, I felt myself becoming awkward and stiff. In my imagination I was again three years old; his look conveyed such contrary feelings—pity and malice both, or so I fancied.

Now I watched him slice off the top of his egg and prayed he would turn his attention to someone else, but Lydia's evil genius prompted her to ask: "Shall you be going to the concert, Papa?"

"Oh, I think not. Unless—" He was looking at me again. "Unless Mary would be heartbroken if I did not." I had not the least idea how to respond and judged it safer to be silent. "While Mary is making up her mind then, I should be obliged if someone would pass me the salt."

It was this sort of treatment—the inference that I was slow-witted, the slighting of my accomplishments, my music especially—that made me harden my heart towards him. (Later, when I was suffering from melancholia, I found the means of similarly wounding him. In response to inquiries after my health—for I was for a time most seriously ill—I would stare at him without speaking and his bemused expression gave me—I confess it—the most exquisite satisfaction.)

But I digress. After breakfast I went to my room to practice, and a little later Lydia and Kitty and young Susan Gardiner burst in without knocking. I was wanted in Mama's dressing room immediately: Aunt Gardiner had finished the new gown I was to wear at the concert.

"And Mama has a present for you," said Lydia.

"And you are to go to Netherfield just as soon as you are dressed," said Kitty. "Papa is to send for the horses."

Lydia now began plunking notes on my pianoforte and Susan Gardiner—a mischievous little two-year-old—was reaching up to touch the keys so that I was obliged to close the lid. Lydia then began her usual moan that I never shared my toys with anyone.

"A pianoforte is not a toy, Lydia."

"Anyway, we know something about somebody at Netherfield that you do not."

"Indeed?"

"You will never guess what. Me and Kitty are the only ones in this family who know."

"Maria Lucas told us in confidence. You will never guess."

"Very well then, I will never guess." (I knew the exchange could last a quarter of an hour if I did not concede as much.)

"Mrs. Rovere and Mr. Frederick Purvis are betrothed."

"It is to be announced at your concert," said Kitty. "They are to make their home in London."

"And George and Sam are to go with them."

The realization that I would no longer be able to go to Netherfield—that I would revert to my former friendless state—so shocked me that I could not immediately reply.

Lydia seemed to read my mind. She said, not unkindly: "Poor Mary. You will lose your little playmate."

My new gown was laid out in Mama's bedchamber. Aunt Gardiner helped me on with it, and as she tied the sash edged with beautiful old Buckinghamshire lace she asked me if anything were the matter: "You are not worrying about playing a wrong note, I hope?"

I shook my head. The gown was so fine it seemed to make my face look less plain, and I took comfort from that. And when I walked into the adjoining dressing room where the rest of my family had gathered, I experienced the novel sensation of being the center of attention.

Lydia ran to seize my hand, making me turn about, whereupon everyone clapped and little Susan Gardiner in imitation of Mama cried out: "Oh la!"

Mama now presented me with a black onyx cross on a gold chain, and Aunt, perhaps observing that I was a little overset, then said: "Come, my dear. We must have the gown off so that Nan may give it a last press."

When I was once more in Mama's bedchamber with Nan in attendance I heard Lydia boasting that she knew something about somebody at Netherfield, and a moment later she was repeating the secret of Mrs. Rovere's betrothal.

"Are you certain of it?" Elizabeth's voice sounded a little breathless, and shortly afterwards she came to me and said: "You are going to Netherfield soon, Mary?"

I told her that Papa was to send for the carriage just as soon as the horses could be spared from the farm.

"They will all be leaving I imagine. The lease will be canceled. He will give up the place."

I had not seen her so agitated since the time two years back when she had accidentally pushed Jane down the back stairs. But then her mouth curved into the smile that always unsettled me—it was so like our father's. She said: "Perhaps it isn't true. I shall not shed tears until I'm certain."

11.

As soon as I saw George though, I knew that it was true. He was up in the old schoolroom, and I saw at once that he had been crying.

"I have heard the news, George." (I spoke as if to one bereaved.) "When is the wedding to be?"

He went to the window, averting his face. "I neither know nor care. But we are to remove to London the day after tomorrow. He has taken a house for us in Russell Square."

"So soon!"

"Mother says Sam is to have his own pony to ride in the park every day—trying to turn him up sweet. And Sam is such an idiot, he thinks we will all live happily ever after."

When next he spoke, his voice was not quite steady. "Nonna says she will not go with us. She will remain here with my uncle."

"Mr. Coates means to stay on at Netherfield?"

He was now fiddling with the window-catch, twisting it this way and that. "My mother says it is because of your sister—she says he cannot bear to leave his little Lizzy. She calls your sister *la lucertola*, 'the lizard,' you understand—cold-blooded and with black, unblinking eyes. She was harping on about her forever last night."

George went on twisting the window-catch. I felt sick in my stomach, unable to think clearly. The tangle of loves and jealousies was past understanding—certainly past the understanding of my twelve-year-old self. If Mrs. Rovere loved Mr. Coates, why was she marrying Mr. Purvis? If she did not love him, why was she so jealous of Elizabeth? And did Nonna too still love Mr. Coates? Why else had she chosen to remain at Netherfield? And what were Mr. Coates's feelings towards them both? What were his feelings towards Elizabeth?

George meanwhile had pushed open the window and was now looking out across the yard (the schoolroom overlooked the stables and, beyond them, the walled kitchen garden and orchard).

"Mary," said he suddenly, speaking soft. "Come and look here."

"What is it?" All I could see was one of the grooms leading Mr. Coates's horse back to the stable-yard.

"Your sister Elizabeth," he whispered. "Cannot you see?"

I could then (but dimly) make out the figure of a girl standing beside a clump of hollyhocks in the shadow of the garden wall. "Are you sure it is she?"

"Cannot you *see*?"

"No," I whispered, annoyed. "Plainly I cannot."

"Well it is her, I swear."

We both watched, and after about a minute Mr. Coates appeared, walking from the direction of the stables. The figure straight away emerged from the shadow of the wall (I saw then that it was indeed Elizabeth) whereupon Mr. Coates went swiftly to her, taking her arm and leading her—bundling her almost—along the path to the orchard. I could barely make them out once they reached the cover of the trees, but George continued to peer after them.

"Well?" I whispered, and then in a normal voice: "Can you still see them?"

He did not reply, so intent was he on looking.

"George?"

He pulled shut the window and I saw that he was no longer looking sullen and despairing—in fact quite the reverse. "Seems my mother was in the right of it after all."

"What do you mean by that, pray?"

"Good heavens, Mary, they were kissing! Don't pretend you didn't see."

"I don't believe you!"

He shrugged. "Have it your way." I heard him mutter something in which only the word "blind" was audible.

"What? What did you say?" (He had now turned back to the window and I slapped his arm.) "You and your sotto voce rude remarks. *What did you say?*"

"Oh, stow it."

The sight of his back—so upright whilst spying on my sister—enraged me. "How dare you speak to me like that!—You know I cannot see as well as most people. And look at you now! The use you're putting *your* eyes to. Oh! you should be ashamed."

He ignored this, whereupon I pinched him—I confess it—but the shame of Elizabeth's behavior—of his witnessing it—provoked me so. "You're no better than Peeping Tom."

He then opened the window as wide as its hinges would permit and leaned out to better view the lovers.

I longed to push him headlong out. Instead, I said that I was glad he was going to London, and when he did not answer, I ran from the room.

I did not at first know where to go. I was desperate to sit quietly, to check my murderous thoughts—the desire to defenestrate George was so strong—and in the end I went down to the little ground-floor chapel. The room was never used for worship by the present tenants but occasionally George and I went there to play upon an old spinet housed in an oak case designed to resemble a Bible.

After praying for forgiveness and saying over the 121st psalm, I opened up the spinet and began tremblingly to play. But whereas I could usually rely upon music to rescue me from myself, now it quite failed me. I did not know with whom I was most angry—George or Elizabeth. They had both behaved disgracefully. And then the thought that George would in two days be gone began to work on me. What after all had he done to deserve being slapped and pinched and insulted? He had spied on a couple of lovers, one of whom was my immodest sister. What normal thirteen-year-old boy could resist such temptation?

And just as I was about to go in search of him to apologize, there was a knock at the door and he poked his head around.

"Mary. I have been looking for you everywhere." (approaching with mock trepidation) "You are not going to hit me again, are you?" And although not normally a demonstrative boy, he now gave my arm a pat. "Your sister has left. My uncle sent her home in the carriage." A pause and then: "I ought not to have spied on her, I know."

"Oh! let us not talk about Elizabeth."

"No, I have been thinking about her—about the whole business. A girl like your sister—she would never do that sort of thing I'm sure, unless she really cared for someone."

"No." I was not interested in finding excuses for Elizabeth but if George was, I would humor him.

"And when people fall in love, you know, they go a bit mad."

"Is that so?" I forbore to ask how he could possibly know.

"Especially a girl of spirit, like your sister."

And now I felt the familiar pang of jealousy: Elizabeth it seemed had won herself another heart.

"What is it, Mary? I will not speak of this to anybody, I swear. Your sister's reputation is safe with me."

I looked up at him. He was now dressed for the concert in a black velvet jacket and matching trousers, his dark hair carefully combed. He looked flushed and anxious, and I saw that his concern was all for myself, for my feelings as a sister. I said: "Should you like us to practice the sonata now?"

He at once sat down beside me and for the next couple of hours, in spite of everything, I believe we were both very happy.

Only Mrs. Rovere was present when George and I went up to the drawing room. She was standing at one of the long sashed windows and looking quite magnificent in a gown the color of old gold and with a great rope of pearls about her neck. She said: "This promises to be an interesting evening."

George then said something under his breath but I cut in quickly: "I have heard the news, ma'am—the news of your betrothal. I'm sure I wish both you and Mr. Purvis very happy."

She smiled her unsatisfactory smile. "I am on the watch for him now as you may gather. I do not want anyone to snub him— my mother has been saying some very cutting things, calling him *il botteguio* and saying he smells of the shop."

"Which he does," muttered George.

His mother then rounded on him, telling him in Italian he was a rude, ungrateful boy: "I do this for you and for Sam—not for myself!"

Before George could answer back, I said: "I hear you are removing to London the day after tomorrow, ma'am?"

"Yes and not a moment too soon. I tell my mother she should be grateful. She may stay on at Netherfield now and have Jasper all to herself." She paused and then addressed me in a conspiratorial whisper: "What think you of my pearls? Frederick bought them for me as a wedding gift."

"Very fine." (Privately, I thought them quite vulgar; some were the size of sparrows' eggs.)

"I confess I did not look to receive *quite* such a magnificent proof of affection."

Again George said something sotto voce but fortunately his mother did not hear; she was peering out the window. "Here comes a carriage! Certainly not Frederick's—the horses look to be great lumbering farm beasts."

"No, it is my family's, I believe."

"Oh good God, I did not mean—" (laughing) "But Frederick's carriage horses are particularly fine—matched grays and beautiful steppers, costing every bit of three hundred pounds."

I marveled how in a remarkably short space of time she had so immersed herself in Mr. Purvis's world, informing herself about his business and possessions—particularly his possessions. But it would surely have been the same with Mr. Coates. I imagined her in the early days of their love—sitting beside him while he wrote, mending his pens and admiring his prose.

My family's carriage had now drawn to a standstill. Mama was the first to alight, followed by Aunt Gardiner, Jane, and Elizabeth. And after them, to my astonishment, I saw my father emerge.

Mrs. Rovere was equally surprised. "I'm sure I did not expect to see Mr. Bennet."

"No more did I, ma'am." (I was secretly delighted however.)

George joined us at the window, and the three of us watched my family mount the stone steps. Jane I saw was wearing her new gown of blue Italian taffeta, and Mama and Aunt had on their best silks. Elizabeth wore her favorite cream sarcenet and a little bronze beaded cap which suited her clear brown complexion admirably.

I felt a pride in their collective good looks—a new experience this, since I had always felt my own inferiority too keenly to appreciate my family's personal claims. It was also a novelty to feel gratitude towards my father for overcoming his usual indolence. I wondered who—Aunt Gardiner or Jane—had persuaded him to come. Elizabeth would not have had time to think of me or my concert. By itself, the walk to Netherfield must have taken her at least an hour.

Another carriage was now coming down the drive. It was a closed Berlin, bright yellow and highly varnished, pulled by a pair of gray horses—Mr. Purvis's, I guessed, and Mrs. Rovere soon confirmed it: *"Benissimo! It is him!"*

She almost ran from the room. And a few minutes later the other pair of lovers—accompanied by my mother and followed by footmen bearing trays of decanters and glasses—walked in.

12.

Even had I not witnessed their earlier clandestine meeting, seeing Elizabeth and Mr. Coates together I am sure I should have guessed their secret. I had never seen my sister look lovelier. She was like the gypsy girl in an old picture-book of mine, dark-eyed and vivid-faced. And Mr. Coates, though he affected interest in what my mother was saying, seemed also happily abstracted.

All conversation was swamped by Mama's effusions: "Oh, Mr. Coates! I am so happy to hear you will not be leaving Netherfield. I have a presentiment about this place. When first I came into the neighborhood—when Mr. Bennet brought me to Longbourn as a bride—I said to him that of all the houses hereabouts, there was but one that truly *spoke* to me, and that one was Netherfield Hall." Turning to Papa, who was following with Aunt Gardiner and Jane: "Did I not say as much, Mr. Bennet? And if it were not for the fact that it is undoubtedly haunted— else why should the owner not choose to live in it?—I should dearly love to live here myself."

Mr. Coates then said something about having heard tales of a resident ghost: "A maiden who haunts the kitchen garden and hides behind the hollyhocks." (Here a swift, sly smile at Elizabeth.)

Mrs. Rovere and Mr. Purvis now showed themselves, and after Mama had made Aunt Gardiner known to them, they

immediately moved off—as if they had rehearsed it—to the opposite end of the room. The sight of them together—the dyed-
haired old dandy and the beautiful, still youthful woman—was
at once comical and shocking. I found it impossible not to stare,
and they seemed to want to be stared at, bowing and smiling like
a couple of players.

The footmen went up to them with wine but nobody else approached more nearly. Following on the mention of a Netherfield
ghost, Mr. Coates and Elizabeth began to talk of novels of phan-
tasy with Mr. Coates taking out his pocket book and writing
down the title of a "horrid" romance she was urging him to read.
Laughing the while, their heads together, they seemed oblivious
to their company.

Papa and Aunt Gardiner now joined George and myself—
Papa was always kindly disposed towards George—and after
Aunt had retied my sash and otherwise assured herself that my
gown was in order, she kept glancing (uneasily I thought) in
Elizabeth's direction.

The Lucases were the last of the guests to arrive, and Nonna
came rustling after them, vivaciously assaulting in quick succession Mama and Jane before advancing on her daughter and telling her to speak to other persons "subito." Short of making a
public scene, Mrs. Rovere had no choice but to comply. And
Mr. Coates, perhaps conscious that he too had been paying attention to only one person, put away his pocket book and moved
to talk to Mr. Purvis.

No sooner had we all entered the dining room, however, than
Mrs. Rovere found fault with the seating arrangement, insisting
that she be placed next to Mr. Purvis and as far away from Mr.
Coates as possible. There followed several chair changes (during
which Mr. Coates jokingly offered to eat his dinner in the nursery

with Sam) before we were placed according to Mrs. Rovere's liking, with Mr. Coates at the head and Nonna at the foot of the long table.

And so began the last meal I would eat at Netherfield for over six years, for I did not dine there again until the arrival of Mr. Bingley. I look back on it now as a sort of unholy Last Supper, for there were thirteen of us seated around that table and a lot of wine was drunk—at least by Nonna—and it all ended in tears.

It began with my father quizzing Mr. Purvis about the latter's acquisition of a Meryton ale-house. (Mr. Purvis loved to talk about his properties, the improvements he was planning and the profits he was making. He loved also to talk of his humble beginnings when he worked as a waiter in the Bedford Coffee-house in Covent Garden.)

I now heard him tell my father that he thought of making the ale-house into such another coffee-house. "A meeting-place for Meryton's finest minds, where good conversation and fine food may be had for a modest subscription. What do you say to such a scheme, sir?"

I saw from Papa's expression that he did not think much of it. "Meryton's finest minds, eh?" He glanced up the table at Sir William Lucas. "I fear the number of subscribers would make such a scheme impractical, Mr. Purvis. A little market town such as Meryton—"

"But there must be many gentlemen who would welcome such a place, sir. I do not mean the townsfolk merely—"

Nonna turned on Mr. Purvis. "You listen to what Mr. Bennet is telling you. He is living here always and you know nothing about it."

This was too much for Mrs. Rovere; she began to abuse her mother in Italian. Nonna merely hunched her shoulders and addressed herself exclusively to my father: "It is very strange to me, Mr. Bennet, how the Englishmen want always to be together in the coffee-house or the club. Always they want to be without the women."

"Aye, we're an uncouth lot," Papa agreed.

"My first two husbands, they were English, so I know. Christina's papa, always he is in the coffee-house."

There was laughter at this—although Mrs. Rovere did not look amused—and Nonna held up her wineglass to be refilled, saying: "Christina thinks I should not talk so about her papa. Always he is the perfect one and I am not to say bad things about him."

"I couldn't care less, Mama, I assure you."

"My *second* English *sposo*—when I go with him to London he is in White's club always." She called to Mr. Coates: "Jasper! I am telling Mr. Bennet about your naughty papa."

Mr. Coates was talking to Elizabeth, but Aunt Gardiner had been listening to Nonna: "You were married to Mr. Coates's father, ma'am?"

"*Scusi?*" And after Aunt repeated the question: "Ah. But if I talk about that, Christina will be cross."

"Oh, say what you like, Mama. It makes no odds now."

"You hear that, Mrs. Gardiner? My daughter, she is telling me to say what I like. *Bene.* I say then that Jasper's papa and me—we marry and I love him dearly—but he was much older man. We marry for one year only, and then he die. Very sad, *si?*"

I saw Aunt Gardiner and Papa exchange glances. Nonna's history was beginning to sound dangerously like the plot of *Paola.*

Nonna again held up her glass for the footman to refill. "After he die, Lady Lucas, I do a very stupid thing."

There was a hush. By some mysterious alchemy, everyone seemed alert to the possibility of high drama. Mr. Purvis said: "I am sure you could never do anything stupid, Mrs. Falco."

Nonna was looking at Mr. Coates: "A month after he die, I do like Hamlet's mother."

My own mother now burst forth: "Oh, Mrs. Falco! I know what you are about to say, I can guess. I know I should lose my mind if Mr. Bennet were to die—I should go distracted. And not merely because of the entail."

"I not lose my mind, Mrs. Bennet. I marry again. A month after Jasper's papa die, I marry Falco."

There was a shocked silence during which Sir William cleared his throat and said in his best mayoral manner: "Might I remind everyone that there are children present?"

"I marry Falco and I am very unhappy. And Jasper—" (looking across at Mr. Coates) "He help me. Always he is so kind to his papa's widow."

I looked at Mr. Coates then. He was staring at Nonna and I saw that he was very angry.

Next moment, there came a crash of china: Mrs. Rovere had knocked over a sweetmeat dish from the raised display. And while the footmen moved to pick up the pieces, Mr. Coates took out his watch. "Our concert begins in just half an hour, and our other guests will very soon be arriving—"

"No, Jasper," said Nonna. "Your watch, it is much too fast. And I have still some things to say."

Mr. Coates continued as if she had not spoken: "You may go to the music room, George. You too, Mary. We will join you presently."

13.

Apart from one or two things I was able to piece together later, I never learned what was said in the Netherfield dining room after George and I left. But when at last the whole party entered the music room, it was clear that there had been some sort of denouement. They looked like a funeral party, for there was not one cheerful face amongst them, and Mrs. Rovere had unaccountably changed her gold gown for one of black.

As they took their places in the eleven gilt chairs of the first row, I saw that Elizabeth chose to sit between Papa and Aunt Gardiner and quite away from Mr. Coates.

But the concert itself was a brilliant success. Perhaps because of all that had gone before, I felt amazingly calm throughout—a nerveless, near exalted feeling where a wrong note was inconceivable. And George seemed to share the feeling, for immediately after we ceased playing he described the performance as "almost" perfect.

The applause too was such as I have never known, with people coming up to congratulate us. (I fondly recall Mr. Knowles coming with his mother, who was wiping away tears. I also remember Mrs. Rovere coming forward with Mr. Purvis, and while my head was being turned with compliments, I still possessed the wit to wonder why she had changed her gown.)

In all the excitement I did not notice the absence of Elizabeth, and I was therefore quite unprepared when Aunt

Gardiner took me by the arm and whispered: "We are to go home at once, Mary. Elizabeth is unwell." (urging me forward as she spoke) "The Lucases are to take you in their carriage."

On the journey home, it was clear that Sir William and Lady Lucas knew something that they were at pains to keep from me, and when at last we reached Longbourn and I was set down— after which they immediately drove off—I had to nerve myself to sound the knocker.

It was Nan Pender who let me in. And it seemed that she too knew something, for she would not suffer me to enter the drawing room before first going ahead to announce my arrival. I followed her with fast-beating heart—a visitor in my own house—and upon Papa opening the door, I saw Elizabeth sitting white-faced on the sofa, still wearing her little beaded cap, with Aunt on one side of her and Jane on the other.

My mother sat slumped in a chair nearby, but on catching sight of me, she cried: "Here she is at last! Little Miss Mary Quite Contrary. Never a thought for what *we* have had to endure while she is a-playing her precious music."

And when Papa—having first dismissed Nan—bade her hold her tongue, she cried out afresh: "Had it not been for her, none of this would have happened. But she must needs go to Netherfield every day and live in his pocket."

Here, Elizabeth spoke: "I beg you, Mama. It is not Mary's fault."

She was unable to continue, and Papa then placed a hand on my shoulder and made me walk with him into the hall. Closing the door behind us, he motioned me to go ahead a little before saying: "Now, Mary."

There followed a pause during which I was once more conscious of my fast-beating heart.

"George leaves for London in two days' time, does he not?" And upon my confirming it: "Then you will not mind so much when I tell you that you are no longer to visit Netherfield. Whilst ever Mr. Coates and Mrs. Falco are living there, we none of us will visit. The acquaintance is to be entirely given up. You understand me, child?"

"Yes, sir."

"Mr. Coates has imposed on us, Mary."

It was one of the few completely serious exchanges I had ever had with him—but as he turned away, there was a glimmer of his old sarcasm: "I am sorry this had to happen on the night of your great triumph."

When he opened the door to the drawing room, I once again glimpsed Elizabeth. Only now her face was pressed against Aunt's shoulder and she was crying, her little cap all awry and her hair tumbling down.

14.

I slept very little that night and the thought to which my tired mind kept returning—the regret which in the end swallowed up all else—was that I had not said good-bye to George and that I would now in all likelihood never see him again.

I blamed Elizabeth. Had she not thrown herself at Mr. Coates, I reasoned, Mrs. Rovere would never have engaged herself to Mr. Purvis and George would not now be leaving Netherfield. I blamed Mr. Coates too of course—although not half so much as everybody else did. My childish understanding of his crime was necessarily partial and imperfect but at no time did I think of him as a hypocrite, still less a libertine, and his installing two mistresses under his roof I even now impute more to convenience—a lack of resolution and misplaced kindness—than to corrupt habits.

Elizabeth judged him, however—almost as severely as she judged herself—and for a while her fondness for jokes entirely deserted her; a silent censoriousness made itself felt, and even when her old playfulness returned, it was not the same. Her manner might mask it, but she made far fewer allowances for human frailty.

But once again I am running ahead of myself. Before I awoke the following morning, Elizabeth had left for London. I knew nothing of it until Lydia informed me that Aunt and the two little Gardiner girls had gone—and that Elizabeth and Jane had accompanied them.

"Nobody told us they were going," said she. "We heard them creeping about and Nan getting out the boxes—and then we heard the carriage."

"Nobody said good-bye to us," said Kitty.

"Did you know of it, Mary?" said Lydia, sharp-eyed.

"No indeed, I promise you."

"Mama has shut herself up in her room," said Kitty. "And Nan says that on no account are we to bother her—"

"But I *shall* bother her," said Lydia. "I mean to find out why they have all gone away."

She did not find out, however, for Papa, placing no dependence on his wife's discretion, arranged for Uncle Philips to collect Kitty and Lydia that same morning. They were to go to Uncle Philips's sister, a Mrs. Jervis, who lived in a very retired way at Kings Langley. As for myself, Papa informed me that I was to spend my mornings at Lucas Lodge. "You will take your lessons with Maria Lucas. Mr. Knowles will welcome the opportunity of a holiday."

I knew by his manner that it would be useless to protest. But to be deprived of Mr. Knowles at a time when I most needed his counsel, I felt to be most cruel. Papa gave me permission to write to him, however, and after Lydia and Kitty left, I spent the rest of the morning composing a letter, confiding a small part of my present suffering—I could not relate the whole without exposing Elizabeth—and asking that he point me towards such texts as might best offer solace.

He wrote back immediately—I still have the letter— quoting Mr. William Cowper's beautiful lines:

"God moves in a mysterious way,
His wonders to perform."

Remember there is one Friend who will never forsake you, my dear
Mary. Mother joins me in praying for your happiness.

And so began an interlude which, after the first pain of
missing George subsided, was not unpleasant. In Charlotte
Lucas, I found a teacher who was both intelligent and good-
humored—a wise old head on young shoulders, as the saying
goes, for Charlotte at the age of one and twenty was burdened
with many domestic cares quite apart from her teaching load.
She was constantly being called away to superintend the baking
or to settle some silly argument between her younger brothers
and sisters, and her father's fatuous remarks and oft-repeated
anecdotes must have also tried her patience. (This early training
in tolerating fools would be put to good use when she married
Mr. Collins.)

My friendship with Maria Lucas dates from this period. I
had always regarded Maria as something of a scatterbrain—she
for her part probably saw me as a bore and a bluestocking—but
now, sharing our lessons as we did, we were able to form a fairer
estimate of each other's abilities. And without the constraint of
my elder sisters' company (for Jane and Elizabeth were objects of
great awe to Maria), I found her to be touchingly deferential towards myself and grateful for any help I could give, especially on
matters musical.

In the meantime I kept up my correspondence with
Mr. Knowles, and since both Mama and Papa were dilatory in
such matters I also corresponded with my sisters. My letters
must have made dull reading, however. Life at Longbourn and
Lucas Lodge was very quiet, and apart from a severe snow-
storm in the last week of November I had little to report. (Several roof tiles directly above my attic room were dislodged, and I
was obliged to move into Elizabeth's room.)

The one exciting piece of news—Mr. Coates's departure from Netherfield—I was forbidden to write about, as Papa had banned any mention of "that worthless fellow and his Italian comic opera." It was Maria Lucas who told me that he had finally gone—he had written to Sir William saying that urgent business called him to London. At the time I wondered whether he had gone to seek out Elizabeth, but on hearing that Mrs. Falco had accompanied him and that the two of them had taken a house in Half Moon Street, I concluded that Nonna Paola was once more his mistress—if indeed she had ever ceased to be.

A second, more surprising, instance of revived passion—of a return to lukewarm conjugal felicity at least—was that of my own parents. The absence of their daughters seemed to promote a better understanding between them. When I returned after my lessons at Lucas Lodge I would often find them seated together on the drawing room sofa, my father reading a newspaper while my mother played with her bracelets. My father even condescended to share the odd piece of news with her, usually gossip about the Royal Family, in which she delighted. I once heard him inform her without the least hint of sarcasm that the Queen's preferred luncheon was a simple dish of chicken broth—chicken broth being Mama's favorite nerve restorative. But this too was something I could not write of to my sisters.

Their letters to me were equally dull. Kitty and Lydia wrote very short letters at very long intervals, and although Jane and Elizabeth wrote regularly, they described their activities without mentioning their thoughts or feelings. Elizabeth's letters were especially dull; impersonal accounts of engagements, visits to the theater or books she was presently reading—mere lists of titles for my father's benefit.

But Elizabeth also corresponded with Charlotte Lucas. And now once again I must confess something of which I am ashamed, for I actually *copied* a page of one such letter. Charlotte had accidentally dropped it when called away to settle some domestic dispute and on picking it up, I at once recognized Elizabeth's hand. Maria was busy putting together a map of Europe, and almost before I knew what I was about, I began to read:

A sort of madness seized me—I can describe it in no other way—I could not rest until I knew if he intended to quit the country. Even now all these weeks later I cannot think of my conduct without amazement, for I had ample time to consider what I was about during the three-mile walk to Netherfield. It is this more than anything that disgusts me—that in the grip of strong feeling, I should have lost all self-command. It was his discretion which saved me, for I was utterly careless of discovery. (I have spoken of this to Jane, but such is her sisterly partiality she cannot credit the extent of my folly. My aunt Gardiner also makes light of it, declaring that she never for a moment doubted my good sense.)

In truth though, Charlotte, the scales did not fall from my eyes until Mrs. F made her shocking disclosure—for he had already told me of his relations with Mrs. R. There followed the edifying spectacle of Mrs. F and Mrs. R screaming abuse at each other with Mrs. R having to be forcibly restrained after her mother emptied a glass of wine over her. As if this were not enough, we were then obliged to endure a further hour of purgatory for there was no escaping Mary's Mozart. I bore up quite wonderfully until the end—

On hearing Charlotte's returning footsteps, I hid the page inside my book, but upon her almost immediately being called away again, I once more took it out. A second reading did not improve my feelings towards the writer. On an impulse I seized a sheet of paper and copied it out.

At the time I felt no shame. I wished to preserve some proof of Elizabeth's folly, a tangible reminder that behind the screen of propriety there lurked a very different creature. And now I am not sorry for what I did, for afterwards it was as if the entire episode had never happened. Papa's ban on any reference to Mr. Coates persisted long after all my sisters had returned home, and Mama—although regularly lamenting that Netherfield continued to stand empty—spoke only of the previous inhabitants as "that dreadful foreign family with whom Mary was wondrous thick."

15.

I had eagerly awaited the return of my four sisters. But no sooner had we all crowded into the Longbourn breakfast room than I saw—in the midst of the hubbub and embraces—that I was not necessary to the happiness of any of them.

I saw that the minds of the two eldest and two youngest were now so perfectly and exclusively attuned as to make them quite closed off to me. I saw, in short, that none of them gave three straws about me—that Jane's universal benevolence was a matter of course and counted for nothing.

For me, it was as blinding a revelation as Saint Paul's on the road to Damascus. I had hitherto believed that however much they might prefer each other's company, my sisters nevertheless loved me—that I dwelt at least in the suburbs of their affections. I recall sitting before the breakfast room fire, staring at Nan Pender's back—she was roasting chestnuts for us all—in a great terror lest one of them should speak to me before I had sufficiently composed myself. And then Lydia had cried out: "Good Lord! Only look at Mary. She has seen a ghost, I think."

Had I been able to go to my room that evening and collect myself, all might yet have been well, but the bad weather had delayed the roof repairs and I was obliged to share Elizabeth's bedchamber. My feelings of exclusion were not helped by our father's coming to the door while Elizabeth was unpacking to make her a present of a novel (Fanny Burney's *Camilla*) and to tell her how much he had missed her. Elizabeth must have indicated my presence—my bed was concealed behind a folding screen—for he said with a sort of laugh: "Yes, to be sure. I had quite forgotten. Good night to you too, Mary."

He had come a second time too—but it was to speak to me rather than to Elizabeth. He had received a letter from Mr. Knowles, which he had only that moment thought to open. "I fear you must prepare yourself for a disappointment, Mary. Mr. Knowles writes that it will not be in his power to return to Longbourn until after Easter."

And upon my coming from behind the screen clad only in my nightgown: "Come, child, 'tis not the end of the world. His mother wishes to go to Bath, that is all—but perhaps you would prefer to read it for yourself."

So saying, he handed me the letter and left, and Elizabeth— seeing my distress—lit some work candles and bade me sit by the fire so that I might read in comfort.

The letter stated merely that Mrs. Knowles's rheumatism had worsened during the recent cold weather and that the doctor had advised a course of treatment in the warm baths and the continuing companionship of her son.

Elizabeth tried to console me. "But you have been going on very well with Charlotte these last months, have you not? You have enjoyed taking your lessons with Maria?"

"'Tis not my lessons!" I was now utterly careless of what I said. "He is the only friend I have left—the only person who really cares about me."

"My dear Mary—you must know that is not so."

And here she actually kissed me on the forehead. I stared up at her openmouthed, my tears dripping down so that I must have been a comical sight. She handed me a handkerchief, saying: "Is there time for you to pay him a visit before he goes? Should you like me to apply to Papa?"

I thanked her, sniffing, and in a rush of gratitude, said entirely the wrong thing: "I am sure that Mr. Coates cared about *you* a great deal, Lizzy."

Her expression changed—hauteur replacing affectionate concern. "We will not speak of him, if you please. He is to be forgot."

She turned away to continue her unpacking. I kept my place at the fireside meanwhile, hoping she would relent towards me. Instead, she took up her candle saying she must bid Jane goodnight, and although I sat up for a further hour she did not return whilst ever I was awake.

But in the morning there was no applying to Papa for permission to visit Mr. Knowles. While we were dressing, an express came from London—my memory of this is preternaturally clear—and Hill, the new housekeeper, came running upstairs to tell us that she doubted not it was bad news, for the master had shut himself away in his library. Jane and Elizabeth ran on ahead of me—Elizabeth taking the stairs two at a time—and when I reached the library after them, the door was shut fast.

I knocked, and after what seemed a long time Papa bade me enter. Elizabeth and Jane were standing beside Papa's desk and Jane was weeping unashamedly.

Papa then told me that little Susan Gardiner was no more. She had been knocked down by a carrier's cart outside her home in Gracechurch Street. The accident had happened the previous evening when, in defiance of the nurserymaid, Susan had run out onto the road to retrieve a ball. She had died some six hours later.

Elizabeth then handed me Uncle Gardiner's letter. It was brief—a dozen or so neatly written lines—with only the scrawled signature giving a clue to the perturbation of his mind. Susan had not appeared at first to be seriously injured; she had complained only of a pain in her left side. A physician was then appointed to examine her but Susan had died before he could attend her.

I could not straight away submit to God's judgment in all this. Susan was a most loveable, albeit willful, little girl—impossible to believe that she would never again run off with my spectacles or open the lid of my pianoforte without my leave. After breakfast—a miserable meal attended only by Kitty, Lydia, and myself—I returned to Elizabeth's room to pray for resignation: "Let the Almighty's will be done. God gives and God takes away. Blessed be the name of the Lord."

Elizabeth happened upon me while I was on my knees, and instead of quitting the room she began opening and closing drawers, saying, "I beg your pardon, Mary, but could you defer your prayers for the present? Jane is to accompany Papa to London, and she is in need of black gloves and ribbons and a great many other things. Could you not try for once to make yourself useful?"

Before I could ask how I might be useful, she went on: "You will be thirteen soon, Mary. You are old enough to offer help without being prompted. You know that our mother's nerves prevent her—" (shutting a drawer with more than necessary force) "You must know that everything falls upon poor Jane."

I was shocked that she could speak so to me—as if I were an unsatisfactory maidservant. "I am afraid I have no black gloves or ribbons. But Jane is welcome to my black onyx cross—the one that Mama gave me to wear at the concert. It is in my trinket box."

I left the room, banging the door behind me, but there was no peace to be found anywhere in the house. Mama had been thrown into hysterics, and those of the servants who were not soothing her with sal volatile or taking her tea and toast were busy getting up mourning clothes. Nan Pender, red-eyed from weeping, was cutting up black crepe to fasten around Papa's hat and the laundry maid was running in and out with armfuls of clean linen.

Kitty and Lydia meanwhile were waiting for Nan to take them to the Lucases, and I determined to go with them. But even as I put on my pelisse, I felt guilty. I knew very well I should be helping. And as it turned out I was properly punished, for on returning to Longbourn, I learnt that Mr. Knowles had called in my absence, and on entering Elizabeth's room I saw that a book had been placed atop my bureau. There was no mistaking the red leather cover, the gold scroll about the title. It was the first volume of *Paola*.

Elizabeth followed me into the room—ostensibly to collect a black fur tippet for Jane to take to London. "Oh, Mary," said she, her color much heightened. "I found that book when I was looking for your trinket box. How did you come by it, pray?" And when I did not immediately reply: "Did he—did Mr. Coates make you a present of it?"

"You told me yesterday that Mr. Coates was not to be spoken of. You told me he was to be forgot."

She gave me a furious look before snatching up the tippet: "I am sure it cannot be a proper book for you to read."

The strain of sharing a bedchamber now became intolerable. I was frightened to say my prayers lest Elizabeth find me on my knees, and yet I had never felt the need to commune with my Maker more urgently. I had expected her to remove to Jane's room after Jane and Papa left for London, and when that did not happen, I offered to move myself.

"Why, Mary," said she in the cool, arch tone she adopted whenever anything threatened to unsettle her, "I had no idea you found my company so oppressive."

She then turned back to her book but I was not prepared to continue in this way. And without much thinking what I was about, I put on my cloak and boots and quit the house. Even though the light was fading, I determined to go to Lucas Lodge and pour out my troubles to Maria.

It was snowing a little when I set out but I did not regard it. In my overheated state I even found it exhilarating. The blessed relief of being alone! Of saying the twenty-third psalm as I walked along: "The Lord is my shepherd. I shall not want. He maketh me to lie down in green pastures." I spoke the words over, mindful of little beyond the reassuring steam of my own breath and the tears running down my face. Anybody passing would have thought me quite mad.

I still have no idea how it happened. Certain it was that I suddenly found myself to be nowhere near Lucas Lodge. I had taken one of the paths to Collins Cottage, the house where the Bushells had once lived but which was now no longer occupied. As far as I could make out though (for the snow was falling fast), it appeared to be lighted up. But when they found me afterwards—chilled to the bone and still babbling of green pastures—they told me that it had been my imagination.

16.

The experience left me badly shaken, and for weeks afterwards—
even when I was once more in my own room—I had trouble
sleeping. Nan had difficulty persuading me to get up as a consequence, and I spent hours in bed dwelling on my misfortunes,
feeling ill-used by my family, and thinking constantly about
death and dying. At one stage I was convinced that George had
died. I dreamt that he had been thrown from his horse and tram-
pled upon. Similarly Mr. Knowles: I dreamt that he had expired
in the Bath Pump Room after drinking purgative liquid. And
every morning on waking I feared that my father had died in the
night. I was terrified that we would all be cast out of Longbourn
to live on the charity of the Gardiners in Cheapside.

I date my melancholia from this time. And although my
mind did not immediately serve me another such trick as happened on the path to Collins Cottage, I began to experience odd
lapses in concentration. I had trouble playing passages of music—
passages I had known for years—and I could no longer read my
daily portion of scripture—the print in the prayer book had become too small. Stronger spectacles were tried to no avail. I could
be looking at somebody seated only a few feet from me, and of a
sudden the person's face would blur and dissolve—or an inani-
mate object would start to quiver, seeming to dance out at me.

My reading and studies were now curtailed. Mr. Knowles returned from Bath only to find his services as a tutor no longer

required. He was invited to visit as a friend, however, to "cheer poor Mary up," as Mama expressed it, for the doctors had begun to entertain grave fears for my eyes. I was not permitted to practice my music for more than an hour at a time but I would continue to sit at the instrument, straining to see the black-and-white blur. I was certain that I was going blind.

Hardly a day passed that I did not have a headache and always in the afternoon my stomach began to churn. And the day before my thirteenth birthday I heard a voice—that is to say I *imagined* a voice—telling me that the Day of Judgment was at hand and to prepare to meet my Maker.

I heard the voice (which sounded remarkably like my father's) whilst lying abed late, and on rising I saw that my sheets were stained with blood.

Mama, Jane, and Elizabeth were entertaining the new tenants of Haye Park, a Mr. and Mrs. Goulding, when I burst into the drawing room. Jane immediately placed her shawl about me and with a gentle pressure forced me from the room. Nan was then called, and I was bathed and given barley water to drink, and after receiving repeated assurances that I was not about to die, I accompanied Jane downstairs to Papa's library, where she read to me a passage from Dr. Hunter's medical book.

After patiently answering my questions, she said: "You ought to have been informed of these matters, my dear Mary."

She then voiced the same concerns she had raised when I was six years old—that I kept too much to myself, that my room was too far off from the rest of the family &c. She invited me to join herself and Elizabeth on their afternoon walks, and in the evenings when they were making clothes for the poor. "I know that you must not strain your eyes with any close-work, but you might safely tack on the odd pattern. Or simply sit with us and chat. And I would be happy to read to you, and so I am sure would

Lizzy. And that way, you know, you might exercise your mind without risk to your eyes. It need not all be on serious subjects. We could read poetry—or even" (smiling) "a novel."

She then urged me to consider removing to the nursery wing next to Lydia and Kitty. "Believe me, dear Mary, too much solitude is not a good thing."

I said I would consider it, but I had no intention of quitting my attic room. I told her, however, that it would be a great comfort to me if we could sometimes pray together.

"Certainly, dear. Whenever you wish it."

But she did not nominate a time, and I felt a stirring of resentment. I watched her walk to the bookshelf and insert Dr. Hunter's book in its correct place—Jane was a little near-sighted herself—and her graceful movements seemed suddenly an affront. How could such a being who clearly enjoyed (albeit unconsciously) the superiority beauty bestowed feel for someone like myself?

A moment later, she was suggesting we walk outside into the spring sunshine and I at once agreed. On quitting the house, however, she directed our steps to the wilderness, saying: "Should you like us to pray together now, Mary?"

Ashamed of doubting her, I bowed my head, whereupon she began to recite the Lord's Prayer. I could not join her in speaking the words, my heart was too full, but on raising my eyes I was able to see her—see her clearly, that is. For an instant, she was no longer a blur of barely recognizable features above a blue dress. I had a clear vision of her lovely face.

Elizabeth joined us soon afterwards and we all walked on together, but jealousy soon reared its ugly head. They spoke of the Gouldings and their hopes of finding them pleasant neighbors, and even though they were at pains to include me in their conversation I soon gave up the struggle to listen. I longed to have Jane to myself, but it was not to be. And later I saw that longing as a weakness and told myself not to wish for it.

About a fortnight after my birthday I once more imagined that I heard my father's voice. As happened before, I was lying abed late, but this time the voice did not frighten me. It was quoting a familiar Bible text—Matthew 5:15: "Neither do men light a candle, and put it under a bushel, but on a candlestick; and it giveth light unto all that are in the house."

But I soon perceived that there was a message for me within the text, cunningly encoded. The bushel was clearly no ordinary bushel but signified the husband of my old wet-nurse, the drunken Bushell who had so terrified my infant self. Once I understood this, the message was clear. Mama had indeed borne Papa a son, but the Bushells had smothered him and placed their own child—myself—in his place and Papa, having now found them out, intended to enlighten everyone as to what had happened. I would then be banished—sent back to the Bushells to live in poverty and disgrace.

Of course I now know that this was all a product of my sick fancy, but at the time I truly believed it. It seemed to explain so much—my plainness as opposed to my sisters' good looks and my father's indifference. I began to look for confirmation in everything they said and did, or more particularly what they failed to say and do, and as everyone knows, "trifles light as air are to the jealous confirmations strong as proofs of holy writ." I was convinced that they all wished for nothing so much as to be rid of me.

And now, mercifully, my memory becomes as clouded as my vision and there are patches of time quite lost to me. Many people have since told me—and I have no difficulty in believing it—that I was behaving very strangely indeed. When I was not closeted in my room, I was spying on my sisters, trying to overhear their conversations, or sitting talking to myself and smiling. On one occasion—which I do dimly recall—I threw a knife at Lydia across the breakfast table. She had been making faces at me and poking out her tongue—perhaps in response to my own strange staring and smiling. I was banished to my room as a consequence and there confined for several days, speaking to nobody except the servants.

Shortly afterwards, a doctor from London was called in to attend me.

17.

The doctor's name was Willis. He was a handsome old, white-haired man and related, so he said, to the Dr. Willis who had treated His Majesty King George. He came recommended by Sir William Lucas, who had met him at the Court of St. James's and vouched for his skill in treating females suffering from nervous disorders—many of whom, Sir William assured my mother, were titled ladies of fashion.

Had Dr. Willis not possessed such credentials, perhaps my parents might have questioned the treatment he prescribed for me. I was made to sit in a darkened room every morning with a vinegar-drenched cloth wound about my forehead, and at night I was given laudanum to drink (three drops in water) to calm my system after a purge of senna and castor oil.

The treatment lasted several months with Dr. Willis talking about *malum hereditarium* and repeatedly asking my father whether the Bennet family had any lunatic ancestors.

As can be imagined, I soon became wretchedly weak and suffered several fainting spells—which Dr. Willis said were nothing to worry about, as my inner corruption was being expelled. The only improvement was to my eyesight: I could now distinguish the keys of the pianoforte. In every other respect I felt myself to be much worse. Fortunately, the Gardiners arrived for their regular Christmas visit—the first since the death of Susan—and Aunt persuaded Mama to dispense with Dr. Willis's services. Had she not done so, I doubt I would have survived.

Another period of confused thinking and another birthday—my fourteenth—followed before another doctor, Dr. Jack, was called in. I disliked him on sight. He was young and fast-talking with an answer, it seemed to me, for everything. With my father, he adopted a man-to-man heartiness I found particularly offensive.

"If Mary were older, Mr. Bennet, I would have no hesitation in recommending marriage. By far the best thing for her in the circumstances, the best antidote, you understand me?" And here he had actually *winked* at Papa and shot a look at me before continuing: "The virgin disease, we call it, melancholia. Because of the weaker texture of their brains, young females are more susceptible."

Dr. Jack then caused a rope to be rigged up in the garden to which a chair was attached, and every morning I was made to sit in this chair while he rotated it, explaining to Papa that my mind and body would thus be forcibly reunited. "The fear I have induced in Mary by swinging her so strenuously will drive out all her *irrational* fears." He added in an undertone: "The rhythmic nature of the exercise will also be beneficial."

But after a few weeks he seemed to forget about the swing; he arrived at Longbourn clutching a tattered old book entitled *Discourse of the Preservation of the Sight; of Melancholike diseases; of Rheumes, and of Old age.* "I turned it up last night, sir," cried he to my father. "It is precisely Mary's condition—explains it all—her weak eyesight—'tis Mary to the life."

He thrust the book at Papa, who took it most willingly. (Papa encouraged Dr. Jack because he found him so entertaining.) "It describes how we all see—the process—we do not see forwards but backwards. Our eyes roll inwards and look at our brains. But the brain of the melancholic is suffused with black bile so that they see only blackness." Here Dr. Jack closed his own eyes as if to illustrate the condition. "Mary must be bled, Mr. Bennet. There's nothing else for it."

So I had then to endure the ordeal of being bled—compared to which the fear of being swung was but a fleabite. I fainted when they first showed me the leeches and when Dr. Jack applied them (two to each temple) they had to forcibly restrain me.

Those were dark days for me. Cure after cure was tried, with Dr. Jack impatient to try everything and failing to test any one thing thoroughly. To quell my so-called religious enthusiasm, he had me inhale ether, and to cure the laxity of my nervous fibers, he dosed me with asafetida. But both treatments were soon left off—to my great relief, I confess—and he moved to dripping hot wax onto my palms in the hope that the pain thus caused would distract me from the pain within my mind.

In the end, however, it was Dr. Jack's passion for Jane that was his undoing. I had long sensed it coming on. Jane was mildly interested in matters medical and she had questioned many of Dr. Jack's measures. In the presence of the beautiful Miss Bennet his glib talk had faltered. On finding that strawberries were her favorite fruit he procured some at great expense from a succession house and presented the Bennet household with a basketful.

Altogether, it was a curiously stealthy sort of courtship, with Dr. Jack exercising all the patience he failed to display in his professional capacity. Apart from the strawberries and sundry medical pamphlets he pressed upon her, he made Jane no token of his affection and she remained quite unaware of his passion for her.

One day, however, his natural ardor asserted itself. On arriving at Longbourn, and learning from Mama that Jane was abed with a cold ("Do pray step up and see what you can do for her, dear Dr. Jack.") he so far forgot himself as to make violent love to Jane. There followed a shocking scene with Jane obliged to flee her own bedchamber (pursued by Dr. Jack, protesting the purity of his intentions) and Mama predictably being thrown into hysterics.

But no sooner did I learn that Papa had given Dr. Jack his marching orders than I felt—not sorry—Dr. Jack had subjected me to too many half-baked cures for me to feel sorry—but I felt that I might have done more to promote my own recovery. I wondered whether I really *wanted* to get well, to have my brain set to right. In many respects the dark world inside my head had become preferable to the loveless reality of Longbourn.

As it turned out, Dr. Jack's final advice—set out in a letter to Papa written the day after his dismissal—was both sound and prescient. He recommended a complete change of scene for me, citing as his authority no less a personage than the Chief Physician of the Manchester Lunatic Asylum. "Dr. Ferriar believes" (Dr. Jack had written) "that lunatics recover faster when removed from home. In his view, the attention they receive at home makes them worse, whereas amongst strangers, they are forced to exert their faculties and behave themselves."

Happily, this advice coincided with an invitation from Mr. Knowles's mother for me to stay with her in Bath, where she was now a permanent resident. And it was in Bath that, finally, I began to recover.

Part Two

1.

I arrived in Bath just a fortnight before my fifteenth birthday, and apart from a couple of unhappy visits to Longbourn, I did not leave the place until after I turned seventeen. Much may happen in two and a half years, and in my own case, with the encouragement of Mr. Knowles's mother, I became by degrees less nervous, less inclined to fancy myself ill, and in company, more cheerful and confident.

My eyesight also improved, and although this was attributed to my drinking the waters, I believe it had more to do with a regimen of regular walks, good plain food, and having to perform many little tasks about the house, for Mrs. Knowles was not wealthy and kept but two servants. Our lodgings were very comfortable nonetheless, a suite of rooms in Edgar Buildings, situated on the edge of the fashionable part of town and within walking distance of the Pump Room.

Soon after my arrival, Mr. Knowles obtained a position as tutor to two young boys in the nearby village of Charlcombe. He always visited us on Sundays, however, escorting us to Bath Abbey for divine service and dining with us afterwards.

With Mrs. Knowles I had much in common. The widow of a clergyman, she was an intensely spiritual woman and extremely fond of music. But here any resemblance ended, for Mrs. Knowles had been a beauty in her youth and was still at the age of fifty a remarkably handsome woman. She had great purple eyes (wreathed with the crow's foot but still brilliantly expressive), a classically straight nose with pinched nostrils, and bright white hair, which she wore elaborately coiled. Despite the discomfort of persistent bouts of rheumatism, she walked always with an upright back and firm step. Mr. Knowles was devoted to her.

She set me a fine example. Whatever the weather or the state of her health, she never emerged from her bedchamber later than eight o'clock, and I was expected to do the same. If the morning was fine, we would repair to the Pump Room, there to drink the waters and to greet her numerous acquaintance. We rarely stayed longer than half an hour, however, as Mrs. Knowles disapproved of idle gossip.

Later, I would go to Queen Square for my lessons, and in the evening, we would attend the concerts of the Bath Harmonic Society. If there was no concert, we might go to a public lecture or to the theater—Mrs. Knowles was extremely fond of the drama. We rarely went to private evening parties, as she did not care for cards. (She did not care for balls either, but for me that was no hardship.)

At home in the evenings we took turns to read aloud to each other, always concluding with a scene from Shakespeare and a portion of scripture. Mrs. Knowles now suggested I transcribe some of my favorite passages into a special book—known ever afterwards as "Mary's Commonplace Book"—so that I might memorize any uplifting thought or wise remark: "No excuse now, my dear Mary, for you to be tongue-tied in company."

But alas it would be the Commonplace Book, or my misuse of it, which spoilt my first visit to Longbourn. On entering the house after an eight months' absence, a host of memories, most of them unhappy, rushed in on me, and the smell of the vestibule—a blend of beeswax and chilly tiled floor—quite overset me. When

Lydia and Kitty ran to welcome me, it took all my self-control not to repulse them.

Small wonder then that I resorted to the Commonplace Book whenever I felt nervous (and there was rarely a family gathering when I did not feel nervous). And the aimlessness of Longbourn days, so different from my Bath regimen, did not help. When I lay abed late in the morning, there was nobody to remind me of my duties—no governess to supervise my studies.

My sisters' lives I saw had gone on in the same old pattern. Kitty and Lydia had both become shockingly idle. Lydia had gained complete ascendancy over Nan Pender, and if Jane or Elizabeth tried to intervene our mother invariably sided with Lydia. Mama had never been interested in our education but now she positively encouraged her daughters to fritter away their time—to walk into Meryton and dawdle about the shops or visit Aunt Philips and play at lottery tickets.

I missed Mrs. Knowles and my Bath life grievously, and I secretly wrote to her, begging her to write to hurry my return. She would not consent to this, but her reply was so full of wise advice that I immediately copied it into my Commonplace Book. Unfortunately, it would be this passage that I chose to quote to Jane and Elizabeth and to Charlotte Lucas.

We were all sewing together in the breakfast room, making clothes for the youngest Gardiner infant, a boy born two days after Christmas—Aunt's confinement having prevented the usual family visit. (And here I should record two earlier additions to the Gardiner family: a girl born one year after Susan's death, and another boy, Edward, born the following year.) A favorable report on the progress of mother and son had reached Longbourn that morning and we now remarked on the good fortune of the four little Gardiners, blessed as they were with such amiable and sensible parents.

A silence followed during which we all sewed very intently, conscious no doubt of the shortcomings of our own parents (for I suspect Charlotte was as embarrassed by Sir William as ever we were of Mama) and it was then that Mrs. Knowles's words came to me. She had written to remind me of my duties as a daughter, citing Exodus 20:12, the Fifth Commandment, but as soon as I started to quote the passage, Elizabeth said: "Mary, you are among family and friends, and to be preaching to us in this way—it is too absurd."

A moment later she cast aside her sewing and came and kissed me. "Forgive me, I spoke hastily. Do not mind me."

From then on, Elizabeth never spoke to me without seeming to weigh her words. And she and Jane also did their best to make Kitty and Lydia mind me. But this merely had the effect of further distancing me from them all, and when the time came for me to return to Bath they none of them seemed especially sorry.

2.

My second year in Bath was every bit as happy and fulfilling as the first. And I might have spent many more happy years there had not a certain retired army officer, one Colonel Philip Pitt, come to live in Edgar Buildings shortly after my seventeenth birthday.

A widower in his fifties, incongruously merry-looking with long dimples fissuring his cheeks, Colonel Pitt so successfully invaded our lives that within a month he was accompanying us everywhere, taking most of his meals with us, even joining us for our nightly Shakespeare and scripture readings. Until his arrival, I had believed myself to be indispensable to Mrs. Knowles. Certainly I had heard her say as much to all her acquaintance. "I simply could not manage without Mary," she would assure them. "Mary is my rock."

But it was soon clear that Colonel Pitt had become her rock. She came to my room late one night to acknowledge the fact, her long white hair hanging down her back and wearing a dressing gown of purple velvet (which I had never before seen, such was her dislike of sloth).

"You must think me the greatest fool alive, Mary, I do myself. And do not think I haven't prayed for guidance—I seem to have done little else these past weeks. But there is no help for it. Philip loves me, and we are to be married."

She seated herself on my bed, her arms folded inside the sleeves of her gown, and it struck me that she had become somehow *ordinary*, that passion had diminished her, rendering her less certain, less queenly.

Perhaps she divined my thoughts, for she said: "When people fall in love, my dear, they are apt to go a little mad, you know."

Somebody had said the same thing to me a long time ago, but I could not immediately recall who, and then I remembered George on the night of our concert talking so of Elizabeth and Mr. Coates.

"Especially at my age." Mrs. Knowles reached for my hand. "You are the first to know, and you must help me break it to my boy." (She always referred to Mr. Knowles thus.) "He will not like it—he and Philip are very different sorts of men—but I trust in time he will be reconciled. And I will need your help in composing a letter to my brother Galbraith."

Here, she made a wry face, an acknowledgment that reconciling her brother to the match would be next to impossible (Mr. Galbraith was a reclusive old bachelor, a prosperous gentleman-farmer who lived not far from Longbourn near the village of Stoke).

She talked on but I barely listened. I was feeling hollowed-out and sick and furious with both her and Colonel Pitt. They had obviously been carrying on behind my back for weeks. And they were both so very *old*—it was disgusting merely to think of it.

But here again Mrs. Knowles seemed to guess some part of what I was feeling. "Now if we were in the other room, you could read me the lecture that Hamlet gives his poor misguided mother. You could tell me that at my advanced age 'the heyday in the blood is tame … and waits upon the judgment.'"

I forced myself to smile and she patted my hand. "These last two years have been very happy ones, have they not? We have been able to help each other in so many ways. Certainly you have helped *me*. But I could not have kept you here with me forever, my dear. You must have returned to Longbourn sooner or later. Your family has claims on you."

I reflected that it was only now, when it suited her, that my family could be supposed to have claims on me. She had never before talked of my returning home.

"But I hope you will consent to stay with me until I am married. Indeed, you must, for I shall need a chaperone." (laughing) "Try not to think too badly of me, my dear. I never dreamt that I could be prevailed upon to marry again. But Philip is so—oh! at the risk of sounding ridiculous, he makes me feel so *young*."

My own distress was as nothing compared to that of Mr. Knowles, however. The news was broken to him by Colonel Pitt without the least preparation over Sunday dinner. "I find I must trouble you for your congratulations, my boy. Your mother and I have decided to make a match of it. What do you say to that, eh? Have we your blessing?"

And when poor Mr. Knowles could not say anything, so shocked was he and looking to his mother for confirmation, Colonel Pitt had slapped him on the shoulder. "Come now, look me in the eye, sir! I swear I shall do everything in my power to make your mother happy. For God's sake give us your blessing."

Having no wish to witness Mr. Knowles being bullied into giving his blessing, I would have quit the room but Mrs. Knowles now went to her son, offering to postpone the wedding if he liked. Whereupon Colonel Pitt was obliged to effect a strategic withdrawal. ("I'm sure I never meant to upset the boy. If he don't wish to give us his blessing, that's entirely a matter for him.")

3.

Mrs. Knowles and Colonel Pitt were married in Bath Abbey on the 26th of November (which was later to be a noteworthy date for me and my two elder sisters), and directly after the breakfast the bride and groom left for London and I left for Longbourn, escorted by Mr. Knowles.

Loyalty to his mother had hitherto prevented Mr. Knowles from confiding his disapproval of the match, but when the maid-servant accompanying me had asked to ride on the box for one stage, he was at last able to talk to me without reserve. He confessed he had grave misgivings as to Colonel Pitt's character. "And I am not alone in my fears, Mary. My uncle Galbraith is convinced he's a fortune-hunter. The fellow has a reputation, you know."

But when I inquired as to the nature of Colonel Pitt's reputation, he turned away: "'Tis not a fit subject for your ears."

A little later he again burst forth, speaking as from an overcharged heart: "I shall certainly never be able to think of him as a *father*." And then in more trembling accents: "I cannot bear to think that people are laughing at Mother, Mary. He has made her a laughingstock. And in a place where she was used to be held in high esteem."

I was shocked to see him so overset. By dint of prayer and reflection, I had managed to conquer much of my own resentment, and Mrs. Knowles had herself helped me in this. She had repeated her evening visit to my room, so that a nocturnal tête-à-tête had become part of our routine—it was the only time I could count on Colonel Pitt not being present. And she had come even on the eve of her wedding—wearing her purple dressing gown—come, as she put it, to play Polonius, to give me advice at parting.

"You must never forget that you have a gift, my dear. Our Lord in his wisdom has endowed you with real musical talent. But gifts entail obligations, Mary. Promise me that when you return home, you will keep to your timetable of early rising and regular activities."

I duly promised and she continued: "Much as my boy respected your father's abilities, it grieved him that Mr. Bennet did not value you as he ought. I know it is improper to be speaking of your father in this way, but I have thought about it—prayed about it—and I believe I am right in counseling you. Your father may never change towards you but if you can bring yourself to forgive him, 'twill be your salvation."

I made her no answer; my feelings were too confused, and she went on: "Your sisters too. Jane and Elizabeth will probably always be first with each other—until one or other of them marries. As will Catherine and Lydia. If you can find it in your heart to forgive them, you will be the happier for it.

"One thing more. Find a like-minded friend, someone your own age who shares your interests. It is wonderful how two sympathetic minds can sustain each other."

She had paused, smiling, but at a spot directly above my head, and I saw that she was no longer thinking of me but of Colonel Pitt. I was able to pardon the lapse, however, and even afterwards to wish her happy. As soon as she left, I wrote the chief of her advice in the Commonplace Book.

I longed now to impart its spirit of forgiveness to her son. But as I looked at him leaning back in his corner of the carriage, I realized that it was much too early to speak of such things. He had worshipped his mother only a degree or two less than his God. It would take time before he could be brought to view her marriage as other than a sacrilege.

4.

My family was not at home when I arrived. A long-standing dinner engagement at the Great House of Stoke was the excuse given by Nan Pender, who, together with the housekeeper Mrs. Hill, had been on the watch for me. And now these two loyal servants fairly laid themselves out to make up for my family's neglect.

They had been charged, they said, with any number of kind messages and there was a great wreath awaiting me in the vestibule, which Lydia and Kitty had been working on all week, entirely made of holly and with WELCOME woven through with red ribbon. My mother had also directed that my favorite dishes be served for my supper buttered lobster and a muffin pudding.

But all this could not do away with the fact that not a single member of my family had seen fit to welcome me home. And they had known for months, ever since Mrs. Knowles had fixed on a date for her wedding, that I would return to Longbourn the following day.

I was determined not to give way to self-pity, however, and after eating my splendid solitary supper, I walked about the house—taper in hand—looking into all the principal rooms to see what changes had taken place. There seemed to be quite a number—new hangings in the drawing room and a Turkey carpet in the dining room and I noticed an oil painting over the chimney-piece that had not been there before.

It was a portrait of three women seated around a table drinking tea. I held up the taper the better to see, and at once recognized the trio—excellent likenesses of Aunt Philips and my mother and Mrs. Long—and the room in which they were sitting was clearly Mrs. Long's front parlor, for there in the background was the oak-leaf wallpaper and the portrait of the late Mr. Long. I looked for the artist's signature then and found it in the lower left-hand corner of the canvas in neat little angular letters: *Cassandra Long.*

My interest was fairly caught. I remembered Cassandra— the elder of Mrs. Long's two nieces—as an intimidating girl, lanky and silent and given to staring intently. I had not the least idea of her having artistic talent. I tried to recall the last time I had seen her. She and her younger sister Helen had certainly stayed with Mrs. Long after the death of their mother and that had happened when I was about ten. But they could also have lived there later when I was ill. If so, I had no recollection of it. And while I knew it was dangerous to dwell on those lost years, I could not help wondering whether Cassandra had observed me then with the pitiless eyes of the artist. It was not a pleasant thought.

My family's welcome next morning was extraordinarily effusive—protesting too much that they had missed me. None of them was much changed except for Lydia. She had grown like a weed and was now at the age of fourteen almost as tall as our father—her figure fully formed, her face fat-cheeked and high-colored.

They were all of them eager to hear about the wedding, questioning me over breakfast; my mother wanting to know about the bride's clothes while Elizabeth and Jane asked about the bridegroom's character and Lydia and Kitty about his appearance. My father wished to know how Mr. Knowles had comported himself. "How did he bear his mother's defection? Did he cry?"

After breakfast, Lydia was eager for everyone to walk into Meryton to visit Aunt Philips. Jane and Elizabeth declined and, mindful of Mrs. Knowles's advice to use my time profitably, I was also about to excuse myself when it occurred to me that I might call on Cassandra—Mrs. Long's house being opposite that of the Philipses.

I went upstairs to put on my cloak and bonnet, and on making my way down again, I stopped outside the old nursery, still the apartment of Lydia and Kitty. The door was open and I could hear their voices within.

"Sure, Mary is much changed," Kitty was saying. "She never used to walk with us to Meryton before."

"Her appearance certainly has not changed. She is so little and pale—she has not grown an inch in the past year. But did you notice her at breakfast? I could hardly keep from laughing— when she picked up her coffee cup, her spectacles steamed over!" (laughing) "She was obliged to take them off, and then when Papa was asking her about Mr. Knowles she would not answer him—she kept wiping her spectacles and blinking like a frightened rabbit."

"You were used to be frightened of Papa yourself," Kitty reminded her.

"Yes, but I do not mean to be made unhappy by him any more. He is so horrid and sarcastic, there is no pleasing him. Shall we go down then?"

I hastily left my listening post. I was not near so mortified by Lydia's remarks as once I might have been. My recent experience with the Bath Harmonic Society—its politics and petty jealousies—had taught me that opinions are invariably colored by personal circumstance. Small wonder that Lydia, strapping and red-cheeked herself, should consider me little and pale. In any case, I knew I *had* grown over the past year, for Mrs. Knowles had kept a record of my height and weight the whole time I was with her.

As for being a frightened rabbit, the collective glare of everybody's attention at breakfast had indeed discomposed me, and I had longed to resort to the Commonplace Book. Only the fear of incurring Elizabeth's displeasure had held me back.

For most of the mile walk into Meryton I had to endure a monologue from Lydia. "Oh Mary! I am so glad you are come back, I can't tell you. You must play all the country dances so that Kitty and me can practice our steps. Lizzy will never play for us—she and Jane are so stuffy nowadays—always wanting us to be *learning* something. But Mama says I may attend the assemblies when I am turned fifteen. Oh! how I wish I was fifteen! And I have still six months to wait—how shall I ever bear it? Well, but now tell me what happened while you were in Bath. You surely did not spend *all* your time going about with old Mrs. Knowles? And now she has got herself a husband and you have nobody. I call that most unfair." (laughing heartily) "But I am glad you are come back. I was beginning to think that you would be in Bath forever."

When eventually I was able to make myself heard, I asked after Mrs. Long and her nieces.

"Oh! they are all well. You may call on them later if you like. Only do not expect me to go with you—Cassandra stares one out of countenance and gives herself such airs, there is no bearing it."

Kitty said: "She thinks herself so accomplished. She draws and paints the whole time and takes no interest in anything else."

"But Helen Long is a nice little thing," said Lydia fairmindedly. "When first they came to live with their aunt after their father died, she would scarce open her mouth, but now she chatters away like anything."

"She has become rather a flirt in fact," said Kitty. "Lizzy said so the other day—that Helen Long was become rather a flirt."

"Dear me, since when was flirting considered a crime, Miss? And why must you always quote what Lizzy says? As if her opinion mattered more than other people's."

They began to squabble then and afterwards Lydia applied to Aunt Philips for *her* views on flirting. And upon Aunt saying that she saw no harm in it—that she liked to see young people enjoying themselves—Lydia rounded on Kitty: "There's for you, Miss!" Whereupon Kitty burst into tears.

When I called on the Longs later, unaccompanied by Kitty and Lydia, Helen Long—a not unpretty but rather bold-eyed girl a bit older than myself—came directly to welcome me. Cassandra, however, took her time. As soon as I saw her though, I felt we should be friends (and she later told me that she had felt exactly the same).

I cannot readily explain the attraction. Cassandra's appearance was unprepossessing and her manner direct almost to the point of rudeness. A large girl, larger than Lydia, she dressed plainly and wore her hair pulled back so that not a tendril escaped, and her light-colored eyes with their small pupils were extremely hard to meet. And yet for all her size and severity, I sensed in her a sweetness—as if an excess of feeling were bottled up within. She was also extraordinarily graceful for so big a girl, quick and deft in all her movements. It was a pleasure, for instance, to watch her make the tea.

She certainly looked at me a great deal during the half hour of my visit. At first, this made me nervous. I was sure that she was watching for signs of incipient melancholia. Even if she had not seen me during the time of my illness, she must surely have heard about it since. Such things are always much talked about and Mrs. Long was a great talker. But as I was leaving she said: "You must forgive me for looking at you so intently but I should very much like to paint you. Would you be willing to sit to me?"

"La!" exclaimed Helen. "What an honor for you, Mary. Cass rarely paints young women, you know. She says they are too unformed."

Cassandra smiled but did not deny it, and after I assured her I would be most happy to sit, an appointment was made for the following morning. I went home with my head so full of it that I scarcely heard the prattle of Lydia and Kitty. Suddenly it seemed that the part of Mrs. Knowles's advice I had thought impossible— finding a like-minded friend of my own age—might not be beyond me.

5.

The portrait took many weeks to complete. Not because Cassandra was especially slow in executing it—she could dash off a lightning sketch when required—but portrait painting in Cassandra's view was much more than putting paint in the right place to create a likeness. ("The artist must strive to capture the subject's *essence*.")

She finally decided to paint me at the pianoforte—not posing but playing. ("I must catch you on the wing.") And as there was no instrument at her aunt's house, she came to Longbourn to sketch me while I practiced. She came almost every morning for several weeks, making dozens of drawings, all the while adjuring me not to mind her, but to concentrate on my music. "You are such a changeable little person and just when I think I have you down pat, I find you have escaped me." Once, in a rare display of temper, she had torn up a sketch she had worked on the entire morning: "If I could but see what I am trying to see *when* I am drawing it!"

Christmas came and went meanwhile, with the Gardiners and their four children paying their usual visit. And on their return to Gracechurch Street, Jane and Elizabeth accompanied them—there to remain until the Easter holiday. I did not especially miss my elder sisters. Increasingly, they seemed to hold themselves aloof from me, and they were especially reticent about the young men of their acquaintance. From what my mother let drop, however, I gathered that Jane at least had formed an attachment during the time I was in Bath, although not of a serious nature. "But Jane liked poor Mr. Houston very well," Mama insisted. "Until Lizzy put it into her head that he was stupid."

Elizabeth herself remained a mystery to me. Certainly she gave her opinions as decidedly as ever and there were the usual sprightly exchanges between her and my father across the dinner table, but her *essence*, as Cassandra would have it, continued to elude me—and this despite our spending a great deal more time together, for we were now taking Italian lessons from the same master. We also shared a music master, one Mr. Turner, who for a short time also taught Kitty. (Kitty had had a brief flirtation with the harp but soon abandoned it, being incapable of pursuing any course independently of Lydia.)

As for Lydia, she was counting the days until the Glorious First of June—the day upon which she was to turn fifteen—with precious little thought for anything else. When Cassandra had first begun to paint my portrait, Lydia had expressed an interest in learning to draw, but before a master could be engaged the fit passed, and apart from practicing her dance steps, the only activity to which she regularly applied herself was taking her hats to pieces and trimming them afresh. But when the Glorious First finally dawned, Lydia declared herself disappointed: "I do not know how it is but whenever I have really looked forward to something, it is never as much fun as I imagined." She unfurled a hand-painted fan, the gift of Cassandra, and scowled over it. "I had expected to feel entirely different this morning."

Foolishly, I then quoted some lines of Dr. Johnson's I had just transcribed into the Commonplace Book: "It seems to be the fate of man to seek all his consolations in futurity. The time present is seldom able to fill desire or imagination with immediate enjoyment, and we are forced to supply its deficiencies by recollection or anticipation."

(I have here set down the passage in full although at the time Lydia did not let me finish, crying out when I was but halfway through: "Oh for God's sake, I shall *throw* something at you if you do not leave off! I will not be preached at on my birthday.")

I told Cassandra of the exchange when I called on her later that morning. "This Commonplace Book of yours," said she as soon as I had done. "Does it contain any of your own thoughts or merely those of other people?"

"Oh! 'tis not the place for my own thoughts. 'Tis not a journal." I felt my face grow hot. "I am more at home with music than words."

She gave me one of her looks. "Have you ever considered putting your thoughts down as music?"

"You mean *make up* music?"

"Why not?"

"Oh I could never do that. 'Tis a man's province, composing."

"Nonsense. Start with a song—a simple ballad. See how you go on."

Her gaze now moved back to the print she was tinting. I dared not call away her attention. I loved to watch her paint and I loved visiting her so-called painting room (in reality a screened-off section of her bedchamber) with its view of Meryton's main street and the nearer prospect of the Philipses' green front door and sash windows. This streetscape was a favorite subject. Cassandra had painted it numerous times and in all weathers and had even—but this was a great secret—sold several such paintings to a print-shop and received very good money for them.

The idea of composing a song, while it seemed an audacious step, soon took possession of my fancy, and I nerved myself to speak to our master Mr. Turner. To my surprise he encouraged me, saying that several females had written songs: "Of course they did not publish them under their own names."

"Anne Boleyn is thought to have written a song," said Elizabeth, who was fond of reading histories of her royal namesake, Anne Boleyn's daughter.

Mr. Turner then remarked that although females were not capable of composing great music as they lacked the necessary mathematical intellect, he did not doubt my ability to produce an acceptable little air. He promised to give me special tuition in harmony and counterpoint, and asked me to consider taking extra singing lessons: "For you will hardly set about the business without first schooling your own voice."

But alas, I ignored his advice. Why bother with solfège exercises when I could be composing? It was only when I came to sing a ballad of my own composition that I realized my mistake. I sang it at the ball given by the new tenant of Netherfield, Mr. Charles Bingley, and my voice then proved much too weak for public display. I shall never forget the humiliation to which my father afterwards subjected me—though the memory, mercifully, no longer pains me. It is now admixed with happier recollections.

But I have yet to describe how it was that Mr. Bingley came into Hertfordshire. I happened to witness his very first visit to Meryton when he came in a chaise and four one fine September morning to call on Mr. Morris the attorney.

6.

On the morning in question, Cassandra and I were in her painting room. She had set up her easel by the window and was painting her favorite street scene while I was reading, on her recommendation, *A Vindication of the Rights of Woman* and extracting passages for the Commonplace Book. One such passage I now read aloud:

> *Children very early see cats with their kittens, birds with their young ones, etc. Why then are they not to be told that their mothers carry and nourish them in the same way? As there would then be no appearance of mystery, they would never think of the subject more.*

Cassandra sighed and said: "Alas, my poor mother would never answer Helen's and my questions about such matters."

I then related the episode of the bloodstained sheets, adding: "Lydia is shockingly curious about such things. As a child, she was forever asking about the farm animals. And now all she ever talks about is flirting and making love. She has done no work whatsoever this past year. It is very bad."

Cassandra was looking at me. "Mary, if you are really concerned about Lydia, you should speak to your father."

"Oh! I could never speak to Papa."

"Nonsense. Tell him that you fear Lydia's education is being neglected. If he shares your concern, he is bound to act."

"The only person Papa would ever listen to is Elizabeth. And do not tell me I should speak to her, Cassy, because I certainly shall not."

Cassandra laughed but a moment later gave an exclamation of annoyance. A chaise had pulled up outside the Philipses', obscuring her view. We both watched as the groom jumped down to open the door. It was an expensive-looking equipage and although there was no crest on the panel, the four horses drawing it were obviously bloodstock. The man who alighted looked equally glossy and well-bred. He was of medium height and wore a blue coat and buff pantaloons but his high-crowned beaver hat obscured our view of his face.

As soon as it became certain that the chaise would not be moving off, Cassandra took up her sketchbook and started to draw the horses. Meanwhile, one of Mr. Morris's clerks hurried over to meet the gentleman, and with a great deal of bowing and scraping escorted him back across the road.

I watched them enter the house from which Mr. Morris conducted his business and although I knew Cassandra would not approve the sentiment, I could not help remarking: "I wonder that such a fine young man should be calling on Mr. Morris."

"I daresay he has come to look at Netherfield Park. Mr. Morris is the owner's agent, is he not?"

"Yes, of course!" (Netherfield still had a hold on my imagination; the mere mention of it excited me.) "What a grand thing for the neighborhood if he should take it. It has been empty for far too long."

Cassandra made no answer, intent on her drawing, and I again took up my book. A few minutes later Helen burst in.

"La, my dears! Have you seen the carriage? The drollest thing—there is a man inside, fast asleep."

And upon my getting up to look out the window: "Oh! but you cannot see him from up here! You must needs come down to see it—the man I mean—he is lying there with his mouth open. I thought he was dead but then Mr. Jones's shop-boy tapped on the glass and he stirred—" (giggling) "Come quick or he will wake."

Cassandra and I followed Helen downstairs—Cassandra still holding her sketchbook—and I could see through the open door, which gave directly onto the street, that a crowd was gathering. Most people were admiring the horses or talking to the groom and the coachman but a few were looking through the carriage windows at the unconscious occupant. He lay sprawled on the seat with his mouth agape—a big man, aged about thirty, fashionably dressed except that his coat was rucked up over his unbuttoned waistcoat.

Cassandra at first gave him only a cursory look, but then she looked again and—seeing a subject worthy of her art—immediately went to work sketching him.

Within minutes a recognizable portrait grew up under her hand. People were watching the progress of the sketch and complimenting Cassandra on her skill when the gentleman in the blue coat returned, accompanied by Mr. Morris. He at once exclaimed at the size of the crowd, crying out (but in the most good-humored way): "Why, what's amiss? What are you all looking at, pray?"

The crowd at once dispersed, but Cassandra did not think to conceal her sketch and in an instant the gentleman was at her side, requesting to be shown it, holding out his hand—elegantly gloved in York tan—in a manner that would not be gainsaid. (I was surprised nevertheless to see Cassandra comply so readily.)

"Oh! this is famous," said the gentleman, laughing. "An excellent likeness. You are to be congratulated."

Helen piped up then: "My sister is a very accomplished art-ist, sir."

"Oh Helen, hush." Cassandra's face was quite pink. "I did it for my own amusement, sir. I meant no disrespect, I assure you."

"I should very much like to have this if I may. And when my brother-in-law wakes I shall make him a present of it." (smiling at Cassandra) "So you must name your price, ma'am, if you please."

"My price?"

Cassandra's face was now bright red and the gentleman, seeing it, said gravely: "It is my turn to assure *you* that I meant no disrespect. But I cannot ask you to give it to me, you know." (taking out his card-case) "I find I must trouble you for a pencil." And upon Cassandra supplying him with her own, he wrote upon the back of the card, saying: "Here is my note of hand, and Mr. Morris will act for me. There."

He bestowed the card on Cassandra, who in turn wordlessly presented him with the sketch. A bow, a touch of his hat, and he was climbing into the chaise once more, followed by Mr. Morris. And before the door was shut upon them I heard him say, "Hurst! Wake up, man, I have something to show you."

The chaise then took off with a great lurch, whereupon Helen linked arms with Cassandra and me, saying: "I'll wager that woke him." And when Cassandra failed to respond (being lost in contemplation of the gentleman's card): "Did you ever see anyone so à la mode, Mary? The other gentleman, I mean. Did you see his coat? Made by a London tailor if I'm any judge. But what business could he have with old Morris?" She turned back to Cassandra." Are you going to show us his card then? Or do you mean to keep it all to yourself?"

Cassandra's response was to detach herself from Helen and head back to the house. Helen caught up with her in Mrs. Long's front parlor. "What on earth is the matter with you?"

"I cannot bear to be patronized, that is all."

I said: "He didn't patronize you, Cassy."

"He has given me a note of hand for two guineas. I cannot—the situation is intolerable."

"Two guineas!" Helen was incredulous. "For that paltry little sketch?"

"It was a very fine sketch," I objected. "And an excellent likeness."

Cassandra handed Helen the card. "See for yourself."

There was no mistaking the two guineas. He had written it in words, not figures, and all as clear as could be. Helen turned over the card to read the name engraved thereon, *Mr. Charles Bingley*, before returning it to Cassandra. "Well, I daresay he is as rich as Dives, so what does it matter?"

"It matters to me. I intend to take it up with Mr. Morris. And in the meantime I must ask you both not to mention it."

"Of course we will not."

"Oh, certainly."

But as soon as Cassandra left the room, Helen laughed and said: "Poor Cass. She is so sensitive about money matters. But *entre nous*, I suspect that there may be rather more to it."

"I'm sure I don't know what you mean."

"La! Do I have to spell it out for you? She has obviously taken a fancy to this Bingley fellow and wants an excuse to recommend herself."

At the time, I thought—and said—that Cassandra was the last girl in the world to adopt such tactics. But later I was forced to acknowledge that she had indeed conceived a *tendre* for Mr. Bingley and that her refusal to accept his two guineas might not have been entirely disinterested. The gesture certainly brought her to Bingley's notice. Within a fortnight of his settling at Netherfield, he had commissioned her to paint a portrait of his sisters.

7.

The news that Netherfield had at last been let spread fast. Mrs. Long carried it to my mother (whose raptures need no repetition here) and within days of his visit, Bingley's name was on everyone's lips. My elder sisters partook of the general excitement. They began at once to refurbish their wardrobes, trimming their hats and so on.

I was astounded at the fuss and said as much to Cassandra: "All that my sisters know of Mr. Bingley is that he is rich—rich enough at least to rent Netherfield—and on the strength of *that* they are preparing to set their caps at him! It is not as if they have heard he is exceptionally clever or virtuous—or even good-looking, for you may be sure that I have not breathed a word about our seeing him. Who would have thought they could be so mercenary?"

Cassandra made no answer—we were in Mrs. Long's kitchen, where she was busy kneading dough. (Both Helen and Cassandra had to help with the cooking, as there was but one servant—a maid of all work—and Mrs. Long had been called away to nurse her bedridden brother.)

"They are exactly like the girls Miss Wollstonecraft writes of in her *Vindication*," I went on. "Marriage is the grand feature of their lives, although they would never admit it."

"You can hardly blame them for seeking to marry well, Mary. Indeed, with your father's estate entailed away from his daughters, it would be imprudent for them to do otherwise."

This was unanswerable, and after a pause I said: "But I have not told you what happened yesterday evening. Papa—after vowing and declaring that he would *not* call on Mr. Bingley— announced that he had actually visited him that morning."

Cassandra stopped kneading. "Did he indeed?"

"Mama and my sisters could scarcely contain themselves. All they could talk about for the rest of the evening was when Mr. Bingley was likely to return the visit. Indeed, Mama was so sure he would call this morning that I made up my mind to come to you early—so that I might avoid him."

I watched as Cassandra covered the dough with a cloth. The subject of Mr. Bingley was not allowed to rest, however. "What did your father think of him, pray? Did he find him agreeable?"

"Oh, there is no telling what Papa thinks. Everyone was questioning him—everyone except me, that is—but he would say nothing to the purpose. My father loves to tease."

"Yes," said Cassandra drily. "That has not escaped my notice."

Helen walked in then with her arms full of parcels. But still the talk was of Mr. Bingley, for Helen had seen his housekeeper Mrs. Nicholls in the street and Mrs. Nicholls had told her that Mr. Bingley planned to attend the following Tuesday's assembly with a large party. "He is very fond of dancing apparently so you and I must go to this ball, Cass, do you hear? No arguments. I am quite determined."

Cassandra smiled but said nothing, and Helen began to undo the largest of her parcels. "Every girl in Meryton will be wearing a new gown I imagine—the Bennet girls certainly will, won't they, Mary? And so too now will the Long girls—voilà!" (The parcel contained a quantity of white book muslin and Cassandra, seeing it, stopped smiling.) "La! You need not look like that. It was not expensive—not really—and I shall make up the gowns myself. But see here, *chérie*—look at these." She tore open a parcel containing two pairs of long white kid gloves. "I just could not resist. French of course, one can always tell."

Cassandra said: "How much did all this cost, Helen?"

"Oh Lord, who cares? Anyway, Aunt gave us that money before she left. She wants us to look our best. She wants us to dance with Mr. Bingley—"

"Aunt gave us that money for housekeeping expenses. And Mr. Bingley may not attend the assembly."

Helen began to open another parcel, addressing her remarks rather pointedly to me: "Mrs. Nicholls told me that Mr. Bingley's greatest friend is soon to visit Netherfield —a single gentleman with vast estates in Derbyshire." (The parcel I saw contained two pairs of silk stockings.) "His name is Darcy and he has a fortune of ten thousand pounds a year."

"Good God!" Cassandra was staring at the stockings. "Are they silk? How much did they cost?"

I thought it prudent to leave the kitchen at that point, and after collecting my book I went upstairs to Cassandra's painting room to await her there. It was a while before she joined me, however, and when she did, she seemed preoccupied. I knew she would not complain to me of Helen—Cassandra was a most loyal sister—but she said as she set out her paints: "I do wish that Aunt had not had to go away just now. But she will return the day before the assembly, thank heaven. I confess I am not at all looking forward to this ball, Mary."

"You mean to go then?" I was surprised. Cassandra never attended the assemblies.

She was now mixing her colors and did not answer immediately. "To say the truth, I have not made up my mind. But if Helen were to make up a new gown for me, I should feel obliged to go, I daresay."

I was astonished—Cassandra was not selfish, but she was single-minded in pursuing her art and to that end everything had to give way—not excepting the claims of family. She had precious little leisure moreover and guarded it most jealously. Yet here she was, talking of going to a silly public ball to oblige her sister!

Looking at her now, still mixing her colors, I could not believe her. And perhaps she saw it in my face—the doubt—for she quickly changed the subject. "But how are you getting on with your song? All this talk of balls has made me quite forget."

"Oh." (I had not been looking forward to this question.) "Well, our music master did not care for the ballad I wrote—did not think it at all tuneful. He suggested I try my hand at a patriotic song—something martial."

"Something martial!"

"Something similar to 'Rule, Britannia!' Mr. Turner thought."

"Oh Mary, what nonsense is this? You know nothing of war or soldiers and sailors—nothing at firsthand."

"Well, but now that the militia regiment is to be quartered at Meryton—"

"Oh good God. 'Tis as bad as your Commonplace Book! No, you must write something from your *own* experience—take no notice of Mr. Turner."

I was silent, mortified by her reflection on my Commonplace Book, and after a pause she said more collectedly: "If I did not think you had talent, I would not care what you wrote. But you have assured me that you are serious about song-writing and that being the case—"

"I am! I am serious."

Cassandra shook her head and after a moment and because she had hurt me, I said: "I'm sure I have never told you what to paint, Cassy—or what not to paint. And it is not as though I were obliged to earn my living writing songs."

The words were no sooner spoken than regretted. She gave me one of her looks but said nothing. I took up my book then and pretended to read. It was the first time we had had a serious falling-out and I felt it keenly. She felt it too (she owned as much to me later) but we kept up a charade of concentration until the maidservant came in to ask about the wash. I used the interruption as an excuse to hurry away.

8.

The Bennets were the first family to arrive at the assembly. Mama led the way into the inn's entrance passage with Jane and Elizabeth following, and Kitty, Lydia, and myself bringing up the rear.

Lydia was talking loudly despite Jane and Elizabeth begging her to lower her voice. "But there is nobody to hear me except the waiters! Nobody is yet come besides ourselves." And then with a snort of laughter as we began to mount the stairs: "Lord, we do look like a gaggle of geese. All of us in white and Mama with her headdress of white plumes."

"And you with your cackle," said Kitty, who was cross because Lydia had crowded her in the carriage.

"And Lizzy with her hiss," said Lydia as once again Elizabeth tried to hush her.

Fortunately we encountered nobody on the stairs but as we were about to enter the gallery leading to the rooms, a dark, gypsy-looking young man came flying up after us. He was clutching a fiddle in one hand and a bow in the other, and in his haste to overtake us, somehow or other his bow caught itself in the folds of my shawl. It was a simple matter to free it, however, and after a hasty "beg pardon" he hurried on towards the assembly room.

"Dear Mary! Your gown is not torn?" Jane with her usual thoughtfulness stepped back to assure herself that all was well with me.

"He must be one of the musicians," said Elizabeth. "Can it be that we have stolen a march on them?"

As we approached the assembly room, now brilliantly lit up with candles, there came the sound of instruments being tuned, and upon our entering the room the four musicians (of whom the young man was indeed one) immediately struck up "Over the Hills and Far Away."

It was a beautiful gesture, both an apology and a welcome, for we were their only audience. Lydia, out of sheer high spirits, executed a couple of dance steps, and at the end of the air we all applauded. I have often since recalled the scene—the six of us standing on the threshold of the long, bright, empty room— standing (it strikes me now) on a threshold not merely literal, for the night would bring Jane and Elizabeth their future husbands, and Mr. Darcy would in turn influence Lydia's fate.

The young man approached me shortly afterwards to make certain that neither I nor my shawl had sustained any lasting injury. His manner was respectful but his hawk-nose and brown face began to make me feel uneasy. I was sure that I had seen him before, and—bethinking myself of the Bath Harmonic Society—I asked him if he had ever visited that town.

"Never been there in m'life, Miss." He gave me a crooked smile. "I lived in London for a spell but I was born and bred in these parts. I once lived in the village of Longbourn—in Collins Cottage."

"You did? Good heavens, what is your name?"

He bowed. "Bushell, Miss. Peter Bushell."

One of the musicians called to him then, and he again bowed and left me—which was as well since I was quite bereft of speech. I could scarcely have been more shocked if he had introduced himself as Bonaparte.

"Mary! Come here, I want you. You too, Kitty."

I moved to obey Mama's summons but my attention remained fixed upon Peter Bushell. During my illness, many childish fears had been revived and magnified, and the memory of Bushell—the mere mention of the name—still had the power to unnerve me. Mama, moreover, had assured me that the Bushells had all left the country. And I did not at all care for the way that Peter—now tucking his fiddle under his chin—was looking across at me and smiling.

"I wonder that Mr. Bingley is not yet come." (Mama, having taken her customary seat by the fire, was beginning to fidget.) "The landlady assured me he would come early."

Here Elizabeth observed that it was an object among fashionable young men to come *late* to an assembly.

"Nonsense, you know nothing about it. Mr. Bingley always comes early. The landlady—Mrs. Curry—she had it from his housekeeper. He always comes early and leaves late." (I saw Jane and Elizabeth exchange glances. Mama's motive in bringing us here so early was now explained.) "And my sister Philips and Mrs. Long promised to give me the meeting. Not that I blame Mrs. Long, for she keeps no carriage and must come in a hack chaise, but I do think my sister could have managed things better."

I mistrusted my mother in this humor. She was liable to find fault for no good reason and I feared now that she would remark on my figure—I had removed the jeweler's wool that she had had Nan stuff into the under-bodice of my gown to make my form appear more womanly. But it was Elizabeth upon whom her irritation finally fastened.

"Upon my word, Lizzy, the more I look at your hair, the less I like it." (Elizabeth had dressed her hair after the Roman fashion—the front in curls and the rest combed back with a bandeau wound about her head.) "That style does not at all become you, you know—it looks like nothing so much as an old bandage—as if you had tied up your head in an old bandage. You had much better change it. There is more than enough time."

Elizabeth's response was a calm: "I am sorry you do not like it, ma'am. But Jane is in great good looks tonight. That must content you."

And Jane did indeed look especially lovely. She wore a frock of plain white silk, cut low, and in her hair, white flowers.

But nothing could long divert my attention from Peter Bushell. The musicians were now rehearsing a reel, and he was sawing away in a lively manner. Watching him, I began to feel less apprehensive. To be sure, he did look like his father (it was the nose chiefly) but his expression was really not in the least menacing. I perceived too that he played extremely well and that the other musicians looked to him always to take the lead. And he clearly enjoyed making music: His every movement proclaimed it. He did not—as many fiddlers do—*hunch* over his instrument; he appeared rather to roll with it, holding himself lightly, his brown face all smoothed over with pleasure.

At the end of the reel he again looked across at me and smiled. I did not know how to respond. I could not possibly *befriend* a person of his order—encourage such familiarity—but neither did I wish to snub him. In the end, it was he who resolved my dilemma. He held up his fiddle in front of his face. I smiled then—I could not help it—but I resolved to look at him no longer. I turned to Mama, who was complaining about the Red Lion's landlady: "What a deceitful woman that Mrs. Curry is. Serving me such a trick. But 'tis all of a piece with her other conduct. She once gave me a receipt for a restorative and I am sure it half killed me. 'Twas made all from sheep's trotters— hark! Is that a carriage? Lydia my love, go to the window. Is it Mr. Bingley?"

It was the Lucases—closely followed by Aunt and Uncle Philips—and after greetings were exchanged, Mama began once more to complain of Mrs. Curry. This was the moment of release for my four sisters. They all moved off, accompanied by Charlotte Lucas, and although Maria Lucas chose to stay and sit by me, she was all of a twitter and could talk only of Mr. Bingley.

"What if he were to ask me to dance, Mary? I would *die*. Oh, do not laugh at me! I am in such a quake—Charlotte has been lecturing me—telling me not to be a goose. But Papa says he has never seen a finer young man than Mr. Bingley—even at the Court of St. James's."

Maria talked on, and I edged back my chair so that I could neither see nor be seen by Peter Bushell (for I was tempted to keep looking at him else) and sought to occupy myself with my own thoughts. The room was now filling fast, but still there was no sign of Mrs. Long or her nieces. I was not looking forward to seeing Cassandra. We had not met since our falling-out of a fortnight back, and although I had written several letters apologizing to her, I had sent none of them—I could not forgive her for scorning my Commonplace Book. And I could not say over my favorite text—Matthew 18:22 on the need to forgive until seventy times seven—without recalling her remarks and feeling freshly aggrieved.

"Suppose he were to ask *you* to dance, Mary?" (Maria was still talking of Mr. Bingley.)

"Oh! gentlemen never ask me to dance, Maria. I am not pretty enough."

"Yes, but suppose he did?"

I shook my head and, perhaps supposing me to be offended, she placed her hand on mine. "For my part, I think a fine mind a thousand times better than a beautiful face. And everyone knows that you are by far the cleverest girl in Meryton." And then what she thought perhaps would please me more: "I must say I do not think Lizzy is in looks tonight. I do not like the way she has done her hair, but pray do not tell her I said so."

Maria was apt to be a little jealous of Elizabeth on account of the latter's intimacy with Charlotte, but it was true what she said—Elizabeth was not looking her best. She was now standing talking to Charlotte, and watching her, I wondered whether something had happened to put her out of humor; so severe was her expression.

"Mary." Maria was whispering in my ear. "Do not look now, but Cassandra Long is come and she has made *such* a figure of herself."

Cassandra and Helen were entering the room in the wake of Mrs. Long, and as their progress was necessarily slow to allow for Mrs. Long's frequent stops to exchange greetings, I had ample time to observe Cassandra. She looked amazingly different—a homemade travesty of high fashion. Her hair was loose and curled in a style similar to Helen's and her gown had a deep décolleté embroidered with gold braid. She had stopped to talk to Lydia and Kitty and my mother now noticed her, saying to Aunt Philips: "Did you ever see such a sight, Sister? Mrs. Long ought never to have permitted—" And then on the nearer approach of that same lady: "Ah, Mrs. Long! How delightful your nieces look to be sure—I declare I should not have known Cassandra. But how is it you are so late? We have been waiting for you this half hour at least."

But there was no time for Mrs. Long to explain about the tardy hack chaise, for the bustle at the entrance to the room— the coming forward of the inn master, Mr. Curry—betokened the arrival of Mr. Bingley and his party. Every eye was on the doorway as five fashionably dressed people—two ladies and three gentlemen—stepped into the room.

They were all of them extremely fine, the ladies especially, but when Sir William Lucas moved to welcome them, Mr. Bingley was the only one of the party who smiled. I recognized him at once and also one of the other gentlemen—the man who had lain asleep in the chaise (now covering a yawn with the back of his hand)—and for one incredulous second I thought I also recognized the third gentleman. On his moving into the light, however, I saw that he was not Mr. Jasper Coates. It was a striking resemblance nevertheless, and I looked across at Elizabeth to see how she bore it.

What I saw quite shocked me. Her face was as white as the bandeau she wore around her head. And whilst I averted my eyes as one would from another's nakedness, the sight stayed with me, so that her later disparagement of Mr. Darcy—her unending criticisms and witticisms—none of it served to convince me that she did not care about him.

But I found I had withdrawn my gaze from one embarrassing spectacle only to be confronted by another. Cassandra was blushing all down her neck. Mr. Bingley had bowed to her. Her curled hair had not prevented him from recognizing her—indeed, he seemed quite overjoyed to see her—but none of the other members of his party joined him when he beckoned. They had stayed talking amongst themselves.

It was then that the orchestra struck up "The Beggarman." At first I thought it must be meant as a joke, an ironic comment on the party's rich apparel, for the pearls and lace of the ladies were beyond anything and quite out of place at a country assembly. I determined then to take a peep at Peter Bushell to see if he looked at all satirical, and to that end edged out my chair. But he was playing most soulfully, his eyebrows in a tender circumflex above his hawk-nose. I concluded therefore that I must have been mistaken.

9.

No two views of a ball will be exactly alike. So many separate little worlds make up the whole (most of them whirling mindlessly about) and my own view of that Meryton assembly cannot help but be different from that of my sisters.

For the first part of the evening I was a mere onlooker. After supper, I may have shocked a few people but before supper I was a fixed observer—unmoving and unmoved. Nobody turned my head with compliments. Nobody asked me to dance. It is true that I was introduced to Mr. Bingley's sisters as the most accomplished girl in Meryton, but it was an epithet frequently bestowed and Miss Bingley's questions made me acutely aware of my *lack* of accomplishments: *Which of the modern languages had I studied? Only Italian and French? Did I have no knowledge then of German? Did I neither draw nor paint? Had I not been taught to dance? What instrument did I play? Aside from the pianoforte of course—everybody played the pianoforte.*

My humiliation, however, was nothing to what Elizabeth had to endure. I was not by when Mr. Darcy slighted her. I had gone to procure a glass of wine for Maria Lucas, who, after having danced the two fourth with Mr. Bingley, had returned to her seat with her senses seemingly disordered. When I came back with the wine, however, she waved away the glass. "Oh, Mary!" (with eyes sparkling) "That odious Mr. Darcy! What do you think? He *refused* to dance with poor Lizzy—even though

Mr. Bingley begged and implored him. He said she was not handsome enough to tempt *him*."

Later, at supper, I heard Elizabeth tell the story herself, and although she laughed as she recounted it, I fancied that she *had* been hurt and was now at pains to hide it. I began to feel quite sorry for her. She was not personally vain but she was used to hearing herself described as beautiful, second only to Jane in looks, and it must have come as a shock therefore to learn that such a fine young man (however disagreeable) did not consider her handsome. She certainly appeared to be in an odd, hectic sort of humor. She had cast aside her bandeau so that her hair was now loose, and this together with her flushed face and all the laughter made me wonder if she had drunk too much of Mrs. Curry's negus.

I left the supper room early—Elizabeth's liveliness was becoming oppressive—and when I returned to the assembly room I found only Peter Bushell present. He was standing by the fire with his back to me, drinking from a tankard, but upon my entering the room he looked around and greeted me in a most respectful way, calling me "Miss Mary" and asking if I was enjoying the ball.

"Oh," said I, uncertain whether to go or stay and wondering how he had found out my name. "I suppose so—that is, not overmuch, I suppose." And because he was looking at me with so much apparent sympathy: "I confess I do not enjoy balls. I have never been taught to dance, you see."

"What, never?" He was drawing up a chair for me so I felt obliged to sit in it. "How did that happen?"

"Well." (I was already regretting having been so frank with him.) "When my elder sisters had lessons, I was considered too young, I suppose. And when my younger sisters were taught—"

I stopped, not wanting to tell him of my long absence from home, whereupon he prompted: "What? You were considered too old?"

I smiled then and he laughed, a loud and extremely ungenteel laugh. He had resumed his place by the fire and was looking down on me complacently. "It was you who my mother nursed, wasn't it?" And upon my admitting that it was, he gave a satisfied nod: "I knew it was you. That makes us almost brother and sister, don't it?"

I took fright at this. "I hardly think—"

"In a manner of speaking." He smiled down at me. "Do you want to learn how to dance then?"

Again, I was moved to confide in him. "It is not so much a case of *wanting*, it is more that I feel I should—as an accomplishment. No woman can be deemed truly accomplished if she has not been taught to dance, you know. It does not come naturally."

I saw then that he looked disappointed, even a little bored, and I realized that I must have sounded condescending. In my confusion I made things worse by resorting to the Commonplace Book: "One is reminded of Pope's lines: "True ease in writing comes from art, not chance /As those move easiest who have learned to dance."

"Yes, well, I wouldn't know about the Pope." He drank from his tankard again and wiped his mouth with the back of his hand. "Nothing like a good tune to get your toes tapping though. Are you fond of music?"

"Yes, very, but I can play only the pianoforte. And everybody can play the pianoforte."

He laughed. "But not everybody can play it well."

He had placed his arm along the mantelpiece, and I saw suddenly that his shirt cuff was frayed. And for some reason that frayed shirt cuff made me forget myself. I felt that I could talk to it without reserve. I told it how I had had a childhood friend who had played the pianoforte extremely well, how the two of us had played duets together, and how we had once given a concert, a performance of Mozart's *Sonata for Two Pianos in D Major.*

He then told me how he had come to play the fiddle. He had had an uncle who played—a ship's carpenter who had made him a fiddle when he was six years old. "It was pretty rough and ready, but it had four strings and a bow and it suited me down to the ground. A fiddle's a good instrument for a youngster—you can pick it up and put it down easy. Not like a pianoforte—you cannot put your arms around a pianoforte."

"I should like to learn how to play another instrument," I said, whereupon he picked up his fiddle and handed it to me.

People were now beginning to return to the assembly room but I paid them no heed. Peter Bushell bade me tuck the fiddle under my chin and handed me his bow, telling me to hold it "light and gentle" as if it were a baby bird. "If the hand is but light enough, you can feel the bow hair on the strings. Soon as you stiffen up though, you lose it— 'tis gone—you feel nothing."

I was holding the bow thus when Mr. Darcy entered the room. He gave me an amazed stare and walked over to the window, there to stand with his back to the room. And just as Peter Bushell was showing me how to roll the bow between my thumb and fingers Mrs. Long walked in. It was impossible to ignore her shocked look and I hastily handed Peter back his bow and fiddle and went to her.

"Mary! Good heavens, child, what on earth do you think you were doing?"

She continued to scold in little bursts: "Men of that sort, my dear Mary—gypsies and musicians and the like—very encroaching—if one gives them the least little bit of encouragement, they become *familiar*—almost impossible to shake off—a young girl cannot be too careful—"

I listened to her without protest, thankful that Peter was out of earshot—he had gone to join the other musicians at the far end of the room. I had heard the same thing many times from Mama and Aunt Philips and even (although more subtly expressed) from Aunt Gardiner. It had never occurred to me to question such sentiments, but now it struck me that they were hardly consistent with Christ's teachings. They could all be countered by quotations from the scriptures: "Thou shalt love thy neighbor as thyself." "The rich and poor meet together; the Lord is the maker of them all."

For a while I amused myself by assembling such texts, although I forbore to quote them. A ballroom is not the place for disputation and in any case I was fond of Mrs. Long and did not wish to set up my opinion against hers. I understood too that her own position in society was dependent on Mama's patronage, and that this might well make her anxious about associating with so-called inferiors. But her lecture was *long* (if I may be pardoned the pun) and provoked contradictory feelings—embarrassment as well as a desire to speak out—and I was also conscious that Mr. Darcy had moved nearby and must have overheard the chief of it.

And what happened next was mortifying, for Mrs. Long had finally noticed Mr. Darcy and addressed him with all the familiarity she had so deplored in Peter Bushell. She asked him whether he was enjoying himself. Mr. Darcy responded merely by a slight inclination of the head, but a few minutes later Mrs. Long again spoke to him—this time asking him how he liked Netherfield. He replied that he liked it well enough but afterwards walked off to another part of the room.

"Well! What a very ill-mannered young man. He seems to think we are all quite beneath him—seems to think he is the Lord of Creation. Your Mama was right, my dear Mary—she told me what he was—the proudest, most disagreeable man in the world."

Mama and Aunt Philips came in then and after Mrs. Long related her encounter with Mr. Darcy, the three of them settled down to abuse him in earnest. I did not pay them much mind. The dancing had begun again, the orchestra was playing "Bonny Bonny Broom," and I rejoiced that I was now at liberty to think my own thoughts.

The extraordinary thing was that what previously had been of such pressing concern—what I would say to Cassandra when we met and what she would say to me—now seemed so unimportant. My thoughts were all of Peter Bushell. I was unable to see him properly from my present seat, as the dancers were in the way. I wanted to be sure that I had not offended him by running off so rudely. I told myself I would not be happy unless I could exchange with him a friendly look before the end of the evening.

In the event, I was to go away unhappy. Every time I tried for a glimpse of him, he had his back to me, and I did not dare move closer to the orchestra for Mrs. Long saw me looking and whispered: "I will say nothing to your Mama, Mary, about what happened earlier, out of consideration for her nerves, but you must promise me to have nothing more to do with that young man."

For the rest, Maria Lucas returned to sit by me. And the encounter with Cassandra, while anticlimactic, was entirely amicable. We shook hands and she invited me to accompany her to Netherfield, where she was engaged to begin painting the portrait of Mrs. Hurst and Miss Bingley in two days' time. "You must read to them during the sitting, Mary—that way, we shall not be obliged to talk to them. They are such fine ladies that I confess I am a little afraid of them."

Maria Lucas said: "I am afraid of them too, Cassy. They are not near so nice as their brother, are they? He is quite the nicest young man I have ever met—and the handsomest. Do you not think?"

Cassandra agreed, laughing, and then aware perhaps that I was watching her, added: "But Mr. Bingley clearly thinks that the nicest young lady *he* has ever met is the eldest Miss Bennet." She looked towards Bingley and Jane, who were now dancing together for the second time. "And there would be few who would disagree with him, I imagine."

So saying, she continued to look at Bingley, quite unblushingly and in the style of her old staring, as if having conceded his preference she now felt free to indulge her own.

10.

I am convinced that on the scale of human emotions fear and fascination cannot be far apart, for after the assembly I lay awake half the night wondering about Peter Bushell. I imagined him living in one of the mean little cottages on the heath occupied by farm laborers—living all alone with nobody to take care of him (the frayed shirt cuff)—and the one bright spot in his otherwise cheerless existence would be music—the business of making music. But without money or connections, how could he hope to prosper?

I determined to find out his circumstances, and to that end conceived a bold plan. I would call at the Red Lion on the pretext of having lost a glove. Mrs. Curry was always disposed to chat—I could talk to her about last night's ball, and (quite naturally) bring up the subject of the musicians. I determined also to ask Mama about the Bushell family, rehearsing several artless-sounding questions. But as soon as I sat down at the breakfast table, I could not utter a single one. I could not have pronounced the name Bushell without blushing. I did, however, manage to settle it with Lydia and Kitty that I would walk with them into Meryton after breakfast.

We were obliged to defer our departure, however, when Charlotte and Maria Lucas and their little brother Tom walked into the breakfast room. I knew that the conversation would again be about Mr. Bingley and his partners—the subject which so engrossed my mother—and sure as check, as soon as Master Tom had taken Papa's vacant chair and Charlotte and Maria had seated themselves, Mama said: "*You* began the evening well, Charlotte. You were Mr. Bingley's first choice."

"Yes." (Here, Charlotte smiled across the table at Jane.) "But he seemed to like his second better."

"Oh! you mean Jane, I suppose, because he danced with her twice. To be sure that did seem as if he admired her—indeed, I rather believe he did—I heard something about it—but I hardly know what—something about Mr. Robinson."

Charlotte obligingly repeated what she had overheard Mr. Bingley say to Mr. Robinson in praise of Jane's beauty, and having satisfied Mama, turned to Elizabeth: "My overhearings were more to the purpose than yours, Eliza. Mr. Darcy is not so well worth listening to as his friend, is he?—Poor Eliza!—to be only just *tolerable*."

Mama burst out at the mention of Mr. Darcy: "I beg you would not put it into Lizzy's head to be vexed by his ill-treatment, for he is such a disagreeable man that it would be quite a misfortune to be *liked* by him."

There was more, but I was no longer listening. I was looking at Elizabeth, and I saw, or fancied I saw, the putting on of a smiling front. And of a sudden I felt for her. I knew the humiliation of being adjudged plain—had known it all my life—and I longed to offer comfort from the Commonplace Book. She would scorn it of course, and me for offering it, but I would not let that deter me.

Before I could decide on a text, however, both Jane and Charlotte spoke, the former characteristically seeking to excuse Darcy's conduct while Charlotte attempted to excuse the inexcusable—his pride. "One cannot wonder," said she, "that so very fine a young man, with family, fortune, everything in his favor, should think highly of himself. If I may so express it, he has a *right* to be proud."

"That is very true," Elizabeth replied, "and I could easily forgive his pride, if he had not mortified *mine*."

And now I could no longer refrain from speaking. I had thought long and hard last night about the sin of pride—how one's view of one's fellow-creatures could be warped by utterly false (not to say unchristian) notions of superiority.

"Pride," said I, trying to speak calmly, "is a very common failing, I believe. By all that I have ever read, I am convinced that it is very common indeed; that human nature is particularly prone to it, and that there are very few of us who do not cherish a feeling of self-complacency on the score of some quality or the other—real or imaginary."

My voice may have betrayed the strength of my feelings—I saw Charlotte give me an odd look—for I was not of course thinking of the pride of Mr. Fitzwilliam Darcy, but of the pride of every single person seated around that table—myself included—how we would all see someone like (for instance) Peter Bushell as being quite beneath us.

I tried then to speak more temperately, making a point of distinguishing pride from vanity, but nobody seemed to be attending. Kitty and Lydia were teasing Tom, heaping food upon his plate. He was a greedy little fellow, forever boasting of how much he could eat and drink, crying out through a great mouthful of egg: "If I were as rich as Mr. Darcy, I should not care how proud I was. I would keep a pack of foxhounds, and drink a bottle of wine every day."

"Then you would drink a great deal more than you ought," said my mother, "and if I were to see you at it, I should take away your bottle directly."

An argument followed with Tom protesting that she should not and Mama maintaining that she should, and under cover of this foolery, Maria Lucas said: "Shall you be going to Netherfield with the others, Mary, to wait on Mrs. Hurst and Miss Bingley?"

And upon my saying that I planned instead to walk into Meryton, she sighed and said: "I confess I would much rather not go. When people are very grand and fashionable, I never know what to say to them."

Charlotte had overheard this last: "You will feel less shy when you are better acquainted with them, Maria."

Maria looking unconvinced, I whispered to her: "I was used to be shy in company, Maria. Until I went to Bath." And as Tom and my mother's silly argument showed no sign of flagging, I began softly to quote from Wordsworth's "The Affliction of Margaret"—a poem that Mrs. Knowles had had me commit to memory in the first anxious days of my stay:

> *My apprehensions come in crowds;*
> *I dread the rustling of the grass;*
> *The very shadows of the clouds*
> *Have power to shake me as they pass;*
> *I question things and do not find*
> *One that will answer to my mind;*
> *And all the world appears unkind.*

11.

By the time Lydia and Kitty and I finally set off, the morning
was well advanced and Lydia in a fever of impatience. "Lord, I
am *so* sick of Mr. Bingley. I wish to heaven he would go back to
wherever he came from—hell or Halifax, I care not—him and
his stupid sisters and his stupid friend."

Kitty said: "If he had asked you to dance, you would not be
so sick of him."

This sparked a quarrel that lasted most of the way into
Meryton, and very glad I was to leave them both at the Philipses'
front door (with Kitty now in tears) and to make my way to the
Red Lion at the other end of the street.

I found Mrs. Curry turning out the inn's best bedchamber.
The militia regiment was expected at the week's end and several
of the officers were to lodge at the Red Lion. Mrs. Curry could
talk of little else. She shook her head over my imaginary lost
glove, saying archly: "It has been known for a gentleman to pos-
sess himself of a young lady's glove. Can it be that you have a
secret admirer, my dear Miss Mary?" And when I denied it,
blushing, she laughed in my face. "Well, I make no doubt there
will be plenty of *that* when the regiment is come—our little assemblies are going to be a whole lot livelier, that's certain."

"I should be sorry if the character of our assemblies were to
change merely because there were officers present." I took a
steadying breath just as Mrs. Knowles had taught me before

adding: "I must say I found last night's ball most enjoyable—the music, especially."

"I am glad it met with your approval, my dear."

"I thought that the musicians played extremely well."

"Aye, they're fine players. And did you enjoy the supper? Curry insisted on adding more negus to the white soup—a mistake, I thought."

To my relief she returned to the subject of the musicians: "Curry talks of inviting the regimental band to play at our next assembly—but I think our little quartet should be given the preference. They're all Hertfordshire lads, and very highly thought of, especially young Bushell."

She then informed me that Peter had run away from home at a young age to play in a London street band. "Ran away on account of his brute of a father. And well for him that he did—considering that his father had taken to poaching and I don't know what else besides—"

"Poaching!"

"Aye." She laughed. "Curry once bought a dozen hares from him at half a crown apiece. But they caught him in the end. He was transported."

"Transported!" I was even more shocked.

"Packed off to that dreadful place—New South Wales, is it? And now poor Peter has his mother and sister on his hands. Not that he ever complains."

She stood back to view the results of her housewifery, adding (with a last tweak of the bed hangings): "He's a good lad, Peter—ambitious too. The joke is that he owes his place at the Great House to his father's disgrace."

"He works at the Great House of Stoke, does he?"

"Aye." (giving me a look) "He's keeper there."

I felt myself blushing again. "Well, he certainly is a fine player—all four of them are fine players."

I was now eager to escape Mrs. Curry's knowing looks. The picture of Peter as a caring brother and son delighted me, and it was reassuring to know he was in the employ of one of the country's foremost families, but I wondered at his being thought ambitious. I wondered whether he might be on the lookout for a rich wife. (To a young man in his situation, I must appear rich.) If so, an assembly would be an ideal hunting ground, and girls who had been slighted by other men—girls such as myself—easy prey.

The suspicion once having entered my mind, I could not rid myself of it. And soon afterwards I had cause to be equally suspicious of Lydia and Kitty and of Helen Long. They were all three waiting for me in the Philipses' parlor, and when I entered Lydia said: "So. Did you find your glove?" And upon my replying red-faced that I had not, she nudged Kitty and the two of them started sniggering. Helen Long then jumped up, exclaiming: "Lord! I had no idea it was so late. Aunt will be wondering what has become of me." (bestowing a Judas-kiss upon me) "You look *très jolie*, Mary— such roses in your cheeks."

I guessed what had happened. Mrs. Long must have told her nieces how she had caught Mary Bennet hobnobbing with one of the musicians, and Helen had in turn told Lydia and Kitty All the way back to Longbourn they went on sniggering, and later I came upon the two of them in the breakfast room with Elizabeth, and from their downcast eyes and quivering lips, I guessed they had now told her the story.

The sight of Elizabeth sitting with her mouth primmed to prevent herself from smiling—sitting and sewing a smock for the poor—suddenly enraged me. I asked her what it was that she found so amusing, whereupon Kitty said that Helen had told them all about "my beau."

"Your beau with the bow." (Lydia here mimed the bowing of a fiddle.)

Elizabeth *did* laugh then, and though she at once checked it, such was my anger that I burst out: "Oh! go on. Laugh if you like. I know how Elizabeth Bennet loves to laugh. Nothing gives her greater pleasure."

Even in my anger I saw that the smile had quite gone from her face, but I was now in full flight: "But if she or anybody else imagines that I—a gentleman's daughter—would so far forget myself as to consort with a common fiddler—"

I could not continue. Elizabeth was on her feet, pale-faced; the other two were observing me much as they had done during my illness—Kitty blinking apprehensively and Lydia looking wary. I took a breath and then with as much dignity as I could muster, walked from the room.

One of them called after me—I believe it was Elizabeth—but I did not stop. I could scarce credit what I had said. I had betrayed Peter—denied him just as the disciple Peter had denied our Lord before the crowing of the cock. And for what? Did I care so much what people might think? People of the likes of Lydia and Kitty?

I went up to my bedchamber and locked the door and wept. And when Elizabeth—and later Lydia and Kitty—came and knocked and said that they were sorry, I refused to speak with them.

12.

I spent the afternoon on my bed, quite unable to get the better of my anger at Elizabeth. I wondered that my feelings towards her should fluctuate so wildly—how I could have felt, at breakfast, so sorry for her and now some five hours later, want nothing more to do with her.

I was confused too about my feelings for Peter, not unaware that I was behaving foolishly—feeding an infatuation for a young man whom I hardly knew—but seemingly unable to help myself, not wanting to help myself. It was not as though he was the first young man to pay me attention—not quite. There had been a boy in the Bath Harmonic Society who had wanted always to sit by me and turn the pages when I played. I had not cared the point of a pin for him, however—Mrs. Knowles had thought him a coxcomb—and when he had left Bath I had not been sorry.

But Peter was different. He interested me. And his being a gamekeeper and manifestly uneducated—none of that now seemed to matter. Had I first seen him out with his gun, killing pheasants, it might have mattered. But I had seen him first with his fiddle, had heard him play like an angel, and afterwards, talking to him, he had been kind to me. He had *charmed* me. I could account for it in no other way.

When people fall in love they are apt to go a little mad. I recalled Mrs. Knowles's words, and the recollection steadied me. If I had gone a little mad, it was surely nothing abnormal—

nothing to do with my melancholia. Undoubtedly people did behave strangely when they fell in love. I thought of how recklessly Elizabeth had conducted herself with Mr. Coates, and of Cassandra's tongue-tied embarrassment in the presence of Mr. Bingley. And I thought of how Shakespeare's lovers had carried on—falling in love at first sight and languishing:

> *My ears have not yet drunk a hundred words*
> *Of that tongue's utterance, yet I know the sound:*
> *Art thou not Romeo and a Montague?*

The housemaid knocking on my door with the hot water woke me. I told her to go away, but soon afterwards there was more knocking and then Jane's voice, asking (so mildly) that I unlock my door and let poor Sarah in, reminding me that we were to dine at Haye Park—that the Gouldings had invited us to meet the Netherfield party: "Once you have bathed and dressed, my dear Mary, you will feel much more the thing. And I have brought you some tea, dear. You will feel much better when you have drunk some tea."

And so I let myself be persuaded—not least because I could hear my mother crying out on the stairs that if I did not unlock my door directly I would be sorry.

Jane and Elizabeth were both in the drawing room when I went down, and Elizabeth at once came to me and took my hand: "Oh, Mary! I did not mean to offend you. And what you said was very true—Jane sees it just as you do—she deplores my levity—thinks me far too apt in general to laugh." She kissed me then, saying: "Come, are we friends then?"

It was impossible to resist such a show of affection, but I would have felt happier if Jane had not been there to witness it. There was between them a kind of collusion—a smiling exchange of glances—Elizabeth's seeming to say, "There. Are you satisfied?" and Jane's look of beaming approval. It was a painful reminder of the bond between them—a bond never more evident than when they sought to include me.

I was conscious too of an air of suppressed excitement about them both. They were wearing their new gowns—Jane a white sarcenet trimmed with glass beads and Elizabeth a white muslin shot through with primrose—and in the combined light of candles and a newly lit fire, their every movement went winking and glinting. We talked on safe subjects meanwhile—about the morning call paid on Mrs. Hurst and Miss Bingley, and how Jane had found both sisters "extremely pleasant and conversable" (Elizabeth got up to poke the fire as this was said) and then about their visit to the wife of one of the tenant-farmers who was badly in need of baby linen (hence the smock Elizabeth had been sewing earlier).

My father came in then. He seemed in a most benign humor, and after pouring himself a glass of Malaga actually complimented my sisters on their new gowns. ("Mr. Bingley will admire them prodigiously.") He also—belatedly—complimented me on mine. ("But of course you are quite above that sort of thing, Mary, are you not?") And upon my mother's entering the room dressed in lilac satin: "My dear Mrs. Bennet, you outshine them all."

The party at Haye Park proved a disappointment, however. While the dinner was excellent and the company select (my younger sisters had not been invited), the conversation was dull. The Gouldings were a middle-aged couple who doted on their only son, William, a wild youth who spent most of his time in the taproom of the Spotted Dog or racing about the countryside in his curricle. In his absence, the parents had little to say for themselves and despite the efforts of Elizabeth and Charlotte Lucas,

Mama monopolized the table-talk. My father, consequently, said very little and Mr. Darcy even less, whilst Jane and Bingley, seated side by side, had eyes and ears only for each other. And after dinner, when we were in the drawing room awaiting the gentlemen, Mrs. Hurst and Miss Bingley talked at length about their grand London acquaintance.

There was a little coldness too on Elizabeth's part towards Mr. Darcy—and a most awkward incident after she finished singing her set-piece, Cherubino's aria from *The Marriage of Figaro*. Mr. Darcy had approached while Elizabeth was still seated at the instrument and had started to look over the selection of music. Taking up a song by Robert Burns, he turned to her, saying (with a most pleasant smile) that it was his sister's favorite air. Whereupon Elizabeth stood, saying: "Indeed? You must ask my sister to play it for you then." She softened the snub with only the smallest of smiles before walking away.

I did not know what to do. I had been waiting to take her place at the instrument but I had my own music, "The Harmonious Blacksmith," to perform. After a moment's hesitation, however, I offered to play the Burns song but Mr. Darcy politely declined and walked away. I had the impression, though, that Elizabeth's rudeness had not offended him. Indeed, he seemed to like her the better for it. He kept looking at her while Miss Bingley was singing "The Lincolnshire Poacher."

But shortly after that lady finished her song, a conversation took place between Mr. Goulding and the three Netherfield gentlemen that seriously alarmed me. Upon Mr. Bingley asking whether we were much troubled by poachers in Hertfordshire, Mr. Goulding replied: "I am not a sportsman, sir, but as a magistrate I could a tale to you unfold."

He then related several instances of gamekeepers being shot at by poachers and the alarming increase in such offences.

Mrs. Goulding called him to order, telling him that he was frightening the ladies, but a little while later I heard him say: "Only last week the keeper up at the Great House was shot at— he and the watch were giving chase to a couple of fellows— called on them to stop and they fired on him. Shot whistled right past his head—lucky he didn't lose an eye."

And upon Mrs. Goulding again checking him: "Well, well. There's no hiding these things, my dear. And these gentlemen have a right to know."

"We do indeed!" Mr. Hurst, having slept through the singing, was now wide awake, observing that if he had his way, every last idler of a poacher would be lined up and shot.

At which point Mr. Darcy remarked that the Game Laws themselves were undoubtedly at fault, being far too punitive.

"Too punitive—!" (This from Mr. Hurst.)

"Their administration too leaves much to be desired." (a nod towards Mr. Goulding) "I mean no reflection on your office, sir. I am a magistrate myself. But the rural justices are often grossly partial in their decisions. They make insufficient allowance for the plight of the poor."

After a short pause, he went on: "A poor man with a large family, living on lands where the game is preserved and under a bad landlord—such a man might well resort to poaching simply to feed his family."

An uncomfortable silence followed: Mr. Goulding blew out his cheeks and Mr. Hurst sniffed, but neither dared dispute with Mr. Darcy. It was left to Mr. Bingley to smooth things over. "I must confess," said he with his engaging smile, "that if I were a poor half-starved fellow and a plump young hare were to cross my path, I could well be tempted. I am extremely partial to jugged hare."

Mr. Darcy and Mr. Bingley then rejoined the rest of the party around the pianoforte while Mr. Hurst talked on in an aggrieved voice to Mr. Goulding about a certain river in Derbyshire that he had been used to fish for trout in as a lad, but which now had been all but destroyed by "the basest sort of people." "In broad daylight, Goulding, have I seen them dam and grope the fish—aye, and bandy words with the keeper when he tried to warn them off."

Our carriage was announced then, and very glad was I to go. I had not the least idea of a gamekeeper's occupation being so dangerous—there had never been such a person employed on the Longbourn estate—and just as I had spent half the previous night wondering about Peter, I spent half the next one worrying about him.

13.

All the neighborhood families were now eager to entertain Netherfield's grand inhabitants and scarcely a day passed without a dinner or an evening party. I attended most of these—my mother would not suffer me to stay home—but I shall not devote space to them here. They were of more concern to my elder sisters.

My mornings were taken up with the Bingley sisters' portrait sittings. I regularly accompanied Cassandra to Netherfield, where it was my duty to either play the pianoforte or read aloud—just as the sisters might wish. Afterwards, Cassandra and I would return to Meryton in Mr. Bingley's chaise.

At first, I resented this claim on my time—I had become used to having my mornings to myself—but I soon learned to be grateful for the distraction. When left too much to myself my thoughts inevitably turned to Peter. I had not seen him since the assembly and had begun building foolish castles in the air—daydreaming about when we would meet again. But I knew it to be a dangerous pastime, and after experiencing one or two unpleasant sensations reminiscent of my illness, I resolved to be sensible, to limit the time spent alone in my room and to take a more active interest in my neighbors.

As a consequence, I made some interesting discoveries.

I had many opportunities to observe Mr. Darcy, for instance. The portrait sittings always took place in the library (Cassandra had posed the sisters side by side on a sofa in the window embrasure) and Mr. Darcy was often present. He rarely said much, but once he had assured himself that Cassandra was no dauber but a serious artist, he unbent towards her sufficiently to describe his own experience in having his portrait painted.

"My late father commissioned George Dawe shortly after I came of age," said he. "But the sittings became a punishment to me—Dawe having persuaded me to smile."

Miss Bingley and Mrs. Hurst laughed heartily at this, but Cassandra said: "I trust it was not too great an ordeal. I believe Mr. Dawe paints extremely fast."

"Yes." (He was smiling properly now.) "Broad brush strokes and the paint very thinly applied. To my mind, the picture looks more like a drawing than a painting."

"'Tis an excellent likeness nonetheless," said Mrs. Hurst.

"Oh! 'tis the most charming picture in the world," said Miss Bingley.

Despite his reserve and occasional rudeness, I saw that Mr. Darcy had the sort of presence that compelled others to perform, and whenever he was not occupied with a book or newspaper, Miss Bingley and Mrs. Hurst laid themselves out to entertain him. Mr. Bingley too devoted himself to his friend's amusement, and could even make Mr. Darcy laugh—no easy task. He frequently sought Darcy's advice on matters of business, speaking in low tones so as not to offend the sensibilities of his sisters, who preferred to think that their family fortune was entirely unconnected with trade.

It became increasingly clear to me that however proud and repulsive his manners, Mr. Darcy was a man of principle. One morning, I overheard a most interesting conversation between the two men. Mr. Bingley had asked Mr. Darcy what he should do about a certain lace factory he owned in Nottingham: "My man of business writes that a quarter of our machines are lying idle on account of this damnable fashion for pantaloons. He says there is simply not the market now for fancy knee-stockings—"

And upon Darcy pointing out that Bingley himself favored pantaloons: "Oh! I am the most unconscionable hypocrite, but seriously now, what is to be done? Harris tells me that a new wide-frame machine has been patented that decreases the need for labor—"

"You are surely not thinking of putting people off work?"

"I do not see how we are to stay in business else—"

"But you cannot turn people off at such a time, Bingley. Half the families in Nottingham have been reduced to Poor Law aid. 'Tis not to be thought of."

"With the best will in the world, my friend, I am not running a charity. Unless some of the frame-workers are turned off, we will have to close the factory. I wish you would read Harris's letter. He sets out the case most persuasively."

So saying, he handed Darcy the letter, and there followed a rapid exchange of questions and answers that I could not easily follow until Bingley burst out: "Upon my word, I would sell the place tomorrow if I could get a fair price—but Harris says nobody but a madman would buy a lace factory now—"

"And what," said Darcy, "would be your idea—what would be *Harris's* idea of a fair price?"

"What a fellow you are!" (laughing) "I see what you are about—you would buy it yourself and retain all the workers and run it at a loss merely to shame me."

"Certainly I would—at least until the overseas trade revives. Cannot you afford to do so?"

"I daresay I could—of course I could. But 'tis no way to run a business. My poor father would turn in his grave."

Miss Bingley now cried out: "What are you saying about Papa, Charles? What are you talking about?"

"We are talking of business, my dear Caroline."

"Oh! business. How tedious." And then before Bingley could address Darcy once more: "By the bye, Charles, Louisa and I mean to invite Jane Bennet to dinner today. What say you to that now?"

"Today?" Bingley looked absurdly disappointed. "But Darcy and I and Hurst are to dine with the officers."

"Let that be a lesson to you not to accept invitations that do not include your sisters." Miss Bingley now rose from the sofa (thereby destroying Cassandra's careful arrangement of the folds of her gown) and moved to the nearby writing table: "Dear Jane. It will be delightful to see her. I shall have Sims ride over with an invitation right away."

She then proceeded to dash off a note on a little sheet of hot-pressed paper, remarking to me as she sealed it: "Jane has no prior engagement, I trust?"

I shook my head, knowing that even if Jane had had such an engagement, Mama would have made her break it.

Meanwhile, Mrs. Hurst's yawnings and stretchings having signaled the sitting was at an end, Cassandra began to put away her paints. Bingley turned back to Darcy, speaking in a more serious manner than before: "You are quite right of course, and I suppose I ought to be grateful to you for pointing out my duty, but I'm going to have a devil of a job explaining my decision to Harris."

When I recounted the conversation to Cassandra, she smiled but shook her head over it, saying: "I fear he is too easily influenced."

"But Mr. Darcy is an influence for good, surely." (I had no doubt which "he" she meant.)

"Oh, undoubtedly." But still she looked a little wistful, as if she would have liked to influence Bingley herself, as a wife perhaps.

"Tomorrow will be our last sitting," said she presently. "I should have liked to have had one more, but Miss Bingley says she cannot spare the time. It is as well perhaps."

I waited. She seemed to be about to confide in me, but then as so often happened, she turned the subject: "So Jane is to dine at Netherfield. Your mother will be pleased."

14.

On reaching home, I was met by the news that Jane had already left for Netherfield on horseback. Kitty and Lydia were eager to explain the circumstances.

"Mama would not let her have the carriage."

"Mama thought it would most likely rain, so then, you know—" Kitty was coughing with excitement, "Jane would have to stay the night."

"A good scheme, was it not?" said Lydia. "For it was coming on to mizzle when she left."

I went to the window. The rain was becoming heavier by the minute. I said that I did not think it a good scheme at all—I wondered that Papa should have permitted it.

But Lydia and Kitty were now whispering and giggling. "You will never guess who we saw in Meryton this morning," said Lydia. "Your fiddler friend."

Kitty was looking at me with sly trepidation. "We saw him come out of the taproom of the Spotted Dog."

I felt my face burn. Nobody had spoken to me of Peter since my outburst of weeks ago, and I was beginning to hope that their own obsession with officers had driven him from their minds.

"Do not you want to know what he said to us then?" said Lydia.

"You want to tell me, and I have no objection to hearing it."

Kitty would have spoken but Lydia cut her short: "Oh no!

No parroting Papa if you please. If you wish to hear what he said, you must ask us properly."

They were both watching me. I took a breath, summoning up the dear image of Mrs. Knowles, but before I could speak, Elizabeth entered and joined me at the window. "This is a bad business, Mary. Jane will be thoroughly soaked."

Even in my confusion, I was conscious of feeling flattered. This was treating me as an equal—as a responsible adult who unlike our silly younger sisters could see the seriousness of the situation. I agreed that it was indeed a bad business, but upon Lydia and Kitty beginning once again to whisper I could not stop myself from asking what it was that Peter had said: "If indeed he did speak to you."

Kitty was now giggling. "He said: 'How is your sister?' And Lydia said—"

"I said: 'Which sister do you mean?' And he said: 'Why, your sister Mary of course.' And then he asked if you were coming to the next assembly."

Here, they both exploded with laughter, whereupon Elizabeth said: "Upon my word, I think Papa was right. You *are* two of the silliest girls in the country." And she comprehended me in her contempt, saying: "Imagine Jane's concern if any of you had been made to ride out in the rain."

She left the room then and for a short while none of us spoke. I was still too overjoyed at Peter's inquiring after me to care about much else, but Lydia soon recovered, pulling a face and saying: "Lord, how she does love to lecture. And what a fuss she makes over Jane—always worrying lest Jane catch cold or some such thing. But she does not give three straws about the rest of us. When Kitty and me had the measles, she never once came near us."

Here Kitty, who had rather more respect for the truth,

remarked that Elizabeth had herself been ill at the time. But Lydia as usual was not listening. "She does not care about you either, Mary. When you were first in Bath, Jane begged Papa to let us visit—I was quite wild to go and so was Kitty—but Elizabeth said that you would go on better without us, and Papa agreed with her—as he always does."

I suspected that neither Elizabeth nor my father would have wished to visit me anyway, and was about to say so when a flash of lightning lit the room. Kitty and Lydia now joined me at the window.

"Lord! she will look like a drowned rat when she arrives."

"Her new riding habit will be quite ruined."

"I pray she does not catch cold."

Lydia laughed. "Pray rather that she catches Mr. Bingley, Mary. Otherwise 'twill all have been for nothing."

The news that Jane had indeed caught cold came the following morning. We had just finished breakfast when a servant came from Netherfield with letters for Elizabeth and for me. Elizabeth at once began to read her own letter aloud. It was from Jane:

> *My dearest Lizzy,*
> *I find myself very unwell this morning, which, I suppose, is to be imputed to my getting wet through yesterday. My kind friends will not hear of my returning home till I am better. They insist also on my seeing Mr. Jones—*

I stopped listening at that point, being eager to read my own letter. It was a very short one and I had no wish to make public its contents:

> *Miss Bingley and Mrs. Hurst unable to sit this morning due to illness in the house. Please to inform Miss Long.*

It was signed "J. Lamrock," whom I knew to be Miss Bingley's dresser—a tall, conceited woman who had wasted a lot of Cassandra's time during the sittings fussing over Miss Bingley's hair and clothes. I read the note through twice in growing indignation before the rising tones of Mama's voice broke in: "How can you be so silly as to think of such a thing in all this dirt! You will not be fit to be seen when you get there."

Elizabeth answered her calmly. "I shall be very fit to see Jane—which is all I want."

My father said: "Is this a hint to me, Lizzy, to send for the horses?"

I had thought myself inured to Papa's favoritism, but I found myself really resenting this indulgence: He would never have sent for the horses for anybody else. And although Elizabeth immediately declined the offer, declaring her intention of walking to Netherfield ("The distance is nothing when one has a motive; only three miles. I shall be back by dinner."), still I felt resentful. I doubted Elizabeth's motive too. I wondered if it were not Mr. Darcy whom she wished to see. And Lamrock's letter continued to work upon me—I could not help comparing Miss Bingley's negligent treatment of Cassandra and myself with the consideration shown towards Jane.

In short, I was beginning to feel decidedly ill-used, and in a fit of pique said sarcastically to Elizabeth: "I admire the activity of your benevolence, but every impulse of feeling should be guided by reason, and, in *my* opinion, exertion should always be in proportion to what is required."

I was ashamed of myself as soon as I spoke, but Elizabeth seemed hardly to hear. Lydia and Kitty were offering to walk with her as far as Meryton, and she appeared to welcome the prospect of their company.

15.

A little later I set out for Meryton myself. The morning was a fine one and mild for November but still I felt cross out of reason. I was conscious of not having behaved well. And the disappointment in store for Cassandra was also weighing on me. I imagined her sitting waiting in Mrs. Long's front parlor, dressed in her best gown and looking out for Mr. Bingley's chaise and wondering what could have happened.

The reality was not as I pictured, however. Cassandra was indeed dressed in her best gown but she was not sitting waiting. She was sketching a remarkably pretty young woman who in turn was talking away as indefatigably as Lydia.

At the sight of me, Cassandra immediately left off drawing, but when I told her there was to be no sitting she was unable to hide her disappointment: "Did not Miss Bingley send any message?"

"I will tell you about it later, Cassy."

Cassandra belatedly remembered her manners and introduced the young woman to me as Miss Harriet Lamb, adding: "I am commissioned to paint a miniature of Miss Lamb for Colonel Forster." (Miss Lamb was now blushing and laughing.) "The Colonel and Miss Lamb are shortly to be married."

Here, Miss Lamb made a face, saying the engagement was supposed to be a secret but that the Colonel was telling everybody so she supposed it made no odds if she told everybody too.

She then began to describe in detail her wedding clothes, informing us that on her honeymoon she would be wearing a corset made entirely of silken bands to mold her form into one of perfect symmetry.

After Miss Lamb finally left (having spoiled several pages of Cassandra's sketchbook attempting to draw her corset), I gave Cassandra the history of Jane's ride in the rain: "'Twas one of Mama's stratagems, and I am afraid it has succeeded all too well."

"But your mother's stratagems usually do, don't they?" Cassandra was tearing out the pages of Miss Lamb's artwork and she spoke with uncharacteristic sourness. She then begged my pardon: "I cannot think what is the matter with me this morning. Perhaps I am envious of Miss Lamb—perhaps I envy her her Colonel or her corset "

"I am sure you do not envy Miss Lamb, Cassy."

I looked at her, willing her to confide in me, to trust me, but instead she began to crumple the spoilt pages and throw them in the fire.

Afterwards, we went upstairs and while she changed out of her best gown, I entered her painting room.

I noticed the painting straight away. It was propped against the wall and there was no mistaking the subject. It was a Kit-Cat portrait of Mr. Bingley. Cassandra must have recalled its being there, for she hurried out with her gown gaping and her face like scarlet and turned the canvas to the wall—realizing too late perhaps that if the painting did not betray her love, then her ill-thought attempt to conceal it certainly did.

When she reemerged from her bedchamber some few minutes later she still looked red, albeit more composed. She at once went and turned the canvas around before going to sit in her usual chair. For several moments we both contemplated Mr. Bingley's image in silence.

I knew now that she would confide in me—her hand had been forced—but I was unprepared for the fullness of her confession when it came. She told me that she had loved Bingley from the first.

"He appeared to me—oh! he seemed the embodiment of every virtue. But I have since asked myself, if he had not been such a fine handsome gentleman and driving a chaise and four and all that sort of nonsense—then would I have been quite so smitten?"

She paused and we both continued to look at the painting. I reflected that although I had always considered Bingley tolerably handsome, he had not appeared to me to be any better-looking than, for instance, young Nicholas Baker, who served behind the counter at Rea's. And if Nicholas Baker had had the benefit of Bingley's fortune and education (and London tailor) then to my mind there would have been little to choose between them— Nicholas being renowned for his obligingness.

"I have never been in love before," Cassandra continued. "I had no idea it could be so all-consuming. I simply had no idea. And there are other, less worthy emotions that I have been quite unable to get the better of." She now looked at me directly. "I confess that I have been very envious of your eldest sister."

"You think then that he cares for Jane?"

"Can you doubt it? Anyone seeing them together—oh! there can be no two opinions about it. But I have been wanting to tell you about this for weeks—"

"Have you?"

She smiled. "I would have told you eventually."

"Even if I had not seen the painting?"

"Oh, what a little doubter you are. But I have sometimes wondered whether you too perhaps—" She gave me one of her looks. "If perhaps there was something you wished to tell me?"

And so I told her about Peter, and when I finished, she owned she had already heard some of the particulars from Mrs. Long. "But you must not blame my aunt for spreading the story. She is a talker, I know, but she has only spoken of it to Helen and myself—she would never make mischief. No, I am ashamed to say that it is Helen who has been indiscreet."

It was the first time Cassandra had criticized Helen to me, and such an instance of trust made it easy to be magnanimous. I said I was sure Helen had meant no harm.

Cassandra shook her head. "I do not know what has come over her lately; she thinks of nothing but officers."

"'Tis the same with Lydia and Kitty—they are all suffering from the so-called scarlet fever."

"Oh! 'tis the same with most of the girls in Meryton, only Helen has contracted a particularly virulent strain."

We stayed talking until the little maid needed help preparing dinner. Cassandra impressed upon me the value of work, both as a discipline and a distraction: "In my own case of course, it is a necessity—Aunt would find it hard to manage without my contribution—but even if we were more comfortably circum-stanced, I would still choose to work. At the moment, thanks to Mr. Bingley's commission, I have been positively *inundated* with requests for portraits."

And upon my shamefaced admission that I had done no more work on my song: "My dear Mary, the song was merely a suggestion. But perhaps you could begin by setting a poem to music, or a psalm. You must have many fine texts to choose from in your collection."

I wondered if she were making game of me and my Commonplace Book, but she appeared perfectly serious, saying: "The thing is to make a start, to use your feelings—turn them to good account. I am sure I have done more worthwhile work these past weeks than I have done in my entire life. I put it all down to love—" (smiling) "unrequited love—it has to be good for something."

I resolved then and there to write a song—to transpose my feelings into music. And on the way home I began to try out a tune, humming it as I walked along.

16.

On reaching Longbourn, I meant to go directly to my room, there to play out the music in my head, but my mother was on the stairs crying out to Nan Pender: "Do not put yourself to any trouble over Miss Lizzy's clothes. There is no occasion for anything fine—she will be spending most of her time nursing her sister."

I retreated to the drawing room, only to find Lydia and Kitty there. As usual, they were full of news, first about Elizabeth, who they informed me was now also to stay at Netherfield: "A servant is just come for her clothes," said Kitty. "Mama is cross as crabs about it. She says Lizzy has no business there and will only be in the way."

"What a good joke if she were to catch Mr. Darcy," said Lydia. "I daresay she is trying for it—for all she finds him so disagreeable."

The two of them began to snigger and Lydia said: "Oh, Mary! We had such a time this morning—you have no idea. We went first to Clarke's Library and Captain Carter came with us and he told us—you will never guess—but Colonel Forster is to be married. To a Miss Harriet Lamb."

"Only think," said Kitty. "Miss Lamb is just seventeen—the exact same age as myself."

"What is that to say to anything?" said Lydia. "But it is the greatest secret and not on any account to be spoken of. Miss Lamb's guardian is yet to give his consent."

She repeated this story at the dinner table, after which my father forbad any further mention of officers. In the absence of Jane and Elizabeth, he went directly to his library after dinner and I was at last able to escape to my room.

Having played over and written down my tune, I now took out all my Commonplace Books in search of a suitable text. But none of the extracts would fit my melody. I saw then that I had gone about the business the wrong way. I ought to have begun with the words, not the music.

Thus it was that I bethought myself of the so aptly named Mr. William Wordsworth. Jane had given me a volume of his verse for my last birthday, and I at once took it down and examined several poems before the pages by a fateful parting revealed to me the following:

> *His station is there; and he works on the crowd,*
> *He sways them with harmony merry and loud;*
> *He fills with his power all their hearts to the brim—*
> *Was aught ever heard like his fiddle and him?*

The verse was from a poem called "Power of Music," an unpretentious little ballad I had barely glanced at before. Now, however, I read it with close attention and fast-beating heart. Never could I have hoped for such a felicitous meeting of music and text! With only a very little tinkering I was sure that I could join them together. I thanked God for the timely discovery.

In the event, the task proved more difficult than I had foreseen. I persevered, however, translating each line of poetry into a musical phrase—a painstaking process that took me the whole of the following morning. I was not altogether satisfied with the finished composition, but my mother that evening forbad me to spend another day working upon it.

"Do you want to get sick again, my girl? Is that what you want? Doing nothing all day except sing like a tomcat?" (Here, Lydia and Kitty began to snigger.) "You would not go with us to Netherfield this morning—you could not spare the time to visit poor Jane. Very well then. Tomorrow morning—I give you fair warning!—you are to go to Lucas Lodge with Lydia and Kitty. There is to be a dancing-class there after breakfast—Sir William has very kindly arranged it—and you are to take part, do you hear? You are to practice your steps. Mr. Bingley is to give a ball at Netherfield just as soon as Jane is recovered and I am determined that *you* will dance at it!"

There was no reasoning with Mama in this humor, and directly after breakfast next morning Lydia, Kitty, and I set out for Lucas Lodge. The class had been formed chiefly for the benefit of Maria Lucas, but some other Meryton young ladies, including Helen Long, had also been invited.

Sir William had engaged the services of a dancing master and a fiddler, but on our arrival these two were nowhere to be seen. Lady Lucas turned hopefully to me: "Perhaps in the meantime Mary might play for us?"

I was only too happy to sit down at the instrument—I was afraid of learning to dance, truth to tell, afraid of appearing awkward and clumsy—and while the set was being formed, I played and replayed my own little tune.

I was playing the opening bars of "The Fine Companion" when Peter Bushell walked into the room.

17.

When one has been constantly thinking about a person, their sudden appearance in the flesh (the god incarnate, as it were) can come as a disappointment. Peter struck me as darker and untidier and altogether more gypsy-looking than I remembered, but then the knowledge that he was actually in the same room as myself was accompanied by such heart-beating, such trembling, as made it impossible for me to go on playing.

I hardly dared look at him but I was aware of his taking up his station beside the window. The strains of a fiddle then came to me and I realized he had taken up the tune precisely where I left off. It took me several moments to compose myself sufficiently to accompany him.

No sooner had the dance ended than Sir William was standing over me: "Now that the fiddler is come, my dear Mary, there can be no occasion for you to keep playing. I promised your good mother that I would not suffer you to sit by. I promised her that I would make sure you joined in the dancing."

And when I did not immediately comply—for I was still so flurried I doubted my ability to stand, let alone dance—he said: "Maria, you see, is now to partner Mr. Howard." (Mr. Howard being the dancing master) "So you are needed to make up the numbers, my dear."

Upon Sir William's moving away I saw that Peter was talking—or rather, listening—to Helen Long while Lydia and

Kitty were in the little group surrounding the dancing master. (I had just sense enough to feel relieved they were not sniggering about Peter.)

I managed then to pull myself together and make my way over to Maria Lucas, who was standing a little apart.

"Oh! Mary." She clutched my arm. "I am *mortified*—they are all so much better than me, and I begged Papa to let me have private lessons." She broke off to look at me. "Why, what is the matter? You are all of a tremble."

I assured her I was perfectly all right, merely a little nervous on account of never having danced before.

"Never ever?" She took my hand. "Well, you and I must dance this next one together then, for Mr. Howard does not partner me until the second set."

Mr. Howard came forward then—a prancing little man with tufted eyebrows and an air of self-consequence. "The beginners must now give place to the more experienced dancers," said he with a condescending smile at Maria and myself. "The best couples must move to the top—so, so—" (taking Helen Long for his partner and placing Lydia and Kitty next) "And the rest of you must watch while you work your way up from the bottom—so that you learn the figure before leading off."

Mr. Howard then snapped his fingers at Peter, ordering him without so much as a "please" or "thank-you" to play "Mayden Lane," before parading with Helen down the length of the room.

For the first time I dared look directly at Peter. In the act of lifting his fiddle to his shoulder, his eyes met mine and he winked at me. And that wink—so mischievous and good-humored—served to banish some of my confusion. From that moment, I was at least able to look at him.

As the figure chosen by Mr. Howard employed only the leading couple, there was at first very little for Maria and me to do. But upon his taking Maria for his partner, Helen Long seized my hands, saying: "Come, *chérie*, you and I will now show the others what fine dancing is."

And with Helen for a partner, I got on surprisingly well. She praised my sense of rhythm and while I did not quite believe her (being far too conscious of Peter in the background), yet it was very pleasing flattery and certainly made the whole thing less of an ordeal. At the conclusion of the dance she whispered: "I have spoken to Lydia, *chérie*, and you need have no fear that she will betray you."

She then called out to Peter: "This is Mary's first dancing lesson, you know. Do not you think she acquitted herself well?"

It was impossible for Helen to speak to any man without flirting, but Peter did not seem to notice. He was looking at me and smiling. "She did indeed."

I felt my confusion returning then, but his expression—his whole manner—seemed so easy and yet free from familiarity that I was reassured. "I confess I enjoyed it much more than I thought I should."

"La!" Helen was looking up at Peter coquettishly, but again he seemed not to notice. He asked whether we would be coming to next week's assembly.

"We might consider it," said Helen. "If you are playing."

This was too obvious a gambit for him to ignore, yet his assenting smile was perfunctory and it occurred to me that he might well be used to females making overtures at the assemblies— forward young ladies who, if gentlemen were scarce, flirted with the musicians. He turned to me then and asked whether I wanted still to learn to play the fiddle, adding: "I give lessons, y'know."

But before I could reply, Sir William interrupted, directing Helen and me to the dining room where refreshments were laid out. "As for you, my good man," said he to Peter, "if you would like to make your way to the kitchen, the housekeeper will attend to your needs."

This from Sir William, who was civil to all the world! The realization that such slights were Peter's daily portion filled me with indignation, and I looked to see how he bore it, but he was packing away his fiddle imperturbably. And without giving myself time to consider—while my courage was still high—I went to him and held out my hand, saying: "Thank you for your music this morning, Mr. Bushell. And I should very much like to learn how to play the fiddle, and for you to give me lessons—if my father permits it."

He took my hand and looked down at me in a curious way— seeking (it seemed to me) to weigh me up while he talked mere commonplace—about being "happy" &c. He was smiling but there was at the same time an odd holding-back. I sensed that I had in some way surprised him.

When I went into the dining room, Lydia pounced on me. "Oh, Mary! Kitty and me are both agreed—your fiddler is a *most* attractive fellow—excellent teeth—and if he were but dressed in fashionable clothes—"

"—If he were wearing regimentals—" (This from Kitty.)

"—Oh Lord! If he were wearing regimentals I would flirt with him myself."

Helen Long now joined us, whispering: "For shame, you two! Cannot you see you are embarrassing poor Mary?" (putting her arm about me) "But I have to agree, *chérie*, he is most attractive."

Whereupon the three of them began to giggle. And I found myself denying Peter for the second time: "I admire him as a musician merely." Their sniggering increased and I threw off Helen's arm. "Why must you turn everything into a flirtation? He is nothing to me, I tell you."

Helen at once begged my pardon. ("I swear I will never speak of him again.") But as we were preparing to leave the dining room she hissed to me: "Quick! Look out the window. Can you see him?"

I was just able to discern two men—Peter and Mr. Howard—walking across the waterlogged fields, presumably taking the shortcut to Meryton. Again, I felt indignant. Why had not Sir William let them have the use of his gig? Had they been gentlemen, he would have offered it—he would have offered them his coach, and welcome. And I bethought myself then of that problematic text from Saint Matthew (25:29): "Unto everyone that hath shall be given, and he shall have abundance; but from him that hath not shall be taken away even that which he hath."

Helen accompanied us back to Longbourn, and in the continuing absence of Jane and Elizabeth, Mama invited her to stay to dinner. I was glad of it—in Helen's presence Lydia forbore to tease me about Peter—and the table talk was almost entirely about officers and their doings. Helen gave us an account of Harriet Lamb's wedding dress: "White satin and lace—and over it a white satin pelisse with swan's down trimming. *Très élégant, n'est-ce pas?*"

Papa objected to the description of finery as well as to Lydia and Kitty's parroting of Helen's French phrases: "A little less *la* if you please." And then almost plaintively to my mother: "When are Lizzy and Jane coming back?"

Mama's reply was evasive. "As to that, my dear Mr. Bennet, I am not entirely sure. I had a note from Elizabeth this morning asking that the carriage be sent for them—"

"Then why in heaven's name did you not send it?"

He lifted his hand to cut short Mama's querulous exculpation: "Very well, very well. The horses were wanted in the farm, I suppose."

Directly after this exchange, I saw Helen do a very odd thing. I saw her deliberately catch my father's eye and mouth the word *la*, dropping down her little pink tongue in a very saucy manner.

At the time, my father laughed but afterwards I heard him say to Mama that Helen was a "pert minx" who would bear watching.

"What nonsense you do talk, Mr. Bennet. Minx, indeed! She is a very pretty-behaved girl—not especially handsome, I grant you—but very good-natured and obliging. She sewed up a torn flounce on Lydia's ball-gown."

To which Papa replied that women were rarely the best judges of what men found attractive and that Helen Long was "quite handsome enough for the purpose."

18.

Jane and Elizabeth did not return to Longbourn until after morning service on Sunday. They borrowed Mr. Bingley's carriage to make the journey, and consequently we were not expecting them. I was in my room working on my song when they burst in upon me.

They seemed delighted to be home—Elizabeth especially—and greeted me most affectionately, asking what I had been doing in their absence &c. (Not wanting to tell them about my song, I was obliged to practice a little deception; I allowed them to think that I had been studying thorough-bass.) But their four-day absence seemed to have changed them, almost as if a spell had been placed upon them—or rather two separate spells, for they were exhibiting quite different symptoms. Jane looked to be living in some sweetly satisfying world of her own whereas Elizabeth was unaccountably restless, roaming about my room and looking at the books on my shelves.

"Why, Mary! You still have Mr. Coates's novel. You still have *Paola*. One of these days I must ask you to lend it to me."

She then picked up my latest Commonplace Book and asked whether there were any new extracts to admire.

Her manner was playful—the sort of manner I mistrusted. I had been pleased to see her, but now I wanted her to go away. To humor her, however, I read out an extract from the first epistle of Pope's *Moral Essays*. But on Jane's beginning to cough, Elizabeth hastily bundled her downstairs.

Mama was not pleased to see her elder daughters. She had calculated on their staying at Netherfield until the following Tuesday, which would have nicely rounded off Jane's week. Papa, however, greeted them with delight, calling for the fatted calf to be killed: "Do I have that right, Mary? Is that the correct text?"

Such was his flow of spirits that I wondered whether he had something up his sleeve—some fresh sport for Elizabeth's diversion—a new neighbor for them both to laugh at perhaps. And as it happened, he did have a surprise in store. The following morning he announced that "a gentleman and a stranger" was to dine with us, and only after Mama's anticipation reached fever pitch (so sure was she that it must be Mr. Bingley) did he reveal the guest's identity. It was none other than our cousin, Mr. William Collins—he who was to inherit Longbourn.

He then read aloud Mr. Collins's letter, and although he read without comment or expression, there were one or two looks at Elizabeth that suggested how much he relished the contents— evidence that the writer was neither clever nor well educated.

Elizabeth enjoyed the letter immensely. The two of them soon had their heads together over it, and their lip-curling was something to behold. Poor Mr. Collins's apology for inheriting the estate was discounted, and his grateful deference towards his patroness Lady Catherine de Bourgh mocked—as was his motive in wanting to heal the breach between our two families.

"He must be an oddity, I think," said Elizabeth. "I cannot make him out—there is something very pompous in his style—and what can he mean by apologizing for being next in the entail?—

We cannot suppose he would help it if he could. Can he be a sensible man, sir?"

My father's reply was entirely predictable: "No, my dear; I think not. I have great hopes of finding him quite the reverse. There is a mixture of servility and self-importance in his letter that promises well. I am impatient to see him."

I then spoke up: "In point of composition, his letter does not seem defective. The idea of the olive-branch perhaps is not wholly new, yet I think it is well expressed."

My father's dismissive glance was the only response I received. I knew of course that my own idea had not been well expressed: I ought rather to have praised the *gesture* of the olive-branch, surely a difficult one for a young man to make in the circumstances. But I could not speak again. My father's contempt was having its usual effect upon me.

Mr. Collins in the flesh did not excite my sympathy, however. He had not been at Longbourn half an hour before the house seemed full of him: his sonorous voice and heavy tread, not to mention the smell of camphor that clung to his person (his patroness Lady Catherine de Bourgh having advised him to store his clothes in camphor to keep off the moth).

And I could not respect his values. As a clergyman, he seemed to be too taken up with the material world, displaying an unbecoming reverence for costly possessions. He boasted of the extent of Lady Catherine's estate, Rosings Park, and the grandeur of her house, with its numerous windows and marble chimney-pieces; he also boasted about his own house—his "humble abode"—and all the improvements he had made to it.

From the hints he dropped—and Mama's gracious demeanor towards him—it soon became clear that he had come to Longbourn not only to heal the breach but also to choose a wife.

And although he assured Mama he had come prepared to admire *all* his fair cousins, it was soon clear he admired one fair cousin a great deal more than the others.

By breakfast-time the following morning, however, he had transferred his admiration from Jane to Elizabeth. I was shocked at this apparent fickleness and said as much to Cassandra when she came in Mr. Bingley's chaise to collect me—Miss Bingley having summoned us that morning for the final portrait sitting:

"Last night he had eyes only for Jane, and this morning he is making up to Elizabeth—complimenting her on her wit and vivacity. What do you suppose he means by it, Cassy?"

"Oh, I imagine your mama told him not to think of Jane—I imagine she told him that Jane was soon to be engaged and to consider one of her younger daughters."

"Well, Lizzy certainly will not have him—she thinks him a pompous fool."

"In that case perhaps" (giving me a mischievous look) "your mama might hope that you could be prevailed upon to accept him."

"*Me!*"

Cassandra burst out laughing. "Oh, Mary! You have the most transparent little face."

"Mr. Collins would never offer for me. I am not pretty enough."

"Nonsense. I won't allow that. You may not have the beauty of your elder sisters, but you have a very sweet, expressive countenance and a fine delicate complexion. Your eyes, I think, are your best feature—it is a great pity that you are obliged to wear spectacles."

But perceiving I was embarrassed, she began to talk of the portrait and the work remaining to be done.

19.

Only the Hursts were present when we were shown into the Netherfield library. Mrs. Hurst, seated in the window embrasure, was leafing through the latest issue of *La Belle Assemblée* while her husband sat slumped in a wing chair before the fire, fast asleep.

At sight of us, Mrs. Hurst placed her finger to her lips. "I shall not wake Mr. Hurst. I know you will excuse him—he is a little out of spirits. He hoped for some sport this morning but my brother and Mr. Darcy had other plans."

Miss Bingley walked in soon afterwards; she too seemed out of spirits, and began conversing in low tones with Mrs. Hurst. Cassandra meanwhile busied herself setting out her paints, and I was about to open my book when Miss Bingley addressed me: "I trust dear Jane is now fully recovered? My brother and Mr. Darcy have ridden to Longbourn to inquire after her health."

I assured her that Jane was much better, adding: "But they will not find her at home, I'm afraid. My sisters have all walked into Meryton."

A look passed between Miss Bingley and Mrs. Hurst as much as to say "running after officers" so that I felt obliged to add: "Our cousin Mr. Collins is visiting us—he has never been to Longbourn before and wanted to walk out and see the town."

"Your cousin is a single man?"

"Does he make a long stay with you?"

And so I had to tell them about Mr. Collins—after which Miss Bingley's manner became more friendly. "My brother charged me to keep you both here until he returns."

Thereafter, the sitting proceeded pleasantly enough—chat alternating with companionable silences (punctuated by Mr. Hurst's snores) and with only one disagreement between the sisters when Miss Bingley opined that Mr. Hurst slept too much. ("It cannot be good for him, Louisa. He should surely be more active—a man of his age." And upon Mrs. Hurst's maintaining that her husband was fatigued because he had stayed up late to oblige the company: "Let him sleep in his bedchamber then. I do not see why we should have to talk in whispers on his account.")

Mr. Bingley, walking in shortly afterwards, likewise remarked: "Hurst still in the arms of Morpheus? What a fellow he is. You must take his likeness again, Miss Long—shame him into exerting himself."

He then turned to his sisters: "Darcy will join us presently." (speaking rather lower) "He is a little out of temper—we ran against that fellow Wickham in the town."

Miss Bingley exclaimed at this. "What! George Wickham actually here in Meryton?"

"Most unfortunate. He has accepted a lieutenant's commission in the ——shire. But pray do not speak of it to Darcy. You know how he hates any mention of the man."

"How dare he show his face in Hertfordshire while Mr. Darcy is staying here! What insolence!"

"My dear Caroline, now you are being absurd. And you have moved your right arm just when Miss Long was working on the sleeve."

Miss Bingley's response was to jump up from the sofa. "Who is the colonel of the regiment? Forster, is it not? Charles, you must speak to him—tell him what sort of man George Wickham is."

This time it was Mrs. Hurst who told her sister she was being absurd. "It has nothing to do with you, Caroline. And Mr. Darcy would not thank you for meddling in his affairs."

Miss Bingley looked not to have heard her; she was now pacing up and down, and Cassandra—in tacit acknowledgment that the sitting was over—began to put away her paints. Mr. Bingley in his usual eagerness to avoid an argument changed the subject: "We saw your sisters in the town, Miss Mary. I was delighted to see Miss Bennet looking so—" He checked himself and colored faintly. "She appeared to be completely recovered."

I saw Cassandra glance up at him and guessed what she was thinking. Lovers, it seemed, found concealment nigh impossible. In his embarrassment, Mr. Bingley changed the subject yet again, asking Cassandra if she were pleased with the portrait: "It seems to me to be a splendid likeness—what say you, Louisa? Caroline? Has not Miss Long captured you both brilliantly?"

But Mrs. Hurst was now trying to wake her husband, and the only reply Miss Bingley gave was an impatient "hmm." Bingley drew up a chair between Cassandra and myself, saying: "One disadvantage of being a younger brother—my dear sisters never listen to a word I say."

He then asked Cassandra about the framing of the portrait— at which point Mr. Darcy entered the room.

After acknowledging Cassandra and myself, he picked up a newspaper, thus foiling Miss Bingley's attempts at conversation. She was obliged to fall back on her brother and Cassandra, who were now talking of portrait painting in general. Cassandra was describing some of Gainsborough's techniques—his use of six-foot handled brushes and his practice of closing the shutters so that the dim light would force him to focus on essentials.

Miss Bingley said in her condescending way: "You might be interested to know, Miss Long, that Mr. Darcy's mother, Lady

Anne, was painted by Gainsborough. As was his great-uncle, the judge."

"You are mistaken." Mr. Darcy spoke from behind his newspaper. "My mother was painted by Joseph Wright."

"Wright of Derby!" exclaimed Cassandra. "Oh! I admire his work so much—particularly his landscapes. *Matlock Tor by Moonlight* is perhaps my favorite—"

"A fine painting," Darcy agreed.

"But then there is his *Blacksmith's Shop* and *An Iron Forge*—both equally fine. And his portrait of Mrs. Swindell, which I was fortunate enough to view at Somerset House—"

"Do you prefer painting landscapes to portraits, Miss Long?" said Bingley with a smile.

"I enjoy painting both. It all depends on the subject. I do prefer to choose my own subject."

"Indeed?" (This from Miss Bingley.) "I must ask then whether you would have chosen to paint us?"

There was a dreadful pause during which Cassandra kept on cleaning a brush. I held my breath: I knew she would not dissemble.

In the end it was Mr. Bingley who spoke: "Upon my word, Caroline—you place Miss Long in a most awkward position."

"No." Cassandra set down the brush. "That is to say—no, I would not have chosen to paint you, Miss Bingley."

"Well, if that don't beat the Dutch." Mr. Hurst was now wide awake and stretching himself before the fire.

"Please understand." Color was now suffusing Cassandra's face. "It has nothing to do with whether or not I like a person. Most artists are obliged—"

Miss Bingley gave an angry little laugh. "I am vastly relieved to hear that!"

"Most artists are obliged to paint portraits in order to earn a living—'phizmongering' Hogarth was used to call it—and they cannot pick and choose their subjects. They must needs paint whoever will pay them."

Darcy said: "And if there were no financial constraints? What subject should you choose then?"

"Well." She picked up another brush. "Last year it so happened that I chose to paint Mary. At the time I hardly knew her, but her face interested me."

It was now my turn to blush, feeling all eyes upon me. Cassandra continued: "As a rule, young faces do not interest me; they are too unformed. But occasionally, perhaps due to illness or adversity, one sees a face grown old before its time. Such faces interest me. Suffering interests me."

"Does it, by Jove?" muttered Mr. Hurst.

I now sought refuge in taking off my spectacles and polishing them. I was conscious that Mr. Darcy was looking at me as if seeing me for the first time. And while the conversation among the others continued (with Mrs. Hurst telling of a London acquaintance who had recently sat to Lawrence), Mr. Darcy remarked: "I wonder I had not noticed it before, but your eyes are remarkably like those of your sister."

I knew of course which sister he meant: Elizabeth and I had both inherited our father's dark eyes while Jane, Kitty, and Lydia all had the light-blue "Gardiner eyes." But Mr. Darcy was now looking embarrassed—adding unnecessarily: "Your sister Miss Elizabeth, that is."

Miss Bingley may have overheard this—she rarely missed a word Mr. Darcy said—and it may also have made her jealous, for she at once said: "I hear that you ran against George Wickham in the town, Mr. Darcy—I could scarce credit it when Charles told me. I understand that he means to join the corps stationed here?" And when Mr. Darcy made her no answer: "I know you do not like to hear his name mentioned—"

"You are quite right. I do not."

"I will not tease you on the subject further—except to say that Colonel Forster might be glad to hear of his dealings—" And in response to a forbidding look: "Very well then, it shall be as you choose. We will not speak of Mr. Wickham again."

20.

I could have wished that my sisters had taken a similar vow of silence on the subject of Mr. Wickham. They were all in raptures over him. Elizabeth sang his praises as loudly as Lydia, so that my father was moved to observe that the fellow sounded rather too good to be true. (Which, as Cassandra later remarked, was as precise a description of Wickham as one could possibly wish for.)

But even Cassandra at first found Wickham perfectly amiable—indeed, I seemed to be the only girl in Meryton impervious to his charms, but from the beginning I mistrusted him. Mr. Darcy, I was sure, would not hold anyone in such aversion without good reason.

I saw him first at the Philipses where several of the officers had been invited to dine, and where my sisters and Mr. Collins had been asked to play at lottery tickets later in the evening. Aunt Philips had also asked Cassandra and Helen to "step across" to partake of a little bit of hot supper.

From the circumstance of my not being present the previous day when my sisters had met Mr. Wickham in Meryton, I was not introduced to him. Uncle Philips said in his befuddled fashion: "I think that you have already met my nieces, Mr. Wickham? My five beautiful nieces?"

Wickham bowed and smiled and soon afterwards seated himself beside Elizabeth. I was thus able to observe him without myself being observed.

He was certainly very handsome and just as certainly very aware of it; there was about him a bandbox perfection—and yet to my mistrustful eye, his hair had on it a little too much Russia Oil and his lower lip pouted as if he were somehow drinking people in—assessing them. I noticed too how even as he talked to Elizabeth, he looked about at the other young women in the room.

He talked first about the weather, but later when we all sat down to play at lottery tickets he began to speak of Mr. Darcy, asking how long he had been staying at Netherfield, and whether Elizabeth was much acquainted with him. Elizabeth's professed dislike seemed to hearten him greatly—as did the news that Mr. Darcy was not liked in Hertfordshire. There was no more looking about at other ladies now: The subject of Mr. Darcy completely engrossed him. He confided that he had been intimately connected with the family since childhood:

"His father, Miss Bennet, the late Mr. Darcy, was one of the best men that ever breathed, and the truest friend I ever had; and I can never be in company with this Mr. Darcy without being grieved to the soul by a thousand tender recollections. His behavior to myself has been scandalous, but I verily believe I could forgive him anything and everything rather than his disappointing the hopes and disgracing the memory of his father."

He spoke earnestly, thrusting the lower lip, and Elizabeth for her part hung on his words as if she were at a play and he the only player. Indeed, Mr. Wickham reminded me of an actor—I imagined him making much the same speech before an audience, nicely calculating the effect of his noble looks and sentiments.

He then told Elizabeth that he had been meant for the church—that Mr. Darcy's father had bequeathed to him a valuable living but that the present Mr. Darcy had disregarded his father's will and given the living elsewhere.

"Good heavens!" cried Elizabeth, "but how could that be?—How could his will be disregarded?—Why did not you seek legal redress?"

"There was just such an informality in the terms of the bequest as to give me no hope from law. A man of honor could not have doubted the intention, but Mr. Darcy chose to doubt it . . ."

A sigh, a shake of his handsome head, but I could no longer believe a word he said—and I wondered that Elizabeth could believe him so implicitly. And could she not see the indelicacy of making such a communication to a stranger? Wickham was now talking to her as if he had known her all his life:

"I have a warm, unguarded temper, and I may perhaps have sometimes spoken of my opinion of him, and to him, too freely. I can recall nothing worse. But the fact is, that we are very different sort of men, and that he hates me."

"This is quite shocking!—He deserves to be publicly disgraced!"

I did not enjoy seeing my clever sister being played like the proverbial trout. Had Wickham imputed such grave misconduct to anybody other than Mr. Darcy she would not have been so credulous. But I was beginning to realize that Elizabeth needed to think ill of Darcy: It preserved her peace of mind.

Wickham continued to talk, but having heard enough from him for one evening I went in search of Cassandra. I found her in the adjoining parlor, where Mr. Collins and Uncle Philips were playing at whist with two of the officers. Cassandra had drawn up a chair the better to observe the game and from her bright glance I guessed that she had been very well entertained. As soon as the rubber ended and the gentlemen returned to the other room she told me that she would very much like to paint Mr. Collins: "I should like to paint him at the card table."

I was astonished. "You cannot wish to paint Mr. Collins."

"Certainly I do. I have never before painted a clergyman."
She began to laugh. "Poor man! The expression on his face as he
looked at his cards. He had not the least idea of the game and
your uncle was becoming quite impatient."

Helen now joined us, looking decidedly deshabille in a low-
cut pink gown. "You should paint Mr. Wickham, Cass—a full-
length portrait of him in his regimentals —now *that* would be a
picture worth having."

"Mr. Wickham is a little too beautiful to my taste."

"La! How can anybody be too beautiful?"

We all contemplated Wickham through the open parlor
doors where he and Elizabeth were still seated at the lottery
ticket table, talking. I had it at my tongue's end to tell them what
Wickham had said of Mr. Darcy. Indeed, had I been confident of
Helen's discretion, I must have told them of my own mistrust of
the man—but Helen was such an unpredictable little creature,
by turns silly and shrewd, and she was now being extremely silly.

"You will never guess where he is to lodge—Lydia and Kitty
were *so* envious of me when they heard—he is to take a room
over Madame Bejart's shop. We shall be able to watch all his
comings and goings, Cass."

And upon Cassandra's giving her an impatient look, she
turned to me: "He owns a gig, *chérie*—a tilbury. I adore those
little open carriages, don't you?—I mean to beg a ride from him
one fine day."

Later, when Wickham finally left Elizabeth's side to chat to
some of the other young ladies, I saw Helen accost him in a
rather bold manner. I was not near enough to hear their conversation, but I saw how Wickham eyed her up and down, how his
eyes went where eyes should not go.

At breakfast the next morning Kitty and Lydia talked
Wickham over thoroughly—from the stabling of his gig (in

Mrs. Long's old coach-house) to who was to do his washing—and I noticed that Elizabeth, who usually ignored their gibble-gabble, was giving it her full attention.

My own thoughts soon reverted to Peter. I was desperate to see him again but uncertain how best to contrive it. There would be no difficulty in engaging him to teach me the violin—my father never questioned the appointment of masters—but I did not want him to give me lessons at Longbourn. I did not want Lydia and Kitty spying on us and sniggering.

My only other path to him lay via the fortnightly Meryton assemblies—but about these too I was uncertain. I could not attend them on my own, and now that Lydia and Kitty were sure of meeting their favorite officers at private parties, the public assemblies had lost something of their appeal.

Before I could decide on a course of action, however, fate—in the shape of Mr. Bingley—took a hand in my affairs. On the afternoon following the Philipses' party he and his sisters called at Longbourn to invite us to their ball. It was to be held at Netherfield on the following Tuesday, the 26th of November. And while Miss Bingley and Mrs. Hurst were chatting to Jane (and ignoring the rest of us) I was seized with the most brilliant idea.

Turning to Mr. Bingley, and in a voice that quavered only slightly, I said: "May I ask, sir, what you intend to do for musicians?"

21.

I had to repeat my question, for Mr. Bingley was hardly aware of anyone's presence save Jane's.

"Musicians? Well, I daresay my sisters will wish me to engage a fashionable London orchestra, although I confess my own preference is for something a little more lively—something more in keeping with the character of a country neighborhood. Do you have any suggestions, my dear Miss Mary?"

I had of course. And much to my delight it ended with his promising to call at the Great House of Stoke that same afternoon, there to bespeak the services of Peter's quartet.

Fortunately, none of my family overheard this exchange, but my happiness was afterwards remarked on. "But you do not care for balls in the least, Mary," Lydia said. "Why are you so excited about this one?" And Elizabeth, in high good humor herself, said: "I think it must be the prospect of dancing with our cousin."

I carefully replied: "While I can have my mornings to myself, it is enough—I think it is no sacrifice to join occasionally in evening engagements. Society has claims on us all, and I profess myself one of those who consider intervals of recreation and amusement as desirable for everybody."

Elizabeth may have divined something of my true feelings, however, for she came to my room later, bringing with her a ballgown of bronze moiré silk that she had worn but once and now proposed giving to me: "There will not be time enough for us all to have new gowns made up and Lydia and Kitty have already bespoke Miss Stubbs's services."

I was extremely touched. "It is very kind of you to think of me."

"My dear Mary, I am not giving you anything new." She held up the gown before me. "It is too long of course but the color suits you admirably—I knew it would. And you may wear Grandmother Gardiner's garnets with it, you know."

I thanked her again and asked what she was planning to wear herself—whether it would be her new white silk with the tiny embossed checks. She professed herself to be undecided, and then, alas, as so often happened with Elizabeth, I said the wrong thing. "I suppose Mr. Wickham will not be coming to this ball?"

"Why should you suppose that?" (She was holding up the gown still, attempting to tuck it about me.)

"Well, he and Mr. Darcy are not exactly the best of friends—"

"Who told you that?"

"They were speaking of it at Netherfield—how Mr. Darcy cannot bear to hear Mr. Wickham's name mentioned—Miss Bingley was speaking of it—"

"Miss Bingley." Elizabeth's tone was dismissive.

"And her brother—they both spoke of it. It seems that Mr. Wickham is not a respectable young man. He has not behaved well by Mr. Darcy—"

"On the contrary. 'Tis Mr. Wickham who is the injured party, Mary. I happen to know that for a fact."

After a pause I ventured: "May I ask *how* you know?" And when she did not immediately reply: "I fear you may be placing too much reliance on Mr. Wickham's word. I could not help hearing what he said to you at the Philipses—"

"Oh, Mary! You should not listen to other people's conversations."

I tried to speak calmly: "I do wonder that he should have chosen you as his confidante—a complete stranger—does not that strike you as a little odd?"

She was smiling but I could tell she was annoyed. "There are some people, Mary, whose candor and warmth of heart predispose them to trust others. And Mr. Wickham, I believe, is such a person."

I saw there was no point arguing further: She had made up her mind. And her generosity in giving me the gown deserved a return in forbearance. I thanked her again for thinking of me and we parted as friends. (It was a struggle nonetheless not to quote to her Oliver Cromwell's words: "I beseech you in the bowels of Christ, think it possible you may be mistaken.")

The mantua-maker came the following morning to begin the work of making and remaking five ball-gowns. It was as well that she had agreed to live and work at Longbourn, for the weather during the next few days would prevent any of us from walking to Meryton. It rained for the whole of Friday, Saturday, Sunday, and Monday, and apart from tradespeople, the only visitor to the house was Helen Long.

Helen came twice to the house, calling before breakfast on Saturday to deliver a note from Cassandra, and calling again some three hours later to tell me to disregard the same note. She did not come on foot—both times she was driven by Mr. Wickham in his gig.

On the first occasion, the maid had brought the note to my room, saying that Miss Helen would not stay for an answer—she "would not keep the soldier waiting in the rain." Cassandra's note—so damp as to be in places barely legible—was as follows:

My dear Mary, I have a favor to ask of you on Helen's behalf, or more
particularly, of Jane. My aunt and I have both received cards of invi-
tation to Mr. Bingley's ball but as yet no invitation has come for
Helen. I would be grateful if Jane could mention the matter to Miss
B. Helen, as can be imagined, is excessively disappointed, and there
will be no peace until the arrival of the all-important card.

Yours &c., Cassandra

Imagine my surprise then when Helen called again, begging me to "forget about that stupid note"—she did not want to
go to the ball after all. "If Miss Bingley does not wish to invite
me, then I am sure I do not wish to go. And I certainly do not
want my friends to be put to the trouble of procuring an invitation for me."

I stared at her in amazement. That Helen should *not* wish to
go to a ball was next to incredible. But she looked to be quite in
earnest—and at the same time remarkably pretty, face all aglow
above her sodden red cloak, which was now dripping water on
the kitchen flagstones (she had insisted we talk in the kitchen so
that Lydia and Kitty might not know she was in the house).

I assured her there would be no difficulty in obtaining an
invitation. "I have spoken to Jane—"

"No, you don't understand!" She pulled me with her into the
scullery, where we were in even less danger of being overheard.
"You see, Wickham does not intend to go to this stupid ball—
and so I do not wish to go either. Oh, Mary! Can you keep a secret?" (pressing her wet cheek to mine) "I am so in love. You have
no idea."

It all came out then—how, on the pretext of running errands, she had spent the last two days driving about the countryside with Wickham, sheltering from the rain in the now derelict
Collins Cottage, where they had (to quote Helen) "plighted their

troth." I was horrified of course and tried to tell her what I had already told Elizabeth—that Wickham was not a respectable young man. She only laughed and embraced me, assuring me that one day I would understand.

"I was used to be a very correct young lady—correct and creepmouse—but I found it did not answer. Good-bye—I must not keep poor Wickham waiting. Tell Jane not to bother writing to Miss Bingley."

She was gone—and such was my unease that I could no longer work on my song. If I had not been so afraid of figuring as a tale-bearer (and of getting my feet wet) I must have walked into Meryton to speak to Cassandra. Afterwards, I wished very much that I had.

22.

After being received by Miss Bingley and Mrs. Hurst in the Netherfield drawing room, I followed my sisters and Mr. Collins into the ballroom (designated the "music room" in Mr. Coates's day), there to join the group of officers and girls gathered about the fire. The room was full of redcoats and I saw Elizabeth looking eagerly about, while Lydia and Kitty questioned the officers directly: Where was Mr. Wickham? Why was he not here?

Having no interest in Wickham's whereabouts (other than devoutly hoping he was not with Helen) I moved away so that I could better view the entire room. I was becoming nervous at the prospect of seeing Peter. Somewhere in the background music was playing but I could not see the musicians. And then I saw that a screen had been placed so as to hide them from view.

It seemed an odd arrangement and I determined to move closer, but there were people in my path: Maria Lucas—who wanted me to stand beside her so that she should not appear "singular"—and after her, Miss Harriet Lamb on the arm of Colonel Forster, and finally, Mr. Bingley, who stopped to say: "You must be wondering why that silly screen has been placed in front of your musicians, Miss Mary—I have this minute given orders for its removal." (speaking low) "My sisters would have it that the lads did not look sufficiently elegant—a great piece of nonsense and so I have told them."

He was gone, steering a course towards Jane, but before I could move on, Cassandra came up to me. "Mary, I must speak with you."

After glancing around to assure herself nobody was listening, she told me that Helen had run away. She began then to question me: Had I seen Helen that morning? Had either Lydia or Kitty seen her? Had she written to anyone at Longbourn?— Left a message with any of the servants?

With growing alarm, I too began to ask questions: Did Cassandra not know that Helen and Mr. Wickham had spent the past few days driving around the countryside together in the rain? Was it possible that Helen had gone off with him?

Cassandra knew only that Wickham had gone to town on business the day before and had not yet returned. The last time she and Mrs. Long had seen Helen had been at tea the previous evening, after which they had retired to their rooms— Cassandra to paint and Mrs. Long to sleep—while Helen helped the little maid Betty clear away the tea-things.

"Next thing I knew 'twas past midnight—when I am working I am forgetful of time—and I went down to see if everything was in order—the doors locked and bolted and the fires banked— Betty is sometimes careless with the fires. The back door was locked but not bolted, only I thought nothing of it until this morning, when I went to Helen's room." (whispering) "She left no note, but Aunt suspected Wickham from the first—"

"Is Mrs. Long not here tonight?"

Cassandra shook her head. "I came with the Lucases. Poor Aunt is beside herself. She has given it out that Helen is ill."

We talked on, not to much purpose, except that it seemed to relieve Cassandra's mind. Her concern now was for Helen's reputation—the need to conceal her absence: "But if Betty keeps quiet, all may yet be well. Wickham cannot afford to stay away long—he has to rejoin his regiment."

"Yes, indeed." I was eager to reassure. "I should not be surprised if they were to return tonight—while everybody is at this ball."

One of the officers, Mr. Pratt, then approached and requested Cassandra's hand for the first two dances. And much to my amazement, another officer, Mr. Chamberlayne, applied for my own hand.

23.

The screen concealing the musicians was still in place as Chamberlayne and I took our places in the set, but moments later I saw two footmen enter and approach the dais. After a short parley, they lifted up the screen and bore it away. Three musicians stood revealed—but Peter was not among them. My disappointment was acute, the more so for never having doubted that he would be present—I felt absurdly let down.

"I trust you do not regret taking me for a partner, Miss Mary?"

Chamberlayne was looking at me anxiously. A slight, elfin-faced young man, I perceived he was just as inexperienced a dancer as myself. Compared to Mr. Collins though, who was now dancing with Elizabeth, his footwork was exemplary—at least he did not keep blundering into people and apologizing; Elizabeth I saw was red with mortification, the more so perhaps because Mr. Darcy was standing nearby observing it all.

In the intervals when he did not need to mind his steps, Chamberlayne was disposed to chat. He spoke of his fellow officers as a "very respectable body of men." I asked him then whether he was much acquainted with Mr. Wickham, to which he replied with a sigh that "all the ladies" wanted to know about Mr. Wickham: "A dozen ladies have asked me where he is tonight."

The movement of the dance then separated us but when we were once more face to face, I asked if he knew when Wickham meant to return.

"Still harping on Mr. Wickham? Well, there is an eight o'clock roll-call tomorrow morning and a drill before breakfast—he will need to be back for that."

As soon as the dance ended I sought out Cassandra to tell her. She had received the same information from Mr. Pratt and in consequence was looking more cheerful. "But look behind you, Mary." She nodded towards the dais. "One of the musicians seems to be trying to attract your attention."

It was Peter. He was standing on the dais smiling across at me. My delight at seeing him was such that I could not disguise it—did not try to disguise it—and I made my way to him directly. "How is this? I looked for you earlier and did not see you."

Before he could answer, the other players spoke up:

"Pete had to speak to His Nibs about the screen."

"The lady of the house thought us too shabby to be on show."

"Didn't like the cut of our jibs."

Peter was laughing. "D'you think we look shabby, Mary?"

I blushed, denying it, although they did look a little shabby, the flautist especially in an outmoded velvet coat and buckled shoes. But Peter at least looked neat, with not a frayed shirt cuff in sight. I had noticed the absence of the "Miss" of course, but when he came to introduce them to me, he said:

"May I make the lads known to you, Miss Mary? This is Will Waldron and his brother Rob, who play with me regular—" He indicated two red-haired youths whom I vaguely remembered from the Meryton assembly. "And this here is Jim Payne—" (nodding towards the flautist, who executed a courtly bow in keeping with his old-fashioned finery) "Miss Mary Bennet, boys."

They all bowed again—Jim Payne almost bending double—and thanked me for recommending them to Mr. Bingley:

"He's a right one, Mr. Bingley," said Will Waldron. "Sent his carriage to collect us and all."

"Not like the lady of the house."

"Stubble it, Jimbo." (This from Peter.)

"Aye, man," said the other Waldron, "she'll put the screen afore you again if you don't mind your manners."

It was then that Miss Letty Stoke, the daughter of Peter's employer, came up, calling for her favorite tune to be played— "The Hound and the Hare."

I was about to move away when Peter called to me: "What is your favorite song then, Mary?"

His voice, deep and carrying, must have been heard by many, for there was a ripple of laughter and Letty Stoke said: "Oh! Mary Bennet does not care for songs—she only likes *serious* music."

I was prevented from replying by my father who, in the first of the humiliations he was to inflict on me that night, now stepped forward saying: "Come, child. You are keeping the musicians from their work." He then made me walk away with him, saying in his most sarcastic manner: "They have not come here to make conversation."

He left me by the side of Maria Lucas, where I stood, eyes smarting, and watched while he resumed his station next to Elizabeth.

The music started up again—they were playing "Highland Mary"—but I was unable to regain my composure, for Maria was questioning me about Peter, wanting to know if he was "the same gypsy fellow" whom Sir William had engaged for the dancing class. And upon my admitting that he was: "You seem to be wondrous great with him, letting him make free with your name."

I lost patience then. "The musicians have been treated very badly, Maria—and since it was I who recommended them, I feel responsible. And I shall be civil to them—I *shall* talk to them— and if one of them makes free with my name, so be it."

After this, Maria fell silent. But when Cassandra joined us she started questioning her about Helen, wanting to know the exact nature of her illness and whether Mr. Jones had been called in. Cassandra had at first answered her politely, but finally, forced to utter falsehoods, she too lost patience: "Upon my word, Maria, you are becoming a regular little poke-nose."

Poor Maria at once begged pardon, and the three of us then stood watching the final movement of the dance. Elizabeth now had Captain Carter for a partner, and in contrast to her earlier passage with Mr. Collins, looked to be enjoying herself. Again, I noticed Mr. Darcy watching her.

Maria noticed too. "I wonder Mr. Darcy does not ask Lizzy to dance. He is forever looking at her."

When the dance ended, Elizabeth joined Charlotte Lucas. And soon afterwards Mr. Darcy began a slow but purposeful advance towards her.

"Look!" Maria clutched at my arm. "He *is* going to ask her."

For the first time that night Cassandra laughed. "I'll wager you he won't, Maria."

I said: "Even if he does, she won't accept him. She has sworn never to dance with him."

"Of course she'll accept him." Maria's grip on my arm tightened as Mr. Darcy approached Elizabeth, bowed, and began to address her. "There! What did I tell you? I may not be clever like you two, but I always know when somebody likes somebody."

And a little later, as Darcy led Elizabeth onto the floor to the stately strains of "Sellinger's Round": "Oh! what a handsome couple they make. And so alike too, don't you think? Dark and haughty-looking—the sort of people one is terrified to talk to for fear of saying something stupid. And only think, a few short weeks ago he would have none of her—do you recall, Mary?—at the assembly when he said she was not handsome enough to dance with. And now he cannot take his eyes off her."

Maria continued to comment on the progress of the dance and its principal couple, but Cassandra's attention soon reverted to Bingley (now dancing with Jane), while my own remained fixed on the dais and one of its four dark, distant figures.

24.

The nearer I approach a certain distressing event, the more reluctant I am to relive it. But there is no escaping it.

When we went in to supper, a Welsh officer, one Mr. Monk, poured me a glass of punch instead of the lemonade I had requested. It seemed an innocuous enough beverage and I allowed Mr. Monk to pour me a second glass. It very soon went to my head, and when there were calls for singing I unhesitatingly stood up and—cheered on by Mr. Monk and armed with my song-sheet—made my way to the instrument.

En passant, I noticed Elizabeth. She was staring at me and shaking her head. Plainly, she did not wish me to perform. There was now no turning back, however, and as soon as Mr. Monk placed my music on the stand, I struck the opening chords.

The sound of my own voice seemed at first entirely satisfactory. It was not until I caught sight of Peter that the bubble burst: He was standing in the doorway with Jim Payne. His expression was peculiar—I could not read it—but the shift in perspective was fatal. It allowed me to hear myself—the words I was actually singing:

> *He fills with his power all their hearts to the brim—*
> *Was aught ever heard like his fiddle and him?*

I felt my mouth go dry, my throat constrict. What possible interpretation could Peter place on those words other than that they were about him?—that the entire song was about him? I tried not to look at him. I heard myself falter. One uncertain high note was followed by another: "She sees the Musician, 'tis all that she sees!" Somehow I managed to go on—heaven knows how, for the room had begun to revolve. And yet when it was over, I continued to sit there. And when they pressed me for another song— Mr. Monk among the most importunate—I instantly obliged with "My Father Was a Farmer." Perhaps I had some wild idea of proving myself to Peter. I could not now see him, for the room was still revolving, but I had a dizzy glimpse of Elizabeth. She was no longer looking at me: Her eyes were fixed upon our father, who shortly afterwards I beheld rising from the table.

Even now—even as I write—the image of that implacable white shirtfront advancing towards me fills me with horror. Stationing himself before the instrument, he pronounced: "That will do extremely well, child. You have delighted us long enough. Let the other young ladies have time to exhibit."

Mr. Monk having long since decamped, there was no one to escort me back to my old seat, and as the room was still spinning I was obliged to sit at the nearest table. I found myself among a set of people I did not know—fashionable London ladies and gentlemen all—and although I tried to appear unconcerned I was now shaking so that I could not pick up a glass of water.

It was Mr. Collins who saved me. Unable seemingly to resist the temptation to address a congregation, he suddenly started sermonizing on the duties of a clergyman. The people at my table were at first amazed and then amused—one gentleman holding up his eyeglass to better view such a "specimen."

But I could only be grateful that Mr. Collins's peroration lasted long enough for me to recover. As soon as I felt steady enough to stand, I left the room.

I went first to the library, where, for a wonder, I found Mr. Hurst wide awake and playing a card game with himself. I then tried Miss Bingley's bedchamber but a housemaid came and fussed over me with smelling salts. Finally in desperation I directed my steps to the little ground-floor chapel. No matter if it were not lighted up; nobody would there intrude upon me and I might easily light it with one of the candelabras in the corridor.

I found the room without difficulty. By candlelight, it appeared unchanged—the same pine pews and threadbare cushions, and the little oak spinet shut up in its Bible case. But I was shocked to see a bundle of old coats draped over the altar rail.

Having removed this desecration, I knelt and without further ceremony told my heavenly father how his earthly counterpart had humiliated me. The tears flowed then, a great self-pitying flood, after which I wrapped myself in one of the coats and lay down upon the bench.

But then came the sound of music overhead—the dancing had begun again—and the thought of Peter brought fresh pain. I resolved not to give way to it, however. I would open the spinet and see how it sounded.

It proved to be surprisingly well tuned, and I played until weariness and the cold overcame me. It now wanted twenty minutes to midnight, but overhead the dancing continued. I calculated they would be at it for hours yet—Lydia had earlier declared her intention to dance until dawn—and after removing my spectacles and placing them atop the spinet, I again covered myself with a coat and lay upon the bench.

The last of the music I recall hearing was another Burns air. I knew one of the verses—it made me think of Peter:

What though on homely fare we dine,
Wear hoddin gray, an' a' that?

Gie fools their silks, and knaves their wine,
A man's a man for a' that.
For a' that, an' a' that,
Their tinsel show, an' a' that,
The honest man, tho' e'er sae poor,
Is king o' men for a' that.

Part Three

1.

I awoke to find Peter standing over me, holding a branch of candles. I believed myself to be dreaming, but his face as he bent over me seemed so solid that I unthinkingly reached up and touched it. I encountered warm flesh—the shock of a shaven chin—and fast drew back my hand as from fire.

"Mary Bennet! What on earth are you doing here?"

Somehow I managed to sit up, to speak. "Is the ball over?"

"It is, yes. Miss Bingley gave us the order to stop playing."

"Oh good heavens! Is it very late? Are they all looking for me?"

"Don't fret yourself, 'tis only just gone twelve."

He had turned away to set down the candles, and for the first time I sensed in him an awkwardness. I wondered if perhaps he were wanting to distance himself from me—whether having heard me sing, he had conceived a disgust for me. The idea was dreadful.

I got up, saying: "I must go."

But I made no further move. I was furiously thinking of something to say. He in the meantime picked up my spectacles from off the spinet. "Are these yours?"

"They are, thank you."

He was smiling now—looking more like his usual self. He said: "I thought there was something missing."

"I wish I did not need to wear them, they are the bane of my existence." I was so pleased to see him smile that I began to gabble from the Commonplace Book: "But I console myself with the thought that had I been blessed with perfect vision, I might not have appreciated music so much."

"Ah, that sounds like an old woman talking."

I was momentarily taken aback. "Well, yes, I did live with a lady in Bath for several years—a very kind and cultivated lady who taught me to think on subjects worth thinking about—her name was Mrs. Knowles—Mrs. Pitt, I should say—but yes, you're quite right, that was indeed her opinion."

"Take good care of you, did she?"

"Very good care, yes."

"That's all right then."

He began to collect the coats that I had spread upon the bench.

I said: "Oh, I found those old clothes over the altar rail—"

"Old clothes! I'll have you know, Miss Mary Bennet, that this is m'best coat."

He may have been laughing but he certainly wasn't joking. He appeared even to take a perverse pride in his poverty— holding up a moth-eaten old gray coat for my inspection. The thought of him appearing in public in such a garment distressed me, and as if he could read my thoughts, he said: "Rob Waldron's coat is a lot worse than mine—at least my coat's clean." And then suddenly he became serious, thanking me again for recommending them to Mr. Bingley. "He's paid us handsomely and 'twill make a great difference—this time of year especially. Jim Payne has seven mouths to feed."

"I could have wished that Miss Bingley had treated you as well."

He shrugged. "We're just the pipers—they call the tune."

After a pause I said again: "I must go. They will be wondering what's become of me."

I held out my hand and he took it. I said: "I've not forgotten about the violin lessons. I will speak to my father."

But at the mention of my father, his expression changed. He let go my hand, saying: "No, don't do that—let's forget about that for the present."

I was sure then that my singing had given him such a poor opinion of my musical abilities that he no longer wished to have me for a pupil. And he now seemed most anxious to leave, bundling up all the coats and picking up the branch of candles: "Are we all set then?"

I went on ahead of him but at the open door I paused and, with my back to him, spoke his name. "Peter." It was the first time I had used his name. "You heard me sing tonight, did you not?"

"Yes, love."

The endearment took my breath away—made me forget what I had meant to say. I stood there with but one thought: *He must care about me.* But when he spoke, it was with a touch of impatience: "Come now. We must get back."

We walked down the passage, not speaking until we neared the end, where he stopped and asked me whether I went often to Clarke's Library.

Upon my assuring him that I did, he said: "I'll leave a message for you there."

"When?"

"Soon." He was smiling—amused at my eagerness perhaps. "I'm not my own master, Mary."

At that point a housemaid entered the lobby, and we were obliged at once to go our separate ways: he to the servants' quarters, I to the drawing room above.

In all the bustle of leave-taking and carriages being called for, it was easy for me to slip into the room unnoticed. I had never in all my life felt so elated. Peter cared for me! It was a miracle I longed to celebrate—to tell all Hertfordshire—and I had to hold my hand to my mouth against an involuntary smile.

The Lucases, I saw, had already left, and with them Cassandra. I was glad of it, being in no fit state to endure either Maria's questions or Cassandra's scrutiny. All the members of my family were present, however—Lydia and Kitty talking to the remaining redcoats, Elizabeth sitting silently beside our father and mother, while Jane stood a little apart talking to Mr. Bingley. Mr. Collins was making one of his long speeches, thanking Miss Bingley and Mrs. Hurst for their hospitality to himself—"a stranger, and ye took me in."

The room was fast emptying and before long my mother spied me and began to scold: "And where have you been hiding yourself, pray? In the library with your nose in a book I'll be bound." But upon two of the officers coming up to make their adieux she forgot about me and was in such good humor (frequently looking at Bingley and Jane) that I felt myself safe from further notice.

Our family was soon the last party of guests remaining, and Miss Bingley and Mrs. Hurst no longer tried to disguise their weariness. Mr. Darcy had moved to a more distant part of the room—away from Mr. Collins—where he stood with folded arms and closed lips, looking from time to time at Elizabeth (who preserved an equal silence) but almost as frequently at Jane and Bingley. My father was also silent, but I could tell from the creases about his mouth that he was enjoying himself. Lydia was slumped in a chair, yawning, while Kitty complained in fretful accents about the lateness of the carriage.

At long last we took our leave, with Mama issuing a general invitation for them to visit Longbourn and in particular asking Mr. Bingley to "take pot luck" with us just as soon as he returned from London (he was to go to London for a short visit the following day). Bingley accepted with pleasure, but there was a marked lack of enthusiasm on the part of the others. Mama seemed satisfied, however, and on the journey home was full of self-congratulatory talk, confessing that she had arranged for our carriage to be delayed on purpose to prolong the visit.

2.

So intent was I that night on revisiting the Netherfield chapel and recalling Peter's every word and look that I hardly slept. But from time to time the memory of my father's unkindness would rush in on me and while it could not extinguish my happiness, it did stir up some bitter feelings that I had long labored to get the better of.

Being sure that he would never apologize, I was startled when he bestowed a small smile on me at breakfast and said that he wished to see me in his library in half an hour. I retreated to my room in the interval and when I emerged I knew at once that there was something going on—some domestic drama—for Kitty and Lydia were on the landing, peering over the banister to the vestibule below. At sight of me, Lydia looked as if she might explode, so red-faced was she.

"You will never guess."

She was unable to go on, whereupon Kitty whispered: "Do not go into the breakfast room. Mr. Collins is in there proposing to Lizzy."

Lydia then unstopped her mouth to gasp: "Tell her what he said to Mama."

"He asked Mama if he could solicit—" (here Kitty began to snort) "—solicit for a private audience with her 'fair daughter Elizabeth'—and when Lizzy tried to run away, Mama *made* her stay and hear him."

I could not help smiling. "Poor Mr. Collins."

"Lord! who cares about Mr. Collins."

"Say 'poor Lizzy,' rather," said Kitty. "Mama is going to be so angry if she does not accept him."

"Mama will make him offer for you then, Mary," said Lydia. "You are the next in line."

They were soon giggling afresh at the idea, calling me "Mrs. Collins" &c., at which point I left them to make my way downstairs.

The library door was ajar, and on my approach, my father laid aside his book and picked up a letter lying open on the desk-top.

"This came several days ago," said he. "It is from a young man—a very talented young musician—" (Here he paused and eyed me in a speculative, slightly malicious way.) "—someone with whom you were once extremely friendly. Can you guess who it might be?"

Wild thoughts of Peter crossed my mind but I said with a fair assumption of calmness, "I collect you refer to George Rovere, Papa."

"You collect right." Having had his sport, he now turned back to the letter: "He and his stepfather, Mr. Purvis, are to stay at West Hall, and the young man writes— very properly—to ask permission to call at Longbourn when they are in the neighborhood. And while I was at first reluctant to agree to it—" (giving me a look) "—on further consideration, I think it not a bad thing. Young people like to be together."

So saying, he handed me the letter but upon my venturing to ask whether he had replied to it: "Not yet, no. Perhaps you would like to do it for me?"

And then taking pity on my tongue-tied discomfiture: "Well, well. I shall certainly write before Christmas."

I wondered then whether this was his way of making amends. But for that, George's letter would surely have been consigned to the fire or left to lie unanswered with all the other letters gathering dust upon his desk. He may have seen me looking at these for he picked up two that were unopened, saying: "Mr. Jones's shop-boy brought this round for you this morning—" (handing me a sealed note from Cassandra) "—the other came in the morning post."

It was from Mrs. Knowles. (To me, she would always be "Mrs. Knowles.") I thanked him, but he had already returned to his book—his customary sign of dismissal. I was on the point of quitting the room when my mother burst in, crying out as she pushed past me: "Oh! Mr. Bennet, you are wanted immediately; we are all in an uproar. You must come and make Lizzy marry Mr. Collins, for she vows she will not have him, and if you do not make haste he will change his mind and not have *her*."

I did not wait to hear more; I escaped into the drawing room with my letters, closing the door against the clamor in the rest of the house—my mother's continuing shrill tones and the clatter of footsteps as the maidservant ran to fetch Elizabeth.

Cassandra's note was short, but it told me what I wanted to know:

My dear Mary, we shall all be at home this morning (the *all* was underlined) *and look forward to seeing you as soon as is convenient.*

I thanked God, reading it, and was most heartily ashamed of myself for not having thought of Helen before; I had even forgotten to pray for her—for her safe return. I now determined to walk to Meryton directly. Mrs. Knowles's letter would have to wait. And the idea of seeing George again did not particularly excite me: I felt sure that he would have changed beyond recognition—it would be like meeting with a stranger.

3.

The house was still in an uproar when I left—Mama pleading with Elizabeth to accept Mr. Collins, and at length resorting to scolding and threats. On my way out, I met with Charlotte Lucas, who had come to spend the day. I did not need to inform her what was going on—Mama could be heard from the rooftops and beyond.

In contrast, the Longs' front parlor seemed a pattern of domestic harmony. When I arrived, Mrs. Long, Cassandra, and Helen were all seated around the fire and gainfully employed Mrs. Long with her carpet work, Helen sewing, and Cassandra sketching.

But it was soon clear that all was not well beneath the surface. Since breakfast, they had had to endure a stream of morning callers—all enquiring after Helen's health and lamenting her absence from last night's ball—and the strain of repeating careful lies was beginning to show. Cassandra looked quite worn down from civilities and Mrs. Long's unease was revealed in a flow of inconsequential chatter. Only Helen seemed serene—sewing away with smiling concentration.

Cassandra cut short Mrs. Long's account of Helen's illness, saying: "Aunt, I have already told Mary what happened. She knows it all."

Mrs. Long put down her carpet work. "Well, I must say—I question whether that was wise, Cassandra—"

"My dear aunt, you know that Mary is to be trusted—she is almost one of the family."

"Nobody said she wasn't to be trusted—" (here Mrs. Long gave me a forced smile) "but I'm sure Mary will not mind my saying, if her dear mother were ever to hear of it—one of my oldest friends but her discretion is not—I am sure Mary will not take offence if I speak plain."

"I will not speak of it to anybody, ma'am, I promise."

The door opened then and Helen spoke just one word under her breath: "Murder." (It may have been a French word she spoke, but let it stand.) It was not another visitor, however, only Betty with the coffee-pot. Both Mrs. Long and Cassandra were at pains to thank her, and as soon as she left the room Mrs. Long said: "To be sure Betty is as good a girl as ever lived, but there's no denying that we are all in her power now."

At which point Helen jumped up and declared her intention of going for a governess.

"Don't talk nonsense," said Cassandra.

"It is not nonsense. I am an accomplished needlewoman, my French is excellent, I can dance, I can sing—"

Mrs. Long cried out: "This is your home, Helen, and so I have said a hundred times—and for you to talk in that wild way—let us have no more of it, I beg you."

"I will not stay to bring disgrace on you, Aunt."

"Oh for God's sake!" Cassandra finally lost patience with her sister. "Running away never solved anything, and you have caused poor Aunt quite enough anxiety." She continued more calmly: "We must conduct ourselves so as to give the neighbors no more food for gossip. We must be careful to be polite to everybody." She gave Helen a look. "And I do mean *everybody.*"

"Just as though nothing has happened," said Mrs. Long.

Helen addressed Cassandra in a low, choked voice: "So you would have me be polite to *him*, would you?"

"To him especially."

The silence that followed was dreadful. They were eyeing each other like two cats, and in my nervousness I made things worse by quoting from the Commonplace Book: "It is said that politeness is the currency of a civilized society."

Helen's response was to quit the room, and a moment later Mrs. Long got up to go also.

Cassandra said: "Best leave her be, Aunt."

"My dear Cassandra—I am only going to help Betty with the sandwiches."

She was absent quite long enough for Cassandra to tell me what had happened. Helen had apparently agreed to go with Wickham to London on the Monday night in the belief that they were to be married on the Tuesday morning. Wickham had told her that he was acquainted with a London bishop and that there would be no difficulty procuring a special license. The attendant secrecy would, he assured her, make everything more romantic and when Helen returned with a ring on her finger, all would be forgiven—her aunt and sister would almost certainly "come round."

Once in London, he had taken her to the house of a Mrs. Younge in Edward Street. It was by then too late for him to call on the bishop, but in the meantime he considered himself most solemnly bound to her—he was her husband in all but name and in God's eyes therefore their union was already sanctioned.

At this point in her narrative, Cassandra reached for the coffee-pot. "I am sure I do not need to go on, do I? You must have read the same stuff in any number of novels. Wickham knew he had nothing to fear—Helen having no male protectors, there was no one to call him to account. And Mrs. Younge was of course his confederate—Helen could not appeal to her.

"In the morning, there was no more talk of calling on the bishop. Helen saw then that she had behaved like a fool and, what was harder for her to bear, that Wickham had proved himself a complete scoundrel. On the journey back to Meryton, they scarcely spoke. At the end, he had the effrontery to assure her that she might rely on his discretion. He even told her that he would always regard her as a friend."

"And she must be *polite* to him?"

"She cannot expose him without ruining herself—you must see that. 'Tis the way of the world."

After a moment I said tentatively: "Perhaps it would be better if she were to go for a governess—for a little while at least."

"Indeed, it would not—governessing is a degrading trade and Helen would never submit to an employer's authority. No, I want her here under my eye. And once things have returned to normal—"

She stopped and the thought occurred to me (as I'm sure it did to Cassandra) that for Helen, things might never return to normal.

"As I see it," said Cassandra after a pause, "there are three things to be feared. First, that someone may have seen them returning together last night—although Helen assures me that she took care to cover her face as they came into Meryton. Second, that either Wickham or Betty will talk—although here again I think it unlikely: Wickham has his own reputation to consider and Betty has always been a most loyal servant."

"And the third thing?" I prompted.

"Well, she could be with child, God forbid."

"Oh, Cassandra!"

But at that point, Mrs. Long came back, closely followed by Betty with the sandwiches, and it was not until Cassandra and I were upstairs in her painting room that the conversation could be resumed. Cassandra now spoke of another fear:

"I worry that she may try to harm herself. She is so very angry—she blames Aunt for allowing her too much liberty. But then in the next breath, she blames herself. Her spirits are very unequal. Last night she was really in a most pitiable state— walking about and crying and cursing in French—Aunt eventually persuaded her to take some laudanum to help her sleep—and then this morning she *insisted* on sitting in the parlor with us."

"These things take time, Cassy. You must be patient."

Cassandra put up her hand: "Please! No platitudes—none of your Commonplace Book today."

I was hurt but tried not to show it. I bethought myself of Mrs. Knowles—how she had helped me to lead a more useful and disciplined life. I said: "If she can just keep busy—perhaps take up some new study—something musical to lift her spirits. Thorough-bass, for instance—Helen has a fine natural singing voice—she could come to Longbourn and take lessons with me."

"That reminds me. I have something to tell you about your Peter Bushell."

"You have?"

"Oh, Mary!" (laughing) "Your face is the most infallible little barometer. There." (kissing my cheek) "I am sorry I was cross, but for the past two nights I have hardly slept. But back to Bushell. Last night at the ball—after supper, when you had sung your song, you will recall that your father—"

"Yes, yes—"

"Yes, well shortly after you had left the room, Bushell came over and spoke to your father. I was not near enough to hear what he said, but Maria Lucas told me afterwards that he had been—" (smiling) "amazingly impertinent."

"Peter actually *spoke* to Papa?"

"He did. According to Maria, he had the impudence to criticize Mr. Bennet for his treatment of you. I must say it gives me the most favorable idea of his character."

"But what did Papa say?"

"Very little, apparently. Afterwards, Sir William Lucas urged your father to report Bushell to his employer, Sir John Stoke."

"Oh no! And what did Papa have to say to that?"

"Oh, he just laughed and said Bushell was undoubtedly in the right of it. A very strange man, your father."

4.

So much did Peter's "impertinence" engross me that I failed to observe certain developments at Longbourn (of which more later) and forgot about Mrs. Knowles's letter until the crackle of paper in my cloak pocket reminded me. I then read it a little impatiently for it seemed to be all about her poor health (her rheumatism had returned but Colonel Pitt had discouraged her from going into the warm bath and quacking herself).

But there was also a postscript announcing her son's betrothal—Mr. Knowles was to marry a parson's daughter from Taunton in March—and this was followed by a quotation from Montaigne about marriage being like a cage with the birds outside desperate to get in and those inside desperate to get out. I wondered then whether she was alluding to her son's marriage or to her own.

I prayed for her that night, for her health and happiness, and I also prayed for Mr. Knowles, although perhaps not as fervently as I should have—or as I once would have. The prayer I offered up on Helen's behalf was pretty perfunctory too—though I had at least remembered to consult Elizabeth about including her in our weekly singing classes. I also made a point in the days that followed of inviting Helen to accompany me to Clarke's Library. I had my own selfish motive for visiting the library of course, but at the same time I did sincerely wish to be of use to her.

Fortunately, we did not encounter Wickham on any of our walks. During this period he was as often as not at Longbourn, ingratiating himself with the rest of my family (my father now deemed him a "very pleasant fellow") and telling anyone who would listen how shockingly he had been treated by Mr. Darcy.

But I am not relating this at all methodically. Far too many things happened in the days immediately following the Netherfield ball for me to give a precise account of them all—and I have neglected to mention Mr. Collins's *second* matrimonial essay. Three days after his offer to Elizabeth, he proposed to Charlotte Lucas—and was accepted.

Like everybody else, I was amazed when the news was made known. I was also relieved—my mother would now stop bothering me, for she had begun to entertain hopes that *I* might be prevailed upon to accept Mr. Collins.

I must now touch on a more painful subject: the continuing absence of Mr. Bingley. Two days after the ball, a letter came for Jane from Caroline Bingley. It was delivered when we were all in the drawing room (my sisters having just returned from Meryton with Wickham and another officer) and I was beside Jane when she opened it. I saw her countenance change as she read it. But I had thought no more about it, and when Jane later announced that the whole Netherfield party—Miss Bingley, the Hursts, and Mr. Darcy—had gone to join Mr. Bingley in London, she appeared quite calm and matter-of-fact. It was Mama who expressed dismay.

But Jane, as I afterwards learned, had not quite told us the whole. Cassandra had also had a letter from Miss Bingley, stating that her brother would not now be returning to Hertfordshire, that they were all fixed in London for the winter, and that Cassandra was therefore to apply to the attorney Mr. Morris for payment for the portrait. Miss Bingley also furnished Cassandra with the Hursts' London address, to which the portrait should be consigned.

Cassandra was quite miffed by this. "It was Mr. Bingley who commissioned the portrait, not his sister. And at the ball when I spoke to him, he said nothing about spending the winter in London. But perhaps Jane knows the reason for the change of plan?"

I shook my head. "Jane was most surprised to receive Miss Bingley's letter, I assure you."

Cassandra was regarding me intently. "Was she though? You know, Mary, I begin to think this is none of his doing—I suspect it is Miss Bingley who wants to winter in London. And that being the case, we may confidently expect him back within the week. He will not want to be parted long from your sister—he's besotted with her."

There was a faint acid tone to this observation but I let it pass: Cassandra tried hard not to envy Jane, but occasionally an ignoble sentiment escaped her. She was wrong in her prognostic however—Mr. Bingley did not come back within a week, and his being settled in London was soon confirmed in a second letter from Caroline Bingley. And this time I did notice that the news affected Jane. Her serenity—her air of sweet composure—seemed quite cut up. She and Elizabeth now spent a lot of time closeted in their dressing room or walking together in the shrubbery. And once after a prolonged rant from Mama on the subject of Bingley and Netherfield, I overheard Jane say to Elizabeth: "Oh, that my dear mother had more command over herself! She can have no idea of the pain she gives me by her continual reflections on him."

Witnessing Jane's distress, my own self-absorption was at last punctured, and I now prayed for the sister I loved best. I reminded

God of her goodness and asked that Bingley not keep her in suspense too long.

I was myself in a fair amount of suspense over Peter. I had been haunting Clarke's Library and had as yet received no message from him. And while I told myself to be patient, that Peter was not free to come and go as he pleased, yet I could not help feeling uneasy.

Another source of unease was Wickham's frequent presence in the house and Elizabeth's obvious delight in his company. I tried once again to warn her against Wickham, but as I could not supply evidence of his misconduct without exposing Helen, she would not listen to me. My parents too were both partial to Wickham, and I therefore looked to Aunt Gardiner to penetrate his character when the family came for their usual Christmas visit.

But in this too I was to be disappointed. Aunt certainly disapproved of Wickham as a prospective husband for Elizabeth, but it was his lack of fortune to which she objected, not his lack of integrity. He successfully bamboozled her by talking about Derbyshire—the particular part of Derbyshire where Aunt had spent her formative years—and of all their mutual acquaintance, including the Darcy family of whom Aunt knew only by report.

After Christmas, the Gardiners left for London, taking Jane with them. And despite Aunt's saying that there was no hope of Jane meeting Bingley as they lived in such a different part of London, I did not consider the gulf between Grosvenor Street and Gracechurch Street impassable. It would not prevent Jane calling on Caroline Bingley, and Mr. Bingley might thereby hear of her being in town.

Cassandra also took this view: "Oh, he will certainly hear of it—and as soon as he sees her again, it will all be resolved." She even added magnanimously: "And I'm sure I hope that they will be very happy."

With the departure of Jane and the Gardiners, the marriage of Charlotte Lucas to Mr. Collins now loomed. Lady Catherine de Bourgh did not believe in long engagements, and the wedding was accordingly fixed for the third Thursday in January. On the Wednesday, Charlotte, accompanied by Maria, paid us a farewell visit, and while my mother was expressing insincere wishes for Charlotte's happiness, Maria plucked at my sleeve and whispered: "I thought that you should know, Mary—pray do not be angry now!—but after the Netherfield ball, Papa saw it as his duty to speak to Sir John Stoke about your fiddler friend."

"I assume you refer to Peter Bushell?"

"Oh, pray do not be angry! It has been on my conscience for weeks now and I could not rest until I told you."

"I am not angry, Maria." (I was of course—I was furious.)

"You must know that Bushell was amazingly impertinent to Mr. Bennet—'tis true, Mary, he was! And Papa saw it as his duty—"

"I take it that Peter has been dismissed from Sir John's employ?"

"Oh dear, no! Sir John said he was too good a keeper for him to turn off—no, he has merely forbidden him to play the fiddle in future, either at private balls or the assemblies, lest he be offending some other gentleman. Sir John thinks—he told Papa— that Bushell has grown a bit too big for his boots."

I had it at my tongue's end to tell her that if anyone had grown too big for their boots it was surely her father—poking his nose into what did not concern him. But Maria, having made her confession in form, was anxious to change the subject. She confided that Charlotte on the eve of her wedding seemed amazingly calm and collected: "I am to visit her and Mr. Collins in March, and I know that she also means to invite Elizabeth." (whispering) "But Mama fears there may be a little awkwardness, you know, on account of Mr. Collins having wished to marry Lizzy first."

5.

The wedding went off without incident—the bridal couple leaving for Kent from the church door—but when we returned to Longbourn, my mother could no longer contain herself: "Well, I hope you're satisfied, Miss Lizzy. I hope you're happy with this day's work—making paupers of us all."

There was more—much more—there being no-one to check her, no Jane to intercede and my father having shut himself away in his library. Elizabeth sat silent while the storm raged on: "And so now Jane has lost Mr. Bingley—no help from that quarter. Not that I blame her—she would have got him if she could—*she* knows where her duty lies."

In the end, it was the sound of a carriage that diverted her. Kitty—always first to the window at the prospect of a visitor—exclaimed: "'Tis the most elegant curricle—far smarter than William Goulding's—and there is a young man driving it—I have not the least idea who he may be."

Lydia then joined her sister and the two of them stayed staring out until Kitty suddenly said: "I know who it is!—'tis that boy who used to live at Netherfield—the one who played the pianoforte."

"Netherfield!" Mama was alive again.

"I'm sure 'tis he. Mary, do you not recall? You used to play duets with him."

I went to the window then, but a little too late. George (for as it turned out, it was indeed he) had already entered the house,

A few moments later Hill was ushering him into the drawing room.

Six years on, I was surprised that Kitty should have recognized him. Certainly his distinctive dark eyes and full lips—the way he held his head—all these were as I remembered, but he was now quite a tall young man and slender, and his face had completely lost its boyish ruddiness. His manner, however, was as friendly as before and he seemed especially pleased to see me, shook my hand, and asked if I remembered Mozart's *Sonata for Two Pianos in D Major*.

The first part of the visit was taken up with establishing the Netherfield connection, and inevitably, Mr. Coates's name came up. I could not help glancing at Elizabeth to see how she bore it but she seemed quite unembarrassed, even asking George whether his mother had accompanied him into Hertfordshire. Upon learning that he had come only with his stepfather, Mr. Purvis, she politely expressed a wish that they would both enjoy their visit, adding: "I'm afraid the neighborhood is rather thin of company at present. So many families are in London for the winter."

Unfortunately this provided a perfect opening for Mama to bemoan Mr. Bingley's departure from Netherfield, and had it not been for a quick interpolation of Elizabeth's, she would undoubtedly have given George the whole history of Jane's abortive romance. I then inquired after Nonna, and this too led to an awkward pause before George replied that he had not seen his grandmother since leaving Hertfordshire.

Safer subjects were then tried. I asked George how he liked living in the country again: "I remember you were used to prefer the country when we were children."

"And so I do still. The only thing I miss about London are the concerts."

After another pause, I said: "Your mother likes London, does she not?"

"She does indeed—which is another reason for my preferring the country."

I had no idea how to respond to this, but fortunately Elizabeth came to the rescue, asking about the London concerts. We began then to speak of music, whereupon George disclosed (with a blush that brought the boy very much to mind) that he had written an oratorio.

"An oratorio!" I thought of my own poor little song and blushed in turn. "What is its subject, pray?"

"'Tis about Goliath and is called *The Philistine*."

Lydia and Kitty now begged to be excused and shortly afterwards Mama also quit the room, saying: "I shall just let Mr. Bennet know that you're here, my dear George—I'm sure he will wish to talk to you—you were always a prime favorite of his, you know."

My father of course did not come, but Elizabeth stayed and a most stimulating discussion on all things musical followed. George had clearly used his time to good effect. He had been taking private lessons from a Professor Crotch in London and had composed a pianoforte sonata as well as his oratorio. "My stepfather now wants me to give a concert here in Meryton and I do not like to disappoint him. He has been very good to me— to all of us."

"A *public* concert, George?" I was shocked.

"Vulgar, isn't it?" He grinned. "But poor Purvis is vulgar— surely you remember that?" And then seeing my embarrassment: "I was used to hold him in such contempt on that account—I hope I know better now."

My mother returned then to issue an invitation for George and Mr. Purvis to dine at Longbourn the following day: "Just a quiet little family dinner, you understand, but I can promise you two courses—and afterwards you and Mary must play for us. I declare it will be quite like old times."

I could see at once what she was about, and could only hope George did not. He accepted the invitation with apparent pleasure but left soon afterwards, and when Mama went with him to the door I said to Elizabeth: "It is very pleasant to see George again after all this time but I do wish Mama would not misconstrue things."

Elizabeth gave a small sigh. "You are not alone in that wish, my dear Mary."

"It is so very embarrassing."

"Yes." The impropriety of criticizing our mother may have struck her then, for she suddenly proposed a walk: "I have some books to change at Clarke's—should you care to come with me? Can you spare the time?"

I agreed to it at once of course, delighted at the excuse to visit the library, and flattered that she should ask me until I recollected that there was now no Jane to bear her company.

6.

Elizabeth was in an unusually expansive mood as we walked, holding forth about George: "He is an example to us all. I am ashamed of my own idleness and from now on mean to practice at least an hour a day—Mary, you are my witness—an hour a day at the very least."

I did not know quite what to make of this. She already prac ticed an hour a day and applied herself to her music most conscientiously. However, she did not like people to know how hard she worked, either at her music or her Italian, and would turn away compliments with self-deprecating humor: She did not "take the trouble" to practice as much as she should; she was "but a poor Italian scholar," in fact, a poor scholar altogether, and not at all well read. More than anything, Elizabeth hated to be thought bookish.

She was still talking about George—marveling that over six years had passed since the family lived at Netherfield—when much to my astonishment she began to speak of Mr. Coates: "I saw you look at me when his name was mentioned, Mary, but I assure you I no longer think about him other than to wonder at my own folly in loving him. My excuse must be that I was but fourteen."

I was tempted then to quote from the Commonplace Book that "love is the folly of the wise," but I held my peace, and after a moment she went on: "In one respect, the experience did me a great deal of good. I was able to reassure Aunt Gardiner that I was not at present 'in love' with Mr. Wickham." She smiled. "I could not, alas, promise her that I would not be in love with him *in future*."

And now I felt bound to speak out—to warn her yet again about Wickham: "I have tried to speak to you before, Lizzy, but you would not listen—Mr. Wickham has behaved shamefully to a young lady of my acquaintance."

Immediately her manner changed. "How shamefully? What exactly was the nature of his offence?"

"I cannot give you the particulars but I do solemnly assure you—"

"Who is the young lady?"

"I am not at liberty to say."

"What evidence can you adduce—other than this nameless young lady's word?"

"I knew you would not listen to me."

"On the contrary, my dear Mary, I *have* listened—this is the second time you have seen fit to denigrate Mr. Wickham without offering a shred of proof. What am I to make of it, pray?"

I shook my head, and after an interval during which we walked in silence she suddenly turned to me, saying: "I thought Helen Long looked very pale and tired at the wedding this morning—I thought she seemed sadly out of spirits."

I realized then that she had been mentally reviewing all the young ladies of my acquaintance—there were not, after all, so very many—and had finally fixed upon Helen. I said: "Oh! Helen has not been well lately, that is all."

Under Elizabeth's gaze, I felt my face grow hot. I dreaded further questions, but when she spoke, her tone was surprisingly gentle: "I am sure you mean well, Mary, but Aunt does not disapprove of Mr. Wickham's *character*, you understand. Her concern is solely about his lack of fortune. And for that, as we all know, Mr. Darcy is responsible—abominable man that he is."

"I do not consider Mr. Darcy abominable. On the contrary—"

"Well." (still trying to be conciliatory) "There we must differ, Mary."

"I do not see why you are so eager to think ill of him. He likes you well enough—admires you even—"

"Nonsense!" She gave me a look. "What makes you say so?"

I longed to make her a Lydia-like answer—a "wouldn't you like to know?" retort. Instead, I said that I had often noticed him looking at her and listening to her conversation with others: "I wonder you did not notice it yourself."

Her response to this was to quicken her pace. She appeared to find the idea of Mr. Darcy liking her disturbing, for she walked on for several minutes in frowning silence. But presently she turned to me, saying: "That young man who plays the violin—whose family used to live in Collins Cottage—Bushell? Is not that his name?"

My face burning, I agreed that it was.

"I hope you will take this in good part, Mary, but if Aunt saw fit to advise me as to the imprudence of encouraging Mr. Wickham, you must not mind my cautioning you. Bushell is a very good sort of man I daresay, but he is not your equal, and for you to be making a friend of him is unwise."

I was too confused to speak. For while I was obliged to acknowledge (in a worldly sense) that she was right, yet I longed to defend Peter's claims to be considered my equal—to quote from Burns and the scriptures. I also felt that in customary elder-sister fashion she was now seeking to put *me* in the wrong.

Approaching the town, we met with Captain Carter and Mr. Fox, who insisted on accompanying us to the library. And there, the most embarrassing incident of all occurred, for the clerk at the desk recognized me, calling to me in the library hush: "Miss Mary Bennet! You will be pleased to know that your message has come at last. I have it here—" (hunting in the pigeon-holes behind the counter) "I was not by when the young man delivered it, but I made certain it was for you—" (finally extracting a folded paper and handing it to me) "I trust it was the one you were expecting?"

7.

Knowing Elizabeth's eye to be upon me, I pocketed the paper and did not dare read it until I was safely back at Longbourn. There, with trembling fingers, I unfolded my treasure.

Like most long-looked-for things it was a disappointment, being but two scrawled lines without salutation or signature:

We play at the Assembley Tuesday fortnight and hop to see you there.

On reading it, my first feelings were shame (at the misspellings) and annoyance that he intended to play at the assembly in the face of his employer's prohibition. But these feelings soon gave way to more tender reflections, and I was then ashamed that at the first stirring of resentment all my old prejudices should have surfaced. I tried to consider the situation dispassionately—whether I ought to try to dissuade him from playing. On the other hand, I so longed to see him! In the end I could decide on nothing. I kissed the paper—paper that he had handled—and placed it in my bodice next to my heart.

Next morning, when Elizabeth and I were awaiting the music master, she suddenly turned to me and said: "I heard what the library clerk said to you yesterday, Mary. You are not engaged in any clandestine correspondence, I trust?"

It was smilingly said, but she was watching me closely and without thinking, I denied it. But even as I spoke, I knew myself to have taken the first step down the slippery slope—for although I had not *yet* written to Peter, I had every intention of so doing. I sat, heart beating hard, recalling the words of the Ninth Commandment while Elizabeth regarded me with a skeptical little smile.

Fortunately Mr. Turner then entered the room, followed by Helen Long—Helen now regularly attended our Friday singing classes—and we were at once required to turn our attention to breathing exercises and scales.

And now I must confess to something shameful. I had become increasingly jealous of Mr. Turner's praise of Helen's singing. I could not understand why such an untrained voice—Helen could not sing above F—was judged superior to my own. According to Mr. Turner, Helen's voice was God-given and all she needed to do to perfect it was to practice her high notes. And the fact that she had never learnt Italian seemed not to matter either (previously Mr. Turner had held that a knowledge of Italian was essential for any serious singer).

Amazingly, Helen seemed indifferent to all the praise—Elizabeth also paid her many compliments—and this too had provoked me. But Helen now seemed indifferent to most things. She was in every respect an altered creature—uncommunicative and paying little attention to matters of dress. Everybody remarked the change in her: Lydia declared her to be a dead bore and my father was especially struck, opining that she had been crossed in love.

Belatedly, it occurred to me that she might be unwell. She was frequently obliged to excuse herself during class, and the previous Friday I had met her coming from the privy, pale and perspiring and with a handkerchief pressed to her lips. However, when I had offered to ask my father to send for the carriage she cut me off most ungraciously.

She was much more civil to Elizabeth, chatting to her while I sang my solfeggio. These conversations were always initiated by Elizabeth and covered a diverse range of subjects, but so far as Helen was concerned, there was an embargo on one subject at least. Whenever Mr. Wickham was mentioned—and Elizabeth mentioned him quite often—Helen would sit in smiling silence like the proverbial Patience on a monument.

On this particular Friday, Elizabeth seemed especially determined to speak of Wickham, remarking on his forbearance in his dealings with Mr. Darcy. But this time it seemed that Helen could bear it no longer. With more animation than I had witnessed in her in weeks, she jumped up, exclaiming: "Lord, I have but just now remembered! Aunt particularly asked me to speak to your cook about a receipt for oyster soup—Aunt is particularly partial to oyster soup—"

So saying, she fled the room. She returned a little later, looking extremely unwell—and while Elizabeth was singing a duet with Mr. Turner, I again offered the carriage, assuring her I would be happy to accompany her: "I have several errands to discharge in Meryton myself—I need to change my books at Clarke's—"

But again she cut me off, speaking in a manner so curt that I could not help taking offence. As a consequence I did something that was really most unkind: I failed to warn her that Wickham was to dine with us that day. Helen always stayed to eat her dinner at Longbourn after our class, and I began to relish the prospect of her discomfiture.

8.

No sooner did I catch sight of Helen's face upon Wickham entering the drawing room than I was sorry for what I had done. I saw her half-rise from the sofa and glance swiftly about, momentarily bent on escape before sitting again and submitting to the ordeal of being civil to him.

And I was even more sorry when I saw that Wickham seemed to be completely at his ease, smiling and acknowledging Helen with a graceful bow before moving on to greet Elizabeth. Elizabeth had also been observing them both—and had perhaps drawn a false conclusion from Wickham's sangfroid. (He was to display a similar brazen assurance when he and Lydia visited Longbourn after their patched-up marriage.)

But then if Helen had *not* stayed to dinner, she might never have met George. For George and Mr. Purvis were also among the guests, and although George did not appear to be much struck with Helen at first—having sat next to her at dinner and barely exchanged two words with her—afterwards, listening to her sing, he was overflowing with admiration.

Mr. Purvis was also struck, remarking to my father: "That little lass could make a career for herself on the concert stage. But I daresay she's too proud to sing for her supper."

Except for the color of his hair, which had changed from caramel to chestnut, Mr. Purvis had altered little. He and the new Mrs. Purvis seemed to lead quite separate lives. I heard him tell my father during dinner that his wife did not care for the country: "Christina prefers London. Always in London when she's not off on her travels. Italy's out of the question now of course with Boney rampaging about—she has to make do with Brighton or Bath."

At the mention of Bath, Elizabeth glanced at me. Her glances were chiefly directed at our father, however. The two of them were up to their old trick of laughing at their neighbor—in this case, Mr. Purvis. My father was again quizzing him about his properties: "They tell me you are planning to rebuild West Hall, Mr. Purvis? And we are now to call it 'Purvis Lodge,' I understand?"

Mr. Purvis nodded and smiled. Under his stiff dyed hair, his face was curiously boyish and unlined. My father's mockery did not seem to bother him. He told us he was presently rebuilding the Meryton banqueting hall: "And as soon as the work is finished, young George is to play his whatchamacallit there."

I saw a quiver pass over my father's face and Elizabeth trying to repress a smile. But I considered Mr. Purvis cleverer than they gave him credit for. For one thing, he was awake to Wickham. When the latter began to talk as usual about Pemberley, Purvis heard him out patiently. But when Wickham related how the present owner had robbed him of the living, Purvis said: "That's all very well, sir, but it don't pay to be dwelling on past grievances, you know. Whenever I've been cheated—and it's happened a few times over the years—I've called in my good friends the lawyers and if they couldn't get me my money back, I made up my mind to forget about it. I'd advise you to do the same, sir."

Wickham was listening, lower lip outthrust, and I saw him redden. Purvis had not yet finished: "A fine, upstanding young officer like yourself shouldn't find it hard to make his own way in the world. I had to earn my own living when I was twelve years old, you know. Of course, there are short-cuts—you can always marry money."

The rest of the evening was uneventful, but right at the end while we were awaiting the arrival of Mr. Purvis's carriage (which was also to convey Helen to Meryton) Lydia began to urge Wickham to attend the next assembly: "Me and Kitty will be there—and Lizzy too, I daresay. Do say you will come."

Wickham temporized: "I thought you were tired of public balls, Miss Lydia."

"Lord, no! I prefer private ones of course—who does not? But seriously now, why will you not come? You have no other engagement, have you?"

Alas, Wickham had to confess that he had. The newly married Colonel and Mrs. Forster were to give an evening party that same night, which he felt obliged to attend.

Lydia was extremely put out. "Lizzy! Did you know that the Forsters are giving a party Tuesday fortnight?—to which *we* have not been invited. It is too bad."

Elizabeth was looking embarrassed: "The Forsters may have thought that you and Kitty would prefer to attend the assembly, Lydia."

"So you have been asked then?—And Mary too, I suppose?"

I assured her that I had not been invited, but this seemed only to enrage her more. She had lately become friendly with Harriet Forster and doubtless felt herself slighted. I saw her turn away, and her furious red face recalled to mind the four-year-old who had so resented being excluded from the Gardiners' wedding feast.

9.

I wasted no more time wondering about the rights and wrongs of acknowledging Peter's message. I wrote to him on Saturday morning, having composed the letter lying awake in the small hours. I now took pains to write it out fair and to include the words he had misspelled. I did not seal it, however. I wanted Cassandra to cast her eye over it before I left it at Clarke's Library.

Lydia and Kitty agreed to walk with me to Meryton, but much to my relief Elizabeth declined to accompany us, saying she had letters to write.

The three of us set out shortly after breakfast. It was a fine frosty morning and Lydia was her usual bumptious self. She intended, she said, to call upon Harriet Forster and "make" her invite her to their party: "And if she does not oblige me, I shall tell everybody about her wedding gown—how she had it padded out to make her bubbies look bigger."

I left my sisters at Aunt Philips's while I went to call upon the Longs. The little maid Betty answered the door, saying that all three ladies had gone out and that she couldn't say when they would return.

"They had an engagement, Betty?"

"I really couldn't say, Miss." And then putting her face up close to mine, she whispered: "Miss Helen had a bad night and Miss Cassandra insisted she see the doctor first thing."

"And so what was Mr. Jones's opinion, Betty? What did he have to say?"

"Oh, Miss!" Betty stepped back inside the house. "She didn't see no Mr. Jones. Please don't ask no more questions, Miss Mary. I really couldn't say."

And before I could utter another word, she shut the door in my face.

With somewhat ruffled feelings I then made my way to Clarke's where—without allowing myself time to think—I took my letter to the desk, sealed it with a wafer, and handed it to the clerk.

It was only after I returned to Longbourn that I began to have doubts—not about the propriety of corresponding with Peter, but about the letter itself. As always, the doubts were strongest in the early morning, and after much tossing and turning, I got up and lit my candle and walked around in an embarrassed sort of stupor.

The letter, I now realized, was a terrible mistake. I had wanted to reach out to him—to tell him something of what I had been doing and thinking, and instead, I had written an over-familiar, prescriptive little sermon. Every line of it now made me cringe.

The salutation "Dear Peter" was far too familiar. He had not used my Christian name in his message.

"I hope to see you at the Assembly Tuesday fortnight." The sentiment was unexceptionable—but I had then had the happy idea of underlining the "*e*" of hope and the "*ly*" of Assembly to indicate the correct spellings.

"—Although I am not entirely happy at your playing in the face of Sir John's prohibition." (Was that really any of my business?)

And compared to his, my letter was so long! Not only had I described George's musical achievements, (was I hoping to make him jealous?) I had also written about Helen Long—of Mr. Turner's extravagant praise of her voice &c. (Was I seeking reassurance about my own voice?)

But the coup de grâce—the thing that now made me blush over and over—was that I had signed myself "Your friend, Mary."

I determined to set out for Meryton after breakfast to retrieve the letter and then recollected that it was Sunday—the library would be closed. I resolved then to collect it first thing on Monday and in the meantime not to think about it. I snuffed my candle and went back to my bed, and thought about nothing else until Sarah came in with the hot water.

10.

As it happened, I was obliged to wait until Wednesday to visit Meryton—and then to go in the carriage with Mama and Lydia and Kitty. On Sunday evening it had snowed and the road afterwards was too slippery to venture forth on foot. The delay only made me more anxious to recover my letter.

I was also impatient to see Cassandra. None of the Long ladies had attended church on Sunday, and after the service Aunt Philips had told Mama that she had seen the three of them mounting the London mail coach early Saturday morning. Mama had since talked of little else.

"Mrs. Long is always so secretive about her affairs—secretive and sly—aye, and selfish too—she thinks of nobody but herself and her precious nieces. Now if I had only known she was going to London, I might have given her a little parcel to take to Jane."

Lydia then disconcerted me by saying: "I'll wager Mary knows the reason for their going."

I assured her that I did not, but of course I had had ample time in the past few snowbound days to think. And if Mrs. Long now feared—as well she might—that Helen was with child, I could see why a London doctor would be preferred to a local one, especially such a one as Mr. Jones, whose shop-boy was forever prating about his master's patients.

On reaching Meryton, Kitty and Lydia went directly to Aunt Philips's but Mama would not permit me to go on to Clarke's, insisting that I first accompany her to call upon the Longs. There was a little delay upon Betty admitting us—I glimpsed Helen running down the passage—but Mama seemed not to notice, so intent was she on finding out why they had all gone to London.

Mrs. Long had her story prepared, however. Her bedridden brother was the reason for their going: An express had come early Saturday morning to inform them of a sudden life-threatening seizure.

Cassandra said: "My uncle was not in any danger as it happened, Mrs. Bennet, but we were not to know that at the time."

"Yes, but why did you *all* have to go?"

I saw Cassandra compress her lips, and was never more ashamed of my mother. Mrs. Long knew how to distract her old friend, however: "Oh! but I was very glad of their company, and my brother is now completely recovered, thank heaven. But my dear Mrs. Bennet, have you heard the news? I was never more astonished. Mary King's grandfather has died and left her a legacy of ten thousand pounds. I had it not half an hour ago from Madame Bejart—Mary and her mother were in her shop to see about their mourning clothes."

Mama took the bait. "—*Ten* thousand pounds!"

"'Twill make a vast difference to her prospects, for she is not at all handsome, poor girl."

"Handsome! I should think not—with that dreadful sandy hair and all those freckles. But how was it that the old man came to leave her such a sum? I thought the Liverpool family was to have it all."

Cassandra now judged it safe for us to withdraw. We went to the kitchen, where sat Helen with her feet up on the settle, eating an apple. She did not look at all pleased to see me, saying: "Oh Lord, is your mother still here then?"

Cassandra said: "Try for a little conduct, Helen, for heaven's sake."

"I don't see that there's much point now really. Now that I am become a fallen woman." She caught sight of my face. "Hasn't Cass told you, *chérie?* I am enceinte. Oh, don't look so horrified. I suspected it was the case all along."

Cassandra drew out a chair for me. "We only returned yesterday, Mary, and would have called had it not been for the snow."

Helen spoke through a mouthful of apple: "But of course it is one thing to suspect something and quite another to have it confirmed. Why should that be, I wonder? Do you have any thoughts on the subject, Mary? Some words of wisdom to reconcile me to my fate?"

Cassandra said: "How dare you speak so to Mary! She is not to blame for your predicament."

Helen pitched her apple core into the fire. "Why did you not warn me, Mary, that he was to dine at Longbourn? I think I might have been spared *that* at least."

Again Cassandra tried to take my part, but I was now determined to speak for myself: "Indeed, it was very wrong of me and I am sorry."

Helen sat in silence for several moments but presently she said without looking at me: "I know I have not been behaving well towards you lately, Mary—I know that—but when you look at me, there is always an expression—a kind of pious condescension— and there is just no bearing it. But I know I have been behaving badly and I am sorry."

A pause while Cassandra—looking pleased—went to the cupboard to take out some port wine, after which I ventured: "Do you still care for him, Helen?"

For a moment I feared I had said the wrong thing, for her countenance changed completely. "Lord, no! The very sight of him makes me—" (shuddering) "And the worst part is not being able to expose him—to have to just *sit* there and listen to people sing his praises. It makes me—well, if you will pardon the expression, it makes me want to puke."

Cassandra now poured out three glasses of port wine, and Helen joined us at the table. An amazingly frank discussion followed. I heard how Helen had been taking "female pills" to bring on her monthly flowers, and that it was only when these failed to produce the desired result that a doctor had been consulted—one Dr. Carey, a reputable London accoucheur known to Mrs. Long's brother.

Dr. Carey had given them all a severe talking-to, telling them to throw away the pills, that they were endangering Helen's health. He reminded them that Helen's situation was not the end of the world, that it called for careful planning rather than risk-taking and recriminations. He had even offered his services for the lying-in.

I then heard how they proposed to manage in the months ahead—where Helen would go when she began to "show" and what story they would give out to account for her absence &c. If their humor was somewhat forced (and in Helen's case, even a little coarse), their courage was exemplary. I felt privileged to be their confidante, and would have been happy to sit listening to their plans all morning if I had not been worried about my letter. I could not be easy until I had retrieved it and after first asking that Mama be told where I had gone, I took my leave of them.

Clarke's Library was but a short walk from the Longs' house, and on entering I went directly to the desk. A new impudent-looking clerk in a red waistcoat informed me that my letter had been collected not five minutes before.

11.

The degree of vexation and shame I now suffered was such that, for days, I could settle on nothing. No sooner did I recover from one bout of embarrassment than another would engulf me. One minute I would resolve not to think about it, the next saw me obsessively reviewing what I had written and imagining Peter laughing at it—at me.

Likewise, my resolve not to attend Tuesday's assembly weakened when Lady Lucas—on hearing that Lydia and Kitty had been invited to the Forsters' party—offered to chaperone me with Maria. But no sooner was I climbing the staircase of the Red Lion behind the broad back of Sir William than I wished myself elsewhere. Maria had persuaded me to leave off my spectacles, assuring me that I looked a thousand times better without them, and I feared that at any moment I might trip on the train of my new gown. (The gown was silk, the color of pale wheat, far too fine for an assembly but I had been unable to resist wearing it.)

Entering the room, everything seemed a blur of candlelight. The dancing had begun—the musicians were playing a lively reel—but I could not see them clearly. I could not see anyone clearly unless they were within a few feet of me. When Sir William and Lady Lucas stopped to exchange civilities with the innkeeper, Maria urged me on, complaining she had never seen the place so thin of company: "There are hardly any officers— only Monk and Chamberlayne– I suppose they are all gone to the Forsters. But Lady Stoke and Letty are here—I did not know that they had come back from London. Now we do not want to be *too* close to the orchestra, do we?" She gave my hand a significant squeeze. "'Twill be impossible to hear ourselves speak, and I have such a lot to tell you."

As soon as we sat down, she began: "You will scarce credit it, my dear, but Mr. Wickham is now making up to Mary King. I had it this morning from Ann Watson—she saw them out driving in his gig. Mary had on her new mourning clothes—all dressed up in black bombazine and smiling all over her freckled face. Can you believe it? The hypocrisy!"

She then turned to her own news: "We had a letter from Charlotte this morning and 'tis all settled—Papa and I are to go to Kent in three weeks' time, and Elizabeth too of course. Think of it, Mary! I shall soon see Lady Catherine de Bourgh."

I managed to make the correct responses although her words scarcely registered. A fog of unreality was walling me off—not unlike my experience of melancholia.

"Charlotte says that they dine at Rosings at least twice a week. I do not know how I shall go on in such exalted company—a footman behind my chair and the Crown Derby dinner service that Mr. Collins is always talking of . . ."

She chattered on until the dance ended and the music ceased, whereupon I burst out: "I wish I had not let you persuade me to leave off my spectacles."

"Oh! but you look so much better without them." She took my hand. "You look like a completely different person."

At that moment a solitary violin struck up. But the music was not dance music; it was more like a song—a solemn, sweet song. (I know now that it was Beethoven's "Romance in F Major.") I listened and suddenly it was as if the fog that surrounded me had been penetrated, as if I were being spoken to.

I sat transfixed, gripping Maria's hand. The other stringed instruments were also playing but it was the solo part I waited for, the melody that wove itself in and out with such astonishing trills and turns and grace-notes. I knew it was Peter playing. I fancied he was trying to tell me something—an absurd idea but it persisted: *I may not be able to spell but just you listen to this.*

Maria said: "Your fiddler friend is certainly in fine form."

"Oh, hush!"

"He should not be playing such stuff. People cannot dance to it—'tis a concert piece."

Sir William came up then, huffing and puffing. "If I do not mistake, Miss Mary, that is the same gypsy fellow who was so impudent to your father at the Netherfield ball. Bush—is not that his name? Sir John Stoke's keeper?"

I let go Maria's hand because my own was trembling so. "His name is Bushell, sir."

"Well, he has no business to be playing here tonight—playing in defiance of his master's prohibition. I shall speak to Lady Stoke."

I could not think what to say—I was afraid of saying too much. Maria spoke before I could: "Best not interfere, Papa."

I found my voice. "I beg you will say nothing, sir. He—the young man—his family used to live on the Longbourn estate and I know a little of his circumstances. He has a mother and sister to support. If he were to lose his place, it would be very hard."

"If he chooses to flout Sir John's authority, then he must take the consequences. People should never try to rise above their station, my dear Miss Mary."

I made a further effort: "Permit me then, sir, to speak for him as a musician—as a fellow musician. Music is such an important part of my own life that if anyone were to forbid me to play or sing—"

I could not go on, and after a moment Sir William said: "You feel these things a little too much, my dear. 'Tis only a common fiddler, after all." And then with his usual gratuitous gallantry: "But here is young Mr. Rovere just come. I make no doubt he is eager to dance with you."

George stood before me, bowing and smiling, and did indeed ask me to dance. It was of course charming to be sought for a partner—it was the kind of thing that happened to my sisters—only I wanted him to move out of the way in the meantime. I wanted to keep a close watch on Sir William.

Next thing, Mr. Chamberlayne approached and also applied for my hand, declaring that he had been practicing his steps since dancing with me at Netherfield. "I assure you I have im proved no end, my dear Miss Mary."

I was speechless. To receive two such offers in the space of as many minutes! And so I had now to refuse a man—a new and distressing experience—whereupon Chamberlayne turned and (quite cheerfully it seemed to me) solicited Maria.

Sir William meanwhile had moved out of my limited range of vision, and I could only pray that he had not gone to complain of Peter to Lady Stoke.

It would be absurd to say I was the belle of that Meryton assembly, but undoubtedly I received more attention—more male attention—than I had ever done in my life. It may have been because I was not wearing my spectacles, or because I had on a fine new gown, or because so many Meryton young ladies had gone to the Forsters' party—but whatever the reason, George and Chamberlayne vied to partner me for every dance and a late-coming officer, one Mr. Liddle, paid me many foolish compliments.

I did not forget Peter in all this. While I was never close enough to see him clearly, I hoped very much that he could see me. But not since the long-ago musical evening at Netherfield had so much notice been taken of me and I confess it rather went to my head. George took me in to supper and Chamberlayne hovered with supernumerary glasses of negus, and by the time I returned to the assembly room (with Mr. Liddle as my train-bearer) I felt quite giddy.

It was then that Maria came to me and whispered that my fiddler friend had just left and that the other musicians were playing on without him.

12.

Next morning, I was extremely ill. Not only had I drunk too much negus, I had convinced myself that Peter wanted nothing more to do with me. But with my head over a basin "casting up my accounts," it did not seem to matter, and in the limp intervals between I craved only oblivion.

Sir William, it seemed, had *not* spoken to Lady Stoke. Maria assured me that Peter had left of his own accord: "Papa had nothing whatsoever to do with it, I promise you."

The rest of the evening had passed in a blur of negus. Maria told me afterwards she had heard Mr. Liddle say he considered me to be quite as pretty as my younger sisters: "He thought you looked so lovely without your spectacles—he thinks you have the most beautiful eyes."

She repeated this when visiting my sickroom the following morning. I told her that I had no taste for such compliments but choked (quite literally) on the words, and after poor Maria held up a basin and ministered to me, I no longer had the strength to argue.

I continued unwell the whole of Wednesday, beset by such shiverings and streams of coldness about my shoulders that Mama called in Mr. Jones to prescribe to me. He recommended that I be moved from my attic room to a bedchamber on the floor below where a fire might be lit, and Mama then ordered that Jane's room be prepared for me. In all the subsequent

bustle I heard her say to Mr. Jones: "'Tis the best place for her—
the sun comes in all morning and there are the new chintz hangings to cheer her up. We cannot have her falling into another
melancholy."

Mr. Jones diagnosed my complaint as a nervous fever, for
which he prescribed his own special physic and a regimen of
rest. But after the first few days I was allowed visitors, and soon
it became a regular thing for me to receive them in the adjoining
sitting room. In this way, not only Maria Lucas and Cassandra
and Helen were accommodated, but George was also admitted
to my "salons" (as Elizabeth was wont to call them). Mama even
arranged for my pianoforte to be brought down so that we might
have music, and many agreeable hours were then spent listening
to George play his own compositions. (He was now writing an
opera about two orphaned sisters living in an English country
village, the elder a gifted artist, the younger a talented singer.
But any resemblance to the Long sisters was—he assured me—
entirely coincidental.)

Elizabeth was also very generous with her time—giving me
the latest news of the Collinses, as well as an edited version of
Jane's London doings. I heard how badly Caroline Bingley had
treated poor Jane—waiting a whole fortnight before returning
Jane's call, and then only sitting with her for a quarter of an hour
before hurrying away. "But we will not speak of it to Mama, if
you please, Mary."

Lydia and Kitty when they came talked chiefly of Mr.
Wickham's defection. Mary King's many imperfections were
dwelt on—her sandy hair and freckles and how she looked like a
coal sack in her new mourning clothes. Lydia declared her to be
quite the plainest girl in Meryton: "Harriet Forster says Wickham
does not care for her in the least. But Harriet says he has no

choice—he must marry money, poor fellow—only Mary King is such a stupid little fool, she thinks he likes her for herself."

I now feared that I had been equally credulous over Peter. I thought of him constantly. Occasionally, I even entertained the possibility that he had *not* left the assembly in order to avoid me. Cassandra certainly thought that he had not: "You are a great deal too apt to fancy the worst, my dear Mary. 'Tis much more likely that he wished to steer clear of Lady Stoke and her daughter."

Cassandra had lately adopted a rallying tone when talking to me that I did not at all care for. I believe she thought that my family was indulging me in my invalid regime, and there may have been—I am sure there were—conversations with Elizabeth about my earlier illness. Also, I worried that she felt obliged to sacrifice her precious painting time in order to visit me.

For this reason, I asked if an easel might be set up in the sitting room and for Cassandra to be furnished with a supply of artist's materials. Mama was happy to oblige and overrode Cassandra's objections, saying: "Oh! my dear—if it means you are able to spend more time with her, I am sure I do not grudge the expense."

Not every one of our salons was harmonious, however. The last such one ended most unhappily— an exchange having occurred very hurtful to my feelings. Helen was present and George had pressed her to sing a newly finished aria. She was in a wayward mood, however, wanting first to know why it was written in Italian.

"I know nothing of Italian. Why cannot Mary sing it?"

George gave me a quick look. "I do not think Mary is quite well enough yet." And on my assuring him that I was: "I think I should prefer Miss Helen to sing it."

Helen shrugged off the compliment. "Then someone must first tell me what it is I am to sing about."

I said: "The opera is about two sisters who live in an English country village—"

"Miss Helen does not need to know the *plot*, Mary." He turned back to Helen: "The song is the second of the sisters' duets—'O! mia bella sorella'—the elder is warning the younger not to trust men."

But Helen now wanted to know why, since it was an English village, the sisters were singing in Italian. And when George explained that operas were always written in Italian: "That's no reason! You had much better change it—change the whole thing to English so that everyone will understand."

And because George had hurt my feelings I took Helen's part, reminding him that *The Beggar's Opera* was written in English.

An argument followed with Helen telling George he must translate his opera forthwith and George refusing to consider it. His stiff-necked obstinacy reminded me of how he had behaved as a boy and, rather unwisely, I said as much. Whereupon he picked up his music and marched out of the room.

Cassandra had continued to paint throughout the quarrel, but after George left she remarked: "I shall probably paint over this canvas—but I should not like anybody telling me that I *must*. I imagine George feels pretty much the same."

13.

My sojourn in Jane's room lasted nearly three weeks, and I might
have prolonged it—I might have stayed there with Mama's goodwill until Jane returned—had not Cassandra given me a talking-
to: "What would your Mrs. Knowles say if she could see you
now? Lolling about like this. Why cannot you come downstairs?
You are no longer ill, are you?" And more gently: "My dear, if
you want to see Peter Bushell, you will have to *go out.* He cannot
call on you."

I made her no answer, averting my face, and after a moment
she went on: "I confess I am in no mood for painting this morning. I would much rather go for a walk—if you would care to
come with me." And upon Mama entering the room, she treach-
erously turned to her: "I am trying to persuade Mary to forsake
her sofa, Mrs. Bennet. It is such a fine morning, I think it would
do her good to take a turn in the garden."

Mama thought so too of course, and while I was cross with
Cassandra for adopting such tactics, I allowed her to help me on
with my boots.

We hardly talked at first—I was sulking, truth to tell—but
the mildness of the morning, the scent of spring in the air, soon
had its effect and I said: "I fear I have tried your patience lately,
Cassy."

"Not at all."

"You have been a very good friend to me."

"Well, I am sure you have been a very good friend to me. And to Helen. We are going to need good friends in the months ahead."

She then began to speak of their plans for Helen's lying-in in August: "We will need to leave Meryton long before of course— perhaps as early as next month. It all depends. Our uncle has been uncharacteristically generous, offering us accommodation in the meantime—a suite of rooms over a butcher-shop he owns in Islington—"

"A butcher-shop!"

Cassandra laughed at my horrified face, assuring me that she and Helen thought themselves extremely fortunate: "We have quite made up our minds to be as stoic as the sisters in George's opera—'twill be a case of life imitating art."

She talked on, determinedly cheerful, but I burst out: "Oh! listening to you, I feel so ashamed. I have thought of nobody but myself these past weeks—"

"Nonsense, Mary. You have not been well."

"—wasting my time feeling sorry for myself—"

"We are all—all of us—more or less selfish. I know I waste an unconscionable amount of time thinking about Mr. Bingley still." (catching my surprised look and coloring) "I no longer have such a high opinion of him, however—I do not think he has behaved well by your sister."

After a pause she went on: "Work is the answer, as I have said a thousand times. By the bye, you will be pleased to know that George is now hard at work translating his opera. Yesterday he sent round his aria and a note addressed to Helen: 'Herewith English translation, which I trust meets with your approval.'"

I took a moment to digest this. "Well, he has certainly not sent round anything for *my* approval."

Cassandra gave me one of her looks. "Jealous?"

"Helen has no knowledge of Italian that I am aware of."

"Ah, Mary." She drew my arm through hers. "He has asked Helen to sing at his concert, you know. But Aunt is not happy about her appearing in public. She wants Helen to leave Meryton as soon as may be."

"And you will go with her?"

"My dear, I must."

Next morning, I managed to bathe and dress in time to take my place at the breakfast table. My father and sisters were present, but not my mother, and the welcome I was accorded was a pretty tepid one. Elizabeth kissed me and set a chair for me but the post had come—she had received a letter from Jane—she knew I would excuse her if she read it right away.

My father congratulated me on coming downstairs but when I remarked that I felt rather like a caterpillar emerging from its cocoon, he said: "A butterfly, surely?" And then disconcerted me by saying: "But I approve of the metamorphosis. You have filled out. There is more of a bloom about you."

I was unsure if he were being sarcastic—It was the first personal compliment I could recall ever having received from him. He then asked after George: "But what has happened to young Mr. Rovere? He has not come to see you these past few days. You have not had a lovers' quarrel, I trust?"

This of course made Lydia and Kitty snigger. I said: "He is not my lover, sir, I do assure you."

"Indeed? I fear your mother will be disappointed to hear that."

To my relief he then turned his attention to Elizabeth, who was folding up her letter with a pleased expression. "Uncle Gardiner has taken a box at the theater for Wednesday night," said she. "We are to see *Macbeth*." And in answer to his look of frowning inquiry: "I leave for Kent on Wednesday, Papa. We are to spend the night in London en route—Maria Lucas, Sir William, and myself—do you not recall?"

"How long will you be gone?"

"About six weeks—but Sir William will only stay a sennight."

"Six weeks! You choose to spend six weeks with Mr. Collins!"

She was laughing, reaching for his hand. "I will write to you, I promise."

A low-toned conversation between the two of them followed, with my father saying he did not like her to be going away and almost promising to answer her letters.

14.

On the morning of Elizabeth's departure I walked into Meryton with Lydia and Kitty, and after parting from them at Aunt Philips's door I went to Clarke's. There, the first of the day's disappointments awaited me, for despite telling myself that there would be no message, still I had been hopeful, and when the clerk (he of the impudent face and red waistcoat) declared that there was nothing, I felt dreadfully let down.

I went to the Longs then, hoping for a tête-à-tête with Cassandra, only to be told by Betty that both sisters had gone out—she really couldn't say where—but that Miss Helen might possibly be with Mr. Rovere in the banqueting hall.

And so I walked across to the banqueting hall, where a workman let me in by a side door, and there I found Helen and George rehearsing with Letty Stoke. Helen and Letty were singing one of the newly translated sororal duets and George was accompanying them on the pianoforte. Nobody noticed me come in and I stood silently as Helen and Letty sang:

> *We must stem the tide of malice!*
> *Overturn the poisoned chalice!*
> *We must comfort our poor father and our mother,*
> *And pour into the wounded bosoms of each other*
> *The balm of consolation—a sisterly oblation.*

Listening, I found myself growing more and more indignant. Nobody had consulted me about translations or rehearsals. For the past four days George had not come near me. He had conducted the whole business furtively and I recalled how as a boy he had been equally sly—spying on Elizabeth and Mr. Coates and making sotto voce remarks.

He may have felt the force of my indignation, for he suddenly spun round, turning quite red at the sight of me and saying: "Good God, Mary, how you startled me!"

"*Chérie!* What brings you here?"

Helen tripped over to bestow a kiss on my cheek. She had a shawl around her and despite my angry concentration on George, I saw that her figure was looking fuller. I curtseyed to Letty, and would have taken my leave had not Helen detained me: "Were you looking for Cass? She has gone to the print-shop, I think."

George was making his way over. "Do you approve of the translation, Mary?"

My resentment then got the better of me: "Are you actually asking *my* opinion? Goodness. I suppose I ought to feel flattered."

"You don't like it?"

"I preferred the Italian version, if you must know. In English, it sounded rather mawkish."

"La!" Helen was laughing. "If you two are going to argue, I shall take myself off."

So saying, she went back to Letty, and the pair of them were soon warbling away sweetly in contrast to George's and my own discordant strains. I said: "I thought you valued my opinion, George." (I gestured towards the singers.) "I have heard nothing of this. Helen has been consulted, it seems, while I have been cast into outer darkness."

At first, he tried to conciliate me: "I have been remiss, I know—and I do value your opinion—" He threw up his hands and gave me a silly smile. "But when composing I forget all time. Who was it who said that, now? Was it Shakespeare?"

"No, it was Milton and you have misquoted—'tis from *Paradise Lost*—Eve says to Adam, "With thee *conversing*, I forget all time.""

"Of course, yes, I was sure that you would know. Dear me, without you to put us all right, where would we be?"

After that, the gloves were off. We might have been back in the Netherfield schoolroom trading insults, and presently I heard myself saying: "I wonder that anyone should be silly enough to hold a public concert in Meryton. You will be lucky if a dozen people come. And this old hall is not at all suitable for concerts. The workmen will never make anything of it."

"I will tell you something, Mary." George's face was now alight with malice. "Nobody has ever had the courage to tell you this—they were afraid you'd fall into a melancholy—but I think it's kinder to tell people the truth—"

He paused, looking at me. I said: "Go on then. Tell me."

Another pause—after which he spoke in a little rush: "The fact is, you can't sing. There. I've said it. One day you will thank me for it."

He did not wait for a response. He went straight back to Helen and Letty. For maybe a minute I just stood there, feeling extraordinarily calm. Everything around me seemed to be going on like clockwork with the workmen hammering and the voices singing. I walked out without saying good-bye.

15.

A truth that's told with bad intent
Beats all the lies you can invent.

I had written William Blake's words in the Commonplace Book long ago, and I now very much feared that George had indeed spoken the truth—with or without bad intent. I resolved to seek an opinion from someone whose musical judgment I trusted (but here the tears threatened because the first person to come to mind was Peter).

In the end I wrote to Mrs. Knowles, charging her as she loved me to tell me the truth:

You once told me that Our Lord in his wisdom had endowed me
with musical talent. Did you mean my singing as well as my play-
ing? If I cannot sing, I would rather know it. I will not conceal from
you that it is not only George Rovere who thinks I cannot. My father
also has a poor opinion of my voice . . .

It occurred to me then that I was harping on about myself—that Mrs. Knowles had herself been unhappy of late. Belatedly, I looked at her last letter:

I confess to you, my adopted daughter, that I have been grossly de-
ceived in the character of Colonel Pitt. He has accused me of lying
about my pecuniary circumstances to entrap him into wedlock.

There followed an account of the Colonel's cruelties—how he had hurled a Bible at her head and sworn at her old servant— and how her health had suffered as a consequence.

> *However, it is an ill wind that blows no good and my brother Galbraith and I are now reconciled. He and my boy are working to re- lease me—Colonel Pitt having agreed to sign Articles of Separation— and as soon as the lawyers have settled the business I shall return to Hertfordshire and make my home with my brother at Stoke Farm.*

The letter was dated the 27th of February—I had received it over three weeks ago, on the day of the assembly—and it had remained unanswered, shut up in my writing box ever since. I hastily rewrote my own letter and sent it to the post.

I tried then to put the matter out of my mind, but when Helen came for the Friday singing class—the first I had attended since my illness—she insisted on talking of George: "I am afraid he will never take back what he said to you—about your singing. But I know he admires your playing."

"I am not interested in George's opinion—about anything."

"Do not choke yourself on your pride, *chérie*. I know he wants you to accompany Letty and me at the concert. Will you?"

"Play at a public concert? No, I thank you."

"If Letty Stoke can perform in public, why not Mary Bennet?" She came to sit beside me. "George is very attached to you, you know. He has told me what good friends you used to be. And he is a good man, do you not think? He would make someone a good husband." And when I did not reply: "Oh Lord! Cannot you guess why I am here?"

"For your singing lesson, I collect."

"He has asked me to marry him, Mary." (speaking quick) "I know he is under-age—I know that—but he says there will be no difficulty in obtaining Mr. Purvis's consent. But I want your advice—you have known him for so long—would he forgive me? If he were to find out afterwards? Would he understand?"

And when I continued to sit speechless: "I have not dared tell Cass—she would never countenance it. But I am not like Cass! I am weak and frivolous and the thought of having to live over a butcher-shop—"

"You would never marry him without telling him, Helen!"

"Oh God!" She jumped up. "How can you be so naïve?"

I let this pass. "Have you told Mrs. Long?"

"Aunt has been wanting me to set my cap at him for weeks. She has become quite desperate—she is terrified people will guess."

"So you have not told her?"

"I need first to make up my own mind."

She was now pacing up and down, and again I noticed how her figure had thickened. I said: "Well, if it were anything else— any other sort of misconduct—I daresay he would forgive you, but not this." I hesitated. "I know that he judges his mother—for being unchaste."

She was looking at me through narrowed eyes. "Is this a fling at me, Mary? Because I assure you that apart from Wickham I have never—"

"It is not a fling at you. I am going to tell you something in confidence. Some of it relates to my own family so I rely on your discretion."

I then told her what had happened at Netherfield six and a half years ago.

She was, I think, shocked, although affecting not to be. "A ménage à trois! Lord! and with her own mother! 'Tis better than a French farce. And this man—this Mr. Coates—you say he was also making up to Elizabeth? But she would have been—what?—thirteen at the time? Fourteen? My God."

Mr. Turner came in then and we were obliged to concentrate on our singing, Helen so unsuccessfully that Mr. Turner reproved her: "If it were someone else, Miss Long—someone without your God-given gift—I should not mind."

As soon as the lesson ended Helen was impatient to be off, gathering up her music and refusing to stay for dinner. Already she seemed resentful: "It would just make everything so much easier."

I must have glanced at her waistline then for she laughed and said: "Cass was certainly right about you. She said she can always tell what you are thinking no matter how many wise opinions you may quote."

I did not like this reflection. "You asked me for my advice, Helen."

"Would *you* care to live over a butcher-shop?" And before I could answer: "You have never been poor, Mary, not poor like Cass and me. We were a pair of shabby little orphans when Aunt took us in. I swore I would never live like that again if I could help it."

But on the point of leaving she suddenly stopped, exclaiming: "I knew there was something I had to tell you. Letty Stoke told us yesterday that Peter Bushell had been shot."

"*What!*"

It was as if I had been shot myself—I was quite beside myself, clutching at her. She was laughing now. "He is perfectly all right, I swear. Only it is all rather a rigmarole—and when Letty was telling us I did not at first realize it was Bushell—she kept saying 'our keeper,' 'our gamekeeper'—Letty is like that—everything is either 'ours' or 'mine'—"

"Oh please. Just tell me what happened. Please."

"Well, and so I will if you will let go my arm. There. I did not mean to frighten you—Bushell is all in one piece, I swear."

After a couple more gibes at Letty's feudal possessiveness she then told me that Peter had accompanied Sir John into Norfolk—the Stokes having an estate there—and that while out after rabbits, Sir John's young nephew had accidentally shot Peter in the arm: "Nothing serious but the wound became infected—"

"Which arm was it? Was it his right arm?"

She was laughing again. "I have no idea, but he is perfectly all right now. Sir John called in a physician from Cromer—'our physician'—and he soon set things to right. But Letty did say that at first her father was quite concerned."

16.

And so I dared to hope again (not that I had ever really left off), and again took to haunting Clarke's. I even agreed to accompany Helen and Letty when they rehearsed their duets in the hope of hearing Letty speak of him.

Fortunately for my sanity, there were other distractions. Sir William Lucas returned from his week in Kent to boast of the grandeur of Rosings and of Lady Catherine de Bourgh's gracious hospitality. Letters also arrived from Maria Lucas and Elizabeth, and Maria's letter mentioned (as Elizabeth's did not) that Mr. Darcy was expected at Rosings the following week:

> You may be sure I shall be on the watch for developments. (This last being heavily underlined.)

Lydia and Kitty brought fresh news of Wickham. They told how Mary King's uncle from Liverpool was coming to look him over and how nervous poor Wickham was at the prospect.

I also received a letter from Mrs. Knowles, replying to my own letter in a strangely evasive manner:

> While I know enough about music to confidently pronounce on your playing (which is positively inspired), I doubt whether I am a fit person to judge your singing. I suggest you apply to the Bath Harmonic Society for their opinion . . .

I read no further. I felt she had failed me in an important test of friendship—I had asked her to be honest with me and she had equivocated. (Alas, in putting aside her letter I did not discover that she had also invited me to spend the Easter holiday at her brother Galbraith's farm—which farm was the home-farm of the Great House of Stoke and a mere hop, step, and jump therefore from Peter.)

The concert was set down for the Tuesday before Easter, and Helen held fast to her intention to stay for it. Of her intentions regarding George, however, I heard nothing more and could surmise nothing from her manner towards him. George's manner towards her was not at all lover-like either—at least not in my presence. He was obsessed with his concert. He had earlier announced that his mother would be coming, speaking of her in the most unfilial fashion: "I would far rather she stayed in London. Poor old Purvis will run round trying to please her—a futile exercise—and we will all be made miserable." And then as if it were all my fault: "But I have to tell you, Mary, that she is most eager to see you again."

"And I shall be happy to renew the acquaintance."

George and I were now careful to be civil to each other but I was no longer easy with him. He had disabused me of a long-cherished illusion and perhaps one day I would thank him for it, but not yet.

I had been invited to take a bed at the Longs' house on the night of the concert, and on the afternoon of that day Betty let me in with a warning that her mistress was in a rare taking. She directed me to Cassandra's bedchamber, where lay Mrs. Long, clutching her smelling-salts.

Cassandra was packing a trunk, pausing in her labors to

greet me, whereupon Mrs. Long cried out: "Not a word of this to your mother, Mary! And if she asks where the girls have gone, you must tell her they have gone to Cornwall—to their cousins in Cornwall."

Cassandra said: "We leave for Islington tomorrow morning, Mary."

Mrs. Long burst out again: "I do not deserve this! To be woken at four in the morning and told that she had made up her mind to refuse him—that her conscience had spoken—"

"George has made Helen an offer, Mary—"

"The answer to all our prayers! And now she means to refuse him. She has made up her mind and will not listen to a word I say. 'My conscience has spoken'—that is what she tells me at four o'clock in the morning."

Helen entered in time to hear her. "Poor Aunt. I am a sad trial to you, I know."

I saw that she was already dressed in her costume for the concert—a round gown of brown cambric in keeping with her village-maiden persona. George had commissioned Madame Bejart to make it weeks ago and now of course it was too tight.

Mrs. Long must have noticed this too, for she said: "Are you wearing your corset?"

"Yes, I am wearing my corset." (The corset was a kind of under-waistcoat drawn tight about her stomach and with a lace behind. Helen had only consented to wear it to placate her aunt.)

"I do not deserve this."

"Well, you won't have to put up with me much longer, Aunt. I shall be gone in the morning." She turned to me then and handed me a sealed letter directed to George care of Purvis Lodge. "You must post this to him tomorrow, Mary, after we're gone. I simply have not the courage to tell him to his face."

Much to my dismay, Mrs. Long began then to cry. Cassandra went to her and after a moment so too did Helen, saying: "Dear Aunt, I cannot accept him. My conscience has spoken." And then in an aside meant only for her sister's ears: "Damn it."

17.

Contrary to my spiteful prediction to George, there was a large audience for the concert. But if Mrs. Long had attended instead of taking to her bed, she would have been relieved at the lack of interest shown in her niece. Neither Helen's figure nor her singing was remarked; everyone was too taken up with Christina Purvis. There was a collective drawing-back when she entered the banqueting hall—a "parting of the Red Sea" as it was afterwards described (there being a number of officers present)—and Mr. Purvis had followed in his wife's wake, bowing to left and right and delighting in all the attention.

Thereafter, the two of them contrived to be a cynosure. It helped that they were seated beneath a great chandelier, the candles of which lit up Mrs. Purvis's jewels (notably a diamond tiara in a design of ivy-leaves all set *en tremblant,* which sparkled whenever she turned her head). And when it might have been supposed that people had grown tired of staring, the Purvises obligingly staged a whispered quarrel—this during the "Tide of Malice" duet.

They approached me directly the concert was over, Mrs. Purvis asking with uncharacteristic hesitation if I "remembered" her.

Purvis fatuously exclaimed: "How could she *not* remember you?"

Her old impatience showed itself: "Oh go away, Frederick. Cannot you see I wish to talk to Mary?"

She then complimented me on my playing before finding fault with George's compositions: "But of course I am no music lover—as you no doubt recall." And here there was a sort of conspiratorial smile, an acknowledgment perhaps that she had not forgotten bringing down the pianoforte lid upon my hand.

"But let me look at you, Mary. Come into the light now so that I can see." She led me to beneath the chandelier. "Upon my word, I never thought you would grow to be so pretty. Of course you will never be a *toast*, as they say—" (And here again the conspiratorial gleam, confident that she herself was such a one.) "But all things considered you have turned out remarkably well. 'Tis a thousand pities you have to wear spectacles though."

At that point, several people came up—ostensibly to talk to me but really to get a closer look at Mrs. Purvis. Wickham was one of them, ogling her even while he was complimenting me on my playing. But Chamberlayne at least had eyes only for me: "I had hoped to hear *you* sing, Miss Mary."

Mrs. Purvis then drew me aside, saying that she had a thousand questions to ask of me. I soon realized though that she wanted only to ask about Helen. "Pray, what sort of a girl is she? Purvis tells me that you are friendly with her family. Do they have any money?"

I recalled this was what I had most disliked about her—her mercenariness. "Not very much, no."

Coincidentally, she now recalled something she had not liked about me. "Those dark, judgmental eyes!—how could I forget?—you and your sister Elizabeth—is she here tonight?"

"No, she is in Kent." And fearing I sounded a trifle curt: "Both my elder sisters are presently from home. Jane has been in London these past three months."

But she was not interested in Jane: "Elizabeth Bennet. What a sad tangle that was, to be sure. Poor Jasper. He was

270

quite smitten with her, you know. And I behaved very badly—all things considered—very badly indeed. But—" (recollecting herself) "I would not have married Purvis otherwise so perhaps it was all for the best. And now you are giving me that look again!"

"No indeed, I assure you—"

"Never mind, never mind. But this girl—this Helen—according to Purvis, George is quite desperately in love with her." She paused, perhaps waiting for me to speak, and when I did not: "This is all 'according to Purvis'—George never tells me anything."

It seemed safe to say: "I believe he does care for Helen, yes."

"Oh! you must not fear my making mischief. Young people are forever fancying themselves in love—I am sure there is some young man of whom you dream, hey, hey?" (laughing) "But George is *very* young and I do not want him to be taken in. Has he made her an offer, do you know?"

"I—yes, I believe so." And seeing her expression change: "But she—Helen has not accepted him."

The face beneath the diamonds had now set hard. "He is under-age, you know."

"I know that, ma'am."

"Oh! you need not think I will forbid the banns—George will have his own way, he always does. But he is an exceptionally gifted boy and I confess I had hoped for something better."

"Is that all you wished to say to me, ma'am?"

She now smiled her unsatisfactory smile. "I perceive I am getting 'that look' again. When you are a mother, you will understand. Are your parents here tonight, by the bye?" And upon my saying that they were not: "I fancy your father was always more my enemy than your mama. And your younger sisters? I fear I have forgotten their names."

"Catherine and Lydia. They are here with my aunt Philips."

"Lydia! The naughty one. I feel sure she is still very naughty. Like my Sam—he is always getting into scrapes."

Mr. Purvis interrupted us then, and I was not sorry. I went to join George and Helen and Letty Stoke on the stage of the hall where they were still receiving tributes—bouquets of flowers and, in George's case, a brace of snipe presented by one of the officers.

And now at last I heard Letty speak of Peter. She questioned the officer about bagging the snipes out of season, saying: "Our keeper thinks it is not sporting to shoot birds on the ground—he says you should only ever shoot 'em flying."

Whereupon Helen asked the question I so wanted to ask myself: "Is this the same keeper who was lately shot at? How does he go on?"

"Oh, pretty well. Considering."

"Considering what?"

I spoke the words—blurted them—and Letty gave me a look. "Considering he refuses to take our apothecary's drugs and has not rested the arm as he should. But 'tis useless lecturing him—he always likes to go his own way to work."

Thinking about this afterwards kept me awake for hours. Neither Cassandra nor Helen were able to reassure me. Helen only laughed at the idea of Peter having nobody to look after him—to make him take his medicine—and Cassandra was far too busy for late-night confidences.

18.

Helen and Cassandra left for London on the mail coach early next morning, and Mrs. Long fretted after they were gone, seeking assurances that nobody last night had noticed Helen's figure and that nobody would now wonder at her sudden departure. In the end, I resorted to the Commonplace Book: "Foolish tongues will always wag, ma'am, but people of goodwill ignore them."

She was not so easily comforted, however. A talker herself, she may have doubted the truth of the assertion—she certainly doubted my mother's goodwill, confiding that she had chosen Cornwall precisely because my mother knew nothing of that county and had no acquaintance there.

Luckily for Mrs. Long, my mother at this time was preoccupied with her own girls—principally with our failure to find husbands. She now despaired of Jane's ever getting Mr. Bingley and considered Elizabeth to be wasting her time in Kent: "All this visiting at Rosings sounds like very dull work to me with only Lady Catherine and her daughter for company. She had much better have stayed in Meryton and met with more of the officers. Wickham is now taken to be sure, but there are plenty of other fish in the sea."

My mother had felt Wickham's defection almost as keenly as had Lydia and Kitty, and so when she heard that his engagement to Mary King was at an end she was just as overjoyed.

Lydia and Kitty brought the glad tidings to Longbourn on Easter-day. They had called on Mrs. Forster after church and she had told them that Mary King's uncle had forbidden the match.

"Apparently he believes poor Wickham to be a fortune-hunter," said Lydia.

Said Kitty: "Lizzy will be pleased."

This sparked a quarrel, with Lydia disputing Elizabeth's claim to Wickham, whereupon I quitted the room. I was finding it increasingly hard to tolerate my youngest sister. In the absence of Jane and Elizabeth, she had become even more unruly. But I was at fault too. I was feeling lonely and irritable. I feared I would never see Peter again—that he had never really cared about me—yet still I could not stop thinking about him. I worried about his arm. Chamberlayne had told me of a fellow officer whose arm had been shot and how the physician had had to work to save it, applying flannels and fomentations, and finally, leeches. It had been a very close-run thing, Chamberlayne said.

In my loneliness, I bethought myself of Mrs. Knowles. She had not been candid about my singing but she had proved herself a true friend at the time of my melancholia and did not deserve to be slighted now. I took out her last letter and this time read it in its entirety—including the invitation to stay at Stoke Farm:

Should you like to come to me here at Easter, my dear? My boy is to pay us a visit with his bride and you would be a most welcome addition to our family party . . .

I was very distressed. Not only had I missed the chance to see Mr. Knowles, but also, possibly, Peter. And I was angry with myself for neglecting Mrs. Knowles. I wrote her a full explanation and an apology—and began then to count the days after which I could reasonably expect a reply.

And now suddenly it seemed that everyone I knew was writing to me—everyone except Mrs. Knowles. Cassandra and Helen wrote from Islington, Jane and Aunt Gardiner from Cheapside (in the absence of Elizabeth, Jane and Aunt always wrote to me because I was the only Bennet to write back), and Elizabeth and Maria Lucas from Kent. I also received a letter from the Secretary of the Bath Harmonic Society who—in response to a letter from Mrs. Knowles—had written to praise my "prodigious knowledge of vocal art and great industry." (I was not taken in by this for a moment.)

The only letter to contain any surprising news was Maria Lucas's; it was full of what she called "interesting developments" and was in two parts. The first, dated Easter-day, read as follows:

At last, dear Mary, there have been some interesting developments! Lady Catherine's other nephew, Colonel Fitzwilliam, is also staying at Rosings and has taken a great fancy to Lizzy. When we went there this evening to drink tea, he and Lizzy talked and laughed together like anything. (You would have enjoyed their conversation, dear, but I fear it was too clever for me.) Anyway, I could see Mr. Darcy did not like it that his cousin and Lizzy were so talkative and merry. He kept looking at them and not listening to Lady Catherine, and in the end Lady C. ordered Colonel F. to tell her what he and Lizzy were talking of because she wanted to have her share in the conversation too. I was so frightened for I could see poor Charlotte was worried lest Lizzy say something impertinent. However, it all passed off and then Colonel F. again got Lizzy to himself by persuading her to play for him.

And this time Mr. Darcy really *did not like it because Colonel F. was leaning over Lizzy and turning the pages for her. And so then in the middle of Lady Catherine telling us the proper way to launder lace (it must* always *be washed in milk, dear, did you know?), Mr. Darcy got up and walked over to the pianoforte and just stood there and* stared *at Lizzy. After a minute she stopped playing, and then the three of them—Mr. D., the Colonel, and Lizzy—started talking but they were too far away for me to hear, and as soon as Lady C. called out to know what they were saying, Lizzy started playing again.*

My dear, I must conclude; it grows late and Mr. Collins has just now knocked on my door to remind me to be saving of candles.

Yr affectionate friend, Maria

The second part of the letter was dated the following day:

I had meant to post this when I went with Charlotte to the village this morning, but unluckily forgot to take it with me and I am glad now that I did, for there have been more interesting developments! Who do you think Charlotte and I surprised in a tête-à-tête with Lizzy just now when we came back from our walk? None other than Mr. D.! Charlotte afterwards told Lizzy that she thought he must be in love with her to call in such a familiar way, but Lizzy only laughed. (Charlotte thinks it would be wonderful if Lizzy were to secure Mr. D., as he has extensive patronage in the church.)

M.L.

19.

About a fortnight later, I finally heard from Mrs. Knowles:

> *I confess to feeling disappointed, dear Mary, for I never could have put away one of your letters unread. My brother and my boy were disappointed too—my boy especially...*

The letter continued in this vein; I felt wretched reading it. And she did not renew her invitation to visit Stoke Farm, although the conclusion was kind enough:

> *I note that your friend Cassandra has left Meryton and will be absent for several months. You must keep to your timetable of early rising and not neglect your prayers or your practice.*

A few days later I received a second letter from Maria Lucas. Again, it was in two parts, the first of which was dated merely "Friday":

> *Dearest Mary, there have been the most dramatic developments—a proposal, no less! Mr. D. called here yesterday evening when Lizzy was all alone. I heard about it from Hannah, the housemaid who opened the door to him. Hannah feared she had done wrong in ad-mitting him——*(Here, the pen had spluttered and the rest of the letter was written in a different-colored ink.) *Pray excuse the*

change of ink, but I thought it best to write this in my bedchamber. I will start at the beginning. Yesterday evening just as we were about to set out for Rosings to drink tea, Lizzy begged to be excused, saying she had a headache. And when we arrived at Rosings without her you should have seen Mr. D.'s face! He was standing by the fire and frowning so, he looked like Lucifer. As soon as tea was over he said he had some "pressing business" to attend to—which pressing business consisted of going to call on Lizzy.

Anyway, Hannah as I told you opened the door to him but afterwards she wondered whether she should have for she heard them having a dreadful argument and Lizzy saying that she would never ever have accepted Mr. D. even if he had behaved towards her in a "more gentlemanlike manner"! (Hannah thought he might have tried to force himself upon her! Can you imagine?) Hannah said he left the house soon afterwards—he let himself out—and a few minutes later she spied him through the window of Mr. Collins's bookroom, striding down the lane looking like a mad man.

So there you have it, my dear! Can you believe it? He has proposed but Lizzy has rejected him. And he is leaving Rosings tomorrow—he and Colonel Fitzwilliam both—so there is little chance of his renewing his offer.

The second part of the letter was dated "Monday" and written in the same violet ink:

Oh Mary, I do so wish you were here so we could talk. Mr. Collins has lectured me about gossiping with Hannah, but I am often lonely here at Hunsford. Charlotte has her housekeeping and her hens and when she and Lizzy are talking together, they do not want a third. Anyway, I have now done something much worse than gossiping with Hannah, for Lizzy has been carrying around this great thick letter for the past three days—taking it with her everywhere, and this morning my curiosity finally got the better of me. Lizzy had shut up the letter in a book, you see, and so when she stepped out of the room I opened up the book—just to see who the letter was from, you understand, and of course it was from Mr. D. (his first name is Fitzwilliam, did you know?) Only it was not a love letter—it seemed to be all about Mr. Wickham. But I did not really read it, I promise you. Do you think it was very bad of me to look at it? I do so wish you were here so we could talk.

20.

I was very happy to see my elder sisters when they first came home but the old jealousies soon made themselves felt. Jane had been absent for over four months and my mother now hung about her, exulting that the Cheapside air had not injured her looks and eager for news of the London fashions. My father kept saying to Elizabeth during dinner: "I am glad you are come back, Lizzy."

The Lucases all came to Longbourn to meet Maria and it was impossible amid their competing claims to have private speech with her, and then I had to endure Lydia's boasting of how she and Kitty had gone to meet the coach: "Oh! Mary," (bouncing about on her chair) "I wish you had gone with us, for we had such fun! As we went along, Kitty and me drew up all the blinds, and pretended there was nobody in the coach . . ."

When she at last paused for breath, I gave her a sarcastic answer—of which I am sure she heard not one word: "Far be it from me, my dear sister, to depreciate such pleasures. They would doubtless be congenial with the generality of female minds. But I confess they would have no charms for *me*. I should infinitely prefer a book."

The truth was that I was furious with Lydia. She had deliberately humiliated Chamberlayne—made him dress up in woman's clothes on purpose to trick Wickham. Chamberlayne had confessed it all to me the day before: "But what was I to do, Miss

Mary? Your sister is so very determined. And she had borrowed one of your aunt Philips's gowns—pink satin it was and with a trim of pointed lace—only I did not at all want to put it on, I assure you, except your sister was pulling me about so, laughing and persuading me to take off my coat—and so one thing led to another—you know how it is."

I had been more shocked by Lydia's disregard for Chamberlayne's feelings than by her lack of propriety—the incident was typical of the sort of vulgar romping she delighted in—but I very much wished for Cassandra to confide in. I was missing both her and Helen dreadfully.

And George was now plaguing me for Helen's direction in Cornwall. I had begun to dread his visits and had taken to telling the servants to say I was not at home. On the morning after my sisters' return I went outside and hid in the shrubbery for precisely that reason.

It was there that I overheard a conversation between Jane and Elizabeth. They were walking together and Elizabeth was saying: "There is one point on which I want your advice. I want to be told whether I ought, or ought not, to make our acquaintance in general understand Wickham's character."

I sat, hardly daring to breathe, before Jane replied: "Surely there can be no occasion for exposing him so dreadfully. What is your own opinion?"

"That it ought not to be attempted."

They were moving off, and I could catch no more than: "Mr. Darcy has not authorized me to make his communication public. On the contrary."

I was quite bewildered by this exchange. If Mr. Darcy had finally convinced Elizabeth that Wickham was a scoundrel, why should she not now speak out? Why should she not warn people what Wickham was really like? *I had not been in any position to* expose him—without exposing Helen—but why should *she* hesitate? I could not understand it.

And even though I knew she had acquired the knowledge dishonestly, I determined to ask Maria Lucas what she could recall of Mr. Darcy's letter. To that end, I called at Lucas Lodge after breakfast the following day. (My motive was twofold—I hoped thereby to avoid George.)

Maria, however, could recollect very little of the letter: "I remember it began, 'Be not alarmed, madam,' I remember that perfectly. But I really only looked at the *end* of it you know, just to see who it was from. It seemed to be all about Mr. Wickham—about his misconduct."

"What sort of misconduct?"

"I really cannot remember, Mary. Why do you not ask Lizzy?"

Maria now wanted to talk only of Brighton—of the regiment's imminent move to Brighton. "They are leaving in two weeks, did you know? Lydia and Kitty are wild to go too."

I perceived that just as Maria had been infected by the fever surrounding Mr. Bingley's arrival, so now she had been led to mourn the regiment's departure. She accompanied me back to Longbourn, there to lament with Lydia and Kitty, who themselves could only exclaim: "What is to become of us? What are we to do when they are all gone to Brighton? It will be the most miserable summer."

This weeping and wailing had gone on for days when an invitation came from Mrs. Forster asking Lydia—and only Lydia—to accompany herself and the Colonel to Brighton.

Lydia was of course ecstatic and poor Kitty inconsolable. Jane and Elizabeth tried to reason with her and I reminded her to be grateful for what she had rather than what she wanted.

"I want to go to Brighton!"

"I meant *want* as in *lack*, Kitty."

"I *want* to go to Brighton!"

But I am bound to say that Lydia's leaving Longbourn was a blessing. It was as if a great weed had been uprooted, letting in light upon the rest of us, especially upon Kitty. There had been tears at first of course and Lydia's early letters had stirred up envy—nevertheless within a couple of weeks Kitty was much more resigned and rational. Her appearance improved too—or rather, her expression, for Kitty was pretty enough, being a sort of watery version of Jane, with the same blue Gardiner eyes and regular features (only with not nearly so good a figure).

Elizabeth was now especially kind to Kitty, anxious to include her in our music classes and taking the trouble to talk to her and walk with her into Meryton (although Meryton minus officers held few attractions for poor Kitty). Elizabeth was also kinder to me, deflecting many of our father's shafts. Indeed, she seemed intent on appraising her whole family afresh—examining us all through new glasses, as it were. Certainly she looked to be less flattered by our father's favoritism.

Happily, this enlightened period lasted through May and into the beginning of June, with even Mama regaining her usual brittle good humor. However, as the weeks went by I found myself becoming increasingly restless. I had been leading a disciplined life—rising early and keeping myself occupied—but three quite separate incidents had shaken me, although later I perceived a common thread. In each case strong feeling had broken through a polite façade.

21.

The first of these was a proposal of marriage. Chamberlayne wrote to me a fortnight after the regiment left, offering me his hand. His letter shocked me—its passionate language; he wrote at length, quoting Burns:

> *O Mary, canst thou wreck his peace Who for thy sake would gladly die? Or canst thou break that heart of his, Whose only fault is loving thee?*

I saw that I had been deceived by his gentle manner into thinking Chamberlayne girlish, even characterless, and now the account of his sufferings (for he had long tried to master his feelings) moved me almost to tears.

I refused him of course, but I did not confide his proposal to a single soul, and fortunately my mother had not the least suspicion of it. She believed still that George was trying to fix his interest with me.

The second incident concerned George. One of the maidservants confessed that George had asked her to extract from the Longbourn post-bag (which bag was held in my father's library but never locked) any letters addressed to either Cassandra or Helen. He had offered Sarah a crown for any letter she so intercepted.

The fact that there had been no such letters (I always took them to the post myself) did not make me any less angry. When I confronted George with it, he was unrepentant. "I merely wished to sight the direction—I told Sarah as much."

"To bribe a servant, George! 'Tis unforgivable."

"You have obviously never been in love, else you would understand."

"How do you know I have never been in love?"

"Why cannot you tell me where they've gone?"

"I *have* told you! They have gone to their cousins in Cornwall—"

"Yes, but where exactly? Why is it such a damned secret?" And for the first time pleading with me: "If you will not tell me where they have gone, cannot you at least send her my letter? I would do as much for you." (extracting a letter from his coat pocket as he spoke) "Just hear me out, Mary. I'm not one of those fellows who make a habit of falling in love. I saw too much of that kind of thing growing up—men making fools of themselves—you know what I'm talking about. I'm not like that."

And perceiving he was beginning to sway me: "One letter, Mary. That is all I ask. And then I won't bother you again, I swear."

I had taken the letter—at the time it seemed easier—but I did not send it.

The third incident was more disturbing. One afternoon when our parents and elder sisters had gone to dine at the Gouldings', Kitty asked me to hear her play an air on her new double-action harp. (Our father had bought the harp at Elizabeth's urging to help keep Kitty's mind off Brighton.) I did not immediately comply—I was busy with my own music—and when I later looked for her in her own apartment, I found her engrossed in a pamphlet.

"Do you still wish me to hear you play, Kitty?"

"Oh! I do. Yes." She hurriedly put up the pamphlet. "Thank you."

And when I asked her what she was reading: "Oh! 'tis just something Wickham gave Lydia. If I were to show you, you must promise not to tell."

I duly promised, whereupon she handed me the pamphlet. It was a report of a recent "criminal conversation" case, complete with salacious details of the wife's adultery. I read it in silence, and Kitty meanwhile went to Lydia's closet and collected more pamphlets. As soon as I finished one, she handed me another. I went on reading the things and Kitty joined me before I came to my senses: "Kitty, these are really—they are quite shocking."

"Yes," (without lifting her eyes from the page) "shocking."

"We must burn them, Kitty."

"Oh! yes, we must."

We took them down to the kitchen then and burnt them, but the memory of them was not so easily destroyed. For days I was troubled with lewd images of servants spying through key-holes on copulating couples with one adulterous wife witnessed in her dressing-gown "riding" upon her lover's lap, and another half-naked under a dining table with her lover (who was also her footman) atop her. One couple was even seen having "criminal conversation" in a chaise: they had been followed by the wife's groom into an alley on the outskirts of London where, such was the vigor of their love-making, the back of the chaise collapsed so that the groom was able to see inside.

I realize now that I must have been as much stirred as re-pelled by the images, for I kept thinking of one couple in particular—the lady was a duchess and her lover a young farmer—who had committed adultery in a turnip field in broad daylight. But at the time I was so afraid I had been corrupted

that I wrote to Cassandra for reassurance. She wrote back directly (Cassandra was an excellent correspondent) reminding me that I had grown up in the country and must surely have seen the congress of animals:

> *If I understand you correctly, it is not so much the sin of adultery that disturbs you as the idea of such intercourse. But do you not remember once reading to me a passage from Miss Wollstonecraft's Vindication?—about how children should always be told the truth about such matters? Did not you copy it into your Commonplace Book? Knowledge cannot of itself corrupt, Mary—and pray do not write to me about Adam and Eve now! I have never understood why God should have forbidden them to eat from the tree of knowledge in the first place.*

There was a postscript:

> *If you are still anxious, speak to Jane. She will give you good advice and help you to feel comfortable again.*

I could not have confided in Jane, however. Since her return from London she had become far less approachable—fenced off by Elizabeth—so that I felt shy with her. There was still the same sweet smile for me of course but behind it I sensed an absence of mind, a sadness even. I could never have gone to her with my troubles.

But we were all more or less struggling now to keep up our spirits. Of the four of us, only Elizabeth had something to look forward to: She was to tour the Lakes with the Gardiners at the end of June and was now deep in Gilpin and Wordsworth's recently published *Guide to the Lakes*.

A few days after I received Cassandra's letter, however, Elizabeth had disappointing news: Mr. Gardiner's business would not now permit his leaving London until July—there would not therefore be time enough for them to visit the Lakes—they would have to confine their tour to Derbyshire.

Elizabeth read out this part of the letter at the breakfast table where sat Jane, Kitty, Maria Lucas, and myself, and Maria at once exclaimed: "Derbyshire! Mr. Darcy is from Derbyshire, is he not?"

Elizabeth made her no answer, seemingly intent on her letter, and Maria then kicked me under the table. But I scarcely felt it, for I too had received a letter. It was from Mrs. Knowles and I had but just realized it contained an invitation to stay at Stoke Farm:

> We should be happy for you to spend a fortnight with us from the 26th of July, my dear Mary. My brother will have a little leisure then between the hay and corn harvests. But please answer this promptly, dear, and take care to address me by my former name and to direct your letter care of my brother Galbraith.

Part Four

1.

It was not until the second week in July that Elizabeth and the Gardiners finally left on their Derbyshire tour. I set off for Stoke Farm a week later.

My feelings on that nine-mile journey changed by the minute, but any excitement—pleasurable excitement—was soon overlaid with doubt, and the closer I came to Stoke Farm, the stronger the doubt. I had not seen Peter now for eight months—not since the Netherfield ball (I did not count the assembly in February)—and apart from the note he had left for me at Clarke's, he had made no inquiries after me, had sent no other message. I blushed to recall the letter I had signed "Your friend, Mary"—the letter in which I had so kindly corrected his spelling mistakes. The thought of it still made me feel ill. I told myself he could not possibly care about me. I had not the slightest hope.

The carriage was now passing through the village of Stoke but there was still half a mile to the farmhouse. I had passed by it often on the way to the Great House and knew it for a tidy, old red-brick place with a mossed-over roof and tall chimneys. I told myself that I would be content to live there very quietly for the next two weeks with only Mrs. Knowles and her brother for company. I told myself that I did not care whether I saw Peter or not. I told myself that several times.

The house had no carriage approach. A high hornbeam hedge screened the front garden from the road, and we entered by the back way. Mrs. Knowles greeted me affectionately, declaring she had never seen me look so well: "You must have grown a whole two inches in the past eighteen months. Either that or I have shrunk—which is quite possible given all that has happened. But I have made a vow not to talk of Pitt—I have nobody but myself to blame, after all."

She led me into the brick-floored kitchen and thence on upstairs to the room I was to occupy. I saw that she was not so straight-backed as before and had lost weight so that her gown rather hung upon her. This, and the great bunch of keys she wore about her waist, made me feel she had become something of a stranger. But she threw open the door to the bedroom with her old theatrical aplomb, saying: "Observe that the window faces east—no excuse for your ladyship to lie abed late! And there is an old dunghill cock down in the yard. I defy anybody to sleep through his crowing."

It was a pretty, albeit rustic room with whitewashed walls and a ceiling of exposed beams. I recognized the patchwork quilt from my old bedchamber in Bath. Mrs. Knowles showed me the spacious closet and the night-table with its cunningly hidden convenience. She then went to the window to point out the picturesque view: "But you cannot see the Great House from here, merely the beginning of the avenue leading to it, and the lodge that is now the keeper's cottage . . ."

The keeper's cottage! I strained to see the place more clearly: It was a single-storied little stone house with casement windows and a thatched roof on which was perched a turreted look-out. I wondered if Peter could possibly live there—if anybody could live there—it looked like a fairy-tale house. And now Mrs. Knowles was describing the inhabitants: "A family by the name of Bushell. The mother is rather a poor honey, but the son and daughter are very obliging and hard-working. The son and my brother are great friends—whenever Galbraith goes rat-hunting in his barn, Peter is always happy to help."

I had it at my tongue's end to tell her that I knew the Bushell family—that they had once lived in Longbourn village and that Mrs. Bushell had been my nurse—but Mrs. Knowles was now talking about the Stoke family: "Lady Stoke is a very kind neighbor—she sent me a receipt for a bread poultice for my rheumatism. But we do not mix with many families hereabouts. Galbraith is—" She lowered her voice. "Truth to tell, Mary, music is about the only way to lure my brother out—last week he went with me to the Great House to hear Miss Letty Stoke sing. She has a lovely voice, Letty—"

Here she paused, possibly recollecting that she had declined to give an opinion on my own voice. It was only a momentary check, however, and soon smoothed over: "I have hopes of forming a little musical society here with Letty—something similar to our old group in Bath. But pray do not think I wish myself back in Bath—rural life suits me very well."

We then went down to the kitchen where the young cook, Sylvia, was busy making apricot jam and seemingly in need of close supervision. All Mrs. Knowles's attention now went to the pot bubbling on the stove—she wanted to know when the jam was going to set—whether Sylvia had put in *all* the apricot-stones. I had to remind myself then of what Mrs. Knowles had had to endure over the past year and a half—the bullying and humiliation. It was foolish of me to have expected the same straight-backed, regal creature.

I was impatient now for more news of Peter, but it was not until after dinner that his name was again mentioned—not by Mrs. Knowles but by Mr. Galbraith. I had but just sat down to the pianoforte when I heard him say to his sister: "We must have Peter Bushell in one evening, Imogen. He could accompany her on his fiddle."

(I knew Mr. Galbraith from my Bath days as a plainspoken farmer with none of his sister's social graces.)

Mrs. Knowles was hemming a tablecloth and did not reply, but when I finished playing, Mr. Galbraith said: "We must certainly have Peter in. I shall ask him to come the day after tomorrow. Imogen? The day after tomorrow?"

Mrs. Knowles inclined her head but I sensed that she did not really want to invite Peter. She might be happy for him to go rat-hunting with her brother in the barn, but Peter in the parlor was a different matter.

Her reluctance was not missed by Mr. Galbraith: "My sister disapproves of Peter—don't you, Imogen?" (Here, Mrs. Knowles smiled and shook her head.) "Before she came to live here, Miss Mary, I used to take my meals in the kitchen—I preferred it, if you must know—and sometimes Peter would drop by and we'd blow a cloud and have a bit of music. But that's all over now. We eat in the *dining* room now—don't we, Imogen?"

"We do. Just as we did when our dear mother was alive."

In response, Mr. Galbraith grunted and picked up his newspaper. It seemed to me that the rift between brother and sister had not completely healed. And afterwards—when Mr. Galbraith had gone outside to blow his cloud—Mrs. Knowles acknowledged as much: "You must excuse him, Mary. It has been hard for him—not having had a woman in the house for so long. And I fear I irritate him. The truth is he has not really forgiven me for marrying Pitt."

I said: "He was always very attached to you, I remember."

"Ah, my dear." She was shaking her head. "I have cost him so much one way or another—what with the lawyers' fees and the shame of it all—but I am determined now to make it up to him. I want him to have a comfortable home in his old age—to have all the things—the *finer* things that he has missed."

"That which should accompany old age," I said softly. "Honor, love, obedience, troops of friends."

I had been thinking more particularly of Peter and the music in the kitchen, but Mrs. Knowles said: "Exactly. He must be persuaded to go out more and mix in good society."

2.

The dunghill cock woke me at four next morning, its crowing counterpointed by the chimes of the clock in the upstairs hall. For a while I lay looking at the window blind—the light growing gradually behind it—listening to farmyard noises and then to stirrings inside the house. I guessed Mr. Galbraith was up and about; Mrs. Knowles had warned me that he rose early and made a deal of noise.

I rose myself then and went to the window, lifting the blind a little to look out. It was a beautiful, pale-skied morning but I had eyes only for the keeper's cottage. Smoke was ascending from its single chimney and the thatched roof shone wetly in the early sun. I longed for a telescope so that I might better spy on the inhabitants. I imagined them sitting down to an early breakfast—prepared perhaps by Peter's sister or even by Peter himself—certainly not by his slothful mother. (I had not forgotten the frayed shirt cuff nor the moth-eaten gray coat.)

After about five minutes I saw a girl in a bed-gown coming from the back of the house with a pail in her hand. I watched her go to the rain-water butt beside the house and ladle water into her pail. A liver-and-white dog followed her out, lapping at the puddle of spilt water before rushing around the front of the house, barking.

Next thing, I heard a whistle and a man's voice calling. The dog raced back and I heard a door slam and then both man and dog appeared—the dog trying to jump up at the man.

It was Peter—it was certainly him—but I could scarcely believe that I actually *beheld* him. I knelt at the window, peering out beneath the blind, hardly daring to breathe. And perhaps he felt my gaze—the intensity of it—for he suddenly looked up, looking (it appeared to me) directly at me. I at once sat back, too afraid to look out again lest he see me. And after a couple of minutes—just as I was nerving myself to look out again—there was a tap on the door and the maidservant entered with the hot water.

When I arrived late for breakfast, Mrs. Knowles, I could tell, was annoyed with me.

"One cannot lie abed in the country, my dear Mary. One must be up and doing."

I thought it best to say nothing, and after a moment, she said: "And so how do you propose to spend the rest of your morning? After you have practiced your music, that is. Perhaps you might care to walk to the Great House? But I'm afraid I cannot go with you. I have to see to the baking."

I was relieved that she could not accompany me. I wondered if she had always been so managing and at once felt guilty for being ungrateful. "May I not help with the baking?"

"Goodness, no!" She patted my cheek. "I will walk with you another time. I ought to exercise more —Galbraith is always at me to take up riding—he says it would improve my posture— restore my figure."

She then told me how Mr. Galbraith had commented favorably on my own appearance: "He thinks you wonderfully improved, dear—your face, your figure—he declares he would not have known you for the same girl."

I felt myself reddening and Mrs. Knowles again patted my cheek: "You must not mind being complimented by an old bachelor."

After breakfast, I went to the parlor to practice. But an old book of Samuel Webbe's songs was lying atop the instrument and I could not resist opening it and then playing and singing "I'll Enjoy the Present Time."

I had not sung since George had told me that I could not sing—but now, believing nobody could hear me (I had taken the precaution of closing the window), I sang with increasing brio. I had just begun a second song when Mrs. Knowles walked in, saying in her most melodramatic way: "Mary! I have brought you a visitor."

And before I could prevent her, she was beckoning George into the room.

I do not know who was the most red-faced, George or myself, for Mrs. Knowles—still in her floury apron—was carrying on like my mother, suggesting that we might like to walk out together: "Mary meant to walk to the Great House this morning, didn't you, dear?"

I was too flustered to speak. I had denied myself the pleasure of singing for so long and that George of all people should have heard me was maddening.

As soon as we were safely outside, he tried to placate me: "I saw your sisters yesterday in Meryton—they told me you were here and that I might call."

He still held his riding whip, flicking it about before bursting out: "I could not help coming. I had to ask you—I had to know—did you send my letter?" And when I did not immediately reply: "You didn't, did you? I guessed as much."

"You swore to me before that you would stop bothering me."

"I swore I'd stop if you sent my letter." He lashed out with his whip at a passing shrub. "I've written another—'tis the last I'll ever write. I would do as much for you if our situations were reversed. I should not hesitate." And finally: "Well, you won't have to put up with me much longer—Purvis is now planning to return to London. I shall probably never come into Hertfordshire again."

We were now skirting the orchard and back-garden of the keeper's cottage, and I was beginning to feel extremely hot and bothered. It was by now late morning, the sun was beating down, and an *avant-courier* of smells—not all of them pleasant—was coming up to meet us. I could now see that there was a pig-sty behind the cottage and a muck-hill next to it, and beyond the clipped hedge sheltering a row of bee-hives was a larger bee-hive-shaped building, unmistakably a privy.

I heard myself say then what a few minutes before I had vowed not to say: "If you have a letter for Helen, you may as well give it to me. I shall be writing to Cassandra today."

To my own ears I sounded ungracious, but George's expression—the deep color of his face as he thanked me—put me in mind of the boy of whom I had once been so fond, and I was glad then that I had relented. He dropped his whip and grasped both my hands: "Bless you! I knew I might count on you."

It was then that I saw Peter. He was coming from the other side of the cottage with the liver-and-white dog at his heels.

3.

The dog bounded over, barking, and before George could retrieve his whip, it pounced. There followed a tug-of-war with George grabbing the whip-end and the dog holding on and growling.

Peter meanwhile was approaching—I could *feel* him coming up, I could not look—and George was shouting: "Call off your damned dog, sir!" Whereupon Peter seized the dog, forcing it to release the whip—thus causing George to stumble heavily backwards.

George—swearing under his breath—then rejected Peter's hand to help him to his feet.

I stood by, saying nothing. I knew not what to say. Certainly nothing from the Commonplace Book came to mind. George was dusting himself off and the dog was barking again.

It was Peter who spoke first, cuffing the dog to silence: "Sorry about that, sir—he's a young dog—bit of an idiot. You've not hurt yourself?"

And when George continued to dust himself off without re-plying, Peter turned to me. "Hello, Mary."

It was like hearing a note of divine calm after a dissonant passage of music. My confusion died away. I found I could greet him composedly. I could introduce him to George. I could even look at him.

He was hatless and coatless, tanned and untidy, wearing old leather breeches and a white shirt open at the throat with a limp collar. (George, in contrast, was very correctly attired in a fitted tailcoat of striped wool, waistcoat, and stiff shirt collar and stock.)

Both men seemed ridiculously reluctant to talk to each other—George kept on slapping the dust from his clothes while I introduced Peter, and Peter then turned back to me: "You're staying at Stoke Farm, are you? For how long?"

George answered for me. "Miss Mary is here only for a fortnight." (stressing the "Miss")

I then made matters worse by telling George that Peter played the fiddle at the assemblies. "He plays really well. I have never heard anybody play half so well."

George said: "A folk-fiddler, are you? Self-taught?"

I burst out· "George! Upon my word!"

"Pretty much." Peter spoke with unimpaired good humor. "But I did take lessons in London for a spell." He turned back to me: "So you're here for two weeks, are you?"

George cut in again: "Now I have it! You're the keeper here, aren't you? Yes, Miss Stoke has told me about you. Yes."

There was a pause with George nodding to himself in satisfied recall while Peter and I waited. When nothing more was forthcoming, I said to Peter: "Mrs. Knowles has invited me to stay with her and her brother. I used to live with Mrs. Knowles in Bath."

"Yes, I remember you telling me about her."

He was smiling down at me and had we been alone I am sure I should have disgraced myself—I should have asked him whether he had received my message and if so, why he had not replied.

George meanwhile was becoming restless: "We should be getting on, Mary. If you mean to call at the Great House."

There was a proprietary edge to his voice—as if I had been his sister or his wife—and the dog also seemed to sense something in his tone (a lack of goodwill towards its master perhaps) and started barking again. Peter speedily collared it, saying: "I'm going that road m'self as it happens."

I said quickly: "You could show us the way then."

And so we set off with the dog racing ahead and George again lashing out at leaves with his whip and refusing to take part in the conversation. For a while I worried that such boorish behavior might make Peter draw the wrong conclusion, but then I wondered if that might not be a bad thing.

At first, we did not talk about anything of consequence. He asked after my family, and laughed when I told him that Lydia had gone to Brighton: "Followed the regiment, did she?"

"She went as the guest of Colonel Forster's wife."

"You would've liked to have gone too maybe?"

"To Brighton? No indeed."

He appeared pleased with this reply though he said nothing. He was throwing sticks for the dog. I was able now to look at him at my leisure and (with the benefit of bright sunlight) appreciate how handsome he really was. It was not a regular handsomeness—the hawk nose and brown skin would not be to everybody's taste—but his figure was extremely good and his shabby clothes in no way detracted from it. They could even have been said to enhance it. I might not have noticed his neck—how well formed it was—if the collar around it had been high and starched.

We were walking now without talking—George's presence was a constraint—and upon entering a little copse, the path became less even. There was a fallen oak tree trunk to step over, and Peter now placed his hand under my elbow to steady me. I then inquired (in a voice that was not quite steady) whether the tree had been struck by lightning and upon Peter confirming it, I quoted the old proverb: "Beware the oak, it draws the stroke."

"What a lot of wise old sayings you have in your head."

We walked on in this way for a while and then the path narrowed and George went on ahead. Whereupon Peter began to tell me about the night-school he was attending in the village: "'Tis chiefly for lads who've not had any sort of book-learning—farm-workers and the like—but the schoolmaster was willing to take me on."

"But you can read and write, can't you? Surely?"

"Aye. But not all that well. You know that."

I could no longer look at him. I was thinking of my letter. I felt dreadful. His hand tightened on my arm briefly. "Don't fret yourself. I can read 'n write enough to get by. But the only schooling I ever had to speak of was when we lived in London." He stopped but then went on: "I did think at one time—Sir John Stoke spoke to me about becoming his bailiff. But there'd've been letters to write—estate business and the like—and I don't think of it no more." (correcting himself) "*Any* more. I've other plans now."

I longed to ask what those plans were but we were coming out of the wood and the path was once again wide enough for three. George now dropped back and Peter released my arm.

"And so for how long have you been playing the fiddle?"

To my ears, George sounded insufferably condescending but Peter seemed not to notice, briefly recounting his childhood experience before asking George about his own musical background. The two of them then talked in fits and starts, with George seeking always (it seemed to me) to condescend. "So which bowing technique do you favor?" And before Peter could answer: "But I need not ask—folk-fiddlers invariably play in the first position." And a little later: "Do you entertain your audience with imitations of cuckoos and the like?"

Peter finally showed hackle. "O aye—and with donkeys braying and dogs howling. If it makes 'em happy, why not?"

I was relieved to see the Great House looming. And Peter now seemed eager to part company, whistling to the dog before taking leave of us. "Goodbye then, Mary."

"Goodbye." (I did not dare call him by his Christian name with George standing by.)

"Good day to you, sir."

George merely touched his hat in return. He scarcely waited until Peter was out of earshot before rounding on me: "What's that fellow to you?"

"What business is it of yours?"

"How comes it that you are so intimate with him? Letting him walk with you arm in arm. Letting him call you 'Mary.' Where did you meet him? At the assemblies, was it?"

George and I were too keen to quarrel to waste time calling at the Great House. With one accord we turned and headed back to Stoke Farm.

Nothing George had to say to me was new—it had all been said before. He told me that Peter was not my equal, that he belonged to the lower orders: "It is very dangerous to encourage men of his stamp—don't you know that? How can you be so damned naïve?"

I completely lost patience with him then. "Oh! this is just how you used to be with Mr. Purvis! Looking down your nose at him and saying that he was vulgar and smelt of the shop."

George seemed momentarily taken aback. "But the cases are not the same—surely you must see that. I grant you that Purvis is not an educated man, but there was never any question of his taking advantage of my mother—"

"Peter is not taking advantage of me! And he is not uneducated."

George gave a snort.

I said: "There's more to being educated than learning Latin and Greek. You should hear him play before you sneer at his abilities."

"Actually," said George with a smile that made me long to hit him, "I think you like him because he *is* uneducated. That way, you can better show off your own knowledge and accomplishments."

"How dare you! You know nothing about him—or me for that matter."

We were now reentering the wood and our raised voices must have disturbed a woodpecker. George waited for its harsh laughter to subside before saying: "Actually I do know something. Letty Stoke told me something."

I was afraid then that Letty had indeed said something to Peter's discredit, but it was no worse than: "His father was transported to New South Wales for poaching."

"He is not responsible for his father's crimes. And poaching is not—" (I tried to recall what Mr Darcy had said in defense of poachers.) "A poor man might have to resort to poaching to feed his family."

To my surprise, George did not challenge this. Instead, he said: "I have sometimes thought that Letty might have a *tendre* for Bushell herself."

I stopped. "What exactly are you trying to tell me?"

"She is always talking about him. I know she frequently lends him books."

My face must have betrayed my disquiet and George gave another of his knowing smiles. He cast no more aspersions, however. Possibly he was content to have sown the seeds of doubt. Or possibly he had remembered his letter to Helen—that it would be impolitic in the circumstances to provoke me further.

But as we were nearing the keeper's cottage, he suddenly stopped and said: "I just don't want to see you get taken in, Mary. I care about you, you know. I cannot stand by and see you getting into a scrape."

He was now very much in earnest, telling me how fortune-hunters cast out lures to innocent young girls like myself. But looking up at him—at his flushed face, the beads of sweat upon his upper lip as he lectured me—it struck me that George was himself something of an innocent.

"You've not been listening to a word I've said!"

"Yes, I have." I started to walk again. "Have you brought your letter for Helen? You may as well give it to me now. If Mrs. Knowles were to see you handing me a letter, she might wonder—she already believes you to be in love with me."

Mrs. Knowles greeted us on our return with complacent smiles, and upon learning that George was soon to leave Hertfordshire she asked him and Mr. Purvis to dinner the following day: "I can promise you only a neat, plain dinner, Mr. Rovere—farmhouse fare—but I shall invite Miss Letty Stoke to meet you, and afterwards I hope you will play for us one of your own compositions."

Up in my room, I mulled over what George had said. His view of Peter as a fortune-hunter I at first dismissed. I prided myself on my discernment (I had never been taken in by Wickham, after all) but then of a sudden I remembered what the landlady of the Red Lion had said of Peter—that he was "ambitious." From there my thinking became increasingly confused. I began to question Peter's sincerity, and thence to argue with myself: "But did he not seem pleased to see you? Did not he declare by his manner, his looks, that he liked you?" "Perhaps," came the doubting reply. "And perhaps Letty Stoke believes that he likes her too."

I had been lying upon the bed but now I leapt up and went to the window—peering out from beneath the blind at the keeper's cottage—willing Peter to appear. And from there it was but a short step to fearing I had gone a little mad.

If thou rememberest not the slightest folly
That ever love did make thee run into,
Thou hast not loved.

Fortunately Shakespeare's words came to me before I had worked myself into an absolute fever of mistrust. I had written them in the Commonplace Book not long after writing my foolish letter to Peter. They served to calm me before I went downstairs.

I found Mrs. Knowles and Mr. Galbraith arguing in the parlor. "But I have not invited his *wife*, Brother! I made sure she was fixed in London before ever I gave the invitation."

"You might at least have consulted me."

"Well, 'tis all settled now—young Mr. Rovere assured me that neither he nor Mr. Purvis had any prior engagement and I have just now received a very pretty note of acceptance from Letty." She offered this up for Mr. Galbraith's inspection. "Sylvia is to cook a goose and there is not the least little thing for you to worry about."

Mr. Galbraith waved away the note. "I suppose now you'll have Sylvia and Matty and young Bert—" (Bert was the yardboy) "You'll have them all running around preparing fancy French dishes—"

"No indeed!" Mrs. Knowles was laughing now. "I promise you there will be none of that. And afterwards we will have some splendid music because Mr. Rovere has promised to play one of his own compositions—and Letty will sing—" (recollecting herself) "—and Mary too of course."

"Very well." Mr. Galbraith picked up his newspaper. "But I hope you have not forgotten that Peter Bushell is also coming here tomorrow evening. *That* is 'all settled' too. I have asked him to come round after dinner and play for us, and I have no intention of putting him off."

4.

Dinner at Stoke Farm was at the unfashionably early hour of three o'clock (a point on which Mr. Galbraith remained immoveable) and at half past two the following day therefore Mrs. Knowles, Mr. Galbraith, and I repaired to the parlor to await the guests.

I was beginning to feel very uncomfortable. I had slept very little the previous night and had helped in the kitchen for most of the morning—sieving gooseberries to make a sauce for the goose. (Contrary to Mrs. Knowles's promise, there had been a lot of running about, for besides the goose Sylvia had cooked a raised giblet pie and, because it was Mr. Galbraith's favorite, a Savoy cake.) At the time I had been happy to help—it had taken my mind off Peter—but I was now tired and becoming increasingly nervous at the prospect of seeing him, especially in the company of Letty Stoke and George. I feared that he might be carrying on some sort of flirtation with Letty and that George would again be uncivil to him. I was afraid too that I would make a fool of myself. I resolved not to sing—even if everyone were to press me.

"You look pale, Mary." (Mrs. Knowles was always observant of my looks.) "Can I get you a glass of wine, dear?"

"I'm not surprised she looks pale." Mr. Galbraith spoke from behind his newspaper. "You've had her slaving away in the kitchen all day."

"She has not been *slaving.* How you do exaggerate."

Brother and sister began to bicker then—or rather Mr. Galbraith began needling Mrs. Knowles, who defended herself but at the same time sought to placate him. Eventually she said: "Brother, you cannot put a good dinner before six people without a little extra work. And a Savoy cake—Sylvia wanted to make you a Savoy cake—and it takes time to prepare. Twelve eggs— and the whites to be whisked into a froth. Ask Mary if you don't believe me—she helped—you cannot just wave a magic wand."

Mr. Galbraith subsided then. And a few minutes later he folded up his newspaper and got me a glass of wine. "There you are, my dear—Sercial—the very best old Madeira. Imogen, can I get you a glass?"

Letty Stoke was the first to arrive. I have not yet described Letty so I shall now set down her chief points. She was a healthy-looking girl, short but well made, with a thick head of red hair and a sharp face. Her conversation consisted chiefly of hunting anecdotes. (Lydia once unkindly observed of her that she looked like a fox herself.) In one respect I envied her: She had a fine, strong singing voice about which she seemed to be not in the least conceited. Her vanity lay rather in pride of family—she was fond of telling people that the Stokes had come over with the Conqueror.

Today though, she seemed more interested in the Long family. "Now tell me, Mary, how are they getting on? Have you had a letter from them lately?" And after I assured her that Cassandra and Helen were both well: "But now you must admit, Mary, 'tis very strange. They have been in Cornwall for months now and nobody has heard from them except you."

I then said what I always said—how the Cornish cousins lived in a very remote village and the consequent difficulty and expense of keeping up a correspondence.

"Yes, yes." Letty had an unfortunate habit of darting out her tongue when excited. "But my father could have franked my letter, you know, and so it would have cost them nothing. And who exactly *are* these mysterious Cornish cousins? I'm beginning to think that they don't exist."

I was very relieved when the knocker sounded and Mr. Purvis and George were shown in. More Madeira was handed round, after which Mr. Purvis and Mr. Galbraith began exchanging views on fine wine and Letty embarked on one of her hunting anecdotes. Nobody checked her—George being himself fond of hunting and Mrs. Knowles too polite to interrupt—and I pretended to listen, drinking more Madeira than was good for me in the meantime.

When we went into the dining room, Letty started speaking of Peter: "Now I understand our keeper is to come here later in the evening—I understand he is to play for you?" And upon Mrs. Knowles confirming it: "Well, you are in for a rare treat, I promise you—Peter plays superbly—better than anyone. Have you ever heard him, Mary?"

"Indeed I have—"

"After the accident we feared his fiddling days might be over—after the shooting accident on our Norfolk estate—for his arm was quite badly injured, you know. But our physician soon put things to right. And so you have all heard him play, have you?"

George said: "I have not had that pleasure."

Emboldened by Madeira, I declared: "I have heard him at the assemblies and also at Mr. Bingley's ball. He plays extremely well."

"Yes, well, you will hear him this evening without those other musicians, Mary, and a good thing too. I have told him that he will never amount to anything while those yokels are accompanying him. 'Shake 'em all off!'—that was my advice!" She was laughing and flicking out her tongue. "Give 'em their marching orders!"

George had been looking at me during much of this with a "what did I tell you?" expression, and indeed Letty's proprietary tone—the intimacy it implied—was making me most uneasy.

Mr. Purvis then entered the conversation. "It's not pleasant, giving people their marching orders, I can tell you. I had to turn off an old carpenter yesterday—he'd been working on the attics at Purvis Lodge." Turning to Mr. Galbraith: "My wife would have it that the attics don't matter—she's been at me not to spend any more money on the place."

George then said (more as a sarcastic aside to me): "My mother, you perceive, considers the servants' quarters quite immaterial."

There was an awkward silence. Mr. Purvis always ignored George's criticisms of Christina, but Letty held her own parents in high esteem and gave George a disapproving look. It was Mrs. Knowles who came to the rescue. "That puts me in mind of a very good joke. Why is the soul like a thing of no consequence?" She looked smilingly around the table. "Because it is quite immaterial of course."

Thereafter things went smoothly albeit predictably, with Mr. Galbraith helping himself to all the fancy dishes and telling Mr. Purvis how much he preferred plain cooking, and Mr. Purvis reminiscing about the meals of his impoverished childhood. George fell silent, and as the effects of the Madeira wore off, so too did I. It was left to Letty and Mrs. Knowles to keep up the conversation—a very lopsided one since Letty wanted only to talk of hunting and headed off poor Mrs. Knowles whenever she tried to change the subject.

5.

George was the only gentleman to return promptly to the parlor, and on Mrs. Knowles inviting him to play one of his own compositions he sat down at the pianoforte and started playing the sisters' duet.

Letty lifted her little fox-head to give tongue and we had just reached the "Tide of Malice" when there was a burst of laughter from the adjoining dining room. Mr. Purvis's loud voice could now be heard: "'Tis wonderful to see a farmer and a keeper on such easy terms."

Next thing, the parlor door burst open and in walked Mr. Purvis and Mr. Galbraith—smelling of cigar smoke—and behind them Peter, looking very neat and sober in black coat and breeches. He was carrying his fiddle and some music sheets.

Because I was sitting directly opposite the door, Peter saw me first and smiled at me. But such was my delight and confusion I then looked away and did not see how he greeted Letty. The little farmhouse parlor seemed of a sudden very crowded. Everybody was talking loudly; Mr. Purvis was almost shouting. "And it's very much to your credit, Galbraith, I'm sure. Because if the hares had been eating up *my* wheat crop I would most certainly have shot 'em."

Mr. Galbraith was a little the worse for all the wine he had drunk. "Between you and me, Mr. Purvis, I did shoot a few—and one or two pheasants, if you must know, but Peter wisely turned a blind eye."

"Sir John a strict landlord, is he?" (Mr. Purvis seemed to have forgotten Letty's presence.) "He has the look of it."

Letty had cried out at this. "'Tis only natural Papa should wish to preserve our game, Mr. Purvis!"

"Sir John is a *splendid* landlord, Mr. Purvis," said Mrs. Knowles. "And a thoroughgoing Christian gentleman."

In the midst of all this, I saw that George and Peter had struck up a conversation. I heard Peter say: "Oh, I doubt there's much that'd interest you, sir—it's just some old songs."

"I like old songs. Show me." George held out his hand peremptorily.

"Just some Robbie Burns's songs, sir. Nothing you've not already seen."

"Show me."

Peter then extracted some sheets and handed them over, saying with a little smile at me: "I thought Mary might wish to hear 'em. I know she likes Burns."

"And how do you know what Miss Mary likes, pray?" George was shuffling through the sheets.

Peter paused for a moment. "Well, I know she likes that work of yours, sir—*The Philistine*, isn't it?"

I was surprised and delighted. Not only was Peter quoting from my letter, but his voice now had an edge to it. George looked equally surprised. "Upon my word, you are certainly well informed."

Letty caught this last. "Of course he is well informed. He is *incredibly* well informed about music. He can read it at sight, you know."

"Can he indeed?"

George handed back Peter's song-sheets and I heard Peter mutter to Letty: "I'm for it now."

And sure enough George now took out one of his own scores, saying to Peter: "I have a sonata here for piano and accompanying violin—shall we play the first movement then?"

"Whatever you say, sir."

But Mrs. Knowles would not permit this. "Oh! but first we must hear the rest of that song from your opera, Mr. Rovere." And then in a minatory aside to Mr. Galbraith, who was still talking to Mr. Purvis: "I want you to listen to this, Brother. 'Tis a splendid song and Letty sings it beautifully."

Thus directed, Mr. Galbraith and Mr. Purvis seated themselves and Letty took up her previous station beside George at the pianoforte. Peter meanwhile moved over to stand behind my chair.

George in his usual contrary fashion played from the beginning of the passage, thus leaving Letty with little to do other than to wait and lick her lips. Peter was now standing very close—as if he wanted to comfort me—as if he knew how hurt I felt that Mrs. Knowles had not asked *me* to play or to sing. And I did feel comforted. It was as if a tide of warmth was carrying me out of myself, inclining me to trust him and to conduct myself well. The words of the 101st psalm came to me straight: "I will sing of mercy and judgment; unto thee, O Lord, will I sing. I will behave myself wisely in a perfect way."

I found I could listen without envy to Letty's singing, and afterwards when the applause came I did not mind that Mrs. Knowles was heaping praises upon her. Peter's hands were on my chair-rail and when I leaned back I could feel them against my shoulders.

But now George was wanting Peter to play and Mr. Galbraith and Letty were adding their voices to his. George placed his

score on the stand, saying: "We will play the second movement only, Bushell—the adagio—the violin's part there is far
less taxing."

I felt Peter's hands leave my chair-back. I watched him walk
over and pick up his fiddle. As always, he moved in an unhurried
way and it struck me anew what a *relaxed* person he was—how
rarely he betrayed any sign of nervousness. There was a brief
exchange with George while the latter explained some notations
on the score, after which Peter tuned his instrument and at a
nod from George, began playing.

I was familiar with George's sonata. I had heard him play it
unaccompanied many times and knew it for a charming composition, the second movement especially. But now Peter's execu-
tion lifted it to a new level. I am not competent to judge the finer
points of the art of playing a stringed instrument but I am sure
that everybody felt it—I am sure that they did—for the atmosphere in the room seemed charged and for a short time it was
as if we were all somehow connected. I suspect that George felt
it more than anyone—it was, after all, his creation—although
when the movement ended he did not speak, merely sat with his
head bowed. But everybody else was also quiet (that sweet hush
before the applause!) and then of course came the compliments.

Peter appeared not to relish them, at one point chiding Letty
for "emptying the butter-boat" over him. I said very little in consequence, and George continued to sit in silence. Presently he
stood and gathered up his music. I saw then that his hands were
shaking, and I marveled (not for the first time) how someone so
sensitive could be so stupidly stiff-necked. I was sure he would
not be able to bring himself to praise Peter—certainly not in
front of me.

Mrs. Knowles was begging both men to play again and as
Mr. Galbraith soon echoed her pleas, they were obliged to

comply—George with none too good grace. This time, however, the collaboration was less happy. They played the final movement of the sonata, and although it began sweetly, a darker theme was presently introduced by the piano. There was much thumping of chords by George—shortly to be matched by furious double-stopping on the part of the violin. It was as if the two instruments were at war and I could not help thinking that the two players partook of the rivalry.

Everyone else seemed delighted, however. There was as much clapping and complimenting as before, and Letty now laid possessive hands upon Peter's arm, hanging on him while the others gathered round. I went over to George instead, but when I praised the performance, he asked in a low voice if I had posted his letter to Helen.

"Yes indeed. It was posted yesterday." (I had in fact forwarded it to Mrs. Long.)

"You wouldn't consider sending another?" And when I shook my head: "The thing is, we leave for London on Tuesday and if my mother has her way we won't ever be coming back."

I saw then that he was upset and asked if he would like some wine: "A glass of Mr. Galbraith's Madeira—shall I bring it to you?" Whereupon he reached for my hand. "I shan't ask you again, Mary, I swear. But if I were to give you our London direction, perhaps you would consider—at least let me know when she returns—"

"Of course," I said quickly, conscious now that Peter was looking at us.

George pressed my hand. "You're a good girl and I'm very sorry I said you couldn't sing."

Somehow this seemed worse than the humiliations inflicted by my father—worse because kindly meant—and I was sure that Mr. Purvis must have heard, for he later assured me that clever people could seldom sing in tune: "It might interest you to know, my dear Miss Mary, that Bonaparte can't sing. A dear friend of mine has connections in the opera world—the Paris Opera, you know—and he assures me that Boney can't carry a tune."

The party broke up soon afterwards. I did not have an opportunity to speak privately with Peter until just as he was leaving, when he handed me one of the Burns song-sheets and (with a most earnest look) told me to read it before I went to bed.

The song was "My Love Is Like a Red, Red Rose" but it was not until I was up in my bedchamber that I saw he had written on the inside page:

> *My mother would be honered if you visited her after church tomorrow.*

6.

I had not wanted to go, but I could not at first bring myself to admit it. Only when I was on the path to the keeper's cottage with the smells of the pig and the privy coming to meet me did I finally acknowledge it. I was afraid of becoming intimate with people who were not my equals. And the fact that I had once enjoyed the closest of connections with Mrs. Bushell made it that much more distressing.

I could see smoke rising from the chimney and wondered whether they were preparing a meal for me. The thought of sitting in a hot little house, being served an ambitious dinner by Mrs. Bushell, made my gorge rise. And had I not seen Peter at that moment, I might have turned tail and run.

He stepped out onto the path to meet me. He was wearing the same clothes he had worn the previous evening, his black coat and breeches—presumably his Sunday-best—and I saw that he was looking anxious.

"I thought you weren't coming."

As he spoke, he grasped my hand. And if the sight of him had not quite restored the magic, the touch of him most certainly did. "You're not wishing yourself someplace else, Mary?"

"No."

"M'mother will be so happy to see you."

"And I will be delighted to see her. I just wasn't perfectly sure I would be welcome. You know what they say about unbidden guests—'welcomest when they are gone.'"

He was smiling now (I at last found the courage to look up) but all he said was: "But you have been bidden." He pressed my hand before releasing it. "We'd best go in. M'sister's making tea."

As we entered the house, the liver-and-white dog rushed at me but Peter bundled him up and put him outside. Inside, the house was dark and before my eyes were quite accustomed to it, a girl came to me and curtseyed. Peter introduced her as his sister, Ruth, and then led me over to the corner of the room, where a woman sat.

"Here is Miss Mary Bennet come to see you, Mother."

Mrs. Bushell stood up. "Well, this *is* an honor, I'm sure." And before I could forestall her, she too curtseyed.

I begged her to sit down but she would not. "Oh no, we can't have that, Miss Mary. First we must set a chair for *you*."

Peter then drew up a chair for me and—much to my disappointment—walked away.

The following few minutes were among the most uncomfortable of my life, for Mrs. Bushell stood staring at me with a sort of melancholy curiosity. "I never thought you'd come. I told Peter you wouldn't. I'm happy to be proved wrong of course but I never thought you would."

I did not know how to propitiate her without sounding condescending, and the consciousness of once having been so close to her made me even more tongue-tied. I realized then that I ought to have called when I first arrived at Stoke Farm—I should not have waited to be invited. Plainly she saw the omission as a slight.

At last she sat down again, saying: "Well, it certainly is wonderful to see you after all this time, Miss Mary."

There followed the most stilted conversation—she simply would not stop Miss-Marying me and thanking me for coming. She called to Ruth to hurry with the tea: "Miss Mary hasn't got all day, you know."

I could see my surroundings clearly now. There looked to be but three rooms—the door to the second one was shut—and the one wherein we sat had a stone floor with rag rugs and some old oak furniture. Everything looked to be clean and well cared for, although the dim light made it seem mournful—the window shutters having been closed (so Mrs. Bushell informed me) lest the sunlight fade the furniture.

Of Peter there was still no sign, but Ruth was busying herself at the other end of the room with the kettle and tea-things.

"'Tis wonderful to be waited on, isn't it, Miss Mary? To sit here and chat while someone else does all the work."

Again, I knew not how to answer her. I feared she was being sarcastic, and at length I resorted to the Gospels, quoting the Savior's words to Martha when she complained about having to do all the work while her sister sat at His feet and did nothing.

Ruth came up with the tea tray in time to hear this. "That text is mighty unfair. I reckon Jesus should've taken Martha's part."

And while Mrs. Bushell exclaimed ("What *will* Miss Mary think of you?") Ruth went behind her back and winked at me.

It struck me then that Ruth was like Peter—irreverent yet good-humored. She looked like him too: She had the same brown skin and dark eyes and—less happily—the hint of a hawk nose. I decided that I liked her. Mrs. Bushell, however, was beginning to irritate me.

Just as we were finishing our tea she turned to me and said: "Has my son told you, Miss Mary, that he plans to go out to New South Wales?"

I was horrified of course, and quite unable to conceal it. Ruth said: "Now, Mama. You know Peter told you not to talk about it."

"Well, it's no more 'n the truth, I'm sure. My husband has made a wonderful success of things in New South Wales, Miss Mary. He's a man of property now."

I was dumbfounded. "But I thought—I understood—forgive me, but is not your husband a convicted felon?"

Mrs. Bushell sat up very straight. "Not any more, he's not! The Governor has granted him a full pardon. *He* at least believes that when a man's served his sentence, he should be treated same as anybody else."

Peter had come in to hear the end of this. "What are you telling Mary, Mother?"

"I've been telling her the truth. I'm not ashamed of my husband, thank you very much. And it might interest Miss Mary to know that my husband's farm—*one* of my husband's farms—is at least the size of Longbourn. And he owns a general store what's more and an inn besides—a grand inn in Sydney Town." She turned now to Ruth. "Go fetch that sketch from the other room, Ruthie—the sketch he made of the inn."

Peter said: "Mother, Mary must be going."

"This won't take a minute."

Ruth was soon back with the sketch. It was a pen-and-ink drawing of what looked like a very ordinary tavern with a shingle that proclaimed it to be the Jolly Poacher.

I could think of nothing complimentary to say, and in desperation quoted Dr. Johnson's famous encomium: "There is nothing which has yet been contrived by man by which so much happiness is produced as by a good tavern or inn."

Peter said again: "Mary must be going, Mother."

"Oh yes, I knew she wouldn't stay long—I'm surprised she came at all." (getting up from her chair) "Well! It's been a real honor, Miss Mary, I'm sure."

And once again before I could prevent her, she curtseyed.

Ruth accompanied Peter and me to the door and as I shook hands with her, she whispered: "Don't mind Mama." And as soon as we were clear of the cottage, Peter said: "Don't fret yourself over my mother."

But I was much more upset about New South Wales. I said: "You're not really going out to that dreadful place, are you?"

He looked down at me: "You don't have to go back straight away, do you?"

7.

We walked over the same ground as we had two days before. Peter said his intention to go to New South Wales was fixed. For him—for his father—it offered opportunities that were not to be had in England.

He spoke of the place as if it were the Promised Land: "It's got one of the finest climates in the world, and the Governor there now—a man called Macquarie—m'father says they could not have a better man rule over 'em."

He spoke of Macquarie as if he were the Messiah: "For him, it's not just a penal colony—he's building bridges and schools and proper roads—as far as he's concerned, the place has a future. And he visits all the convicts when they come and gives 'em hope. See, the barriers there, Mary, they're nowhere near as high."

I was struggling not to cry. The word *barriers* had done it— the fear that between us, the barriers were well nigh insurmountable. "But there are prospects for you *here*—in England—why must you go to the other side of the world?"

"What prospects? There are no prospects here for the likes of me. Not unless I was to do something underhand. And what would people say then, I wonder? 'Like father, like son'—that's what they'd say."

I stopped to take out my handkerchief and blow my nose. I said: "So much for the village night school and becoming

Sir John's bailiff. And all the books Letty lent you so that you might better yourself."

"*Better* m'self!" But he was smiling. "Did she tell you about the books, did she?"

"You cannot possibly want to go there—even if your father were king of the place, it would still be vile."

"Now you can't say that until you've seen it."

"Well, you haven't seen it either!"

"I've been reading about it in Miss Stoke's books."

Some demon then prompted me to say: "I don't see how you can be sure that your father's telling the truth. About the inn and the farms and everything. I mean you can't really trust someone like that, can you?"

He was annoyed now, I could tell. It was the first time I had known him to be annoyed with me and for some reason I found it exciting. He said: "What do you mean, 'someone like that'? What do you mean?"

"Well, he's not exactly a law-abiding citizen, is he? Your father."

He looked down at me. "You know I thought you were different from the rest of them. I thought you didn't judge people— that you weren't . . . prejudiced—is that the right word?"

And when I nodded: "Course I should've known when you wrote me that letter. I told m'self then it'd never work."

I was appalled. I had credited him with a superhuman degree of confidence but I now perceived that he was as sensitive as George—as sensitive as myself—at least upon certain subjects. It was my first apprehension of him as vulnerable and although it did not make me love him less—indeed, I think from that moment my love for him "grew up" as it were—I knew I must tread carefully.

He walked on without taking my arm. I caught him up and said: "I should not have said that about your father." And when he made no reply: "I'm sorry about the letter too. I knew it was wrong—condescending—almost as soon as I'd sent it, I knew."

After a long pause he said: "See, you've never had to go without, Mary."

I was tempted to quote something about the uses of adversity but held my tongue.

"I'm not talking about gewgaws—I'm talking about food on the table. That was what drove m'father to poaching in the first place. Later he didn't have that excuse—he'd got himself a good place and we all had more 'n enough to eat—but by then he was in the way of it and he'd got into bad company. It was that and the drinking that did for him. When he was in his cups there's no denying he was a pretty ugly customer."

Memories of Bushell in his cups still haunted me and I tightened my hold on Peter's arm. "You must find his conduct hard to forgive."

"Oh, he's a reformed character now—swore off the drink before he was transported—promised m'mother that if she stood by him, he'd never touch the stuff no more."

Fine talking thought I to myself, though I said nothing.

"He always said it was the loneliness that made him drink. He said being a gamekeeper was the loneliest of jobs. He reckoned it made you an outcast from your own kind—always having to look out for the master's interests."

I longed to remark that Bushell's new occupation must suit him perfectly—an *inn*-keeper being surely the least lonely of jobs. Instead I said: "And you? Do you feel that way? About the nature of your work?"

"The nature of m'work. Well, I don't much like having to search some poor laborer's cottage for snares, or chase after lads collecting pheasants' eggs. And I certainly don't enjoy wet-nursing gentlemen-sportsmen."

"Or being shot by them," I said, remembering Sir John's nephew.

"You heard about that, did you?" He was smiling again. "But I had the best of care you know—Sir John had his own physician to me."

After a moment he added more seriously: "I don't get as angry as m'father used to about things. Or maybe I'm just better at hiding m'feelings."

"I fear I'm not very good at hiding my feelings."

He covered my hand with his own. "That's what I like about you. I liked it from the first. You're so different from the others."

I did not care for this compliment. "Oh! you don't have to tell me that. All my life I've heard myself described as 'different'— different from my sisters—"

"I wasn't thinking of your sisters specially—"

"I lack Lydia's high spirits and Jane's saintly disposition—not to mention Elizabeth's wit."

He was laughing now. "No, I meant the people in your—walk of life. Different from them."

"Oh." But woman-like, I was not satisfied. "In what way different?"

"You don't put on a mask when dealing with the 'lower orders.'" (He spoke the words much as George would have—that is to say, loftily.) "You don't try and set yourself apart from us."

Again, I felt myself blushing—but from guilt rather than gratification. I knew that the old prejudice was ever ready to surface. And soon he was giving me more undeserved praise— telling me what a good girl I was: "I don't know anyone who tries so hard to do the right thing—do what their Bible tells 'em."

He was looking at me now with such warmth that in my embarrassment, I began to gabble: "You must not impute to me—I am not as virtuous as you think." But this only made him laugh and in desperation I resorted to the Commonplace Book: "I think you are making game of me. 'Most men admire virtue who follow not her lore.'"

"What, you're trying to tell me I'm no good?"

Before I could reply he had picked me up, literally swept me off my feet, and kissed me. And afterwards, when I tried to speak, he silenced me in much the same manner. It was a shock (but not at all distasteful) to be so caught up. Later—when he at last set me down—he handled me more gently. He took off my glasses and told me that he loved me.

We did not talk of New South Wales again, not directly. But I told him that I was prepared to go to the ends of the earth with him, which so far as I was concerned amounted to the same thing.

8.

If I had set out from Stoke Farm filled with doubt, I returned to it in a state of blissful certainty. Blessed with the love of a good man, I felt equal to anything—even the prospect of living out my days in the Antipodes. Only the thought of Peter's father gave me pause—and it was but a moment's pause—before the text came to me: "Perfect love casteth out fear."

Had I needed reassurance, I was given it that same evening by Mr. Galbraith. He had been drinking his Madeira at dinner and by the time he rejoined us in the parlor he was more than a little "disguised." I saw Mrs. Knowles glance at him but she said nothing until he asked me to play a Haydn sonata.

"Oh, Mary is much too tired to play for us now, Brother. She was obliged to visit Mrs. Bushell after church you know—and there was no getting away from the poor woman—"

My face burning, I jumped up. "You wish me to play the entire sonata, sir?"

"Look at her now!" Galbraith sat back in his chair. "Don't she look lovely flying her colors?"

Fortunately the music was lying atop the instrument and I seized it and sat down. But Mr. Galbraith kept talking—saying how he liked to see a lass "fired up"—how it was "boo'ful to behold." Mrs. Knowles (her own color heightened) tried to hush him but he took no notice, finally bursting out: "Puts me in mind of m'little Sukie Holloway."

For one horrible moment I thought that he was going to cry, but instead he blew his nose in a watery sort of flourish and got up and left the room.

Mrs. Knowles said: "You must forgive him, my dear Mary."

"Dear ma'am! There's nothing to forgive."

She stretched out her hand to me. "She was a farm-girl—her father was a mere laborer—marriage was out of the question, as our mother rightly adjudged."

I was afraid then that she too might cry, but she was made of sterner stuff: "It was a long time ago but I fear that my own misadventure has brought it all back to him. 'At least you followed your heart, Imogen.' He said that to me last night. He thoroughly disapproved of Pitt of course but—" She released my hand. "Oh, Mary! Who's to say that our decisions are right or wrong without the benefit of hindsight? At the time I truly believed that he would one day meet someone more suitable."

Peter and I had arranged to meet at the blasted oak at ten the following morning. Mrs. Knowles placed no difficulties in my way—she had shut herself up in the kitchen with Sylvia—and I set out punctually, arriving at the exact same time as Peter.

He was wearing his old work-clothes (which suited him much better than his Sunday-best) and had brought with him the liver-and-white dog. The dog took exception to our embracing, however, even to our holding hands, and as a consequence I felt awkward and talked to hide it. I told Peter of Mr. Galbraith and Sukie Holloway.

To my surprise, he knew all about it. "She was supposed to've been very beautiful—but then they always say that, don't they?"

He was throwing sticks for the dog, and there was a something in his manner—a levity—which I did not like. He must have seen this in my face for he turned back to me. "What is it? What's the matter?"

"Oh, it's such a pathetic story. Poor Mr. Galbraith."

"He had a choice, Mary."

"But he must have been so young."

"He was of age—he could've married her if he'd wanted to."

And then perhaps because I still looked troubled, he kissed me and—with the dog dancing round us hysterically barking—told me I was not to fret myself because *he* was not about to let anyone talk him out of marrying me.

Afterwards we walked to the coverts on the other side of the Great House, where Peter fed the young pheasants. We then went on to a little grove of late-blooming elder-trees (the scent of elder-flowers will ever transport me back to that sweet morning), where we talked of what we were going to do.

Peter was not planning to leave for New South Wales for several months, but I now learned that neither Mrs. Bushell nor Ruth would be accompanying him on the voyage: "I want to see the place for m'self first. Ruth wouldn't mind roughing it but m'mother would be unhappy if things weren't to her liking."

I saw then that he *was* a little mistrustful of his father's account, but it was too sensitive a subject to dwell on and I asked him instead about the voyage: "How far away is Sydney exactly? How long does it take to get there?"

His answer shocked me. "'Tis over thirteen thousand miles—nautical miles—depending on the route. The voyage takes at least four months."

"Four months!"

"At least. It's a long way, love."

He kissed me then (the dog was asleep in the shade): "I shan't be leaving for a good while yet—I have to stay for the shooting, I owe it to Sir John."

"Could I not come with you?"

"Oh, Mary." He kissed me again. "Let's not think about it now, love—let's just enjoy the present time."

And so we talked no more about the future—instead, as is the way with new lovers, we talked about when we had first fallen. For Peter, it had been at Sir William Lucas's dancing class. "It was when you come up to me—*came* up to me and shook my hand—I just didn't expect it. There you were—your dear little serious face—saying how you wanted to learn to play the fiddle."

"You saw that I liked you perhaps?"

He laughed and colored faintly. "And you?"

"I suppose it was at that first assembly. I noticed that your shirt cuff was frayed."

"You felt sorry for me, did you?"

I denied it but he would not believe me and from there we descended into the childish sort of nonsense lovers delight in— nay-saying and yea-saying with kisses interspersed—whereupon the dog woke and we were obliged to be sensible once again.

We arranged to meet at the oak-tree at two o'clock the following afternoon and then talked of what we would do in the remaining days of my visit. (Mrs. Knowles had filled the evenings with engagements but the mornings were pretty much mine to do with as I pleased.)

There was one matter, however, on which we did not see eye to eye. Despite my telling him that my father would never consent to our marrying, Peter insisted that he would speak to him—that it would be "underhand" not to do so.

"But not just yet," I pleaded.

He kissed the top of my head and told me not to fret myself: "We'll talk about it tomorrow."

9.

But there was no tomorrow. Shortly after breakfast the news of Lydia's elopement was brought to Stoke Farm by Mr. Purvis and George. Mr. Purvis had not waited for Matty to quit the dining room before bursting out: "I don't like being the bearer of bad news but we've just come from Longbourn—a take-leave call—and the place was in an uproar—"

George said hastily: "They're all well, Mary. Be assured they're all well. It's Lydia—the silly chit has run off with Wickham—they left Brighton two days ago."

"We've come to take you home, my dear Miss Mary." Mr. Purvis now handed me a letter. "'Tis from your sister, 'tis from Miss Bennet—it explains it all." And then as I took it with trembling hands: "Shocking business, shocking! I could've told 'em the fellow was no good. First time I laid eyes on him I knew him for a smooth-talking rascal."

Jane's writing was nowhere near as neat as her normal hand:

My dear Mary, I have some very distressing news to relate concerning poor Lydia. She and Mr. Wickham left Brighton Saturday night, bound—as was then believed—for Gretna Green, but we have since learned that marriage was never his intention and that they are now in all likelihood living together in London. Our father has gone with Colonel Forster to try to discover them.

Excuse the scrawl, dear Mary—I write in haste—our poor mother is in need of constant attention.

Yr affec. sister, Jane

I have written to Lizzy in hopes of hastening her return from Derbyshire. Aunt Philips is just now come to help with the Gardiner children.

In all the flurry of departure, I was not able to write to Peter but I sent a message to Mrs. Bushell saying that "family concerns" had obliged me to cut short my visit. Mrs. Knowles bade me farewell with dramatic fervor, presenting me with a bottle of her homemade cherry brandy to be used judiciously as a composer: "And let me assure you, my dear Mary—" (clasping me to her bosom so that her housekeeping keys hurt) "—as one who has recently known scandal—let me assure you that it *will* pass. I shall pray for you, dear—and also for poor Lydia."

Releasing me, she adjured Mr. Purvis and George to re-member the Savior's words: "He that is without sin among you, let him first cast a stone at her."

Mr. Purvis had not appreciated this, and when we were seated in the carriage he said: "I'm not in the business of casting stones at anybody, but if I were, 'twould be at him, the deceitful dog." And a little later: "Nobody was wise to him besides m'self— and now it's too late, goddammit."

He then begged my pardon, saying: "But there's only one way to persuade such a rascal to do the right thing and that's to bribe him—there's nothing else for it—and so I should tell your father, my dear. 'Twill cost him a fortune but 'tis the only way."

At Longbourn, Aunt Philips met us with a cheerful face. I heard her say to Mr. Purvis: "My poor sister keeps to her room—

it has been a sad shock to her—Mr. Wickham was always such a favorite."

Mr. Purvis spoke of his own misgivings then, while George took the opportunity of writing down his London direction, whispering as he handed me the piece of paper: "You will be sure to write to me now?"

As soon as they left, Aunt turned to me with sparkling eyes. "Well, pet! I see you have an admirer. Oh! don't try to deny it now—I know your mother always had hopes of him—but if I were you, I'd secure him mighty fast because this business is bound to frighten away the men."

When I went up to my mother, she was asleep, with Jane dozing in a chair beside her. The two of them made a fine picture—I wished Cassandra was there to capture it—a couple of sleeping beauties (my mother was then but two and forty) with the afternoon sun slanting on their faces and lighting up the bottles on my mother's bureau—the cordials and smelling salts and jar of wilted pinks, gathered, I guessed, by the Gardiner children.

I closed the door and retreated to my own room. I had been craving solitude all morning. I had never been so confused about the rights and wrongs of anything in my life. My first feeling had been one of shock—that Lydia could have done such a thing. Ever since the time of my melancholia I had had a horror of notoriety, and now it seemed that Lydia had not only forfeited her own reputation, she had brought disgrace on our whole family. But I was also angry with Elizabeth. If she had spoken out about Wickham, this surely could not have happened.

I then began to wonder what Wickham and Lydia would be doing now that they were alone together. My own recent passages with Peter—the exciting strangeness of being kissed and caressed—made me alive to certain possibilities. I recalled the "crim con" pamphlets: what had hitherto seemed disgusting I now conceded might—with a particular person—be not wholly disagreeable.

I even wondered—I am ashamed to confess this—whether Lydia's disgrace might make it easier for me to marry Peter. If, as Aunt Philips opined, all the eligible men were likely to be frightened away, then would not my mother be obliged to look lower for suitable sons-in-law?

When I went back to my mother's room, I found Aunt Philips there with Mrs. Long. Mama held up her arms to me. "Oh, my dear Mary! I hear such tales of Wickham now as make my blood run cold."

Mrs. Long hastily assured me that she was not the talebearer: "'Tweren't me, my dear. I've not heard a word of this till now—I've been in London this past week."

Aunt Philips said: "Lord, Sister, you would not wish me to hide it from you, would you? Everyone knows it was he who debauched Lucy Fry—"

A moan from Mama caused me to intercede. "Dear Aunt! This can do no good now."

But I soon realized that my mother in a perverse way wanted to know the worst of Wickham: The more he figured as a depraved monster, the less Lydia could be held accountable. She blamed everybody except Lydia (and of course herself) for the elopement. She blamed my father for not agreeing to take his family to Brighton in the first place; the Forsters, for not taking proper care of Lydia; and lastly, poor Kitty, for concealing the couple's plan to run off together.

It was wearying to have to sit and listen to it all, although I was pleased to see Mrs. Long took no joy in her old friend's distress. She was uncharacteristically quiet, patting Mama's hand. Later, in tones not meant to be overheard by the other two, she asked me to call on her next morning: "Come to me after breakfast, my dear. I shall be quite alone." And then in a whisper: "The girls will be coming home soon—if all goes well—very soon."

There was no mistaking the significant look that accompanied this, but before I could inquire of her further, Mama was wanting attention—her pillows plumped and her face fanned—complaining in the next breath that I did not perform these tasks nearly as well as did Jane.

Jane and Kitty and the elder Gardiner girl were in the breakfast room when I went down. Jane embraced me and Kitty kissed me and said: "I am glad you are come back—everyone has been so cross with me. I knew what they were planning—Lydia wrote me."

Jane shook her head at Kitty then, for Virginia Gardiner, a knowing little eight-year-old, was listening to every word.

10.

We now lived for letters. Wednesday's post brought a number, most of them disappointing. My father wrote merely to give his London direction, warning that he would not write again until he had something of importance to relate. There were several letters from Aunt Gardiner and Elizabeth—carefree travelers' letters from Derbyshire written in ignorance of unhappiness in Hertfordshire—and there was also a letter from Cassandra. I went to my room to read it:

> *My dear Mary,*
> *Our friend was last night brought to bed of a healthy boy and is, as I write, sitting up in bed drinking caudle. As for the child, he seems very stout for an eight-month babe; the doctor certainly holds no fears for him, and he is to be taken to the wet-nurse tomorrow. (There is now a little reluctance on his mama's part for this to happen but she knows what must be in the end had best be done soon.) I will write at length in a day or so.*
>
> > *Yours ever,*
> > *Cassandra*
>
> *My aunt returns to Meryton tomorrow and we plan to follow in about three weeks.*

Mrs. Long confirmed all this when I called on her later that morning. At first though, she wanted to talk of Wickham: "Think of it, Mary!—at the exact same time when that devil was making off with Lydia, his son was being born—the exact same time. When your poor mother told me, I nearly died. 'Saturday night, you say? Don't tell me they ran off on Saturday night?' Oh, my dear! It nearly killed me."

Presently she said: "He has a look of Wickham, you know, the child. 'Tis chiefly about the mouth. But when I mentioned it to Helen, she was fit to be tied. 'How *could* you say such a thing, Aunt!' And then we had mutterings in French—always a bad sign—and the next thing, she was saying she could not bear to part with the child, covering its face with kisses and carrying on—after everything we'd been through! Lord! it nearly finished me. But luckily Cassandra came in and made her see sense."

She confided then that Cassandra had urged her to return to Meryton: "She told me—you know her direct way—she said, 'You can do no good here now, Aunt.' And really, I have to admit, she can manage Helen better than I ever could. And there is an excellent nurse in attendance, a very respectable woman who was once nurserymaid to a nobleman's family. And of course dear Dr. Carey—he and Helen are now the best of friends. All of it paid for by my brother of course—he has been most generous. But oh, Mary! My heart misgives me when I think she might yet change her mind and decide to keep the child."

On Thursday, Aunt Philips returned to her own home and it now became easier to divert Mama. To that end, I offered to read to her from Mrs. Brunton's new novel, *Self-Control*. Jane had presently relieved me, however, saying she feared I tired my eyes from too much reading. (Jane in her own gentle way could be quite obstinate, telling me she considered it *her* responsibility to wait upon Mama.)

In the days that followed we heard nothing further from my father, which did not at all surprise me, but Jane now began to worry that she had not had a reply to her letters to Elizabeth: "I hope they have not gone astray—I directed them both to the inn at Lambton."

On Friday, I received a second letter from Cassandra, giving more news of Helen's lying-in:

> *Dr. Carey is happy with her progress, tho' he disapproved of Aunt's caudle, saying it clogged the stomach. He says that provided his instructions are faithfully followed, the patient should be fit to travel in a fortnight. He assures me he has never yet lost anybody to the puerperal fever. (I confess I am half in love with Dr. Carey.)*
>
> *But one may be fit in body and less robust in mind, and when last Monday the child was about to be taken to the wet-nurse, Aunt said something ill-considered and made it all much worse.* (Here there had been a line crossed out.)
>
> *I look forward to seeing you soon, Mary. You had better burn this.*

I was reading the letter at the breakfast table when Virginia Gardiner said: "Pray who is your letter from, Mary?"

I replied that it was from Mrs. Long's niece, whereupon Jane exclaimed: "How does Cassandra go on?—how do they both go on? Are they in Cornwall still?"

I felt myself blushing. "They hope to come home in about a fortnight."

Virginia now nudged Kitty. "Mary has gone all red—p'raps the letter is from her lover—p'raps she has a lover like Lydia."

It was but a momentary flare-up, swiftly checked, but I had never seen Jane so angry. Virginia was sent back to the nursery (after protesting she had heard the housemaids talking about Lydia) and we continued our breakfast in silence.

Afterwards I went to my mother and again offered to read to her from *Self-Control*. I was in need of Mrs. Brunton's wise words myself. I had been back at Longbourn for three days now—three interminable days of waiting for news that never came—and the atmosphere of the house was dreadfully oppressive. Apart from Hill and Nan Pender, Jane had told none of the servants of Lydia's elopement, but they all seemed to know about it anyway, tiptoeing around us with covert glances—the kind of glances I remembered from the time of my melancholia.

I had read only a chapter of *Self-Control* to Mama when Jane again came to relieve me, saying in a tone of gentle reproof: "She has fallen asleep, dear Mary—were you not aware?"

On Saturday we received no letters and I spent the morning in my room writing a song—a ballad about Lydia and Wickham running away to Gretna Green, which was of course really about Peter and myself (though it took me a while to realize it).

Later, I went down to my father's library to while away the interval before dinner with a book. The four Gardiner children were playing on the lawn outside—Virginia strutting about in a gold-paper crown while Edward, the elder of the two boys, marched behind her beating a toy drum. The two younger children were being mercilessly ordered about: I could hear Virginia telling them to bow down and pay her homage.

Peter had ridden right into the paddock before I realized that it was indeed he, and by the time I unfastened the French windows and stepped out onto the terrace, the children had all run towards the fence that marked off the paddock.

I stood irresolute as Peter trotted up to the fence and dismounted. He was riding Mr. Galbraith's roan horse and in response to a question from Edward, I heard him enter into a discussion of the horse's points.

Virginia then asked if the horse was Peter's: "Is it your own horse, pray?"

"No, your Majesty."

The children all laughed at this—Virginia too—and again I marveled at the ease that characterized Peter's dealings with people. I hung back, hoping that the children would return to their game, but the superior attraction of the horse and its rider kept them fixed. Finally, Peter looked up and saw me and said: "Miss Mary Bennet. Fancy seeing you here."

Virginia said: "Oh! you know Mary, do you?"

I said quickly, "I imagine Bushell has brought me a message from Mrs. Knowles, Virginia, that is all."

As soon as I spoke, I knew it for a betrayal. And I compounded it. I said: "You must know that Bushell is gamekeeper at the Great House of Stoke."

Peter stood, regarding me with an odd little smile. After that, everything seemed to happen very fast. The nurserymaid was on the front steps calling to the children. Peter was untying a pair of boots from the horse's saddle—boots I recognized as my own and which I had forgotten in the rush of my departure. The children were following the nurserymaid indoors—all except Virginia, who stayed on the steps to stare at us. A moment later and she was shouting to the others to come back: "There's a carriage coming!—it is Mama and Papa."

Peter was handing me my boots. The children came running back. I tried to take Peter's hand—to thank him—but he turned away to mount his horse. The carriage was coming on. The children in their excitement were jumping up and down. I saw that it was indeed the Gardiners and Elizabeth. Peter did not wait for the carriage to stop before riding off.

11.

I fled without greeting them—running through my father's library and up the stairs to my room.

After several botched attempts, I succeeded in writing:

Forgive me for speaking of you as if you were not my equal. In truth you are my superior, being far above me in every way. Please forgive me. I cannot bear the thought that you are angry with me. I cannot write more, I am too ashamed.

Your Mary

I then locked up the letter in my writing-box, washed my face, and bethought myself of Mrs. Knowles's cherry brandy. It was horribly sour and stung at my throat but I drank a whole glassful and after a few minutes felt much better.

Elizabeth and the Gardiners were in the dining room with Jane when I went down, and Kitty soon joined us. I had had the foresight to bring a book with me (Fanny Burney's *Evelina*) as an excuse for not having come down earlier.

They were talking of their travels—doggedly describing them whilst ever the servants remained in the room—and for some reason (I daresay it was the cherry brandy) it struck me as funny. I sat next to Elizabeth, who greeted me with a deal of reserve. I saw that she was wearing her severe look and without thinking,

I said the wrong thing, whispering: "This is a most unfortunate affair; and will probably be much talked of."

She made me no answer—she was helping herself to a dish of peas—and I noticed that her eye-lashes were wet (Elizabeth has the most beautiful long lashes) and suddenly I heard myself babbling from George's opera: "But we must stem the tide of malice, and pour into the wounded bosoms of each other the balm of sisterly consolation."

Again, she made me no answer. She was handing me the peas. But I was determined now to comfort her: "Unhappy as the event must be for Lydia, we may draw from it this useful lesson: that loss of virtue in a female is irretrievable—that one false step involves her in endless ruin—"

The cherry brandy had undoubtedly befuddled me, for I had not meant to quote such uncompromising maxims. My eye fell on *Evelina* and I repeated the famous passage about a woman's reputation being both brittle and beautiful. Elizabeth was now looking at the ceiling and compressing her lips. I wondered then if something else had happened to overset her while they were away—something more than Lydia—and later when Uncle Gardiner spoke of catching a great carp in the river at Pemberley I guessed that she must have seen Mr. Darcy.

12.

Uncle Gardiner left for London on Sunday morning to help my father look for Lydia, and we were now at least assured of receiving regular letters.

But when I was not worrying about Lydia, I was of course worrying about Peter. I left my letter to him at Clarke's on Monday morning and waited until Wednesday before again setting out for Meryton. Kitty agreed to accompany me but just as we were about to set out, Jane put a letter into my hands. For one heart-stopping moment I thought it was from Peter, but it was from Mr. Collins to our father. (Jane had permission to open all Papa's letters in his absence.) I read it aloud to Kitty as we walked along. It was a disgraceful letter—smug and sententious—and it made Kitty cry.

"How could he have written such a thing? Saying that it would've been better if Lydia had died!"

"It is certainly a most unchristian letter for a clergyman to write."

Kitty was fishing in her reticule for a handkerchief and she now set about restoring her appearance, tucking away a tendril of wet hair. "Do I look as if I've been crying? I should hate anybody to see—they will all be looking at us—Aunt Philips says that everyone in Meryton knows."

I said: "You must miss Lydia very much—you must feel her absence more than anybody."

"Oh! I do. When she first went to Brighton I missed her so I can't tell you. But one grows accustomed, you know. And now I suppose when she is come back—if she is not married, I mean—they will not let us be together. Aunt Philips said she will have to live somewhere far off where nobody knows her—like poor Lucy Fry. But I will tell you something, Mary—if Papa forbids me to go to balls simply because of Lydia I shall think it monstrously unfair."

We parted in the high street—Kitty to the shoemaker's and I to Clarke's. There, the red-waistcoated clerk handed me a folded paper with an impudent flourish. I left the library clutching it and resisted reading it until I was at the end of the street.

"Meet me here Monday at ten" was all he had written.

On Friday we received another letter from Uncle Gardiner informing us that our father planned to return home the following day. Mama cried out at this:

"What, is he coming home, and without poor Lydia? Sure he will not leave London before he has found them. Who is to fight Wickham, and make him marry her, if he comes away?"

My father's imminent return now prompted Aunt Gardiner to bring forward her own return to London. We said good-bye to her and the little Gardiners the next morning and welcomed (if that is the right word) our father when he arrived a little before noon.

Elizabeth, Kitty, and I were in the breakfast room when he joined us for tea, and so forbidding was his face that only Elizabeth had the courage to address him.

"You must have had a wretched time of it, Papa."

"Say nothing of that. Who should suffer but myself? It has been my own doing and I ought to feel it."

Thought I to myself: *Alas, you never said a truer word, sir.*

Elizabeth said: "You must not be too severe upon yourself."

"You may well warn me against such an evil. Human nature is so prone to fall into it. No, Lizzy, let me once in my life feel how much I have been to blame. I am not afraid of being overpowered by the impression. It will pass away soon enough."

Elizabeth then asked whether he supposed Lydia and Wickham to be in London.

"Yes, where else can they be so well concealed?"

Kitty was simple enough to say: "And Lydia used to want to go to London."

A grim smile lit my father's face. "She is happy, then, and her residence there will probably be of some duration."

There was a brief silence during which he continued to look at Kitty and smile, but then he suddenly turned to Elizabeth and addressed her with an awkward sort of seriousness: "Lizzy, I bear you no ill-will for being justified in your advice to me last May, which, considering the event, shows some greatness of mind."

On Jane's coming in to fetch our mother's tea, however, he reverted to his usual manner: "This is a parade which does one good—it gives such an elegance to misfortune! Another day I will do the same; I will sit in my library in my nightcap and powdering gown and give as much trouble as I can, or perhaps I may defer it, till Kitty runs away."

Instead of ignoring him, Kitty rose to the bait: "I am not going to run away, Papa. If *I* should ever go to Brighton, I would behave better than Lydia."

"*You* go to Brighton! I would not trust you so near it as East Bourne for fifty pounds! No, Kitty, I have at last learnt to be cautious, and you will feel the effects of it." He drew himself up like some despotic old father in a melodrama. "No officer is ever to enter my house again, nor even to pass through the village. Balls will be absolutely prohibited—unless you stand up with one of your sisters . . ."

Normally I should have been relieved that it was someone other than myself who was the butt of all this heavy humor, but poor Kitty was taking his threats seriously. Even then he did not relent—he was enjoying himself too much: "Well, well." He patted Kitty's shaking shoulders. "Do not make yourself unhappy. If you are a good girl for the next ten years, I will take you to a review at the end of them."

13.

On Monday I woke early and began many little preparations so as to look my best—plastering my face with crushed strawberries, a complexion beautifier recommended by Kitty, and washing myself all over with ambrosial soap. I put on my new pale-green linen gown with the white collar with Vandyke points and my straw bonnet with matching green ribbon, and at half past nine I set out for Meryton alone. It was a fine morning and I felt optimistic—I felt pretty, even.

When I entered Clarke's, Peter was nowhere to be seen but shortly afterwards a new and courteous clerk hurried over to tell me that a "gentleman in a curricle" was awaiting me in the street behind the building. It was Peter of course and he greeted me with such a smile—such a look—that mistrust and resentment were done away with quite.

I said: "How did you come by the curricle?" And then, paraphrasing Virginia Gardiner: "Is it your own, pray?"

He grinned. "It's Galbraith's. Up with you then."

He reached down to hand me into the vehicle, touched up the horse, and we were away. I did not ask him where—I did not care—but presently he asked (with one quick serious look) whether I was still of a mind to go to New South Wales.

I made a silly joke then—I was so happy—I said: "What, right now?"

He smiled but he was now very much in earnest. "I don't want us to keep on in this havey-cavey way, love. I want everything to be above board. I want to speak to your father."

"Oh please, Peter, not yet." I explained how angry and dejected my father was, having given up the search for Lydia. "He blames himself for what happened. He has been in a dreadful humor—so sarcastic—even to Elizabeth."

"Is there no-one looking for Lydia now?"

"Oh, yes! My uncle will keep searching—my uncle Gardiner lives in London."

Peter was silent, seemingly intent on the road (we were keeping to the back-lanes until we were clear of the town). I touched his arm. "Don't be cross."

"I'm not cross. I only wish to God I could help. Is it certain they're in London?"

"My father believes so. They have certainly not gone to Scotland."

I told him then how Lydia had left a note saying they were going to Gretna Green, but that no traces of them had been found on the Barnet Road. "My uncle now thinks that Wickham's debts could be the real reason for his flight—the disgrace—they were chiefly gaming debts, you see."

"Ah, yes." Peter's tone was scornful. "And they must always be paid before the poor tradesmen's bills, mustn't they?"

"They must indeed. They are debts of honor."

"Oh, Mary." He leant over and kissed me quickly. "What a lot we'll have to argue about after we're married."

I thought it best not to explore this, and he soon returned to our own predicament: "I must speak to your father, though."

I saw then that there was no turning him; the best I could do was to temporize: "Cannot we wait till there is news of Lydia? It is such an anxious time for my father right now."

We were now on the high road leading out of Meryton and after a short pause he said: "I'm going to be away for the next few weeks. Sir John leaves for Yorkshire tomorrow for the grouse-shooting and wants me to go with him."

"To Yorkshire!"

"I'll only be gone a few weeks—but I must speak to your father when I get back." And then before I could object: "You're not going to talk me out of it, love. Any other course would be underhand."

14.

On returning home, I went directly to my mother and read to her half a chapter of *Self-Control*. Kitty then joined us and a few minutes later Jane and Elizabeth rushed in. Elizabeth had in her hand a letter, and after first preparing us all for good news, she gave the letter to Jane, who read it aloud.

It was from Uncle Gardiner and addressed to our father:

My dear brother,

At last I am able to send you some tidings of my niece, and such as, upon the whole, I hope will give you satisfaction. Soon after you left me on Saturday I was fortunate enough to find out in what part of London they were. The particulars, I reserve till we meet. It is enough to know they are discovered. I have seen them both. They are not married, nor can I find there was any intention of being so; but if you are willing to perform the engagements which I have ventured to make on your side, I hope it will not be long before they are. All that is required of you is, to assure to your daughter, by settlement, her equal share of the five thousand pounds—

But my mother was not interested in the details of the settlement. "My dear, dear Lydia! This is delightful indeed!—She will be married!—I shall see her again!—She will be married at sixteen!"

Her concern was now all for the wedding clothes: "I will write to my sister Gardiner about them directly. Lizzy, my dear, run down to your father, and ask him how much he will give her. Stay, stay, I will go myself. Ring the bell, Kitty, for Hill. I will put on my things in a moment."

In vain did Jane remind her how much we were all indebted to Mr. Gardiner. "We are persuaded that he has pledged himself to assist Mr. Wickham with money."

"Well," said my mother, "it is all very right; who should do it but her own uncle?"

Next thing, she was wanting to dictate orders for quantities of cambric and linen from the London warehouses, with poor Jane trying to persuade her to wait until my father could be consulted.

Elizabeth meanwhile had retrieved our uncle's letter and was frowning over it. Under cover of our mother, I ventured: "I suppose one can feel happy as well as unhappy about this."

Elizabeth looked up at me, her dark eyes bright. "I suppose one can, Mary."

15.

A fortnight later, the happy couple were received at Longbourn, having been married that same morning in London.

Their visit lasted only ten days, but it seemed to me a very long ten days. My mother had allotted to them the set of rooms that the Gardiners always used—a south-facing apartment directly beneath my own bedchamber—and because of the mildness of the late summer evenings, the newlyweds opened wide the windows so that I could hear them running about and laughing. Once I heard Wickham groaning and in my innocence I feared he must have hurt himself.

But Lydia was so immodest—so impudent—in her newly-married conceit, coming down to breakfast with her hair all bundled up, yawning, and telling us how tired she was (Wickham in contrast never once put in an appearance at the breakfast table).

Fortunately, Cassandra and Helen had returned to Meryton that same week so that most mornings I was able to take refuge with them. Both sisters expressed dismay at the marriage, believing too high a price had been paid for respectability, and Helen especially was eager for me to come to them whilst ever Wickham was at Longbourn.

But I was not, alas, as comfortable in Helen's company as formerly. It seemed to me that she had hardened, had become combative towards men, flirting with them in an odd, unfriendly way. I heard her quiz the courteous clerk at Clarke's, telling him that the hero of such-and-such a novel was a coxcomb: "*Sans coeur*—completely heartless—just like you and me, I fear."

Cassandra had changed too, I thought. The months shut up with Helen had left their mark and she was occasionally impatient both with her sister and her aunt. To me though, she was unfailingly kind; she had been delighted to hear about Peter—indeed, both sisters had been—but whereas Cassandra praised him unreservedly, Helen said: "I'm sure I wish you every happiness, *chérie*, but do not forget that he is a man, not a god."

I now felt obliged to honor my promise to George to tell him of Helen's return, but having written to him, I lacked the courage to tell Helen what I had done. Instead, I told Cassandra while the two of us were shopping together in Meryton.

"He will return to Hertfordshire now, I'm sure."

"Did he plague you for our direction?"

"Oh! mercilessly. He came to Stoke Farm and it was so very embarrassing—Mrs. Knowles thought he was in love with me."

That made Cassandra laugh, and I continued a little shyly: "Peter thought so too at first and I am ashamed to say I did not disabuse him of the idea. Do you think that was wrong of me, Cassy?"

"Perhaps, but very understandable."

We now turned into the print-shop, where Cassandra had left several sketches for the proprietor to look over. Most of the work had been done in Islington—landscapes depicting the village of Islington Spa and various picturesque inns—but there was also a charming crayon sketch of a sleeping baby. Cassandra hastily removed this from the portfolio, and after the proprietor paid her what I considered to be a trifling amount (but which Cassandra later assured me was a very fair price), we quit the shop.

Because I fancied she was a little flustered by what had occurred, I described my visit to Peter's mother and the sketch of the Jolly Poacher. Cassandra laughed at this and soon afterwards repeated her praise of Peter: "I must say I liked him from the first—ever since I heard how he stood up to your father at the Netherfield ball."

She then went on in rather too casual a manner: "By the bye, have you heard that the tenant of Netherfield may be returning soon?"

"Mr. Bingley is coming back?"

"For the shooting. Aunt heard it from the butcher-boy this morning—the housekeeper Mrs. Nicholls had placed a great order for meat. But I daresay it is all a hum."

It was not a hum, however, and within a week of the Wickhams' departure the servants brought my mother intelligence of Mr. Bingley's arrival. She was of course beside herself, and at the same time furious with my father for refusing to call. But my father was adamant. "No, no. You forced me into visiting him last year, and promised if I went to see him, he should marry one of my daughters. But it all ended in nothing, and I will not be sent on a fool's errand again."

When Mr. Bingley called at Longbourn a couple of days after his arrival, I was not at home—I was at the Longs—but Kitty later interrupted my music practice to tell me about it.

"You will never guess who came with him."

I knew I must observe the childish ritual. "Very well. I will never guess."

"That tall, proud man who never talks—Mr. Darcy."

"But did he not talk to Elizabeth?"

Kitty shook her head, giggling. "He just sat there and looked at his boots—beautiful black ones they were, exactly like the ones Wickham had made for himself in London. But Mr. Bingley had on the same blue coat he was used to wear before—the one

with the gilt buttons. Mama has invited them both to dinner on Tuesday."

"Has she indeed?"

"Yes, and she means to ask Mrs. Long and her nieces too— and Mr. and Mrs. Goulding. And Jane is to have a new gown made up specially."

16.

Fourteen of us sat down for dinner on Tuesday—George having been invited by my mother after he had called at Longbourn the previous morning. I half expected Helen to keep away on that account (she had of course refused all my mother's invitations while Wickham was with us) but both she and Cassandra came with Mrs. Long, arriving a little after Mr. Bingley and Mr. Darcy.

George was the last of the guests to arrive, and I saw him eagerly looking around for Helen even as he was being introduced to Mr. Darcy. But I had forgotten that George had never before met Mr. Darcy, and on being presented, he was unable to repress a start, exclaiming: "Good God! For a moment I mistook you for someone else, sir." He then asked if Mr. Darcy was acquainted with a family by the name of Coates.

"Coates?" Darcy smiled, on his best behavior, perhaps believing Elizabeth to be within earshot. "I have heard of Romeo Coates the actor, certainly. I saw him play Lothario at the Haymarket—"

"No, no." George with his usual impatience cut him off. "I was alluding to a Mr. Jasper Coates. You are not by any chance related to anyone of that family?"

Darcy was no longer smiling. "No sir, I am not."

George said hastily: "I beg pardon—it was an impertinent question—but the resemblance is so very marked."

Darcy merely acknowledged this with a bow before moving off, and poor George then turned to me. "He must have thought I was questioning the legitimacy of his connections."

Helen came up then. "What did you say to him, for heaven's sake? It must have been something quite shocking."

George grinned and took her hand, and this seemed to me such a promising beginning that I at once moved away. But just as we were about to go into the dining room, I heard them arguing. George had written a new song that he wanted Helen to sing before the company and Helen was now refusing to oblige him.

"I've not sung for months," said she in what I now thought of as her "hard" voice. "I've been far too busy. You had better ask Elizabeth or Mary."

"Too busy to sing! Just what *have* you been doing, may I ask?"

"Oh, Cass and I have been out raking every night—haven't we, Cass?"

So saying, she moved off to join the others around the table, taking her place on one side of my father. George was then summoned by my mother to sit next to me.

I now observed that the course of true love was not running smooth for Elizabeth and Mr. Darcy either. They were seated at opposite ends of the table and Elizabeth seemed particularly ill at ease. Darcy's feelings were harder to determine. It may have been that the earlier exchange with George had put him out of humor; he certainly looked not to be enjoying himself—but that may have been because he was seated on one side of my mother.

Of all the lovers or would-be lovers, only Jane and Bingley appeared to be happy. They were sitting next to each other (my mother's contrivance matching Bingley's inclination) and amazingly Bingley seemed not to mind my mother's obtrusive attentions: "Pray take a little more of the venison, Mr. Bingley, and there is frumenty too—our cook makes an excellent frumenty." And a little later: "Can I not tempt you to another piece of pie, Mr. Bingley? Or what say you to a ratafia cake? Or some trifle now?"

In contrast, her exchanges with Darcy were cold and formal, and I realize now that it must have given Elizabeth considerable pain, for nobody except herself and the Gardiners then knew of Mr. Darcy's part in bringing about Lydia's marriage.

After dinner, while we were waiting in the drawing room for the gentlemen to join us, both Helen and Elizabeth seemed especially out of humor. When Mrs. Long tried to persuade Helen to sing, saying that it would make Mr. Rovere very happy, Helen retorted: "I have no *wish* to make Mr. Rovere very happy." Likewise Elizabeth, happening to spill a drop of coffee on Kitty's gown, was impatient with the latter's lamentations: "What a piece of work over nothing, my dear Kitty—'tis barely visible."

And when the gentlemen at last walked into the room, and George and Mr. Darcy approached the table where Jane was making tea and Elizabeth pouring coffee, Helen immediately moved close to Elizabeth, whispering: "The men shan't come and part us, I am determined. We want none of them, do we?"

I thought though that Elizabeth wanted very much to talk to Mr. Darcy, and upon his walking away holding his coffee cup, she looked after him with such longing that I felt for her most sincerely. And when soon afterwards George also walked away— to sit at the pianoforte—Helen seemed equally unhappy at the success of her maneuver.

My mother had earlier given orders for the whist tables to be set up, but George was permitted to remain at the pianoforte, and Kitty having retired earlier with her coffee-stained gown, the twelve of us remaining took our places at the three card-tables.

Beyond ensuring that Bingley and Jane played together and that she secured Mrs. Long for a partner, my mother cared not how we disposed ourselves, and when Mrs. Goulding claimed my father for herself and Mr. Darcy for her husband, Elizabeth was obliged to partner Helen. Cassandra and I then sat down opposite Mr. Goulding and Mr. Darcy.

Ours was the dullest of tables. Mr. Darcy and Mr. Goulding had by far the best cards and as Cassandra soon stopped concentrating on anything other than Mr. Bingley—whose table was next to ours—I began to amuse myself by studying Mr. Darcy.

There was something about him that bothered me. I knew him to be a man of integrity but watching him—his haughty face, his immaculate linen, and white, well-tended hands—I felt a stirring of distaste. The man had been so pampered—had enjoyed so much more than his fair share of the world's blessings. I thought of Peter's frayed shirt cuff. I thought of Peter's hands—*working* hands with the fingers of his left hand calloused from stopping fiddle strings and the back of his right hand scarred from a long-ago accident when the powder horn of his gun had caught fire—hands I would infinitely prefer to touch, and be touched by.

"'Tis your turn to play, Miss Mary." Mr. Goulding sounded impatient.

Mr. Darcy smiled at me. "Miss Mary was woolgathering, I think."

I felt myself blushing; I had forgotten to count trumps. I now led out a low card that Mr. Goulding topped with an emphatic grunt.

"You were miles away, my dear," said he to me afterwards, totting up the score.

"Aye," murmured Cassandra. "In Yorkshire."

Mr. Goulding heard this. "In Yorkshire, was she? What was she doing up there, I wonder?" (sorting his cards with a satisfied smile) "Fine county, Yorkshire. My friend Stoke is up there now for the grouse-shooting—you remember Stoke, Mr. Darcy? Sir John Stoke?"

But Darcy was not listening; he was looking at Elizabeth, and before Mr. Goulding could repeat his question, Mr. Bingley turned in his chair and said: "Sir John is in Yorkshire, is he? I wonder he is not here for the start of the partridge season." Bingley then disclosed that his sisters were presently in Yorkshire: "They have been in Scarborough these past three weeks."

A short dialogue between Bingley and Cassandra on the beauties of Scarborough followed, and I now noticed that Mr. Darcy had turned his attention to Jane. She for her part was listening to Bingley with such unaffected pleasure as to make her face for once very easy to read. And I felt sure that Darcy had indeed read it, and read it correctly, for he was regarding her not in the way a man generally appraises a beautiful woman (although Jane was looking lovelier than she had looked for a long while) but more thoughtfully, even with a touch of disquiet.

"I believe it is your lead, Mr. Darcy." Mr. Goulding was impatient for play to resume and now reminded me, with a condescending smile, that spades were trumps.

And so we played on, accompanied as before by George's music—an eccentric medley of his own compositions, culminating in such a deafening rendition of the last movement of his sonata that my mother begged him to play more quietly.

The party broke up soon afterwards. Contrary to my expectations, George did not offer to take the Long ladies home—they went instead with the Gouldings. And just how Mr. Darcy parted from Elizabeth I did not see, although Elizabeth afterwards seemed as dissatisfied as before. Bingley, alone of the young men,

seemed to have thoroughly enjoyed himself, prolonging his farewell to us all in the vestibule and then glancing back for a last
look at Jane.

As soon as we were by ourselves and my father had escaped
to his library, my mother began to congratulate herself on the
success of the dinner: "And, my dear Jane, I never saw you look
in greater beauty. Mrs. Long said so too, for I asked her whether
you did not. And what do you think she said besides? 'Ah! Mrs.
Bennet, we shall have her at Netherfield at last.' She did indeed.
I do think Mrs. Long is as good a creature as ever lived—and
her nieces are very pretty behaved girls, and not at all handsome:
I like them prodigiously."

17.

Despite several clumsy attempts on my mother's part to force Bingley's hand, Jane's happiness was secured within a few days of the Longbourn dinner. Elizabeth's took a little longer, however, and about a week after Jane and Bingley's engagement, there was a most curious visit from Lady Catherine de Bourgh.

I heard about it from Kitty in the usual fashion: "You will never guess who called this morning."

She was too excited to wait for a response. "Lady Catherine de Bourgh! Are you not astonished? She called to see Lizzy and the two of them walked together in the wilderness."

I was indeed astonished. "Lady Catherine called here!"

"She came in a chaise and four and she wore the most amazing hat with six black feathers in it."

"Did she give a reason for her visit?"

Kitty shook her head. "Lizzy told Mama later that she had nothing particular to say. Mama thinks she must have been on her road somewhere and—passing through Meryton, you know—decided to call."

Neither Cassandra nor Helen seemed especially interested when I told them of Lady Catherine's visit. Cassandra said: "The lady that Mr. Collins was forever talking about? The one with the eight-hundred-pound chimney-piece? Goodness."

Soon afterwards she left to go up to her painting-room and I was about to follow, when Helen said: "Oh, let her be, Mary, for God's sake."

We were in the kitchen and Helen as usual was sitting on the old settle with her feet cocked up. After a moment she said: "Mr. Bingley called here yesterday. He wants Cass to paint a whole-length portrait of your sister and himself to mark their betrothal. It's not that Cass isn't happy for your sister, you understand. It's just that—well, you know how it is."

After a pause I said: "Perhaps it would be better in the circumstances if she refused the commission."

Helen answered me in her "hard" voice: "We need the money, Mary. It seems we will always need the money—unless I decide to marry George."

She looked at me then and laughed. "All very well for you to sit in judgment, *chérie*, but some of us cannot afford principles. I shall make George a proper wife, never fear. I have sown my wild oats after all."

"I hate to hear you talk that way."

The only answer I received was a shrug. I said: "Has George renewed his offer to you then?"

"Not yet, no. But he will."

I took my leave, feeling more than a little vexed. And my mood was not helped by finding there was no letter for me at the post office. Peter had promised to write to me while he was away; I missed him terribly and I found I could not really care about the happiness of Cassandra and Helen, let alone Elizabeth, whilst ever my own seemed so uncertain.

But Elizabeth's happiness at least was soon assured. Two days later Mr. Darcy returned to Longbourn with Mr. Bingley. They called very early and as soon as I saw Mr. Darcy, I sensed he had come on purpose to propose. There was about him an unusual nervousness—a brightness of eye and flicker of cheek-muscle as he looked toward Elizabeth—and when Bingley suggested a walk, he could scarce conceal his impatience to be out of the house and away from my mother.

I declined the invitation, saying that I could not spare the time, but Kitty elected to go with them, and again I saw a look of impatience cross Darcy's face.

The five of them then set off across the fields in the direction of the Lucases—I watched them from my bedroom window—and I soon saw Jane and Bingley fall behind. But of the three figures going on ahead, I saw only one of them turn into the lane which led to Lucas Lodge. It was Kitty of course—I recognized her pink pelisse—and Mr. Darcy and Elizabeth then walked on alone.

18.

My mother had wanted Jane and Elizabeth to be married in London by special license—a grand double wedding to puff the consequence of her two rich sons-in-law—but Bingley asked instead for the banns to be read at Longbourn village church. He wanted a quiet country wedding and for the ceremony to take place on the 26th of November, the anniversary of the Netherfield ball, and on this he was at last permitted to have his way since, as Elizabeth put it, he had been so abominably thwarted in the past.

In my own case there was no such quick and simple resolution. Peter had returned from Yorkshire as determined to speak to my father as before, and indeed, I was at first optimistic that Papa would look kindly on his suit, for after giving his consent to Mr. Darcy and Elizabeth, I heard him call out from his library. "If any young men come for Mary or Kitty, send them in, for I am quite at leisure."

But of course he had not really meant it—or he may have thought that nobody would want Kitty or me—in any event, when Peter first applied to him, my father gave him a flat refusal. Peter told me about it afterwards—we walked together in the little copse while the others were all gone to Meryton—and amazingly he was not cast down by it: "I always knew I'd have a job convincing him. He kept telling me that a thousand pounds in the four per cents was all the money we could ever hope for. Then he changed tack—"

Here Peter paused, drawing my arm through his. "I've never told you this, love, but I once had occasion to speak pretty sharp to your father—it was at the ball at Netherfield when he—when you had been singing—"

I saw he was looking embarrassed—I was myself embarrassed—and quickly I said: "I know to what you refer."

Peter pressed my arm before going on: "Any road—as they say up in Yorkshire—your father suddenly remembered what'd passed between us but he seemed not to hold it against me. That was when he asked me about m'prospects."

"And then?"

"There was no 'and then.' Soon as I mentioned New South Wales, he wouldn't listen. Said it was out of the question—oh, he tried to joke me about it—told me his youngest daughter had just moved to Newcastle and as far as his wife was concerned, Newcastle was the end of the earth. He said: 'What would she say to a daughter's going to New South Wales, I wonder.'"

We walked on in silence then, but upon my remarking that it all seemed quite hopeless, he kissed me and said, "Not a bit of it. With your approval, I mean to ask Mr. Galbraith to give us his support. He's been a good friend to me over the years and I know he'd speak up for us if I asked him."

To this I at once agreed, for my father had long been acquainted with Mr. Galbraith as the uncle of my tutor Mr. Knowles, and two days later Peter again came to Longbourn, this time with Mr. Galbraith. They came in the morning while my mother and sisters were at Netherfield, and my father received them in his library. I waited in the hall, alternately hoping and fearing to be sent for, and after about five minutes my father stepped out and called to me.

Peter was standing by the windows when I walked in. He was wearing his black Sunday-best clothes and looked a little grim.

Mr. Galbraith was leaning against one of the bookcases, arms folded, frowning down at his leather gaiters. I joined Peter by the window while my father took up a position in front of the fire.

For a short time nobody spoke. There was just the ticking of the clock on the mantelpiece and the rustlings of the small fire burning beneath. I knew it was the sort of situation my father delighted in—keeping us all in suspense—and in an effort to check my childish fear, I breathed deep and took a deliberate inventory of the room. I noted that the two wing chairs which always stood on either side of the fireplace had been recovered (the chairs he and Elizabeth always sat in to play at chess) and that on top of the pile of letters on his desk was one that had come from Mr. Collins—I recognized the sprawling, unformed hand. But looking about, I realized how much I disliked this domain of my father's. In spite of its comforts and the smell of books, it was not a welcoming place: It had too many unhappy associations.

"I'll tell you what I will do."

My father was talking, and in such a way as made me think he must have crafted his speech. "I will not consent to an engagement but I will allow you to correspond."

Peter said: "Sir, it takes at least four months for a letter to reach New South Wales."

"I know it does."

The smile that accompanied this was dreadful but Peter was seemingly unaware. "I did not think to correspond with Mary, sir. I thought I would write to her just the once—I hoped that after I'd arrived in the Colony and seen for m'self how things were—"

"Yes, yes, I know what you hoped. But supposing you find this place is not the land of opportunity your father led you to believe—or that his property is not so extensive—would you own as much to my daughter?"

"Certainly I would."

Peter was now looking annoyed and Mr. Galbraith spoke for the first time. "I've known Peter for the best part of seven years, Mr. Bennet. I've always found him to be completely truthful."

My father seemed not to hear; he continued to address Peter: "Mary has many accomplishments as I'm sure you're well aware, but she has no turn for housewifery. She cannot boil an egg even. I fear she will be expensive to keep—even in New South Wales."

I wondered then if he were testing Peter, doubting his attachment still, hoping to expose him as self-seeking. Peter for his part was looking increasingly annoyed. Again, Mr. Galbraith spoke up: "I must say when Miss Mary stayed at Stoke Farm she made herself very useful in the kitchen—she helped our cook to make a Savoy cake."

This made my father laugh. "Mary made a cake, did she? Well, well. Better that than she should make a cake of herself, I suppose."

Peter then burst out: "Why must you always be making game of Mary? 'Tis not fair, 'tis not sporting."

"*Sporting!*"

The smile had quite left my father's face and Mr. Galbraith said quickly: "Mr. Bennet, sir, I do believe these two young people really care for each other. I know there is some difference in their backgrounds—Miss Mary being a gentleman's daughter and my friend Peter—"

"For your information, Mr. Galbraith, my own wife is not a gentleman's daughter."

My father was smiling again but it was the smile I mistrusted most, being a nasty side-twisting of his mouth. It silenced Mr. Galbraith, however, and my father now turned to me: "But what about you, Mary? How do *you* feel about the prospect of spending your days in comparative poverty? Or perhaps you feel that worldly considerations do not matter since your sisters have made such splendid matches? What have you to say, hmm?"

I could think of nothing to say—nothing to quote. The old fear of my father was rapidly getting the better of me.

It was then that Peter took my hand. That steadied me and of a sudden it came to me what I would say. I would quote Shakespeare's Cordelia—I would say, "Nothing."

As soon as I spoke the word, I felt better—cleansed—and inside my head I kept saying it over like an incantation, holding tight to Peter's hand the while.

"Nothing?"

My father, unconsciously, had followed Shakespeare's script. He was frowning, perhaps out of puzzlement, and Peter now addressed him in a more respectful way. "Mr. Bennet, when I first spoke to you, you were concerned about the distance of the Colony. You said how Mrs. Bennet'd want her daughters settled nearby and how far off she thought Newcastle, let alone New South Wales."

My father listened to this without demur. "Well?"

"Well, I can't do anything about that, sir, but if you're concerned about the—the *extent* of m'father's property and whether it'd allow me to support Mary in comfort, I can only tell you what m'father has written me."

Peter then spoke of his father's two farms—how the larger one in a place called Parramatta had a proper stone-built house, complete with verandah and a parlor thirty feet long. "And then there's the Sydney inn and the general store. M'father tells me that his income from the store alone amounts to some three hundred a year. I know it mightn't sound a lot to you—"

"On the contrary. Pray go on."

"I only have m'father's word for all this, but as soon as I'm able to see for m'self I can give you a more detailed account."

Mr. Galbraith then attested once more to Peter's integrity: "He's as sound as a roast, Mr. Bennet. Respected by everyone on the estate. Most keepers—the ordinary folk detest them because they try to lord it over, but Peter always plays fair—"

"Yes, yes." I saw that my father was becoming impatient but Mr. Galbraith kept on: "These young people aren't planning anything rash—they're prepared to wait. *That* will be the proof of the pudding to my mind—whether their attachment will stand the test of time."

His eyes were now glistening and I guessed that he was thinking of his Sukie Holloway. "I'm no advocate for hasty marriages, Mr. Bennet—God knows it cost me a pretty penny to rescue my poor sister from one—but Peter's done the honorable thing by you here. He deserves to be taken seriously."

He blew his nose then, retiring behind a great spotted handkerchief, and because I feared my father might mock this show of sentiment I said: "Papa, I did not give you a proper answer earlier—when you asked what I had to say about living in poverty and I said 'nothing'—I was quoting someone else's words when I should have spoken for myself." I breathed deep. "I want you to know, sir, that I am not afraid of living in poverty—comparative poverty—if Peter and I can be together."

"Well, well." My father was looking almost benign. "Whose words?"

"Shakespeare's, sir—Cordelia's."

"Ah yes, to her tyrannical old father, King Lear." He was silent then, looking first at me and then at Peter and finally down at the fire. At last he turned to Peter. "I shall think over what you have proposed, Bushell. But I cannot consent to any formal engagement at present, you understand. Everything is yet too uncertain. And I shall say nothing of this to my wife. You will not be leaving for several months and after that there will be a four or five months' voyage, and the same amount of time must pass before Mary can receive your letter. Howsoever—" He held out his hand. "We will talk again, and in the meantime I hope you will call at Longbourn—to instruct Mary to play the fiddle perhaps—but the pretext I leave to your discretion."

He then shook hands with Mr. Galbraith. "Perhaps sir, Mary might come to you at Stoke Farm this Christmas? She will of course wish to make herself useful in the kitchen once more."

19.

In the wake of my sisters' weddings, an unusual peace fell upon Longbourn. It was not so much that the place was quieter—Lydia's absence had already brought that about—it was more that by marrying off three of her daughters, my mother's purpose in life had been dulled, at least temporarily, and with it much of the attendant agitation.

The news that George was to marry Helen Long (announced by an elated Mrs. Long a few days after my sisters' nuptials) had upset her, however. George had been *my* rightful property and the fact that the wedding was to be a fashionable London one at St. George's, Hanover Square, and that Purvis Lodge was to be deeded over to George as a wedding present also rankled. She consoled herself by predicting the worst: "They will never be happy together. Helen is such a flighty little thing and George is by far too young—twenty is far too young for a man to settle. I wonder that Mr. and Mrs. Purvis should have given their consent. If he had been my son I should never have agreed to it."

And when my father reminded her that he had attained his majority a mere three weeks before their own wedding day: "Oh! but you were such a sensible, serious young man, my dear, there can be no comparison."

Here, my father had actually winked at me, for in the absence of my sisters he had become kinder to me—or rather he had become less *un*kind. Certainly he considered my feelings

more. He had not permitted Mama to press me to go to Pemberley, for instance, when Elizabeth and Mr. Darcy invited us all
there for Christmas.

"Mary has already accepted an invitation to Stoke Farm,"
said he. "And you would not wish her to slight an old friend, my
dear, surely."

"Oh! as to that, I am sure Mrs. Knowles would understand.
Nobody in their right mind could be expected to pass up an invitation to Pemberley."

"That's as may be, Mrs. Bennet. Mary must decide for
herself."

But there was one area where he did not allow me to have my
way. With Kitty now spending much of her time staying either
with Jane or Elizabeth and my mother being quite unable to be by
herself, I was obliged to mix more in the world—my mother's
world, that is—and accompany her on her morning calls. Whenever I begged to be excused, protesting that the talk was so trivial—
nothing but neighborhood gossip and the latest fashions—my
father would not listen, saying that it would help prepare me for
the society of New South Wales. And I later overheard him telling
the new Mrs. Bingley that it did me a great deal of good to be exposed to such frippery things: "Mary was used to be mortified by
comparisons with her sisters' style and beauty. Now, conceivably,
she may eclipse you all."

And certainly there would come a time after Peter left when
I was glad to have to go out—glad to be diverted—because our
separation was a long one, almost a year and a half, and only on
receipt of Peter's letter some ten months after his departure
from England did my father at last consent to our engagement.

Part Five

1.

Peter's long-awaited letter from New South Wales arrived just before Easter while we were all at Pemberley—Hill having redirected the package from Longbourn—and my father announced the engagement at the breakfast table: "I am happy to inform you all that Mary is to be married," He held up Peter's untidy-looking letter. "To a Mr. Peter Bushell, who lives in New South Wales."

And amidst the ensuing furor, above my mother's hysterics and the incredulous exclamations of Mrs. Bingley and Mrs. Darcy, my father read aloud the letter. There was more than one grammatical error in it but such was my happiness that I felt no shame, only a deep thankfulness that God had at last seen fit to answer my prayers. I said over to myself the words of the 138th psalm: "In the day when I cried thou answeredst me, and strengthened me with strength in my soul."

Later, Elizabeth and Jane spoke to me very seriously. Jane was concerned for my safety: "I cannot help feeling a little anxious, dear. You will be living so far away and amongst such a different set of people."

Elizabeth was more concerned about the society itself: "Who will you mix with, my dear Mary? Are they not for the most part convicts?"

"You have been gently raised, dear. You cannot know the dangers of associating with such people."

"And what of this man's mother and sister? Are they not very low sort of women? And you will be shut up with them on the voyage for many months together."

Here Jane, perhaps seeing I was annoyed, reached for my hand. But the next moment she checked herself on a sharp intake of breath—she was now heavily pregnant—and Elizabeth's concern was immediately redirected. "Are you in pain? Shall I send for Charles?"

And despite receiving Jane's repeated assurances, she hovered over her, seeming to forget all about New South Wales until I remarked: "The tardiness of correspondence is a worry certainly—the gradual estrangement it must produce—unless we are careful to write regularly and at length."

Elizabeth smiled then, still looking at Jane (the old colluding look). "'Tis fortunate then that you are a good letter-writer, Mary. Had it been Lydia, I doubt we would have ever heard from her again."

Lydia was visiting Pemberley for the first time—without Wickham of course—and she now took me aside to tell me she was acquainted with several officers who had served in the New South Wales Corps: "And I know they all made vast amounts of money while they were out there—trading in rum or gin or some such thing. Wickham was tempted to go out himself and try his luck. However, I am very glad that he thought better of it, for I should not have liked to live in a place where there are so many dishonest people." And then hastily: "But I am sure you will be very happy there, Mary, for you will be with the man you love—and that, you know, is more important than anything."

Mr. Darcy too—after his initial astonishment wore off—approached me to say that he had a cousin in the Colonial

Office: "I would be happy to write to him if you wish it. He could at least provide you with a letter of introduction to the Governor."

Of all my acquaintance, only Cassandra expressed unqualified approval, owning that she had a lively curiosity to see the place: "And if Aunt lets her Meryton house and goes to live with Helen and George at Purvis Lodge—as she talks constantly of doing—I shall book my passage tomorrow."

But whether out of indolence or because he had had second thoughts about letting me go, my father did not book my own passage until Mr. Galbraith called on him a week after we returned to Longbourn. Mr. Galbraith was accompanied by Ruth, and while he and my father conferred in the library, Ruth sat with my mother and me in the drawing room.

It was a most uncomfortable quarter of an hour, for my mother kept eyeing askance Ruth's plain stuff gown and unfashionable bonnet and addressed her remarks to the portrait of Mr. and Mrs. Darcy, which now hung over the chimney-piece. (The painting, in the style of Gainsborough's celebrated portrait of Mr. and Mrs. Andrews, depicted Darcy standing in the grounds of Pemberley with his wife upon one side and his favorite pointer bitch upon the other.)

Did Ruth have any idea of the vast extent of Mr. Darcy's estate? my mother now wanted to know. The number of carriages and horses he owned? The army of servants in his employ? And more pointedly: the number of his gamekeepers?

My mother went on to enumerate these while Ruth sat composedly, her ungloved hands clasped in her lap. Later, she got up to look more closely at the painting, saying: "I reckon Mary has got the exact same eyes as her sister."

I could tell my mother was not best pleased by Ruth's calling me Mary. And when Ruth remarked that the row of bee-hives in the background looked "mighty life-like," my mother responded with a snort: "Bee-hives!"

A spirit of murmuring now rose in me and I said: "Elizabeth married Mr. Darcy for himself, Mama, not for his possessions."

"I'll thank you not to preach to me, my girl!" There followed one of the worst rants since before my sisters were married. I was accused of ingratitude, of disgracing my family by contracting a degrading alliance, of preferring the company of servants to those in my own sphere &c.

My father and Mr. Galbraith walked in while she was still fulminating and I now think that this proved decisive with my father, for the following day he informed me he had instructed his agent to book passages for Ruth, Mrs. Bushell, and myself on the first available ship: "Pray tell your mother, so that she may share in the rejoicing."

Happily, the safe arrival of Jane's baby—a boy they christened Bennet—diverted my mother's attention from my departure preparations and I was permitted to pack my trunks in relative peace. There was no talk of placing orders at the London warehouses for wedding clothes of course, but that did not trouble me—Jane and Elizabeth had already made me a handsome present of two dress lengths of white muslin as well as a white silk gown and veil of Honiton lace.

It was not until June though that I at last left for New South Wales, or as Governor Macquarie later liked to call the place, "Australia." And when my father was reluctant to escort me to Portsmouth, Mr. Galbraith stepped in, accompanying Ruth and Mrs. Bushell and myself to the inn where we were to stay overnight and then next morning to the wharf, where we were to embark in the store-ship *Odyssey*.

Mr. Galbraith even gave me fatherly advice at parting, drawing me aside from the mêlée of passengers and saying: "Now you will be cooped up on this ship for a good while, my dear, so do not let little things upset you." A nod towards Mrs. Bushell's back made clear his meaning.

2.

There is nothing like a long voyage to reveal the true natures of one's fellow creatures. In the one hundred and forty days it took the *Odyssey* to sail from Spithead to Sydney I came to know the other cabin passengers extremely well—including, alas, my prospective mother-in-law. Mrs. Bushell's loyalty to her husband made her, in my view, see the world askew. She blamed the Bennet family for things that were not our fault and many of these grievances surfaced on the voyage. But our first falling-out was over my friendship with a young farmer, a cabin passenger called Thomas Cudlipp, who was going out to New South Wales with his elderly father.

The circumstances were these. Much to my surprise I found myself to be an excellent sailor. As the *Odyssey* beat her way down the Channel I was able to eat and drink and with only a little difficulty move about, whereas most of my fellow passengers were prostrated in their cabins. Young Mr. Cudlipp was similarly fortunate and whenever we met on deck we would exchange smug smiles and compare notes about our respective patients—Mr. Cudlipp's father having retreated to his berth a few hours after we weighed anchor, as had both Ruth and Mrs. Bushell.

In this way, and as often happens on board ship, we soon became pretty well acquainted. Mr. Cudlipp was a great reader, an enthusiast for poetry, which he invariably misquoted, but as he never minded my putting him right, we continued to enjoy each other's company. We saw the last of England together. Plymouth was the *Odyssey*'s last port of call and while watching the Devon coast disappear, Mr. Cudlipp began mangling "This royal throne of kings."

Shortly afterwards, Ruth emerged on deck looking frail. Mr. Cudlipp immediately offered her his arm, saying in his irrepressible way: "You must be the sister of the man Miss Mary's going to marry." And upon Ruth acknowledging it with a weak smile: "You must hang on to me until you have got your sea-legs."

By the time Mrs. Bushell left her berth a couple of days later, romance between Ruth and Mr. Cudlipp was blossoming, and Mrs. Bushell blamed me for it. She said nothing at first, however, merely giving Mr. Cudlipp repulsive looks—to which he was cheerfully oblivious—and refusing his arm when we were walking about on deck, saying (while clinging to the rigging) that she was well able to stand upon her own two feet.

Just why she so disapproved of Mr. Cudlipp was a mystery to me. Perhaps she did not like to see Ruth hanging on his arm. Perhaps his brother's farm in New South Wales—a mere two hundred acres in a place called Toongabbie—was not large enough to impress her. Perhaps it was because she could not dampen his spirits—he seemed not to notice her sighs. But one day she was rude to his father and that he could not overlook. Old Mr. Cudlipp was very forgetful, needing to be constantly reminded who everyone was, and when Mrs. Bushell was introduced to him for the fifth or sixth time, she sighed and said she really could not see the point. I quickly quoted Sheridan: "Our memories are independent of our wills."

Tom Cudlipp said sternly: "He don't mean to be rude, ma'am, I do assure you."

The implication was obvious and Mrs. Bushell colored. Thereafter, she directed her sighs at me. She feared that I was "too refined and delicate" for life on a farm. She worried that the harsh antipodean sun would burn my pale skin. And did I know how to ride a horse? Parramatta was at least fifteen miles from Sydney and she was concerned I might feel cut off.

Most of this I could ignore. It fell into the category of the "little things" Mr. Galbraith had warned me about. Also, it was a difficult time on board, with tempers other than Mrs. Bushell's being tried. We were awaiting a favorable wind to get us clear of the Spanish coast and for days the *Odyssey* and the other ships in the convoy were either lying still or being buffeted by contrary gusts. Our captain, Captain Ross, a genial and communicative man, owned when we were opposite Cape Finisterre that we were a little too close to the coast for his comfort.

But one evening when the sea was calm, a dance was held on the poop deck and Mrs. Bushell started on a new tack. A fiddler was playing and some four couples dancing, including Mr. Cudlipp and Ruth. Mrs. Bushell suddenly turned to me and said how the girls were "wild" after Peter whenever he played at the assemblies: "Jim Payne used to joke him about it. He reckoned Pete could eye a girl over the bridge of his fiddle—a girl who was not dancing of course—he could *fix her in his sights* and have her all of a flutter."

She was looking at me in a bright-eyed, malicious way so that I found it hard to breathe. "Indeed?"

"He said for Pete it was as easy as shooting pheasants." She leant towards me. "If Pete'd played his cards right, he could've married Miss Letty Stoke."

Ruth returned in time to hear this. "That is just nonsense, Ma, and you know it."

Later, Ruth came to my cabin and said what she had said when first we met: "You mustn't mind Mama." Then trying to joke me: "Imagine Miss Stoke with her Norman blood and all—imagine her marrying the likes of Pete."

I was not in a humor to laugh, however. I had been sitting in my cot for the past half hour looking through the porthole at the darkening sea. The memory of my first Meryton assembly when Peter had fixed me in his sights—*a girl who was not dancing*—had thrown me back upon my old self. I was doubting him again—doubting myself.

But Ruth was not prepared to let me sit in the dark. She had brought with her a hand-lantern which she now hooked into the slot beside my cot. "I've brought along the bee book, Mary. If you'd be so kind."

The book was one Tom Cudlipp had lent her—a translation of M. François Huber's *New Observations on the Natural History of Bees* (both Ruth and Cudlipp being ardent apiarists). She now scrambled up onto the cot beside me, opened the book, and began haltingly to read.

Ruth was a worse reader than Peter even, and although previously I had been happy to help her, tonight I wanted to be left alone. Gradually though, I found myself becoming interested in M. Huber's description of how bees go about replacing a lost queen—how they select a "young common worm" and enlarge its cell and ply it with rich food, thus transforming it into a royal bee.

I could tell Ruth relished the description, for after she finished she drew up her legs and hugged herself, saying: "Just goes to show, don't it, how small rooms and mean rations can hold you back." She nodded at the cabin, less than eight feet square. "I'll wager this is the smallest room you've ever slept in, eh Mary?"

I could not deny it and she grinned at me, but then her face became serious. "Mr. Cudlipp says they don't have no honey bees in New South Wales, only the little native ones. His brother said someone once tried to bring a hive out but they all died."

It was very much "Mr. Cudlipp says" with Ruth these days but this did not bother me—provided he was not misquoting poetry—and I said: "How sad."

"Mr. Cudlipp says it could be done—shipping out a hive—if the bees had enough wax and honey to last 'em on the voyage. And you could feed 'em sugar and all." (shaking her head) "But they need air. They must have air. I reckon it'd be mighty tricky."

After Ruth left with the lantern, I looked out at the sea once more—except that it was now a different sea, no longer calm, for a fair wind had sprung up while we were reading. My own mood was considerably calmer, however. I was relieved that the *Odyssey* was at last underway and I resolved never again to let Mrs. Bushell upset me—to undermine my confidence in Peter or in myself. I also resolved to forget about the journal entry I had been contemplating—a petty inventory of Mrs. Bushell's recent remarks.

3.

My journal was written chiefly in pencil (opening an ink bottle on board ship can be a risky undertaking) and I kept it throughout the voyage. For the first month or so, I conscientiously recorded daily latitude and longitude readings and changes in the weather. I wrote of the squall off the coast of Madeira when the tiller-rope broke and three poor sheep and a cage of poultry were washed overboard. I described the tropical storm we experienced off the Cape Verde Islands—of how I stood in the stern on the lee side of the ship and said over the words of the 139th psalm. And I did not omit to log the long interval of smooth seas when Captain Ross said we only wanted a little garden to make us believe we were on land.

I also recorded the meals we ate (for dinner, roast mutton or poultry until the livestock was depleted, fresh fish that the crew caught for us, and then leaner pickings with soup and salt beef, but always a pudding and cheese and our daily dose of lemon juice). I did my poor best too to describe the tropical sunsets and the bright moonlit nights when it was possible to read on the poop until midnight.

Later, I wrote more about "little things"—of the amount of crockery smashed between decks, of how troublesome the cockroaches were becoming and how hot the nights, and how for the first time in my life I had left off wearing stockings. I wrote of how Tom Cudlipp was so keen to sleep like a proper sailor that he slung up an old sheet for a hammock to the ceiling of his cabin, and how the sheet could not bear his weight so that he came crashing down in the night causing old Mr. Cudlipp to wake in fright. (Save for a cut on his forehead, Tom was not badly hurt but his father could not be pacified. He kept crying out: "Tom! You have hurt yourself, Tom!" so that in the end, Tom had to fetch the ship's surgeon to reassure the old man.)

I wrote too of how Tom had his head shaved when the ship was crossing the Line. (There is much vulgar horseplay among the seamen when a ship crosses the equator and passengers can be subjected to shocking indignities—"baptized" by buckets of sea-water being thrown over them or having their hair shorn off &c.) When Tom appeared at dinner with a shaven head— and still with a patch of court-plaister on his forehead from the sheet accident—old Mr. Cudlipp was terribly distressed: "Tom! Tom! What have you done to yourself now?"

Ruth and I laughed about it afterwards, for Ruth was an excellent mimic and could imitate old Mr. Cudlipp's speech and mannerisms. This made me hope that I could correct her own speech—her grammatical errors especially—but she resisted all my hints: "You'll never make a lady out of me, Mary. I'll never be like you and Mrs. Bowker." (Mrs. Bowker was a very genteel young woman who occupied the cabin next to my own and whose husband was presently serving in New South Wales with the Forty-sixth Regiment.)

Ruth persevered with her reading, however, and ironically this led to my own lapse from ladylike behavior when two female cabin passengers (I shall name no names) began tittering as Ruth was reading aloud from the bee book. We were all seated up on the poop deck under an awning, it being a hot morning with the sun almost directly overhead, and I overheard the younger of the women say something about Ruth having "a bee in her bonnet," to which the other replied quite audibly, "But not, it would seem, her A *Bee* C."

They both seemed to find this hilarious and the tittering increased. I waited until Ruth went off with Tom Cudlipp (Ruth hated to have Tom sit by her when she read) before speaking out. "I wonder," I said, trying to speak calmly. "I wonder if you have any idea how hard it is to read if you've not been properly taught as a child. You have to *un*learn the bad habits before you can get on. You have to stop guessing and covering up your ignorance." (Peter had explained to me some of this.) "You have to start afresh and it is very hard."

I saw with satisfaction that both women had stopped smiling, but then the older woman said with a sort of sneer: "Thank you, Miss Bennet, for that little lecture." And the younger one added: "Vastly illuminating, I'm sure."

They then walked off and I sat on feeling my heart beat. The women had hitherto been polite to me but negligent towards Ruth and Mrs. Bushell. I guessed that they had somehow found out that Mrs. Bushell's husband had once been a convict—the older of the two talked constantly of convicts, how she had heard they were "incorrigible" and what shocking servants they made, and how the Governor was now "disgracefully" favoring the emancipists over the free settlers &c.

And here I should mention that the *Odyssey*, though a store-ship, was carrying convicts. There were but twenty of them—twenty men—and they were, according to Captain Ross, "the better class of prisoner." Tom Cudlipp felt sorry for them and made a point of saying good-day to them when he saw them in their little work-parties, washing clothes or picking oakum. But they frightened me, especially when they were all assembled on deck for Divine Service and we were obliged to stand quite close, and I think they also frightened Mrs. Bushell. They would have been a daily reminder to her of what her husband had had to endure—that and the fact that her reunion with him was a steadily approaching reality.

4.

When the *Odyssey* was over half-way between the Line and the Cape of Good Hope, cold, blustery weather set in and we were happy to huddle in cabins that only a fortnight before had felt like ovens. Mrs. Bushell now spent days in her cot, sleeping sometimes fully clothed and constantly complaining of the cold and how the sea-water was "flooding" her cabin despite the carpenter tightening the scuttles and stopping the bull's-eye window with a deadlight.

"It puts me in mind of Collins Cottage," said she, eying me malevolently from her nest of blankets. "Your father's bailiff never mended the roof and there was also a broken windowpane. How we did suffer!—pots and pans everywhere to catch the leaks and the wind whistling through—the chilblains on Pete's feet I shall never forget."

This was her new refrain—my father's shortcomings as a landlord—and while I did not believe the half of it, I judged it better to be silent. She timed her attacks well —Ruth was rarely present—and after I failed to respond, she started needling me about the convicts: "I couldn't help noticing, Miss Mary—" (I was always "Miss Mary") "I couldn't help noticing how you turn your face away from those poor creatures—as if you could not bear to look at them—as if they was beneath you."

I said: "I confess I am a little afraid of them." I tried to make a joke of it: "Especially the fierce-looking one with the tattoo on his arm—what does it say? 'I love to the heart NKE.' He certainly frightens me."

She was watching me, ready to pounce, and I heard myself gabble: "And the one who does all the washing—the one without any teeth—the other men call him 'Soapy.' He frightens me a little too."

"Miss Mary." She was actually smiling. "Miss Mary, there are just *twenty* convicts on this ship. How many d'you s'pose there are in New South Wales?"

I had it at my tongue's end to say: "I believe you are afraid of them yourself." Instead I said—it somehow burst out: "Why do you dislike me so?"

"Dislike you! I don't dislike you!"

I said nothing, letting the lie hang there, and after a moment she looked away. A little later though, when Ruth with great difficulty entered carrying a hot plum pudding (Mrs. Bushell had started taking her meals in her cabin), she suddenly said: "Have you told her yet, Ruthie?"

"Told who what, Mama?"

"Told Miss Mary that Cudlipp's brother was a convict?"

I had been sitting on the floor—it was the only safe place to be, the ship was rolling so—but now I struggled up and despite Ruth trying to catch hold of my arm, made my way back to my own cabin. I was extremely hurt that nobody had told me—hurt and bewildered that they had discussed it among themselves.

I had resolved not to let Mrs. Bushell upset me yet now it seemed she had again succeeded. I could not pray—could not go down on my knees with the ship rolling so. Instead, I climbed into my cot, where I had wedged my little writing-box. I had placed therein some letters that I determined now to read, to comfort myself. They were farewell letters wishing me bon voyage—from Cassandra and Helen, and also from my family—from Elizabeth and Jane and Aunt Gardiner—and a long letter from Mrs. Knowles, which Mr. Galbraith had handed to me at parting.

I had not opened my writing-box for over a fortnight, not since we crossed the Line, and I now saw with horror that the wax on my letters had melted—both those I had received and those I had written in the hope of "speaking" another ship—and that they were all stuck together and spoiled.

It seemed to me then that my old life—everything I valued in my old life—was ruined, and my new life cold and comfortless: a foolish thought, but I could not get the better of it.

When Ruth came in presently, she was eager to explain: "He stole a silver wine cup—he were just thirteen years old—he stole it from a church. Tom said he went a bit wild after their mama died."

She climbed into the cot beside me. "Tom would've told you, Mary, but you are so—" She paused, perhaps searching for the right or polite word. "You have mighty strict views. And Tom thought you'd be shocked—that you wouldn't want to have nothing more to do with him. He thinks you such a fine lady and all. 'Course I told him you wasn't." She grinned. "He only told us because of Pa—one of those nasty ladies told him about Pa." Here she paused again. "I don't like secrets. I reckon they're silly things. But it was his secret, not mine."

I saw that she had brought with her another of Tom's books, Wordsworth's and Coleridge's *Lyrical Ballads*, which she now opened at "The Rime of the Ancient Mariner" (Cudlipp's favorite poem). But before she began to read, she put her arm around me—Ruth was a most affectionate girl—and said for perhaps the twentieth time: "You mustn't mind Mama."

The ship drove fast, loud roared the blast,
And southward aye we fled.

By the time the *Odyssey* had reached Table Bay at the Cape, Ruth had not only read the whole of "The Rime of the Ancient Mariner," she had learned several verses by heart—one of which Tom was especially fond of misquoting:

Water, water, everywhere,
And all the boards did shrink;
Water, water, everywhere
Nor any drop to drink.

There was no shortage of water to drink aboard the *Odyssey*, however, for as we set out across the Indian Ocean the rain fairly pelted down—rain such as I had never known in England—pounding the decks as if trying to drive the poor ship under. Later, the waves grew mountainous—great walls of water that the *Odyssey* (miraculously it seemed to me) ascended and descended but with such groanings that Mrs. Bushell took to stopping up her ears, for the noise disturbed her much more than the rolling and pitching. With the other ships in the convoy the *Odyssey* had long since parted company—Captain Ross judged that we were at least a week ahead of them—and towards the end of that tempestuous time (miraculously again) Mrs. Bushell's attacks on me ceased.

We smelt Van Diemen's Land long before we sighted it. On the first fine morning in weeks Tom Cudlipp came rushing into the saloon where we were all at breakfast and urged us to come on deck: "I promise you, you can smell it," cried he. "'Tis unmistakable—the smell of earth."

Shortly after sunrise on the 4th of November, just a fortnight after smelling the earth of Van Diemen's Land, we reached the entrance to Port Jackson—the great rocky "Heads" of the harbor of Sydney Town. Captain Ross fired a gun for a pilot, the flags were hoisted up a flagstaff on the hill above the South Head, and we then began the wait for the pilot's boat.

I was near sick with excitement for I had been up since five watching from the poop. Everything looked so beautiful in the early light—the pink sky, the foam-laced waves, the sun fingering the dark horizontal rocks of the cliff-face. Tom joined me in time to see the pilot's brig approach and draw alongside, and the pilot climb aboard. The wind had shifted to the south-east—a favorable wind, said Captain Ross, to take the *Odyssey* through the Heads and into the harbor.

And so indeed it proved. Within minutes, the motion of the ship to which we had grown so accustomed changed. The deck suddenly seemed oddly stable and the unladylike seaman's stance I had perfected over the past five months—legs apart and braced—no longer necessary. The *Odyssey* was gliding and the full loveliness of the great expanse of water became every minute more apparent. Tom quoted only one line of poetry as we slid past the numerous bays and inlets and the little green islands and beaches of white sand. He breathed the words: "O brave new world."

5.

When I went below to change my gown in preparation for going ashore, the younger of the two women who had laughed at Ruth was standing at the foot of the companionway. She was wearing a purple silk gown and one of the new high-crowned French bonnets and doubtless thought herself very elegant. For the first time in over two months she spoke to me: "Journey's end, Miss Bennet, and everyone's turning out in new trim."

I complimented her on her bonnet and hurried on. I was still unsure what to wear—I did not wish to appear too fine beside Ruth and Mrs. Bushell. When my box was first brought up from the hold, I had taken out my best silk gown but now I determined to wear my plain white India muslin, and for a hat, an old-fashioned straw *bergère* that Aunt Gardiner had given me, and Kitty had fresh trimmed with ties of white ribbon.

It was wonderful to perform the simple tasks of changing my gown and brushing my hair without having to hold on to the side of my cot. I wished though that I could see more of myself in the little looking-glass. My face at least looked healthy—tanned from the past fortnight of fine weather—and I now employed one of Kitty's tricks, pinching my cheeks to bring color into them. I longed to leave off wearing my spectacles but did not dare. I was beginning to feel light-headed from lack of sleep and from not having eaten any breakfast.

By the time I went up on deck again, Ruth had joined Tom. She was wearing what I knew was her best gown, a red cotton print, and a red ribbon in her hair. Both she and Tom were very excited. Tom said that the *Odyssey* would soon be dropping anchor in Sydney Cove: "You can see the town now, Miss Mary. The mate's just been pointing it out to us—the principal buildings. You can see Government House—the white building with the verandahs—you can see the flagstaff and the big tall pine tree— can you see?"

I said I could, but at first it was no more than a vague outline. The light though was remarkably clear and soon I was able to discern streets and rows of houses on the hill beyond the Government House, with several handsome buildings—mansions of honey-colored stone set in gardens of what looked like European shrubs. To the right of the cove were a great many warehouses and wharves. On the ridge above the town I espied a windmill. I was surprised at the extent of it all, but the town struck me as standing apart from the surrounding gray-green countryside. The mass of buildings seemed to be staring out at us—staring out to sea. I fancied I could smell peppermint.

"You look mighty fine, Mary." Ruth had turned her attention from the shoreline to my person.

I said anxiously: "But not too fine, I hope."

She laughed, lowering her voice. "Look at Mama." She nodded to where Mrs. Bushell stood on the starboard side of the deck. "Took me 'bout half an hour to do her hair."

Mrs. Bushell was wearing a gown of pearl-gray superfine that would not have disgraced a gentlewoman and holding aloft an ivory-handled gray silk parasol. She wore no hat, however, and her hair looked very unbecoming. Normally she wore it loosely coiled but Ruth today had plaited it up into a sort of coronet and the upswept style emphasized the downward trend of Mrs. Bushell's face. (She had reached the age, alas, when habitual expressions begin to leave their mark.) There were spots of color on her cheeks. I wondered whether she was wearing rouge.

She was watching the wharf with such an intensity of expression that I felt for her, despite my dislike. I had an impulse to go to her and say something pleasant but I did not act on it, fearing another rebuff. (I now look back on that as a failure of charity on my part—a failure I regret, for there was dreadful disillusionment awaiting Mrs. Bushell in Sydney Town.)

"Look, Mary!" Ruth was pointing towards the wharf Mrs. Bushell was so intent upon. "I think I see Peter."

But it was not until we were being rowed ashore in the jolly boat that I could see him. Even then, until he smiled and waved, I could not be completely sure. He was standing beside another man of a similar height and build, and they were both wearing cabbage-tree hats. From a distance, Peter and his father looked horribly alike.

How to describe our meeting?—the confusion of it—the rush of emotion that made me nearly faint—and on all sides, the sights and sounds and smells of a foreign place. After sixteen months, it was inevitable there was a shyness, but Peter looked so much browner, his teeth showing white in smiling, and under the ugly cabbage-tree hat, seemed such a stranger.

He took off his hat briefly and embraced me, and then it was Mrs. Bushell's turn and Ruth's. Meanwhile Mr. Bushell stood by, impatient to be introduced. "So this is the blushing bride!" he roared. "This is Princess Mary!"

If I had not had Peter's arm to hold on to, I am sure I would have fallen. Some of the other passengers were coming up. Old

Mr. Cudlipp looked to be as dazed as myself. He had a straw hat jammed on his head and was staring around.

Ruth was now eager to introduce Tom to Peter, and there followed a short parley as to the best way of getting to Tom's brother's farm at Toongabbie. I heard Peter say: "'Tis very near Parramatta. I could take you there—I have to go back this evening." He then explained how he had driven to Sydney without knowing even that the ship had arrived. "I had some business here." He smiled at me. "But that can wait."

During this exchange, Mr. Bushell stood rattling the change in his pockets. "Are we all set then?" Belatedly, he offered Mrs. Bushell his arm, telling her to put away her parasol: "Don't want to poke someone's eye out, do we?"

And even though it was now nearly midday and the sun very hot overhead, Mrs. Bushell obediently closed up her parasol.

We set off for the George Street store, which Mr. Bushell informed us was a mere hop, step, and jump away. The Cudlipps accompanied us, walking ahead of Ruth and Peter and myself. I heard poor Mr. Cudlipp say: "Where are we, Tom? Where are we now?"

I was tempted to ask the same question of Peter. I had now reached such a state of light-headedness that I could not properly take anything in. Ruth was chattering away happily on Peter's other arm—telling him how seasick she had been at the start of the voyage and what good sailors Tom and I were in comparison: "They was eating and drinking and walking around when the rest of us were sick as dogs."

I said: "I confess to feeling sadly unsteady on my feet at this moment."

Peter drew my arm more closely though his and said he remembered how strange it felt to be walking on solid ground after so many months at sea. And when Ruth continued to talk and I stayed silent, he bent down his head to peer under the brim of my *bergère*: "Still there, love? Don't fret yourself. We've not far to go now."

BUSHELL'S EMPORIUM read the Gothic gold letters on the fanlight over the double doors. Mr. Bushell punched one door open and then as an afterthought held it wide so that we could all pass through. It was a relief to step out of the sun into the cool interior, but the smell of the merchandise was overpowering. The shop seemed to sell everything—coffee and tea and tobacco and rum, and pepper by the bag and spices. There were shelves crammed with bolts of cloth and long tables set out with shoes and slop clothing and pyramids of candles and soap. I discovered later that they even sold gunpowder.

Mr. Bushell waved a hand at the meek-looking man behind the counter and led us through to the adjoining room—a parlor also full of shop goods—crates of china and glassware packed in straw, bed quilts and chamber pots, and boxes of knives and forks. Mrs. Bushell would have sat down upon a horsehair sofa but her husband stopped her. The sofa was also for sale.

Next thing, he was unlocking a door with bars on it and telling us all to follow "quick smart." We then entered a dining room where a large cedar table was set up and where at last we were permitted to sit down.

Surely a more disparate group of people never broke bread together than the seven of us seated round that table! (I have to say though that the bread was excellent, freshly baked, and there was butter and new-laid eggs and fresh fruit and coffee with cream—all the things one longs for aboard ship.) Peter made sure we were all well supplied while his father talked—and talked.

We heard all about the store and the house, how they were both built of stone because thieves could pick holes in bricks. He drew our attention to the stone chimney-piece and the stone emus standing sentinel on either side. In a curious way, he reminded me of Mr. Collins: There was the same reverence for things—the cost of things. He told us how he had paid the mason "a pony" to carve the emus. Towards the end of the meal, he emptied the change out of his pockets and we were given a lesson on the new currency of the Colony—the coins known as "dumps" and "holey dollars" and how much exactly they were worth.

Old Mr. Cudlipp seemed to revive after he had eaten and he too became talkative. He told Mr. Bushell how Tom had had his hair shaved off when crossing the Line: "'Tis quite grown back now—you can see it is quite grown—but 'tis not the same." He patted Tom's head affectionately. "It used to be more curly."

Mr. Bushell stared at Tom: "Had your head shaved, did you?"

Tom with his usual frankness explained the circumstances, whereupon Ruth piped up: "There was another young man what they set upon but Tom offered to take his place—which was mighty good of him, I reckon."

Mr. Bushell now stared at his daughter. He had paid her scant attention before, tweaking her hair ribbon and telling her she looked like a Bushell. "Mighty good? I call it damned foolish."

Peter spoke then. He asked Tom about his brother's farm at Toongabbie—whether it was near the New Ground.

Mr. Bushell cut in before Tom could reply: "Toongabbie! That place's now good for nothing—soil's completely useless— the whole place's been farmed out."

I saw Peter was looking annoyed and Mr. Bushell must have seen it too, for he said: "Well, it's the truth. No sense hiding from the truth." He turned back to Tom. "They used to send the convicts there—the ones left over from assignment. Your brother a convict, was he?"

Tom colored and glanced at me. "He was, sir. Yes."

"Nothing to be ashamed of—I was one m'self."

Mrs. Bushell now spoke for the first time: "There were convicts on the *Odyssey*—twenty of them. Miss Mary was very frightened of them."

It was my turn now to be stared at and I felt my heart beat, but Mr. Bushell rounded on his wife instead: "What's all this "Miss Mary," for god's sake? Ain't she one of the family now?"

Peter was talking to Tom again, repeating his earlier offer to drive him and Mr. Cudlipp to Toongabbie. "If we leave at four, we can get you and your father there before dark."

Tom thanked him and there was talk of fetching their box from the ship, whereupon Mr. Bushell said: "You'll get your box, never fear—one of m'men'll take care of that. But there's no call for Pete to drive you—you can get the stage—the stage leaves from the Rose and Crown at four sharp—"

"Sir." Peter spoke quietly but firmly. "I said I'd drive them, sir."

Father and son now looked at each other. Mr. Bushell shrugged. "Suit y'self."

With that, he got up from the table and walked off. Mrs. Bushell went out after him and for half a minute nobody spoke. Old Mr. Cudlipp was peeling an orange. I had a mad desire to laugh. I looked at Peter sitting across the table. He seemed his usual imperturbable self. He smiled at me and said: "Want to see the church we're going to be married in?"

It was by far the best part of the day—the visit to St. Phillip's Church. I was overjoyed to escape the company of Mr. and Mrs. Bushell and no longer felt light-headed, having eaten a substantial luncheon. Ruth and Tom accompanied us—Mr. Cudlipp having stayed behind to rest—and as we walked up along George Street, Peter pointed out the various buildings and said how Governor Macquarie had had all the streets new-named and finger-posted.

I was surprised to see so many soldiers lounging about. It put me in mind of Meryton in the days of the "scarlet fever." And I was also surprised at the number of smart bow-windowed shops and the expensive wares therein displayed—jewelry and handsome English furniture. Many of the women looked expensive too—expensively dressed—but conversely there were people who looked to be quite poor. I noticed several shabbily dressed children running about. And there seemed to be no happy medium either in the carriages I saw—they were either shiny new barouches or mean little painted carts. But the place had an undeniable vitality—a sort of vulgar seaport charm. Tom said that it reminded him a little of Plymouth.

St. Phillip's Church was a shock, however. It did not look in the least like a church, having at one end a castellated clock-tower, and at the other, an odd-looking roundhouse resembling nothing so much as a giant mustard-pot. Between these two excrescences, the church itself was a low stone building with multi-paned windows of clear glass.

Peter smiled down at me. "What do you think, Mary?"

I hesitated, having discerned more than a little pride on Peter's part in things Colonial. "Well, it's not—it doesn't look much like a church."

"No." He was laughing. "It's been called the ugliest church in Christendom."

"I reckon it looks friendly," said Ruth.

The only shadow on my afternoon was the appearance of a party of natives, a man and two woolly-haired women, who were walking up Church Hill as we were coming down. They were dressed in a most outlandish fashion, the man especially. He was wearing a battered old bicorn hat and a brass-buttoned military jacket with a single tarnished epaulette. The jacket was unfastened and beneath it he wore no shirt—I could see his bare black chest—and his trousers were full of holes. He was barefoot, as were the two women. The latter were both covered— half-covered—with striped cotton blankets.

Peter scarce had time to tell me not to fret myself—that it was "only Bungaree"—before they were upon us. And now to my horror I saw that the man was approaching Peter, smiling broadly and with his hand outstretched. Peter looked equally pleased. They shook hands and next thing Peter was wanting to intro-duce Bungaree to me—Bungaree and his two wives, Matora and Cora Gooseberry. I could hardly believe it!

Fortunately, Tom stepped into the breach, shaking hands all round. I made a great effort then. I said, "How do you do?" Where-upon Bungaree swept off his greasy bicorn hat and—with as much grace as Mr. Wickham—executed a low bow. "How do you do?"

He spoke the words with a perfect English accent, and it was only when everyone laughed that I realized he had mim-icked my own voice.

But I then heard something that shocked me even more. He was asking Peter for money. "Can you lend me a dump, sir?" Turning to Tom: "Tuppence to buy bread?"

Peter was emptying his pocket of change and Tom bestowed some pennies on the women, who in turn handed them to Bungaree. Another courtly bow and some jabbering from the women and the whole party moved off.

I then heard Peter say to Tom that Bungaree was a "very clever fellow" with a fine sense of humor: "He can take off all the old Governors from Hunter to Bligh—imitates 'em all perfectly— and he's a fine sailor too—been right round Australia with Matthew Flinders."

I was amazed that Peter could so admire a bigamist and a beggar. And I think Ruth was also a little shocked. She had hung back during the entire exchange. Now she touched my arm and pointed back up the hill. I saw that one of the women had divested herself of her striped blanket and was dancing about, completely naked, waving the blanket above her head like a flag.

On our return to the George Street house, we were met with the news that our boxes had all been brought up from the ship and that old Mr. Cudlipp had woken from his nap and was calling for his son. Tom hurried off, after which the housekeeper—a roguish-looking young woman—informed Peter that Mr. and Mrs. Bushell were "resting upstairs" and that Mr. Bushell had given the order they were not to be disturbed.

A peculiar look passed over Peter's face—annoyance and amusement both, or so I fancied—and he said with a slightly heightened color, "Sorry about this, Mary."

"Oh! I quite understand. Your mother must be very tired."

"Mama is *always* tired," said Ruth. And after the housekeeper left the room, she turned to Peter with a stifled giggle: "D'you reckon they're really resting?"

"You watch your tongue." But I saw he was finding it hard not to laugh.

Ruth made a face. "So when are you two planning to get married?"

I said: "The banns must be read for three successive Sundays—"

Peter spoke at almost the same time. "What's it to you, miss?"

"I don't want to live here longer'n I have to. I want to live at Parramatta with you and Mary."

Peter's eyes met mine and I said quickly: "Of course you can live with us, dear."

"Just until I'm married m'self."

Tom came back then with Mr. Cudlipp, and Ruth and I sat with the old man while Peter and Tom went into the yard to see about the box. I thought about Mr. and Mrs. Bushell upstairs "resting" and envied them their married privacy. Ruth may have been thinking the same thing about Tom, for after a little while she burst out: "I wish we could all go to Parramatta right now."

Mr. Cudlipp turned to her. "Are we not going to Toongabbie? Tom told me we were going to Toongabbie."

I said: "You are, sir. You are going to Toongabbie."

It was hard to reassure him, however, and Peter, on seeing the old man's anxiety, judged it best to be off directly. A quick public embrace and the promise of seeing each other tomorrow (Mr. Bushell having engaged to drive us all to Parramatta in his new carriage) and they were away.

6.

For reasons I did not discover until my wedding night, Mr. and Mrs. Bushell quarreled on the evening of the day we arrived in Sydney. Ruth and I first heard raised voices when we came upstairs. The prospect of a proper bath and a feather-bed had led us to retire early, but my bedchamber was next to the one occupied by Mr. and Mrs. Bushell, and the desultory sounds of their argument kept me awake. I lay in a great bed festooned with green gauze (mosquito netting, I later learned) and tried not to listen, but every so often Mr. Bushell would start shouting and in the end I could bear it no longer. I picked up my pillow and went and knocked on the door of Ruth's room.

She was awake and had heard them too. Her room was farther away, however, and the voices less audible. "You can sleep with me," said she. "This bed is more'n big enough."

But as we settled ourselves, there came an especially loud shout, followed by the sound of a door slamming and footsteps. I waited, holding my breath, but the footsteps continued on downstairs. They were a man's footsteps—heavy and booted—and after a few minutes Ruth let out a sigh: "I reckon Pa's an awful bully."

I could not immediately reply. I could not even think of a comforting quotation. Finally I said—it was the best I could do: "My father used to bully me—though in quite a different way."

When I awoke, it was starting to grow light and the house was quiet. Ruth was fast asleep. I picked up my pillow and crept back to my room, but I did not go back to bed. Instead I unpacked my writing-box and began a letter to Elizabeth—a continuation of the penciled letter I had begun on board the *Odyssey*. After relating my safe arrival in Sydney and my happiness at seeing Peter, I embarked on a brief description of Mr. Bushell's store and house. It then occurred to me that I had not yet described Mr. Bushell. I reached for a fresh sheet of paper and suddenly the habitual reserve I practiced with Elizabeth gave way:

> *I have to confess I do not like him. I do not like either of my prospective parents-in-law. Mrs. Bushell is a very odd woman—never cheerful—and he is a selfish bully. Pray do not judge me for speaking ill of them, Lizzy. I must unburden myself to somebody and you are aware of the family history, after all. It cannot come as a complete surprise.*
>
> *But it has just struck me that you and Jane have had no experience of this sort of thing. Neither Mr. Darcy nor Mr. Bingley has parents living—and now that I come to think of it, neither has Mr. Wickham. You are all of you married to orphans! Alas, my future father- and mother-in-law are very much alive—*

I stopped writing. Did I then wish Mr. and Mrs. Bushell dead? I crossed out the last line, but after glancing back over the preceding paragraphs I tore the page into little pieces and on a fresh sheet of paper began an account of Bungaree and his two wives.

I had all but finished when I imagined Elizabeth reading aloud my letter to Mr. Darcy. I imagined how he would look as he listened to the description of Cora Gooseberry throwing off her blanket and dancing about on Church Hill naked. I was about to tear up this page too but then I recalled Maria Lucas telling me how long ago she had heard Mr. Darcy speak disparagingly of dancing—how he had informed her father that "every savage can dance." I added a postscript:

I hope Mr. Darcy will not be too shocked to hear about Cora Gooseberry—she is a savage, after all.

Mr. and Mrs. Bushell did not appear at breakfast—another excellent meal of oatmeal and sweet cream together with bacon and poached eggs and a variety of fruit. Ruth and I both ate well, but I kept thinking of the text in Proverbs: "Better is a dinner of herbs where love is, than a stalled ox and hatred therewith."

Mr. Bushell walked in just as we were finishing. He looked rumpled and untidy and his eyes were red. I had a sudden fear that he had been drinking. He poured himself a cup of coffee with a steady hand, however, and without sitting down said: "You girls are going to have to shift your quarters. M'lady-wife wants a room to herself—and a dressing room besides."

Ruth and I looked at each other. Mr. Bushell cut himself a chunk of bread and bit into it without buttering it. "There's a couple of rooms on the floor above. They're full of shop stuff but I'll have one of m'men clear 'em out."

He looked at me, chewing, and laughed suddenly so that I could see the bread inside his mouth. "All these years I worked like a dog. Even when I were a ticket-of-leave man I never absented m'self—not once—and I never once touched a drop 'cause I gave her m'word. And this is the thanks I get for it."

He gulped down his coffee and then perhaps in an effort to appear more normal said: "Well. What's your plans for the day then? I got to be at the Poacher by ten."

Ruth said: "But you said you was going to drive us to Parramatta."

"That'll have to wait."

"But you promised, Pa!"

I spoke quickly, more to deflect him: "Ruth and I might call at Government House."

"Government House!" It was as if I had said I was going to the moon.

"I have a letter of introduction to the Governor. My brother-in-law has a cousin in the Colonial Office."

"Oh, he has, has he? And which brother-in-law would that be? Not the one what ran off with your little sister?"

I hated the thought that Peter had been talking to this vulgarian about my family. "I was referring to my brother-in-law, Mr. Darcy."

Mr. Bushell grunted. "A letter of introduction? A proper formal letter of introduction?"

"Yes, sir."

"Could I see it?" He was like a child.

When I returned with the letter, I feared that father and daughter had been arguing. Ruth was sitting, studying the table-cloth, while Mr. Bushell stood looking out the window into the yard.

The letter had not been sealed and Mr. Bushell now unfolded it and read it, his lips moving. It took him several minutes. He said: "I met him y'know—not to speak to—I shook his hand. It was in the year ten—not long after he first come. It was at a fete."

Ruth lifted her head. "I don't want to go with you, Mary. I don't want to go to Government House."

I guessed what they had been arguing about. I said: "Of course you don't have to go, if you don't want to."

"Oh yes, she does! If she knows what's good for her." Mr. Bushell handed me back the letter. "One of m'men can show you the way."

Ruth sulked most of the way to Government House—along George Street and down and up Bridge Street—and I found my-self talking to her in the rallying tones Cassandra had once used with me. "'Tis the way of the world, Ruth, and foolish to set your face against it. Connections can be very useful."

I tried again: "I know people are apt to set too much store by such things—an old neighbor of ours was forever prating about the Court of St. James's—but permit me to offer you one of Francis Quarles's little emblems: 'Be wisely worldly; be not worldly wise.'"

Ruth's response was a sniff. Under her best bonnet, her sharp little face was mutinous. I said: "If not for your own sake, then for Tom's. From what I hear, his brother is none too prosperous."

"Don't preach at me, Mary."

We walked on then without talking. I would not speak of my own disappointment at not going to Parramatta lest it seem like a reflection on her father.

Bridge Street is a busy thoroughfare, connecting as it does George Street with the eastern slope of the Tank Stream, and there was much to see—carriages and carts rumbling down and up, gentlemen on horseback, and people on foot. I saw a convict work-gang going to the lumber-yard. They wore garish canary-yellow jackets and overalls, all daubed over with broad arrows. I could not look at them for long, but Ruth gazed after them. I wondered whether she was thinking of her father.

Mr. Bushell's man was keen to point out the sights. He had already drawn my attention to a large brick, balconied house on the corner, which he said was the Female Orphan School. He said that a new institution was now being built for the orphans at Parramatta.

"Are there so many orphans?"

"Aye, mum. Soldiers' spawn."

At the time, I had not known what he meant.

Ruth remained silent as we crossed the bridge over the Tank Stream (an unpleasant-smelling brackish creek) and began the climb to Government House. Mr. Bushell's man now pointed to the Chaplain's house—a pretty cottage with a verandah and two well-grown orange trees standing on either side of the path.

"The Chaplain?" Ruth gave my arm a little punch. "Would that be the one what's going to marry you?"

I was relieved that her sulks seemed to be over, but as we approached the guardhouse of Government House she said: "I don't see why there has to be kings and queens and governors—people holding court and lording it over you. I reckon it's silly."

I said: "If the Governor receives us, it will be only for a very few minutes—it will be a purely formal visit."

In the event, it was anything but formal, and it was Mrs. Macquarie who received us, not the Governor. The visit was to have important consequences nonetheless, although it did not begin well. Mrs. Macquarie struck me as very stiff and Scottish—a tall, white-skinned woman with pale-blue eyes—and at first Ruth's little rusticities met with a chilly response. But everything changed when the child was brought in.

I have somewhere read or heard it said that on every formal visit, a child ought to be of the party by way of providing conversation, and little Lachlan Macquarie answered the purpose wonderfully. He was at the time some eight or nine months old, small for his age but precocious, and while he would have nothing whatsoever to do with me—apart from some solemn, unfriendly looks—he took an instant liking to Ruth, thus furnishing us all with plenty to talk about.

His mother clearly doted on him, and after the nurserymaid placed him in her arms, her reserve disappeared. Ruth then took him on her knee to sing "Ride a Cock Horse to Banbury Cross," varying the words to suit the occasion:

> *To buy little Lachlan a galloping horse;*
> *It trots behind and it ambles before,*
> *And Lachlan shall ride till his bottom is sore.*

I was horrified, but Mrs. Macquarie, I saw, was highly amused: "I have never heard *that* version, Miss Bushell!" And then perhaps seeking to include me in all the fun: "Do you ride, Miss Bennet?"

"Alas, no. I tried to learn when I was twelve but could not conquer my fear of horses."

She nodded. "It has a lot to do with balance—balance and letting the horse know who's in charge."

"You are a horsewoman yourself, ma'am?" (I later learned that Elizabeth Macquarie was capable of spending six hours in the saddle.)

She nodded again. "Yes, I enjoy riding."

Her attention then returned to her son, but as we were leaving (with Lachlan still holding fast to Ruth) she turned to me and asked if I wished to make another attempt to learn: "If so, I could speak to our coachman. I'm sure he could find a quiet, steady mount for you. And you might go out with one of the grooms. Clayton is a very sensible lad."

She cut short my thanks. "I shall arrange it then, shall I?"

My riding lessons commenced the very next day, and very different was the experience from my first nervous attempts at Netherfield. I was given the quietest of horses to ride—a little bay gelding named Bob—and the art of balance I had acquired on board ship (a kind of bandy-legged equipoise) now served me wonderfully. After only my third lesson, I wrote to Jane:

> Give me joy: I have just ridden in the Governor's Domain without a leading rein, and tomorrow we are to complete the circuit, a distance of some two miles. I have quite made up my mind to become as proficient a horsewoman as yourself—Peter having promised to ride with me every day at Parramatta.

7.

Peter and I were finally married on the 26th of November, two years after my elder sisters' weddings and four years after Mrs. Knowles's unfortunate second venture. I wore the white silk gown given to me by Elizabeth and Jane and the veil of Honiton lace, and St. Phillip's Church, so unprepossessing on the outside, looked surprisingly beautiful on the inside, with its clear-paned, arched windows letting in the late-afternoon sunshine. (I like to think of it as somehow emblematic of our marriage.)

Our wedding night had a bad beginning, however, for just as the last guests were leaving the Jolly Poacher and Peter went to see about the horses for our journey to Parramatta, a handsome, overdressed woman hailed me from the verandah. She was sitting at one of the trestle tables under the grape-vine and was clearly the worse for drink, introducing herself as Mrs. Tasker and inviting me in a strongly accented Scots voice to sit with her a "wee while": "You'll be missing your mother, I'm thinking. You'll be wanting someone to tell you what's what on your wedding night."

Seeing me hesitate, she reached up and seized my hand. "Sit down now. It won't take a minute."

It took rather more than a minute, however, and her advice consisted of turning a blind eye to my new husband's philandering. ("He's a chip off the old block and you'd be wise when it happens to look the other way.") She then informed me that she had been Mr. Bushell's mistress, that they had lived together openly as man and wife, but that when Governor Macquarie had issued a proclamation against couples living in sin, Bushell had deemed it prudent that they part. "He just wanted to get into the Governor's good books—he's such an old hypocrite. But we had a high old time while it lasted so I'm not complaining."

The whole time she was talking she kept blotting her face with a fine cambric handkerchief, embroidered with what I first thought were strawberries but which she explained were a species of native flower called waratahs. Mr. Bushell had given it to her as a parting gift: "Practically the only present he ever gave me, he's such an old miser." She hiccoughed and laughed. "Perhaps you'll have better luck with the son."

So shocked was I by Mrs. Tasker's revelation that as soon as Peter and I were alone together on the road to Parramatta I blurted it all out and we had the first quarrel of our married life. Peter defended his father, saying that Mrs. Tasker had received an extremely generous settlement: "You don't want to believe everything you hear, love."

I could not see Peter's face clearly in the growing dark but I fancied I could hear amusement in his voice. I said: "So you knew about her, did you?"

"Course I knew." He was obliged to check the horses, for a small animal had run out from the surrounding scrub onto the road. When he spoke again he sounded more serious: "Mary, you must remember—this place—it's hard for men having to live apart from their wives—a wife on the other side of the world—you have to make allowances."

"I don't have to wink at adultery. Your father has broken the Seventh Commandment."

I felt him withdraw from me then and for a time neither of us spoke. I no longer held his arm. I stared ahead at the horses and breathed to calm myself. This then was the explanation for Mr. and Mrs. Bushell's quarrel: Mr. Bushell must have confessed his adultery to his wife and she had been unable to forgive him. I kept thinking, "But this is my wedding night. Why should I have to worry about Mr. and Mrs. Bushell on my wedding night?" I looked at Peter and thought: "Why does he not tell me he loves me?" And increasingly the darkening strangeness of the place— the smell of the bush, the sound of the insects people called cicadas—everything was making me feel more alienated.

I tried then to conciliate. I described to him Mrs. Tasker's handkerchief: "It made me think of *Othello*—of the handkerchief in *Othello*."

"What handkerchief?"

The realization that he did not know what I was talking about shocked me anew. I felt of a sudden the most awful loneliness. I tried to keep calm. I tried to say over in my head the 121st psalm: "I will lift up mine eyes unto the hills." In suiting the action to the words, however, I perceived that the stars were all wrong.

That was my undoing. I had looked up unthinkingly, anticipating the familiar and, finding it gone, began to cry like a baby. Whereupon Peter stopped the gig and took me in his arms, kissing me so that my face was soon sore both from kissing and crying.

After that, there was no more arguing, and in the early hours of the morning, while the sky was still dark and wearing only our nightclothes, we went out into the field at the front of the house to look at the stars. Peter pointed out Orion ("It's still there, sweetheart, it's just upside-down.") and, lower on the horizon, the constellation that cannot be seen in the northern sky— the Southern Cross.

8.

The first of the very few letters I received from my father came when Peter and I had been married only a week. I well remember the opening sentence: "By the time you read this you will be married and I trust not too disillusioned with your partner in life."

Beyond that, I recall only the news that Elizabeth was now expecting a child and that Kitty was betrothed to a clergyman, one Dr. Slipper, a widower who lived near Pemberley and who was (according to my father) "a hearty old fellow with a costive head."

I lost the letter in rather embarrassing circumstances. We were to dine at Parramatta Government House that same evening and Peter had come in early from harvesting the wheat, sitting down in all his dirt to read the precious missive. I sat beside him, fresh from my bath. And so handsome did my husband look, long legs sprawled in dungaree trousers and frowning over my father's spiky hand, that I could not resist reaching out to smooth away the frown. He caught my hand to his lips, still reading, and then chancing to look up and reading my face more swiftly than he would ever read the written word, pulled me onto his lap.

We arrived late at Government House as a consequence, and the letter—doubtless caught up in a pile of discarded clothes—was never afterwards found. But Dr. Slipper and his costive head entered our private lexicon from that day forward and became (I blush to confess it) a favorite conjugal joke.

I have to say though, that despite being extremely happy in my marriage, I was not at first very happy living in New South Wales. In my letters home, however, I was at pains to paint an idyllic picture. I praised our farm at Parramatta—the fine prospect of the river, the acres of waving wheat, the orchards and olive trees. I praised the house—the spacious rooms, the new library, the colonnaded verandah. I even praised my pianoforte (purchased at a bankrupt-estate auction by Peter) and the superior concerts we attended at Government House and the superior society to be met with there.

The reality, however, was more complicated. I never recovered, for instance, from my first impression of the town of Parramatta, formed on a hot November morning two days after my arrival. Peter had driven Ruth and myself out to see the farm, and having crossed the little wooden bridge spanning the river he had suddenly stopped the gig and climbed down, taking with him one of the water flasks. On the bank nearby was a great stone, two-storied building—the jail, I adjudged from the bars on the windows—and I saw then that an old man had been placed in the stocks outside. He was crying out for water, his face bright red from the sun beating down, and Peter, after first holding the flask to the man's lips, had covered his head with his own wetted neckerchief.

I had wanted very much to write to my sisters about this because it so perfectly illustrated Peter's Christian charity, but I knew not how to describe it without mentioning the stocks or that the old man was a convicted felon. I did not want to confirm them in their prejudices—to portray the Colony purely as a place of correction.

Similarly, I sought to present our farm as an extensive and cultivated estate, not comparable to Pemberley perhaps, but picturesque in its own way and productive. I did not therefore write about the drought that destroyed a third of our wheat crop or how I spent my first Christmas watering wilting rows of vegetables in the kitchen garden. And when I described our new library—the fine craftsmanship of the red cedar joinery—I did not mention that, save for Peter's agricultural journals, the bookshelves were quite bare. Or that when my own books were at last unpacked and placed upon the shelves I was not at first able to read them (my Wordsworth especially) without feeling homesick.

I ignored too the vulgarity and crookedness of Sydney Town and wrote instead of its beautiful harbor, for despite Governor Macquarie's efforts to broaden and straighten streets and erect fine public buildings, the place to my mind had an irredeemably raffish air. (There were too many men like Mr. Bushell and too many women like Mrs. Tasker living in Sydney Town.)

But unlike so many of the officers and their wives, I did not talk of returning to the old country. I did not court nostalgia by singing about cups of kindness. Whenever homesickness threatened, I said to myself the words I had said to Peter when first I had agreed to accompany him to the Colony—uncompromising words from the Old Testament Book of Ruth: "Whither thou goest, I will go; and where thou lodgest, I will lodge; thy people shall be my people, and thy God my God." (That Peter was not particularly religious was another of the things I chose to ignore.)

In the beginning though I was quite blind to the beauty of my new home insofar as it did not correspond with English notions of beauty. Two people in particular helped to open my eyes—Cassandra (who came to the Colony some eighteen months after myself and stayed for over a year) and Elizabeth

Macquarie (the vice-regal couple being our near-neighbors at Parramatta).

Cassandra was especially struck by the quality of the Australian light, its peculiar clarity, and spent hours painting what I first thought very unattractive subjects: the spindly foliage of the eucalyptus trees and the native people—portraits of naked men with white circles of clay around their eyes and one of a bare-breasted native mother suckling her baby in full view of a congregation of church-goers. Cassandra answered my objections in her usual no-nonsense fashion, saying that she considered the people and plants of the New World to be every bit as beautiful in their way as those of the old, reminding me that the ancient Britons had gone into battle stark naked and painted themselves blue.

Elizabeth Macquarie was similarly impressed by the country's original inhabitants, considering them to be of open and favorable dispositions. But just as I have never been able to get the better of my fear of convicts, so have I been unable to overcome my mistrust of the native men. I know I have disappointed Peter in this respect, for he has several good friends amongst them and in general feels that they have not been fairly treated. Indeed, one of our worst arguments occurred after I praised Governor Macquarie's plan to give the natives a Christmas feast in the Parramatta market-place: "He means to feed hundreds of them with roast beef and plum pudding—'twill be just like the miracle of the loaves and fishes." I had then asked Peter to reconsider joining the Committee for the Civilization of the Natives—whereupon he rounded on me: "'Tis nothing more'n the crumbs from the rich man's table, Mary. The natives round here can't even camp on the Crescent. Don't you understand? They have lost everything."

And in time, I did come to understand (though my fears, alas, remained) and Peter for his part conceded that some of his anger was due to guilt—the knowledge that his father must have dispossessed many of the local aborigines when first he came to settle in the area. (Mr. Bushell in turn maintained that there was now no turning back the clock: "If the British hadn't settled here, the Frenchies would've, and they'd've treated them a damned sight worse. 'Sides, who stands to profit from what I done if not you and yours?" He was much more eager to talk about the injustices *he* had suffered at the hands of the free settlers: "Those damned exclusionists—those pure bloody merinos—herd of silly bloody sheep. They never let you forget you was once a convict.")

9.

Perhaps I will never feel completely at home in Australia, although I have gradually grown accustomed to its back-to front seasons and upside-down stars. I miss England most at Christmastime. While we never kept up the old traditions at Longbourn, it was still the season for fires and good cheer, and it seems very odd therefore to be wishing folk a merry Christmas with the glass reading over eighty degrees in the shade.

Some five months after my second colonial Christmas I received a letter from Elizabeth describing the festivities at Pemberley:

As I write, the house has a full complement of guests—Bennets and Bingleys and Gardiners and Hursts—and for the first time since our marriage, Lady Catherine has condescended to visit with her daughter Anne. Mr. Darcy believes in the old English style of hospitality and this evening (Christmas Eve) we dressed the windows of the great hall with holly, the Yule log was lit, and trestles set up with goose-pies and mince-pies and mead. Afterwards, there was a splendid game of snapdragon with the bowl of raisins and brandy set alight—much to the joy of the Gardiner children and little Bennet (our own Fitzwilliam being yet too young to take part).

Tomorrow we will be twenty-six at dinner, for I have invited our housekeeper, Mrs. Reynolds, to sit down with us, as well as Mrs. Annesley, the lady with whom Mr. Darcy's sister Georgiana was used

to live in London. (I have a mind to seat Mrs. Reynolds next to Lady
Catherine.)

Jane wrote to me by the same post:

I think of you in your antipodean sunshine, dear Mary, while here
we have ice underfoot. Bingley and I braved the weather this morn-
ing and went for a glorious walk in the Pemberley woods. Lady
Catherine, I know, thought it imprudent in my condition—I have
scarce two months to go before my confinement—but it has been
delightful to be at liberty these past few days, for Lydia and Wickham
have been staying with us since Michaelmas and we begin to think
that they will never be gone. But this is quite between ourselves,
dear.

These letters at first made me feel low. I calculated it must
be at least another two months before news of the birth of Jane's
baby could reach me—before I could be sure she was out of
danger—and I could not help wishing that Peter and I might
have been part of all the Christmas merriment. The wish, however, was not long-lasting. In England, my marriage must always
be seen as a mésalliance and no amount of personal kindness
from Jane and Elizabeth or their husbands would ever alter that.

In the event, it was Cassandra who brought news of the safe
arrival of Jane's second son when she came to the Colony in July.
She also presented me with a miniature of mother and child,
painted when the Bingleys made a visit to Longbourn shortly
after the birth. (The portrait is very similar to one of the
Madonna and child by Raphael; the blue of Jane's gown matching that of the Virgin's robe.) But there was also sad news to be
communicated. I learned that Helen had suffered a miscarriage

early in the New Year and that for a short while she and George had been estranged. Cassandra explained: "Helen told George about Wickham—about the child—and he took it very badly." After a pause she added: "But they are now reconciled and I believe their marriage is the stronger for it."

When Cassandra first came to the Colony, I hoped that she might be prevailed upon to settle. The place suited her, and if she chose to paint naked native men and women or to consort with artists who had once been convicts (forgers for the most part), it was after all nobody's business but her own. I was hurt though that she chose to live in a room above Bushell's Emporium rather than with us at Parramatta. She explained it to me thus: "For one short year (I have promised my aunt it will not be longer) I intend to do exactly as I please—paint what I please and be accountable to nobody. If I were to live with you and Peter, that would not be possible, but Mr. and Mrs. Bushell will not care."

Oddly enough though, Mrs. Bushell did come to care about Cassandra. Theirs was a peculiar relationship, begun in the dilapidations of the Bushell marriage and consolidated over the time it took Cassandra to paint Mrs. Bushell's portrait. I could never understand it, and beyond saying that Mrs. Bushell had "suffered," Cassandra did not try to explain.

Ruth opined that her mother would feel more at ease with Cassandra than with myself: "Miss Long ain't such a fine lady as you are, Mary."

"I am not a fine lady, Ruth, as I've told you many times."

"Well, why won't you let me learn you to bake bread then? Like a proper farmer's wife?"

This was a longstanding grievance: Since marrying Tom and settling at Toongabbie, Ruth was eager to instruct me in house-wifery (while at the same time resisting my efforts to turn her into a lady). But our sisterly squabbles rarely lasted long, and the proximity of the Cudlipps's farm at Toongabbie—a distance of just three miles—was a comfort to us both. We regularly rode together (myself side-saddle and Ruth astride) and this more than anything helped disperse the little megrims and fits of homesick-ness that were apt to overtake me whenever Peter was away.

I wrote to Jane about these rides, as only a horsewoman could understand (I felt) the pleasure of taking in the country in such a way—the giving up of oneself to one's surroundings. Rid-ing was how I began to acquaint myself with my new home.

I wrote my most comprehensive letters to Mrs. Knowles. To atone for past neglect, I wrote regularly and minutely. I knew she would appreciate descriptions of butter-churning and bread-baking (I had eventually capitulated), and that she would be pleased to hear how I rose early to practice my music and write my songs. And Mr. Galbraith, I knew, would wish to hear about Peter's antipodean farming and Ruth's bee-keeping (Peter hav-ing arranged for a hive of European honeybees to be shipped out from Rio de Janeiro).

But I confided my regret that Ruth's determined rusticities prevented her from mixing with a wider circle of people:

Peter, in contrast, is able to move easily in any company. His pass-port to such polite society as the Colony affords is undoubtedly his musicianship, but his talents and integrity make him everywhere valued and respected. He is equally at home in the taproom of the Jolly Poacher and the drawing room of Government House. I can never be sufficiently grateful to you and Mr. Galbraith for bringing us together.

As soon as I knew I was with child, I wrote to tell everybody. And I wrote my parents—I could not help myself—that I was presently working on a set of baby caps to which I had affixed rosettes of satin ribbons on the *right*-hand side (Peter having wagered we would have a daughter upon learning that Mr. Bushell had bet heavily on having a grandson):

> *I tell you this, my dear parents, not in a spirit of contrariness, for (thank heaven!) we do not have to concern ourselves with an entail, but to illustrate my husband's regard for my feelings. Truly I may say—to quote Ecclesiastes 7:28 and with no disrespect to Papa— "One man among a thousand I have found." I am the happiest creature in the world, or perhaps I should say in the New World, for I do not aspire to be happier than my sisters.*

I had then crossed out the last dozen or so words—they seemed to smack of the old rivalry and resentment—before beginning a letter to Lydia. (I found letters to Lydia the hardest of all to write—she seldom wrote to me and when she did, it was always the same sad tale: friends with whom they had fallen out or debts they had been unable to repay.) I often wondered whether she still loved Wickham—certainly she no longer referred to him as her "dear Wickham"—and in her last letter she had hardly mentioned him.

Cassandra had left the Colony before I knew I was with child, sailing on a returning convict transport in response to an urgent summons from Mrs. Long. But in the weeks before she sailed, she painted a portrait of the Bushell family—Mr. and Mrs. Bushell senior, Peter and myself, and Ruth and Tom—all lined up on the verandah of the Jolly Poacher.

Nearly eight months after her departure, Peter's and my child was born—a girl we named Elizabeth (after Mrs. Macquarie) and on the following day a box containing the latest novels and London newspapers arrived—the gift of George and Helen. In it was a copy of Cassandra's shipboard journal together with her letter. I shall let her have the last word:

> *I called at Longbourn this morning to find your mother and father walking in the shrubbery, arm in arm. My face must have betrayed my surprise, for your father said: "Perhaps the news did not reach you in New South Wales, Miss Long?" "What news would that be, sir?" "Why, that hostilities have long since ceased." Whereupon your poor mother assured me that the war between England and France had ended years ago!*
>
> *They both looked remarkably well, your mother perhaps a little stouter, and when I presented them with the sketch of yourself and Peter on the verandah of the Jolly Poacher, your father said it would make a fine companion piece to the portrait of Mr. and Mrs. Darcy in the grounds of Pemberley.*
>
> *He then said (quite seriously) that despite some inequality in rank he had never doubted your marriage would be happy and that Peter would use you kindly. He also said that he feared that he had not always used you kindly and I did not contradict him.*

Acknowledgments

I'm especially grateful to Suzanne Falkiner for her help and encouragement. I also thank the president of the Jane Austen Society of Australia, Susannah Fullerton, for taking the time to read and comment on an early draft. And for helping the book on its way, I thank Mary Cunnane, Nicci Dodanwela, Vanessa Battersby, Tony Rogers, Diana Dasey, and Rick Evans.

About the Author

Jennifer Paynter was born and educated in Sydney. She has previously written two stage plays: *When Are We Going to Manly?* (produced by the Griffin Theatre Company in 1984 and nominated for the 1984 Sydney Theatre Critics' Circle award and the 1985 NSW Premier's Literary Awards), and *Balancing Act,* produced by the Canberra Theatre Company in 1990 and adapted for radio by the ABC. The author of several anthologized short stories, she lives in Sydney. *The Forgotten Sister* is her first novel.